A Curtain Twitcher's Book of Murder

GAY MARRIS

A Curtain Twitcher's Book of Murder

First published in the UK in 2024 by Bedford Square Publishers Ltd,
London, UK

bedfordsquarepublishers.co.uk
@bedsqpublishers

© Gay Marris, 2024

The right of Gay Marris to be identified as the author of this work has been asserted in accordance with the Copyright, Designs and Patents Act 1988. All rights reserved. No part of this book may be reproduced, stored in or introduced into a retrieval system, or transmitted, in any form or by any means (electronic, mechanical, photocopying, recording or otherwise) without the written permission of the publishers.

Any person who does any unauthorised act in relation to this publication may be liable to criminal prosecution and civil claims for damages.
A CIP catalogue record for this book is available from the British Library.
This is a work of fiction. Names, characters, places, and incidents either are the product of the author's imagination or are used fictitiously, and any resemblance to actual persons, living or dead, businesses, companies, events or locales is entirely coincidental.

ISBN
978-1-83501-011-2 (Paperback)
978-1-83501-009-9 (Hardback)
978-1-83501-041-9 (Trade Paperback)
978-1-83501-010-5 (eBook)

2 4 6 8 10 9 7 5 3 1

Typeset in 11pt Garamond MT Pro
by Avocet Typeset, Bideford, Devon, EX39 2BP
Printed and bound in Great Britain by Clays Ltd, Elcograf S.p.A.

The manufacturer's authorised representative in the EU for product safety is
Easy Access System Europe, Mustamäe tee 50, 10621 Tallinn, Estonia
gpsr.requests@easproject.com

For Mum and Dad

Prologue

The first brick of the first house on Atbara Avenue was laid while Queen Victoria mourned her way through the twilight of her reign; the last brick of the last house when her son had been on the throne for a year. The mortar that bound them was imbued with both the complacency of an empire and the sanguinity of a playboy king. When newly built, each handsome dwelling, with its broad bay windows and gabled roof, was graced with sober iron railings and a gay front path of black and white tiles. London families quickly moved in with their cocker spaniels and their housemaids, pleased to unpack their soup tureens and aspirations into such generously appointed accommodation. They were as green and up-and-coming as the sapling limes planted outside every third house. There was a florist shop at one end of the avenue. At the other stood the modest church of St Francis in the Fields, complete with an ugly hall and even uglier vicarage in its grounds. In those days, fresh-cut flowers were a household necessity, and it went without saying that God was an Edwardian Englishman.

But that was two World Wars ago, and a dog has since orbited Earth. The buildings of Atbara Avenue have stood shoulder to shoulder, on parade for almost seven decades. Gone are the railings, melted down to make munitions, and cracked are the harlequin tiles. Gone, too, are the domestics. Armed with nylon brushes and Liquid Gumption, these days the women of the households scrub their own front steps. Some addresses have been converted to bedsits and several back lawns supplanted with crazy paving. The vicarage and hall lurk in the churchyard, unscathed and as ugly as ever, but St Francis's is more often half empty than half full. The florist's has been replaced by a corner shop, run by Mr and Mrs Singh. They sell all the essentials for a brave new world: *Beano* comics, Sherbet Dips, Instant Whip and Spam. The granite horse trough at the gates of Atbara Park is planted with lobelias. Tube trains rumble beneath the street's foundations. The lime trees, fulsome in their maturity, rain down honeydew onto Ford Escorts and Vauxhall Vivas parked in their sticky shade.

While the Sixties may be in full swing on Carnaby Street, where skirts are short, shirts are cheesecloth and the Beatles are more popular than Jesus, Atbara Avenue retains a sense of restraint. As if something in its very fabric remembers its less cynical roots. Doubtless a little frayed round the edges, perhaps no longer absolutely smart, each pastel-painted frontage still offers a more-or-less respectable face to its smiling counterpart across the road. And, outwardly at least, it seems these decorous qualities rub off on its current population.

It's true that you no longer have to be rich, or educated, or English, to live on Atbara Avenue, but you do have to maintain certain standards. Spick and span, best foot forward, inhabitants are as well presented as their window boxes. Heaven forbid that any bras should be burned in this neck of the woods. Here, children Listen with Mother, Father Goes to Work on an Egg and, on TV, chimpanzees sip their PG Tips from china cups. Many residents have lived on the avenue for years and years, swimming around together in the same bowl of suburban soup. In fact, some of them have never lived anywhere else. It's surprising how often people born on the avenue end up dying there, too. But, in the meantime, they hail each other in passing, with confident waves and nods and simply-must-dashes.

Ask anyone how well they know their neighbours, and they'll answer, 'Well.' They won't hesitate before replying. After all, they see each other every day, as they move through the ebb and flow of their existence. Their faces have become as familiar as the printed daisies on their kitchen blinds. The truth is, however, these people hardly know each other at all. They can't do, since propriety dictates they conceal the truly important details of their lives from view.

The residents of Atbara Avenue observe each other across the vast distance afforded by close proximity, and that is probably for the best.

1

Beneath Suspicion

From a distance, it's easy to mistake Mrs Muriel Dollimore for a sweet little old lady. Plump and stooped, with a halo of wispy white hair framing her round, wrinkled face, it's obvious she's advanced in years. And trussed up in her tweed coat, its horn buttons straining to contain her short, stout body, she gives the impression she's been upholstered rather than dressed. The epitome of the lavender-scented granny who sits, no doubt knitting away, in the mind's eyes of her neighbours. They see her pass their front windows each afternoon, regular as clockwork. *Tic tack*, *tic tack*, *tic tack* go her clickety-clickety walking sticks, quick time on the pavement as she shuffles herself to the corner shop to fetch cat food and Carnation milk. She always looks the same. She always looks lovely. Bless her.

Mrs Dollimore is the longest-standing resident of Atbara Avenue. Not one of the neighbours who witnessed her arrival is alive to remember it, so as far as present-day occupants are concerned, she's been around forever. A treasured constant in the stage play of local life.

When Muriel first moved in, half a century ago, the Great War was over, but London was still in shell shock. Horses were common, young men were rare, and ladies wore gloves to tea. It was her wedding day, but if anyone imagines that a once virile, now dead, Ernest Dollimore proudly carried his blushing bride over the threshold, they're wrong. He was never built for lifting and she preferred him not to touch her. Especially in public. As soon as their hackney carriage pulled up outside Number 17, she alighted, and her slender feet bore her directly up the path and into the house. No dilly-dallying on the way.

Before she married, Muriel Edwards was a professional singer. With a sylph-like figure and a ruthless ability to blow her cigarette smoke in the direction of only the most useful men, she was the quintessence of glamour. Known by her stage name, *Dolores*, she was a rising starlet by the low-pitched standards of the day. She topped the bill in jazz clubs of the coastal resorts of southern England, and around the time she met dependable bank clerk Ernest, she also caught the eye of entrepreneur Vincent Grünblatt, shark-eyed talent spotter and keyholder to West End success. Vincent promised his little lark the stars and the moon. But, to her unending disappointment, she was never to receive such hard-won rewards. When it became clear she was expecting a baby, any interest Vinny may have had in his uncaged songbird evaporated, and it was he who flew away. With a steely instinct for survival, desperate *Dolores* had quickly accepted lovesick Ernest's renewed offer of marriage. Ernest brought her to this city, where they completed the formalities at Hammersmith Registry Office within the month. Ernest was overcome with happiness; Muriel, with resentment.

Pauline Dollimore, daughter of Muriel, is the second longest-standing resident of the street. She was born in the back bedroom of Number 17 and, apart from a brief interlude in her early adult life, she has never left that address. She's lived through a new war and rationing and bombs. She's witnessed the departure of the horses and the gradual recovery of generations blown apart, but she's never drunk tea anywhere smart enough to require gloves. For many years, this sad woman has been slowly reversing away from the world around her, and now she's retreated so far into the background, she's become scarcely more than a spectator in her own story. Viewed from any distance, way off or up close, it's impossible to mistake Pauline Dollimore for anything other than exactly who she is: a nervy, overweight spinster, living at home with her widowed mother. She always looks the same. She always looks wretched.

Deirdre, wife of the Reverend Desmond O'Reilly, finishes a row before resting the knitting in her lap. Lit only by the mellow glow of the setting sun, the vicarage sitting room has become too dim for her to see her work. Although she prides herself on her ability to knit 'blindfolded', her eyes have started to ache. She looks across to her husband in the opposite armchair, snoozing. Head resting on the antimacassar, mouth hanging open, eyes closed. The latest paperback crime novel lies, face down, on his chest. His long, thin legs are stretched out in front of him.

She gives one of his feet a gentle kick with the toe of her slipper. 'Desmond,' she whispers, very loudly, 'are you asleep?'

The vicar lets out a little grunt and opens an eye. 'Not anymore.'

'Oh good. Because I want to talk to you about something.'

'Talk away,' he replies, without adjusting his position. 'I *may* close my eyes again, but I *will* still be listening.'

'You need to sit up properly,' says Deirdre, switching on a standard lamp, 'otherwise you'll just slide back off to sleep again and miss the whole gist.'

'Yes, I suppose you're right,' he yawns, straightening up and reining in his legs. He closes his book, places it on the arm of his chair, and puts on his spectacles. 'You have my full attention.'

Deirdre shuffles her hips a little deeper into her seat, smooths down the front of her cardigan, and begins. 'I'm worried that if a neighbour – let's say for the sake of argument, a fellow member of the Women's Institute – had a problem of some kind, she might not tell anyone. Especially if the individual concerned happens to be a particularly selfless person.'

'What makes you think they wouldn't want to confide in *you*? You're an excellent sounding board.'

'I'm concerned that natural reticence prevents her from offloading. She's afraid, if she were to confess her problem to another person, she'd be inviting that person to worry about it too, obligating the confidante to carry her burden along with their own woes. And, of course, there are boundaries when it comes to one's neighbours.'

'How do you mean?'

'It may be all right to spatter immediate family with emotional slurry, but to do the same to one's neighbours would be extremely...' Deirdre hesitates before landing upon just the right word, '... rude. Good neighbours don't embarrass each other by revealing their difficulties. Good neighbours keep themselves to themselves.'

'Such a disappointing expression.' The vicar shakes his head sadly.

'Disappointing but true,' she retorts irritably.

'How can you tell that your mystery acquaintance is concealing something?'

Deirdre pauses before answering. She can't say it's anything about the way the woman looks, because, now she thinks about it, she's never really looked at her that closely. When the gentle folk of Atbara Avenue meet in the street, they'd no more stare into one another's eyes and risk such unneighbourly intimacy than trespass into someone else's front garden and peer through their sitting-room window. 'I don't know. It's just an uneasy feeling I get around her. She never complains, of course. The brave woman. But it must be stressful for her, still stuck in that house together, mother and daughter, cheek-by-jowl.'

'Rather than guessing, can't you just *ask* her what the trouble is?'

'Certainly not!' Deirdre exclaims. 'Anyway, as I said, I don't believe she'd tell me.'

They both fall into a testy silence. Instead of making her feel better, Desmond has made Deirdre feel admonished. As if speculation about a neighbour's problems is just idle, fireside gossip. Isn't it basic human nature to be curious about those around us? Isn't her husband as basically human as she is? She may not have spent much time watching this woman – or listening to what she says, for that matter – but there's a lot one can surmise about someone, even via the most casual observation. Deirdre takes in what she can see at a glance, and then fills in the gaps with guesswork. The tall policeman must be courageous; grubby boys are cheeky monkeys; tattooed youths probably stole Desmond's bike. Etcetera, etcetera. These portraits of her neighbours, hanging in the galleries of her ever-active mind, may be painted with the brushstrokes of a thousand fleeting glances, but Deirdre's quite satisfied with them. She does know people aren't necessarily so straightforward, but she's convinced she's never guessed wrong yet.

'I'm sorry, Desmond,' she sighs. 'I don't mean to sound like a busybody. I really do want to help.'

'That does you credit,' says the vicar. 'I never imagined otherwise.'

'Thank you, darling.' Deirdre resumes her knitting. 'And the sooner I can reach out to Pauline Dollimore, the better.'

'*Pauline* Dollimore?' The vicar snorts. 'Good heavens!'

'Naturally. Whom did you think I meant?'

'Saintly old Muriel. She's the one *I* feel sorry for.'

It's a fine April afternoon and the weather is breezy and bright. The conscientious housewives of Atbara Avenue have removed their rollers, fastened their pinnies and flocked outside, determined to take advantage of a decent drying day to peg up their Daz-white sheets in the coal-smoke-kissed air. Pauline Dollimore is indoors. She's in her bedroom, redrafting a suicide note, when her mother returns home from the shop.

'Mum? Is that you?' she calls cheerfully from the upstairs landing.

She hears the old lady shuffling about downstairs, grumbling away, but can't make out what she's saying.

Pauline has another try. 'Did you get what you need?'

Again, no direct answer, but a muffled string of complaints. '*Sixpence? For a couple of ounces of desiccated coconut? Daylight robbery...*

but that's no surprise… remember what they charged me for a shampoo and set at that bloody hair salon on the high street… tarts' boudoir, more like… swanning around with their "beehives". Birds' nests, if you ask me. Everyone's on the take…'

'I was just going to put the kettle on. I expect you're ready for a cup of something hot.'

'Never found yourself a man and it's far too late now. Look at yourself! I'm amazed you can bear to show your face… even that fool Ernest would be disgusted to look at you now. Do you hear me? He'd be DISGUSTED!'

As always, Pauline ignores these remarks. She didn't answer back when she was growing up and she doesn't now, no matter how hurtful her mother's words nor how deep the unseen cuts they cause. What would be the point? The result would only be a tirade of abuse and a flurry of slammed doors. Her father taught her his ways well. Don't rock the boat. Don't kick the hornets' nest. Let sleeping dogs lie. Bitch. For so many years Pauline has allowed her loathing to simmer, silently, in its bilious juices. Irrespective of what she hears, or what she feels, it's now second nature to present her mother with an oblivious front.

'Hot chocolate or tea?' she asks brightly.

Not receiving any audible reply, Pauline lumbers down the stairs. As she approaches the kitchen, she catches sight of the hall clock. 'Mum,' she calls again. 'It's nearly time.'

'Better get your skates on with my hot chocolate then, hadn't you?'

Pauline picks up the string bag of groceries she finds carelessly abandoned on the worktop, and neatly stows its contents in the pantry. It takes her a few goes to set light to a ring of the fumy old gas hob. When the vapours eventually ignite, they go up with such a spectacular puff, she steps back to avoid singeing her eyebrows. She warms a pan of milk, preparing her mother's drink first before knocking up a cup of tea for herself. Hastily, she piles a plate with cakes she finds in a tin on the side and manages to make it into the front room with only seconds to spare. Here she finds her mother, ensconced in her particular armchair, a rug over her knees, glued to the television set.

Pauline puts her laden tray down on an occasional table – *'You're in the way of the picture… great fat arse…'* – and settles herself into the chair next to the old lady's. 'You've whipped up a lovely batch of baking this week, Mum,' she says, helping herself to two solid, moist macaroons. 'I can never resist these.'

'I know you can't,' spits her mother, giving her a particularly mean look as she turns up the volume on the TV, just in time for the opening sequence of her favourite programme, *The Galloping Guzzler*.

Pauline isn't remotely interested in this show, but she'll sit through anything so long as it keeps the old bat off her back for at least a little while. It follows its usual format. The host, a velvet-clad, improbably tanned-looking man named Julian LeCheval, begins by inviting two unsuspecting contestants, plucked from his entirely female studio audience, into a studio-set kitchen. Each woman, giddy with excitement, clutches her basket of ingredients while her apron strings are tied by a stagehand. Then, as always, Chef LeCheval challenges them to produce an original dish 'fit for a king', ready to be served up in just 30 minutes. After a frantic and emotionally charged half-hour of chopping and flambé-ing, the successes or failures of the participants' efforts are judged. Not, as it turns out, by royalty, but by a celebrity. Someone from the world of show business sniffs and prods at the lovingly prepared plates of food, while the sweaty, starstruck competitors anxiously await their verdict. Today's prize, a state-of-the-art hostess trolley, has them fit to burst.

Yawning, Pauline studies her mother, bent forwards, no more than three feet from the set, fixated on the screen. The old biddy's eyes are alight as she nods and claps along with the TV audience. She licks her lips as the dishes are tasted and savoured and admired. Pauline has no doubt she's imagining herself to be in the show, centre stage once again.

'Come on down, contestant number two, *Dolores*!' [prolonged round of applause] 'Welcome to the show.'

'Thank you, Julian. It's lovely to be here.'

'So, tell us, delightful *Dolores*, how long have you been interested in cooking?'

'Ever since I was first married, Julian.'

'And what do you like to cook best?'

'Cakes.'

'Well, your husband must be a very happy man. Now, it's time to let the viewers at home know, *Dolores*, what are you going to cook for us tonight?'

'Tonight, Julian, I'm going to cook my signature dish: Coconut Surprise.'

'Can't wait. Put your hands together for our lovely contestants. Ladies, oven gloves on, wooden spoons at the ready. All together, everyone, it's time to get GUZZLING!'

Looking at her mother now, it's hard to imagine her as she was in her prime. No one ever pictures her as anything other than elderly. And sweet-looking. Pauline sighs. She knows their neighbours haven't the faintest notion her appearance is just a pleasant patina, not earned fairly through a long life kindly lived, but acquired through lucky adjustments the aging process has made to far more pointed original features. Soft jowls, as pink and pouchy as marshmallows, conceal a sharp, aggressive jawline. Scribblings of fine wrinkles have defrosted a mean mouth into the fat smudge that now passes for a warm smile. In youth, her cynical gaze smouldered beneath sultry lids. Today she's never seen outside the house without a liberal caking of cornflower blue eyeshadow, which gives a clownlike affability to her expression. Together, these alterations conspire to create a convincing façade.

Perhaps if people were to stop for a minute, look up from their lives and take more than a glance at her mother, they might see something else. Perhaps they'd catch the spiteful glint in her bird-bright eyes as they dart to and fro, scanning the landscape for all-comers. God knows, she doesn't miss a trick. Perhaps if anyone listened, they might hear the bitter diatribe tripping from between her constantly fluttering lips. A whispering, malevolent commentary. But neighbours are all too gladly deceived. They take it for granted that frail old ladies who appear homely and wear comical makeup must be equally benign in thoughts and deeds. So, no one ever does look hard, and no one ever listens to what she's saying. No one, that is, except for Pauline.

'Useless lump.'

Glancing at her wristwatch, Pauline remembers that at five o'clock the Reverend O'Reilly's wife is taking her mother to choir practice. Thank God. As soon as she's on her own in the house she can change the channel. She'll be free to watch her own favourite programme in private.

True Detective screens dramatic reconstructions of real criminal investigations. Although the names of the victims are 'changed to protect the innocent', the policemen involved in the cases play themselves. Most of the stories are about murders, mostly from America. She does enjoy the Texan police officers who call all the female suspects 'ma'am' – even the ones who are prostitutes. Pauline sighs in anticipation. She likes the idea of being called 'ma'am'.

As she picks at the edges of a third macaroon, she wonders what today's case will be about. Another random shooting? She hopes not. Gun crimes are so lacking in finesse. The stories she relishes are about small-town, domestic murders, carefully planned to the tiniest detail, where the means of death is something so much part of the normal fabric of life that it isn't even recognised as a weapon. Not death in a boring old hail of bullets, but by a ruck in the carpet. As for the identity of the murderers, the most satisfying cases are the ones where the victim knows their killer, but it's someone so inconsequential that no one ever thought them capable of any crime at all. She smiles to herself as she recalls her all-time favourite episode, 'The Dog Meat Massacre'. 'I can't believe he did it,' the astonished townsfolk cried on learning that one of their God-fearing community strangled his wife and then fed her minced remains to her own chihuahuas. 'But he was a *marvellous* neighbour, always kept himself to himself.'

Pauline has a great respect for such insidious assassins. Not people who are above suspicion, but people so low they're beneath it.

The vicar's wife arrives late.

'*Slovenly cow.*'

As usual she sweeps through Number 17 like a dose of salts, carried in and then out again on an enormous bow-wave of efficiency. It seems to Pauline that the woman barely ever touches the sides of the hallway in her haste to cross another good deed off her to-do list.

'Oh, ladies, ladies!' blusters Deirdre O'Reilly. 'You must have been wondering where I'd got to. I got held up by Mr Smith's bad foot. That's quite a saga. And then Brown Owl had issues with litter pick-up in the churchyard. But here I am at last, to whisk you off, Muriel. Now, where are your sticks? And your coat?' As she fusses around, she turns to Pauline. 'I wonder if you'd be so good as to fetch me mum's baked offerings for the homeless hostel supper, so I can sling them in the car at the same time.'

Used to following orders, Pauline quickly does as she's asked. To her amazement, in the few moments she's away, the vicar's wife somehow gets her mother dressed and ready, for when she returns, both are waiting for her by the door.

'Here you are, Deirdre.'

'Don't these look wonderful? You've excelled yourself, Muriel.'

'*I've spat on them.*'

'Delicious! I shall rush these to the hostel straight after choir practice. We all know there's nothing staler than a stale iced bun. And remember, Pauline,' calls Mrs O'Reilly over her shoulder as she sails out, steering Muriel by the elbow, 'the choir can always use another soprano.'

'*Pauline? Sing?*'

*

As soon as she's closed the front door behind them, Pauline goes back into the sitting room and switches over to her programme. Too late. She's missed the beginning. But when she realises it's a repeat of the episode 'The Kalashnikov Killings', she chooses to turn off the television and make the most of her temporary solitude. She toys with the idea of having another stab at the suicide note but decides against it. Instead, she sits back in her armchair, the armchair that was her father's, taking in the silence. She closes her eyes, allowing memories of Dad, which are never far away, to come to the fore.

She misses him now as much as ever. From the moment she was born, she was the apple of his eye. He was always saying so. She also knew that right from birth, her mother saw her as a tiresome inconvenience – a fact the old woman likes to remind her of to this day.

As Pauline considers the succession of childminders she had as a little girl, she finds she can still remember some of their names. There was a 'Nanny Sarah', a 'Nanny Susan', a 'Nanny Hetty'. Wasn't there even a 'Nanny Nancy'? She chuckles dryly. These women, who came and went faster than the seasons, had attended to her day-to-day needs while her father did his best to meet her emotional ones. He'd taken her to the park, read her bedtime stories and decorated the Christmas tree.

When she tries to recall the nannies' faces, though, none comes to mind. They seem to merge into one composite figure – essentially female, essentially capable, paid to watch over her while her mother sloped off into the wings. At some point in Pauline's childhood, *Dolores* all but withdrew from family life. She retired to the kitchen, closing the door firmly behind her. Interred within this tiled cocoon, she spent her days maniacally baking, uninterrupted by her husband or daughter, seldom re-emerging until Pauline was older, and slightly less *'repulsive'*.

Pauline summons a hazy recollection from when she was perhaps six years old, of hearing her mother singing at full volume while she mixed and measured; melodies that Pauline later learned were romantic songs from her days on the stage. *'Let me call you sweetheart, I'm in love with you …'*

She pictures her father, listening wistfully at the kitchen door. Poor man. Pretending Mum was singing about him. *'Let me hear you whisper… that you love me too.'*

But over the years, the singing stopped. Instead, her mother began to talk to herself. What was it she used to say? *'Why did you go without me?'* That was it. *'Why did you go without me, Vinny?'* God! She always sounded so angry, even back then. Clattering her baking tins. *'I don't belong here. Trapped here forever, that's what I am.'*

No longer did her father strain to catch his wife's words. Instead he, and Pauline too, endeavoured to turn deaf ears. As more years passed, it was a mercy when the talking became mumbling, and then, finally, a whisper, making it much easier for both to imagine they couldn't hear.

'There has got to be more to life than this place and these people. I am DOLORES!'

Following her stoic father's daily example, Pauline had always striven to please her mother. Together they weathered her rages, ignored her insults, and ate the endless stream of cakes she set before them. He was always encouraging Pauline to 'eat up, like a good girl'. And Pauline knew why. Hungry or not, they both recognised that these self-raised heaps, whipped up in the sanctum of her kitchen, were the closest her mother could ever offer either of them in the way of love. Neither wasted a crumb.

An aching sadness lurches inside her chest, making her gasp aloud. God knows she tried to be a good girl. God knows she's still trying.

Scolding herself, Pauline summons thoughts of better times. She did well at school. Got a decent pass in her secretarial course. Once the war was over, she had no trouble getting that office job, working for Frank. And with four whole pounds a week in her personal back pocket, she was bright enough to leave home quick smart. Rent her own place.

Closing her eyes again, she evokes her modest little bedsit above the baker's shop on the high street. Heaven. The details are vivid in her mind. One room, with a pull-out bed, a stove and sink in the corner, tucked away behind a curtain. The tiny bathroom, with its pink rubber shower attachment for the taps. A windowsill just broad enough to take a pot of geraniums. Although she'd moved no more than a short walk from Atbara Avenue, she'd stumbled out from under the monolithic shadow cast by her mother into a world that shone chromium bright. She was free.

A smile creeps across her face as she remembers the marvellous pleasure she took in keeping house, bleaching her net curtains until they were as white as the purest snow. Best of all, the flat meant she could entertain Frank. He'd come over. She'd make him a meal. Sometimes he brought a bottle of wine, something white and sweet, and they'd drink it together, sitting on her sofa bed, holding hands. Listening to Bing Crosby. Her smile broadens as her thoughts fly back through the years.

'May I kiss you, Pauline?'

'Oh yes, Frank, you may.'

She'd loved Frank and she believed he'd loved her in return. Why shouldn't he have loved her? She was attractive enough in those days. Perhaps not beautiful – not like *Dolores* – but she did make the best of herself. Back then. Sturdy rather than curvaceous, she'd known what clothes to wear to make the most of her figure. The fashions of the day had suited. She really thought they had.

Reaching up to touch her greying temple, Pauline thinks about the trouble she used to go to in order to keep her brown hair nice, treating herself to a monthly wash and set at the salon. She can't imagine setting foot in the hairdresser's now.

She and Frank enjoyed going to the pictures and having picnics in the park. Some weekends he'd take her out for the day… pick her up in his sporty silver car.

'A *Renault*,' breathes Pauline. Just saying its name sounds debonair. It had a walnut-effect dashboard and a built-in cigarette lighter. She inhales as she remembers the smell of its blue leatherette seat covers mingling with the scented cologne she'd bought Frank for his birthday. If the weather was fine they might even have a run out to the coast, stopping for tea in some country village on their way back. Frank was so smart in his demob suit. When he wore a cravat, he looked like Clark Gable. She decided that when Frank asked her to marry him, she would accept.

Her smile fades. It seems impossible she was ever that happy. And impossibly cruel such happy times could have been so short-lived. How long was it after she moved out that Dad's health went up the spout? Less than six months. Two heart attacks, one after the other. He was forced to retire from the bank. Of course, it was far beyond her mother's inclinations to take any care of him.

'Blasted, flaming, bloody nuisance. Always in my way.'

That's why Pauline came home. Just for the time being. Nothing permanent. Just until he was on the mend. But her poor, shattered father never did mend. His decline was rapid and terminal. Their last conversation is one of Pauline's most painful recollections. It was on the final day of his life, although she didn't know that at the time. Propped up in bed, he suddenly grabbed her hand, gripping it so abruptly that it hurt.

'Ow, Dad! Not so tight. You'll turn my fingers blue.'

'Promise me something, princess?'

'Of course, Dad. Anything.'

'Don't leave her on her own, will you? When I'm gone, promise me you'll stay with Mum.'

'But you're not going anywhere just yet, Dad.'

'You've always been such a *good* girl, Pauline. Who else'll take care of her? Just promise me. Promise your old dad.'

She looked into his face. His imploring eyes. 'Yes, Daddy, I promise.' And in the very next moment her flimsy father turned his face to the wall, sighed, and passed away.

The thought of these four words, so casually spoken, makes

Pauline physically cringe. Jesus Christ, how could she possibly have known what was to come?

In the first weeks after her father died, when Pauline was still strong enough to keep turning a deaf ear, she had ways of coping with her mother. She had her bedsit and occasionally retreated there, if only for an hour or two. She watered her geraniums. Saw Frank. Life in Number 17 was unpleasant, but not impossible. But then the firm she worked for, along with Frank, moved to bigger premises away from the borough. She couldn't follow without leaving her mother on her own. She lost her job. With her promise to her father ringing in her ears, and no money to pay rent, she let the bedsit go. Not long after, Frank stopped seeing her. And that was when the dreadful complacency began to set in. Like rising damp.

Her confidence ebbed away, her self-doubts reinforced by the background of constant whispering. Although she was pretty expert at tuning out her mother's vicious opinions, delivered *sotto voce* and unattenuated, enough shards of malice hit their mark to inflict at least one wound every day.

'Hopeless waste of space. I know why you're still here. Too pathetic to be on your own, that's why. "Will ye no' come back again?" Ha ha ha. In the end he didn't want you. In the end they never do.'

Now, sitting alone, kept company by a host of past regrets, Pauline longs for some respite from her mother. Apart from lightning-strike visits from the vicar's wife, callers to the house are rare. A smattering of well-meaning neighbours knocks from time to time, but although the old woman sometimes takes up Reginald Pyles's offers to mow the lawn, and has allowed young Robert Watts from up the road to trim the hedge, she never asks them inside. Pauline knows better than to extend any invitations of her own. It isn't her place to do so. She's painfully conscious that it isn't *her* house, or *her* parlour, or *her* china tea set. Everything inside these walls belongs to her mother.

Her mother is right. Pauline doesn't have any friends – or enemies – to invite. To her abject misery, Pauline has long conceded that she doesn't occupy sufficient space on the planet to warrant either. She simply rolls along, from day to day, in her own shrunken world. No one makes her stay at Number 17 but, miserable as she is, it's become impossible to leave. These are the most depressing facts of all. Somehow, weeks have turned into months, months into years, and today, more than two decades later, she's still here. Left with nothing to do but feed her face with comfortless cooking – an endless round of rock cakes and melting moments that stick to her fat, unmarried hips, anchoring her permanently to her mother's house.

The aching sadness returns to her chest, pressing harder than ever, threatening to actually burst her heart.

His wife draws the sitting-room curtains with such a vigorous *swoosh*, it makes the vicar jump. She looks troubled.

'Something worrying you, my love?' he asks, bashing the ashes from his pipe into the wastepaper basket.

'I was thinking about poor Pauline Dollimore. Honestly, Desmond,' she tuts, immediately emptying the contents of the bin into their empty hearth. 'One of these days you'll set fire to the vicarage.' She passes him a pottery saucer embossed with the likeness of Joan of Arc, which serves as his ashtray.

'Thinking what, exactly?' He takes a generous pinch of fresh tobacco and refills his bowl.

'How low she seems. Do you know, when I dropped Muriel Dollimore home this evening, I found Pauline just sitting in their front room, all alone in the dark. And I could tell she'd been crying. So, so sad. She looks pitiable these days.' She joins him on the sofa, picks up her knitting and attacks a new row.

'Pitiable is rather a harsh word.'

His wife is unapologetic. 'I mean it quite literally. Her appearance makes me pity her. And, for that matter,' she adds knowingly, 'so do some of the things I've heard about her past.'

'You know how we must resist the urge to gossip, however powerful the tempta—'

Her interruption is swift. 'I was *not* gossiping. I was conferring with another concerned member of our community. And during this conferring I found out that, believe it or not, Pauline was once engaged to be married. Well, practically engaged. Let's say "engaged to be engaged". So put *that* in your pipe and smoke it!'

'Who told you that?' His curiosity is piqued.

'I never like to reveal my sources,' she teases, 'but since you're so interested, it was Ursula Peabody.'

'How does she know? Did she say what happened?'

'I don't know, and I didn't ask. Remember it's not our business to pry!' She smiles. 'Suffice to say, something went wrong, and Pauline ended up crawling back to Mother and has stayed with her ever since.'

'Well, it's a blessing that Muriel was in a position to provide a roof over her head,' he says sincerely, suck, suck, sucking on his newly lit pipe.

'Yes, indeed. Pauline would be lost without her old mum.'

'Shouldn't we do something to help her? You're so clever at drawing people out of their shells.'

'I've been trying to get her to join things. Like the Women's Institute, quilting club… I mentioned the choir again tonight as it happens, but she just isn't interested.' Deirdre sighs as she resumes her knitting with renewed gusto. 'I shall certainly keep trying. Not least to get her out from under Muriel's feet. But who knows? Perhaps Pauline has ways of keeping up her spirits that we know nothing about.'

'I pray that you're right, Deirdre. Let us pray that you're right.'

Pauline isn't sure exactly when she first decided to murder her mother. It started as the smallest grain of an idea, hiding in the creases of the most private pages of her consciousness. At first, not even she acknowledged such a dirty little thought. So, for a long time, it just lurked, lost in the crowd, amongst many other unfinished plans jostling for attention in her head: she would move out of her mother's horrid house and find her own bright, airy flat on the new estate. She'd look up her old school friends. She'd find Frank and tell him she'd never stopped loving him. She'd reclaim her life.

Eventually, all these schemes withered to nothing. Over the passing years, the flats in the new estate were sold and sold again, old friends moved to new pastures… and Frank married someone else. But the murder idea festered away, growing in form and lustre with each disappointment, like a black seed pearl. Now it's enormous. It is *everything*.

It's not yet dawn, but Pauline is wide awake. Lying in bed, still enveloped in the gloom, once again she runs through her plan. Although it's a simple one, she likes to go over it in her head at least once a day, checking for leaks. In essence, it goes as follows: she'll dispatch her mother and make it look like suicide. Nice and straightforward.

She began her preparations a few weeks ago, working on the note to be found with the body. She's tried various compositions, but even though her mother's handwriting is similar to her own, she's decided to keep the content brief. The fewer the number of words, the fewer opportunities for scrutiny. In the end, the final version, which she completed just yesterday evening, reads quite simply: 'I have been a burden long enough.' Not that Pauline expects anyone to question the suicide. She's sure it's obvious to even the most casual observer that the old woman must be nothing but an encumbrance to the daughter who's stayed with her for the last twenty withering years, putting her own life on hold so her mother would never be alone. If the obnoxious witch had any decency, she'd have killed herself years ago.

Pauline is pleased the note is, at last, done. But with that out of the way, she must now address her plan's next phase. She sits up in bed and takes in the room that's been hers since childhood: the doll's house her father made, on top of the wardrobe, its unblinking plastic windows staring down at her; her old school books on the shelf; the mother-of-pearl ring box Frank bought her, forever empty, gathering dust on her ridiculous, girlish dressing table. Just as the familiar, creeping ache begins to invade her chest, the whine of a milk float in the street outside shakes her from her reverie. She hears the distant rattle of the number seven bus, the first of the morning, heading off towards the city. Sure signs that the rest of the world is waking up to face the day.

Pauline, too, musters herself. Enough procrastination. She knows that although it will take courage, the time has come to turn her full attention to the real meat of the matter. The means of death.

When Deirdre O'Reilly spots Pauline Dollimore in the ironmonger's, she pounces at once. 'Pauline, how lovely to see you. The slugs are causing merry hell in the vicarage veg plot too.' Seeing that Pauline is nonplussed, she adds by way of explanation, 'You're holding a packet of slug pellets, so I just assumed…'

'Oh, yes, sorry, Deirdre.' Pauline hastily stuffs the packet back on the shelf. 'I was miles away. As a matter of fact, I've finished my shopping. But then I came back to get some string… and,' she adds lightly, 'some wallpaper paste. So, you see, nothing poisonous. I can't think what I was about.'

'Do you know, I believe wallpaper paste might actually *be* poisonous?'

'Really?' A spark of something like interest briefly ignites Pauline's dull eyes.

'Well, if one ate enough of it, perhaps. But we wouldn't want to go sprinkling it on our porridge, would we?' chuckles Deirdre, giving Pauline a little nudge. She peers into Pauline's shopping basket and makes a swift appraisal of its contents. 'Good gracious, you *have* been stocking up. It seems the Plagues of Egypt must have landed upon Number 17. Ant powder, weedkiller, wasp spray! Whatever next? Locust repellent? Mind you, I wouldn't bother with that packet of Drano. It doesn't work half so well as neat caustic soda. That's what I put down the vicarage plugholes and our pipes are beautifully clear. Just ask the ironmonger.' She makes a move to summon him over.

Pauline stops her. 'Oh no, please, Deirdre. I don't want to trouble him. Besides, as I say, I've already made my purchases for today, so, if you don't mind—'

'Well take some of mine then!' says Deirdre, thrusting a packet of the crystals into Pauline's basket. 'I've just bought two of these for myself.'

'No really. I couldn't.'

'Don't be silly. Think of it as a little treat from me.'

Pauline offers no further protest but shifts slightly from foot to foot.

Noticing that Pauline is eying the shop's door, planning her escape, Deirdre swiftly strikes again. 'Anyway, I'm so glad I've run into you. I've been meaning to ask whether you'd like to join my sewing bee. We meet once a fortnight, at the vicarage. Just local ladies.'

Pauline hesitates, as if considering the offer.

'And, of course, you *must* bring your mother.'

'No,' replies Pauline decisively, 'but thank you so much for thinking of me. Now I'm afraid you must excuse me.'

'What about the wallpaper paste?'

'I don't need any after all,' she answers, her tone of voice suddenly distant and vague.

'Are you quite all right?' Deirdre notices Pauline looks tearful, and very pale. 'May I walk you home?'

'Oh. No. Thank you. I'm quite all right,' she mumbles, reeling towards the exit. 'I'm always quite all right.'

'Say hello to Muriel from me.'

Pauline wanders homewards. As always, she walks tight in to the front garden walls, avoiding the centre of the pavement. It's her practice to keep out of the paths of pushchairs, waggy-tailed dogs and the puddles of fallen cherry blossoms that mock her spinsterly progress.

Deciding on a staged suicide was all very well, but finding a way to do it is proving tricky. Despite giving this a lot of thought, so far all her ideas have unacceptable drawbacks. Poison seemed like a good solution, at least at first. But now she's reconsidering. She can't think of a way of buying something over the counter that would be toxic or corrosive enough to kill her mother, without it being traced back to her. She's regretting asking the ironmonger which of the surprising array of rat poisons he stocks is the most easily soluble in hot milk. He tried to sell her a mousetrap. And the bloody vicar's wife! Deirdre has seen – and no doubt made an indelible mental note of – all this morning's acquisitions, so now Pauline can't use any of these either. What a waste of money!

Pauline thinks about the caustic soda that Deirdre foisted onto her. It does look very like granulated sugar, and it could undoubtedly do somebody serious harm if they were to 'accidentally' take some. But Pauline has no idea how to engineer such an unfortunate mishap, short of putting a heap of the crystals in the middle of the kitchen table in a bowl labelled 'sugar', suggesting her mother make herself a nice, sweet cup of tea, and then leaving the old woman to brew up. As if. The hateful slouch hasn't boiled her own kettle in over twenty years.

Anyway, even if Pauline does manage to get her hands on a suitably noxious substance without attracting attention, and she does somehow get her mother to swallow it, how can she be sure of delivering a lethal dose? How many spoonfuls of slug pellets, or wallpaper paste, or drain unblocker, would it take to get the job done? One? Two? Twenty-two? She remembers a disturbing episode of *True Detective*, where an intended victim failed to succumb to a diet laced with antifreeze because the would-be murderess messed up and only managed to get her husband to drink enough to cause convulsions. Just imagine if she were to make a similar mistake. She might be found out or, even worse, stuck with Mum, not dead but perhaps blinded, or incontinent, more foul-mouthed and difficult than ever. What a nightmare! This isn't a risk she can afford to take.

Pauline knows she isn't anything like clever enough with wiring to stage an electrocution. Besides, who 'kills themselves' by sticking their finger in a socket? Not only would it seem too incredible that the old woman would take her own life in this way, but Pauline doesn't want to end up burning the house down. And as for staging a bathtub drowning or a hanging, there were myriad reasons for ruling out anything so physically ambitious.

She arrives back at Number 17 just one bit more discouraged than she was when she left it.

'Yoo hoo!' calls Pauline as she lets herself in. 'Home again.'

On hearing no reply, she scurries into the kitchen and hastily puts away her now redundant purchases. She stows the Drano under the kitchen sink; the ant powder, weedkiller and wasp spray in the cupboard under the stairs. And Deirdre's sodding soda crystals? She stuffs them into an old tin caddy and shoves it right to the back of the top shelf in the pantry. Out of sight, out of mind.

'Are you in, Mum?' she calls again. Still hearing nothing, not even a whisper, her mood lifts. Although she has a mountain of chores to get through, at least she has the place to herself. She'll be able to work in peace for a change.

Apart from withstanding her mother's limitless vitriol, she has to contend with her untidiness. Used to being waited on hand and foot, first by her husband and then by her daughter, she does absolutely nothing to keep their home straight. The old lady moves restlessly from room to room, leaving chaos in her wake. She always makes the worst mess in the kitchen. Although Pauline was never allowed in there as a child, as her mother has grown older and lazier, she now accepts her daughter's presence in what was once exclusively her realm. But purely on a needs-must basis. Her cooking generates daily storms of disarray, and Pauline is the one left to wash the pots and sweep up after her.

When her mother isn't baking, she's constantly rummaging through cupboards and drawers. Whispering and rummaging, rummaging and whispering, she reminds Pauline of a foraging pig. Her favourite quarry is any photograph of herself, of which she has countless examples. She never seems to tire of looking at dated publicity shots of the dazzling *Dolores*, queen of the stage. At other times, she digs for recipes cut out of magazines. Every drawer in the house is stuffed with sticky scraps of paper. Nothing is sorted into any kind of order. Bank statements and bills are mixed in with the litter of her mother's memories. It drives Pauline mad that important documents are always getting lost. Every day is a battle to keep even a semblance of tidiness in Number 17.

Pauline pulls on her shabby housecoat, slips on her shabby slippers, and arms herself with duster and beeswax to begin her regime. As she enters the dining room she gasps in shock. To her surprise her mother's already in there, busily leafing through an old theatre programme, one of many dozens sprawled before her on the dining table. A moth-eaten boa is draped around her neck and she's adorned herself with an assortment of jewellery – some real, some fake, but all gifts from *Dolores*'s stage-door admirers. Pauline guesses her mother must have been in the dining room for some time, given the number of crimson feathers trampled into the carpet.

'Mum! You didn't half give me a fright! I'd no idea you were in here.'

Her mother doesn't look directly at her, but throws her a nasty sidelong stare.

'I just thought I'd have a quick whizz round with the hoover,' Pauline continues, her resolute semblance of good humour quickly restored. 'Spruce things up a bit.'

'*What for? In case you have company? Ha ha.*'

'Why don't I get started on the kitchen, so as not to disturb you.'

'*Tidying? Cleaning? Fetching in the coal? That Cinderella act doesn't fool me. Cinderella was supposed to be beautiful.*'

'The vicar's wife sends her love, by the way.'

*

Over the following weeks, Deirdre O'Reilly makes numerous overtures to Pauline. At every opportunity, which by coincidence often seem to arise in the aisles of the ironmonger's, she extends an invitation to some event or another. She offers to take her, and naturally her mother too, to bridge, flower arranging, even brass rubbing. But all proposals of such companionable pastimes are politely rejected.

'Honestly, Desmond,' sighs Deirdre, 'Pauline Dollimore is an absolute *wreck* these days. So miserable she looks unwell. Sometimes I wonder how Muriel stands it.'

It's Maytime. Spring gambols towards summer. The days get longer, and after school the children of Atbara Avenue play in the street. Released into the teatime sunshine, a bellowing trio of boys rattles a homemade go-cart up and down the pavement, shedding caps, blazers, satchels and splinters of orange-box in their wake. A gaggle of little girls has chalked up a hopscotch grid, right outside Number 17. Hop, hop, hop, split, hop! Festering in the gloom of her mother's front room, Pauline can hear the *tap, tap, tap* of their skipping ropes on the flagstones, and their maddening rhyming chants.

'Johnny gave me apples,
'Johnny gave me pears.
'Johnny gave me thruppence
'To kiss him on the stairs.
'I gave him back his apples,
'I gave him back his pears.
'I gave him back his thru'penny bit
'And kicked him down the stairs.'

She sighs to herself. She looks across at the old lady asleep in her chair, a framed photograph of *Dolores* resting on her chest. Kick her downstairs? If only!

Pauline has been chewing over her options, but after a lot of restive deliberation, she still finds herself no further forward. Resolved to commit her murder, but without a modus operandi fixed in her mind, she's unable to proceed. If *True Detective* has taught her nothing else, it's that the absolute bedrock of an effective looks-like-a-suicide killing 'has to be a cast-iron MO, folks'.

This inability to settle on a strategy – to get the thing over and done with – has greatly added to her abject state. Unable to sleep, eating more cake than ever, she fears the murder plan might never come to fruition. Perhaps she *is* nothing more than a '*hopeless failure*'. Close to the end of her tether, this is the lowest Pauline's ever felt in her whole, low-ebb life.

Much to her disquiet, there've been times recently when her anxious state has been so obvious that it's drawn unwanted attention. In her latest encounter with Deirdre O'Reilly, the blasted busybody practically begged her to seek medical help.

'Pauline,' she burred in a voice steeped with pity, 'you really should see someone.'

'Thank you for your concern, Deirdre, but I can assure—'

'The thing is, my dear, whatever it is that's worrying you,' she went on, raising the palm of her hand to silence Pauline, 'and don't you dare tell me you haven't anything on your mind, because I can see that you do – it's making you ill.'

These comments rattled Pauline at the time, and they still do now. If people can see she's this distracted, that she's ruminating dark thoughts, perhaps they might even work out what those dark thoughts are? Maybe she does need to take steps to improve her demeanour, or risk arousing suspicion?

Deirdre had continued, 'Go and see a professional, Pauline. Ask a doctor to make you feel better. If not for your own sake, then do it for Muriel.'

The recollection of this last remark brings a brief, rueful smile to Pauline's face. Taking care not to wake her mother, she rises to her feet, quietly slips into the hall and picks up the telephone.

When Deirdre O'Reilly next bumps into Pauline, she's delighted to hear her news. She can hardly wait to pass it on to her husband.

She finds him on his knees in the churchyard's memorial garden, pulling up weeds.

'Desmond!' she gushes. 'You'll never *guess* what Pauline Dollimore's done.'

'Stolen her mother's walking sticks and run amok in Woolworths?' offers the vicar teasingly.

'What a thing to say!' she gasps. 'Pauline must be the most timorous person I know. No,' she continues triumphantly, 'she's taken my advice and booked herself an appointment at the local surgery.'

'Has she now? Well done indeed.' He smiles, pulling himself upright to pat her shoulder. 'I can see why you're pleased.'

'Thank you. It's gratifying to know that one really has been of help to a friend in need, even if it is in just a small way.'

When the day of Pauline's appointment dawns, she expects to be seen by her usual doctor, a brusque woman who keeps patient encounters brief and compassion carefully rationed. Pauline has already mentally prepared herself for the long wait in the waiting room, followed by a short but thorough pull-yourself-together consultation, after which she'll trail back home again, still broken. Indeed, she fears the only merit in this exercise will be the break it makes in her grindingly monotonous routine. However, quite by chance on this bright, bright morning that had promised so little, she learns that Dr Gwendoline Berry-Bowness has been called away. To her surprise, Pauline is, instead, seen by a locum GP.

Not long out of medical school, new to the practice, and *such* a caring young man, he is wonderfully sympathetic, Pauline finds. He asks her all about her life at home and, quite unlike her normal self, Pauline lets the whole story come tumbling out. She misses out the bit about the murder plans – obviously – but she does tell him how long she's been living with her mother, about her mother's talking to herself, her own sense of feeling trapped. The handsome young doctor is such a good listener. Pauline notices he doesn't so much as glance at his watch once the entire time she's talking. He looks genuinely sorry for her when she starts to cry.

'Thank you for being so candid about your domestic situation, Miss Dollimore,' he says when she's finished. 'I can see that sharing your circumstances with me hasn't been easy for you.'

He's very charming and though he doesn't call her 'ma'am', when he says 'Miss Dollimore' Pauline experiences a frisson of pleasure that makes her blush. There's definitely something of Frank about him around the eyes.

'I'm sorry for being so emotional, Doctor,' she gulps, trying to blow her snotty nose as prettily as possible.

'No need to apologise. Your feelings are entirely understandable. You, Miss Dollimore, are suffering from what I like to call a "reactive depression". In fact, I'm quite concerned about your frame of mind.'

'You are?' Pauline is so astounded to hear anyone express any concern about anything to do with her, it's all she can do not to burst into tears again. 'Because, quite honestly, I'm at my wits' end.'

'Rest assured, Miss Dollimore, I can see that for myself.' The young doctor leans forward and pats her hand.

Pauline takes in the medicated scent of his soap and the potent, masculine whiff of hair cream, and she swallows, hard.

'For now, I'm going to prescribe a course of tablets, just something to help you sleep, and let's see how that goes. It may be that a proper night's rest will be all it takes to make you feel better.'

'Thank you so much. I can't tell you—'

The doctor interrupts her. 'There is one other thing I would like to suggest, if I may?'

'What's that?'

'I would like to visit your mother.'

'My mother?' Pauline's aghast.

'Yes. Having listened to what you've told me, I'm a bit worried about *her* health too. It may be nothing, but the agitated behaviour you describe could be an early sign of senile dementia. Caring for someone who is suffering personality changes, especially a close family member' – he nods knowingly – 'can be extremely challenging. It might help if I could see her myself.'

'Oh, dear. I'm afraid that she won't like that idea. She really can be *so* difficult, Doctor, I'm not at all sure…'

'Well, why don't you mention it to her when you get home and let's see what happens, eh? You never know. Your mother may just catch you by surprise.' He smiles reassuringly. 'If she agrees to seeing me, give our reception desk a ring to let me know. She doesn't even have to come to the surgery. I can pop in to see her, first house call on my rounds – just to make sure all's well.'

The young doctor makes his proposal sound so easy, but when Pauline leaves the consulting room she's filled with doubts. A stranger 'popping in' to Number 17. Worse still, a 'pop in' elicited by *her* actions. She can't see any way on this earth her mother would sanction it.

She makes her way home, her pace becoming slower and slower as she gets nearer and nearer her destination. By the time she's back in Atbara Avenue she's almost sick with despondency. Nevertheless, not wanting to disappoint the kindly doctor, she does exactly as he's asked.

It's to Pauline's utter amazement that her mother not only consents to seeing the doctor – she actually seems keen to have him come.

The following day, the old woman prepares for his visit with care, plastering on makeup to recreate a ghastly parody of *Dolores*. Even Pauline herself puts on an ironed housecoat in honour of their guest.

'*Pathetic.*'

To the doctor's surprise, on arriving at the Dollimore household he finds the elderly lady bears no resemblance to the character described by her daughter. Quite the contrary, she comes across as calm, collected and the very embodiment of venerable cosiness. Admittedly a little short-tempered with Miss Pauline Dollimore, whom she dismisses to the kitchen to fetch shortbread – *'homemade'* – she welcomes him into her front parlour. After spending just a few minutes alone with her, he's very soon satisfied there's nothing whatever wrong with this patient's mental capacities.

'Sharp as a needle, you are, Mrs Dollimore. Marvellous for your age.'

The only symptom of any note is that she too complains of sleeping badly.

'Ah yes,' he thinks to himself, 'now that *does* concur with the younger woman's account of her mother's restlessness.'

He opens up his brand-new Gladstone bag and fishes out his prescription pad. 'Mrs Dollimore, I'm guessing this is a pretty anxious time for you. Having met you, I see you hide your feelings well, but I'm sure worrying about Pauline's depression must be weighing on your mind, keeping you awake at night.'

Mrs Dollimore mutters something he doesn't quite catch.

'Quite so,' he continues, wagging his index finger in a gently scolding manner. 'But it's important you look after yourself as well, starting with a good night's sleep. I'm going to write out a weekly prescription for some pills – as it happens, the same ones that I've sorted out for your daughter. In fact, she can pick up your tablets each time she goes to the chemist's to collect her own. Killing two birds with one stone, eh?'

Mrs Dollimore mutters something else, which he doesn't quite catch either.

'Well, likewise I'm sure. The pleasure's all mine. Now, I'm certain if you take the tablets things will soon pick up. Try not to worry about Pauline.'

When Pauline returns from the kitchen he pockets the shortbread 'as a treat for later' and makes his farewells to both ladies. He sets off on the rest of his house calls, pleased his bedside manner has been so well received.

*

Pauline continues to wave goodbye to the young doctor until he's completely disappeared from view. As she returns inside from the front gate of Number 17, it's all she can do to contain her elation. A happy day indeed! Just when despair had threatened to overwhelm her, she's been presented with a practical murder weapon; not on a plate, but in white plastic pots. Little sugar-coated tablets. So much more convenient than antifreeze; so much more probable than arsenic. She can scarcely believe her luck.

The way forward is, at last, clear to Pauline. She can use her own supply of medication to kill Mum and, after the event, make sure that empty pill pots are found with the body, along with the note. Her mother will be gloriously dead, dead, dead, and it'll be completely obvious she died by her own hand!

Pauline isn't even worried by the possibility of an autopsy. After all, any pills found in Mum's stomach will match the ones written up for her by the doctor. As for motive or, rather, 'suicidal tendencies' on old Muriel's part, by her own admission she's been sleeping badly too. Not five minutes ago, Pauline overheard her saying as much to the doctor. That's why he prescribed the pills. The *lovely* man. And everyone knows sleeplessness is a sure sign of depression. It's not going to matter whose fingerprints are on what. Not that it'll ever come down to fingerprints. This will be an open-and-shut case. Simple, neat, perfect.

That night, Pauline sleeps better than she has done in years.

Exactly as the young doctor surmised, old Mrs Dollimore rarely ventures as far as the high street, so he was right about Pauline making trips to the chemist on behalf of them both. Each prescription is for only seven days' supply at a time, delaying the execution of her plan until she's stockpiled enough medication to ensure her mother's suicide will be successful. But, as far as Pauline's concerned, the day of the murder can't come soon enough.

Although she faithfully hands her mother a pot of pills each week, Pauline sees no signs she's actually swallowing any.

Judging by the rattling noises coming from the old woman's large crocodile-skin handbag, she can guess where she's hiding them. Pauline makes a mental note: when the deed is done, dispose of that stash! Then no one can question how poor dear Muriel managed to 'overdose' without downing her own hoard. Should Pauline flush them down the lavvy, or will the bathroom plughole do? She'll decide later. Details for another day. But that *bloody* handbag! Her mother has taken to carrying it around wherever she goes. Perhaps she really is going senile? The rummaging habit certainly seems to be getting worse. More restless than ever, day and night, she moves from room to room. Poking about. Rattling and rummaging, rummaging and whispering.

'Sleeping pills indeed! Over my dead body.'

Finally, after twenty-one long days of pill-hoarding, it's time. Pauline goes out. Just down to the local shops, as usual. She wants everything to appear as ordinary as possible. She's learned from *True Detective* that it's very, very important to stick to her normal routine. As she leaves the house, she can hear her mother clattering around in the kitchen, blabbering away, bashing pans and dropping knives. Baking again. Creating bedlam.

'Not long now,' she mutters to herself. 'Not long now.'

Pauline spends an hour or so wandering up and down the high street. She visits a few shops, without buying anything, and takes one last look at her old flat above the bakery. Whoever lives there now hasn't hung any lace curtains, but she notices there's a potted geranium on the windowsill, its red flowers bobbing in the afternoon sunshine.

She rallies herself. 'It must be done.'

Pauline turns into the chemist's. The shop doorbell announces her arrival. She tries to look casual, thumbing through a display of tweezers while she waits for the small queue of other customers to finish their purchases. Miss Cartwright from Number 5 is stocking up on "Bombshell Blonde" hair dye, Mrs Ursula Peabody from Number 34 is stocking up on liver salts, and Mr

Richard Pyles from Number 3 is buying sticks of barley sugar from the large jar on the counter because – as he takes his time explaining to anyone who'll listen – they are his favourite.

'Good afternoon, Miss Dollimore,' says the pharmacist brightly, when at last she hands over the two prescriptions. 'Lovely day for it.'

'Yes indeed,' she replies tautly.

He peers at the pieces of paper over the top of his glasses, holding them at arm's length to decipher the doctor's scrawl. 'That's fine. I just have to ask you to sign for mum's medication again. How is the dear lady these days?'

'Same as always, Mr Chen.'

'Bless her.'

Pauline signs and the pharmacist goes into the back of the shop, emerging a few moments later with the pots of pills in his hand. 'Is it all right if I pop them in the one bag, Miss Dollimore?'

'I won't need a bag, thanks. They'll be fine in my pocket.'

It's all Pauline can do to keep her hand from trembling as Mr Chen gives them to her. Mumbling her thanks, she immediately turns to leave. She's in such a hurry that she's already at the shop door when he calls her back.

'If you would be so good as to wait for one moment, Miss Dollimore, I just need to ask you a couple of questions.'

Pauline feels the blood drain from her face. 'Questions?' She reaches into her coat pocket and touches the small white plastic pots, nestling in the satin lining. She runs her fingernail over the ridges on the side of a pot's lid. She hears it rasp. 'What kind of questions?'

'The ones I always ask you when you come for your pills.' He smiles innocuously. 'Like: "Are you planning to operate any machinery?"'

'I beg your pardon?'

'Remember not to drive, or to operate machinery while taking these pills.'

The ridiculousness of these statements takes Pauline by surprise. She lets out a nervous laugh. 'I won't be doing either of those things, thank you. And nor will my mother.' With that, she pulls the door open and makes her escape.

'And don't take them on an empty stomach,' the pharmacist calls after her. 'Make sure you take them with food!'

Pauline opens the front door and, as she comes in, calls out, 'It's just me, Mum, back from the shops. Why don't I make us both a nice hot drink to have with the telly?'

Good as her word, she bustles into the kitchen and puts the kettle on the gas ring, alongside a small pan of milk to heat through, humming to herself as she works. She has to hum quite loudly to blot out the sound of her mother stomping around upstairs. Pauline hums 'Jerusalem' – her father's favourite hymn. She decides to stop after the first verse, though, choosing to push such disquieting evocations of the man out of her mind. Sorry, Dad.

Pauline doesn't like to think of him watching her actions from some heavenly cloud above. So, as she waits for the kettle to boil, she turns her attention to clearing up the kitchen. It's in a dreadful state. Much worse than usual. Good grief! What *has* Mum been up to? Various open packets of ingredients are strewn about the work surfaces and there's a stack of unwashed mixing bowls. Her mother has even had the pestle and mortar out. A sprinkling of white powder spills over the Formica worktops and snows down onto the sticky brown linoleum floor. Perhaps baking soda? Cream of tartar? Possibly flour? Pauline shrugs her shoulders. Who cares what it is? This is the last time she'll ever have to deal with the old woman's mess, so she decides to just get on with it. She picks up a tea towel, runs it under the hot tap and begins to wipe up. Then, as has been her habit for half her childhood and her entire adult life, she meticulously washes and dries each used item before returning it to its rightful place in the cupboards. In no time at all the room is spotless. No one would ever know Muriel had been in there.

In the middle of the kitchen table, carefully arranged on a cake stand, is the end result of her mother's efforts. Six perfect, moist macaroons sitting on a dainty lace doily, each dusted with icing sugar and crowned with a glistening glacé cherry.

'Irresistible.'

Just as she always does, Pauline helps herself, stuffing one into her mouth as she stands over the kitchen sink. She lifts two cups from their shelf. Into the chipped one with a faded floral design on its side she drops a teabag; into the china coronation one, she tips three heaped spoonfuls of cocoa powder. She has another macaroon. Then, from a hiding place under the sink she retrieves three full pots of pills. She empties these, along with today's haul, on top of the cocoa. For good measure, she adds several generous spoonfuls of sugar to each cup before filling hers with hot water and her mother's with hot milk. She puts the empty pill pots into the cutlery drawer. For later. They need to be found with the body. While she waits for the last traces of pills to dissolve, Pauline polishes off another macaroon. As she stirs and stirs she wonders, idly, if she'll miss her mother's baking.

The hall clock chimes the half-hour. It's almost time for *The Galloping Guzzler*! Pauline scurries into the dining room and, as quietly as possible, eases open the sideboard drawer. Reaching right to the back, she recovers the suicide note. It's looking quite dog-eared. More than she remembers it looking before. But this is hardly surprising, she supposes, considering the number of times that it's been re-read. Well, so what if it does look a little used? Pauline's sure that suicide victims must often procrastinate.

Seeing that it's such a special occasion, Pauline puts her mother's and her own cup onto a little silver tray before carrying them through to the front room. Taking great care not to spill either of the drinks, she places the tray onto the occasional table between their two armchairs. Again, she calls upstairs.

'Drink's ready, Mum. Hurry up! Your favourite programme's beginning… and I've already started on those macaroons.'

Hearing no coherent answer – only a mean, muffled cackle – Pauline settles down in her chair. She closes her eyes and while she waits for her mother to join her, happy thoughts of Frank, Liebfraumilch and geraniums swim around in her tired, tired head.

It's Deirdre O'Reilly who discovers the body, early the next morning. She calls at Number 17 to offer Pauline, and Muriel of course, tickets for the Women's Institute's next coach trip. Having got no answer to her repeated knocking, she steps into the front flowerbed and peers through their bay window.

That's when she sees her, slumped in her armchair, TV still on, a teaspoon resting in her lap. Returning to the front door and realising that it isn't, in fact, locked, she lets herself in.

A cursory examination of the scene tells her what she already knows. Pitiable Pauline is dead, a crumpled note folded in her partially open hand. On a nearby table are two cups; one filled with a milky drink, untouched and skinned over; one empty, save a few dregs of cold tea. Next to the cups, neatly lined up, are four empty pill pots. She kneels down beside Pauline, lifts her wrist and satisfies herself that the pathetic woman's threadbare heart is no longer beating. Rising to her feet, she switches off the TV. She rings for the police, her husband, and the nice new doctor.

These formalities over, blaming herself for not doing enough to prevent this sad event, she goes to awaken poor, poor, *poor* Mrs Dollimore, not yet risen from her bed, to break the dreadful news.

2

Soul Mates

From a distance, Colin Peabody appears to be a natural loner; a self-contained lad, conveniently settling for his own peculiar company. He's very small for his age. And thin. With dark brown eyes, long, long lashes and raven-black hair, he might be of Latin descent, if it wasn't for his bone china complexion. In certain lights his skin has an almost ghostly translucency. The football-boot bruises and riotous acne sported by his peers have overlooked him. Controlled and quiet, Colin is also devoid of his classmates' burgeoning unwieldiness. He is far from a typical twelve-year-old. Because of his slight build, he could be mistaken for a younger boy, but something in the shadows of his face, the sobriety of his countenance, makes him seem much older.

From his viewpoint in the front window of Number 34 Atbara Avenue, Colin watches with great interest as two paramedics manhandle a trolley over the threshold of Number 17, the house directly across the street. Their boiler suits and gloves make them look a bit like dustmen. The local doctor, whom he recognises, is flapping about in the flowerbeds, trampling pansies and getting in the way. Colin can tell by the shape and wobble of the body bag strapped on top of the trolley that it contains the fatter of the two Dollimores. A momentary tightness enters his chest; a sensation some might have supposed to be sadness, but it comes and goes too quickly for him to get the measure of it. He assumes the passing of miserable Pauline has merely triggered a little indigestion.

Ursula Peabody finishes washing the last of the lunch plates and slots it into the draining rack. As she arranges a damp tea towel over the kitchen radiator she calls out, 'Colin! What are you up to? I'm nipping to the corner shop but when I get back, d'you fancy a game of Scrabble? Keep us busy till Dad gets home. I'll let you have first pick of the letters.' Hearing no reply, she puts her head round the sitting-room door to catch her son, parked right in the centre of the bay window, unashamedly observing the commotion opposite. 'What are you doing, Son? Keep away from there or the neighbours'll see you!'

Without shifting his gaze and without answering her question, Colin says, matter-of-factly, 'I think Pauline Dollimore is dead.'

Ursula moves at once to his side. Resting her hand on his shoulder, she says gently, 'I know. The postman told me.'

'How does he know?'

'He caught sight of something going on when he arrived with this morning's mail. I wasn't going to say anything about it.'

'Why not?'

'Well, it's upsetting, isn't it?' sighs Ursula, adding, 'And none of our business,' as she too peers through the net curtains to get a better look at unlovely, unloved Pauline's final exit from Muriel's house. 'You'd think they'd have got a rug or something to cover that up. It doesn't seem decent, lugged out in a zip-up bag. I'll pop over the road later and put a card through her door. Poor soul.'

Colin turns sharply to look at his mother. 'Who's a "poor soul"?'

Regretting her choice of words, Ursula reflects for a moment, screwing her hands into her apron. 'Well, both of them I suppose. Her mum, because she'll be all on her own now, and Pauline herself, of course. Especially when you think how she went. The postman thinks she…' Ursula lowers her voice to a near-whisper and mouths, '… took her own life.' She makes a tut-tutting sound. 'Isn't it awful? Gossiping like that. Although there'll be those of the opinion she's committed a sin.'

'A sin?'

'Yes. It says so in the Bible, doesn't it? One of the Ten Commandments: "Thou shalt not kill". And that means kill *anyone*. Including yourself. Suicide is a "mortal sin" in some folks' books.'

'What happens to people who commit suicide, then?'

'How do you mean "happens to them"? They end up just the same as anyone who's struck by lightning, has a heart attack or, God forbid,' continues Ursula, chuckling at the very thought, 'gets themselves murdered. They end up dead.'

'No, that's not what I mean, Mum. I mean, if they've committed a mortal sin, what happens to their *souls*? Can they still leave?'

'Now that's an odd sort of question. I'm not really following you… Come away from the window, there's a good boy. Wherever did I put my purse?' Ursula unties her apron and trots into the kitchen, returning with her handbag.

Aware his mother wants to change the subject, Colin turns back towards the window in time to see the ambulance pull away. He watches it drive off, slowly at first, but it only gets as far as Number 29 before it speeds up sharply and disappears up the avenue. It seems the length of decorum required to mark due respect for dead Pauline can be counted in just a few yards. He realises he has to rephrase his question.

'I suppose I want to know if their souls still get into Heaven.'

His mother lets out a gasp of surprise, bends down and cups his face in her hands, squashing his cheeks and making his mouth into a silly goldfish pout.

'What a gorgeous boy you are, worrying about a thing like that. There's not many on this earth who'll be fussing about the next life of Pauline Dollimore, let alone handsome young men like you. I may not know all the ins and outs of God's mysterious ways, but *that*, I can tell you, *is* a fact! Whatever took her, her soul's gone to a better place than it's been for years, may she rest in peace. Now, I'm off to get my "With Sympathy" card before they close. Want anything yourself?' She opens the hall cupboard, pulls out her jacket and headscarf and makes ready to leave.

'You could pick me up some of those stomach pills.'

His mother immediately stops fastening her jacket, re-enters the sitting room and once again she takes Colin's cheeks in her hands, scrutinising his features for the smallest of tell-tale signs. 'Are you off colour again, sweetheart?' she asks, anxiety ringing in her voice.

Taking hold of her wrists, Colin gently moves her hands away from his. 'No. I'm fine. Really. A bit of a tummy ache, that's all.'

'Just your insides hurting? Nothing else?'

'No. Nothing else. Get me those minty pills I can suck. The other ones are too chalky.'

'All right then. I'll be back as quick as I can and then we can have that game of Scrabble. Now, come away from the window like I asked. It's morbid gawping at a scene like that.'

Ursula buttons up and sweeps out, slamming the front door behind her.

Colin rolls his wheelchair back, away from the window, but Adam carries on watching. Colin tries to get him to come away too, but he knows that once Adam puts his mind to something, there's no turning him. Colin knows all about Adam and Adam knows all about $C_3.O_1.L_1.I_1.N_1$.

Over the last few years, Colin has had a lot of time to consider Adam and the nature of their very special relationship. By now, he accepts the head injury triggered his modified mental state. He was born sane. Since the accident, he's different. And on these points, Colin and the medical profession are agreed. However, when it comes to the nitty-gritty of his diagnosis, they don't see eye to eye at all. While no one has actually said 'insane', they do use words like 'altered' and 'brain structure' in the same sentence. Here lies the fork in the road, for Colin absolutely cannot accept he's mentally ill. Just mentally 'split'. Adam is of the same mind.

Waiting for his mother to return from her errand, he recalls last week's session with yet another doctor, this time a psychologist, who'd made him explain things all over again. It's not that she was unsympathetic – in fact, she was quite a good listener – it's just that the meeting now seems as pointless to him as all the others.

She'd ushered him into her smelt-the-same-as-the-surgery office, gushing formal informalities like a true pro. 'Hello, Colin. Super to meet you. I'm Sally Bickerstaff, but most people call me Doctor Sally. Come on in and take a seat.' Flushing extremely red, in an effort to diffuse their mutual embarrassment while he positioned his wheelchair opposite her desk, she offered him a drink. 'Juice? Water?' Without noticing that he'd declined, she buzzed the receptionist and asked her to 'be an angel, Lesley, and rustle up two coffees'.

Once settled in her own chair, Doctor Sally cleared her throat and got down to business. 'Okay, Colin. As you know, I've been having a few pow-wows with my colleagues, the guys you normally work with, and they're worried you may not understand what they've told you about your symptoms. So, if it's cool with you, I'd like *us* to have a chat. See if I can help clear up a few points, if that would help you get the whole thing straight… in your head?'

He sighed, deeply. 'It's not that I don't understand. I don't *agree*.'

'Well, why don't you tell me the way you see things, and we'll take it from there?'

He sighed again, long-wearied of telling his story. This inability of doctors to properly listen drove him crazy. But he did try his best to explain himself to this Doctor Sally in a way he hoped would, at last, get through. 'Where would you like me to start?'

'Wherever makes sense to you, Colin.'

He considered for a minute, smiling wryly to himself while he thought of a way to make sense of things to her.

Adam appreciated the 'I$_1$.R$_1$.O$_1$.N$_1$.Y$_4$.'

Then it came to him. 'I know!' he exclaimed. 'Point to the place in your body where you think your soul lies!'

Doctor Sally, with more patience than many he's seen over the years, poked her finger into the centre of her chest.

'I knew it, I knew it, I *knew* it! Everyone does that!' he exclaimed, triumphantly. 'It's such a common mistake. People always point at their heart and that's so wrong. Our souls don't live in our hearts. They live in our *heads*.'

Doctor Sally wrote down something in her notepad, and he took this to be an encouraging sign. Perhaps someone was finally taking him seriously? Taking notes, even.

But then she replaced her pen lid. 'How do you know that we have souls in our heads, Colin?'

'Well, it's obvious. Three years ago, on my actual ninth birthday, Mum took me up to town to get a new pair of football boots. I was going to buy them with my present money. We were about to cross the road and I must've been overexcited or something, because I just stepped right out in front of a bus. The impact sent me flying through the air, I landed on my head, and that made my soul leave my body.'

'You sound very sure.'

'Because we... I mean *I*... am sure. Apparently, when my head smashed onto the tarmac, I let out a series of screams. Mum says I did. Horrible screams they were, like weird animal noises. Now, I don't know if it flew out of my head on a carpet of howls, or if it shot from my ears or stole out through my nose holes. Perhaps all three. But whichever way it happened, that sudden, cracking whack on my skull drove out my soul. "Spooked" it out. That's my word for it. My soul must have been spooked out of my head rather than any other part of me because, really, it was only my head that got bashed up. See?'

'I see. What happened next?'

'Well, technically, the accident killed me. The doctors told my parents I was properly dead for eight minutes, so great was "the insult to my brain". Curious expression, don't you think? "Insult"? As if my brain was somehow offended.'

'But you didn't die, Colin, did you?'

'That's the funny thing. Just as things were beginning to look really bad, a passenger on the bus leaped into action and began CPR on me. That means "cardiopulmonary resuscitation", by the way.'

'$A_1.N_1.... A_1.C_3.R_1.O_1.N_1.Y_4.M_3.$'

'I know.'

'Anyway, she happened to be an off-duty emergency nurse, and she managed to jump-start my heart. She carried on working on me until an ambulance arrived. She was a hero. There was a picture of her in the local newspaper. "*Florence Nightingale Saves Bus Crash Boy*". Would you like to see the cuttings next time I come in? Mum and Dad kept a scrapbook.'

'No thank you. A really kind thought, though. You were saying how this nurse saved your life.'

'Yes. The papers described how she "*brought me back*" and how Mum and Dad "*could never repay her*". In fact, they sent her a box of chocolates and a bunch of yellow roses. But the thing is, she didn't bring me back. Don't get me wrong – I *am* grateful for what she did. She spanked my heart hard enough to make sure that the blood kept flowing through my veins and the air still reached my lungs. She certainly stopped my body from dying, but she wasn't quick enough to stop my soul from leaving. I'd already given up the ghost. Are you following this so far, Doctor Sally?'

Doctor Sally picked up her pen again and jotted down a few more notes. 'Yes, absolutely.'

'Okay. But here comes the bit that sounds, well, "mad": once my soul was out, it didn't fly away in the manner spooked souls must normally do.' At this juncture he checked himself, unsure if he should continue. Experience had taught him that once he started talking about 'spooking', he often lost his audience.

'$S_1.C_3.E_1.P_3.T_1.I_1.C_3.A_1.L_1.$'

Doctor Sally removed her specs, breathed on the lenses and polished them on a corner of her what-looked-like-silk scarf. 'Do go on. I'm fascinated.'

Made brave by this apparent acceptance of his account so far, he carried on. 'Here's what I think must've happened next. I think my spooked soul was about to leave when it glanced back at bashed-up me and, in that blinding-white split second between this life and the next, it saw I wasn't dead. Just stunned. This must've been when that nurse began banging away at my chest. Anyway, I reckon my soul decided to hang around in thin air, invisible, waiting for the right moment to nip back into my vacant head, like a sort of spectre of my own true self. But it… *he*… never got the chance.'

'Why not?'

'Well, the ambulance people arrived, didn't they? Scraped me up. Whisked me off to hospital. For weeks, I lay in a coma in St Agnes' Memorial, teetering between life and death. I can't remember anything about that time either, but Mum and Dad's scrapbook also has cuttings about my miraculous recovery. "*Bus Boy Beats the Odds*". It took three months before I woke up, though, and when I did, I was like a baby. Literally. Couldn't walk, couldn't talk, couldn't even breathe on my own. I'd no idea who I was or any memory of life up to that point. I suppose it stands to reason I was such a mess – after all, the person, the soul who was Colin Peabody, had left my head.'

'Sounds like a scary time for your family.'

'You'd think. But my parents were so overjoyed that I was "back", they didn't notice that I wasn't back at all. They threw themselves and alive-again Colin into the rehab programme worked out by the doctors and, gradually, a new me emerged.'

'A new "me"?'

'Yes, a new soul. I think he arrived at the moment my heart re-started, though I can't be exactly sure. Doesn't matter. The point is, since he was, let's say, "born", I've built him up myself, from scratch. You see, because he was brand new, he didn't know anything. Nothing about the kind of person I was before the accident, the things I could do. Zero. He was like a tiny seed, planted in my empty head, waiting to grow. So, while I learned to sit up, swallow and wipe my arse, my new soul learned things too. I've shown him I must have a spirit that never gives up. It's as if my new soul is actually made out of the day-to-day "you can beat this" types of things that doctors and parents like to say. They're dead proud of me, you know.'

'I'm sure they are, Colin.'

'Perhaps that's why my new soul is so strong. He's pretty much totally built now. Filling up my headspace. Keeping the "Colin Show" on the road. That's why Adam can't get back in.'

At this point, Doctor Sally paused. She looked directly into his eyes. 'Tell me about Adam.'

'Okay.' He took a deep breath. 'So, you know my old soul? The one spooked out in the accident, who didn't fly off?'

Doctor Sally nodded.

'Well, he *never* flew off. He's still here. Waiting. I've named him Adam.'

Doctor Sally wrote that down. To her obvious relief, at this moment angel-Lesley knocked and entered, bearing two coffees in paper cups. It was evident that Doctor Sally needed this interruption to buy time to frame her next question.

'$L_1.U_1.C_3.K_5.Y_4.\ldots B_3.R_1.E_1.A_1.K_5.$'

'When did you first come to believe Adam is with you?'

'While I was in hospital. Around the time I was re-learning to clean my teeth. I was sat in a wheelchair, left alone in a shower room to scrub and spit as best I could, when I heard Adam's voice… well, my voice, I suppose… in my left ear. "Don't you miss me?" he said. Something like that. Creepy, it was.'

'What did you do?'

'I pulled the bell-cord to get nurse, and she got the doctor and he called my parents.'

'What did the doctor do?'

'He said I had to tell him if anything like that happened again and, of course, it did. Loads of times. In fact, since that day Adam has been with me pretty much all the time. He hasn't got much choice, has he? Where else can he go? As he says, "we belong together".'

'What does Adam talk to you about?'

'This and that, but mostly about how *he* should be running things, not my new soul. He wants to come back inside my head. He's always on about it. "I'm still here," he says, "let me come home." He doesn't think it's fair he got spooked out and then I didn't die like I was supposed to. He says the new me is just "$I_1.N_1.V_4.E_1.N_1.T_1.E_1.D_2.$". Funny, really. Everyone else thinks it's Adam who's the invention.'

'How does having Adam around make you *feel*, Colin?'

'Like a cripple!' He almost spat out the words.

'Wow! Does he have the power to make you feel *that* bad?'

'Yes, absolutely! *He* remembers my childhood before the accident, before the wheelchair. I don't, but *he* does. He taunts me about it all the time. Adam says that if I let him back in he'll give me back memories. Not just small stuff like what we did on family holidays and the name of Granny's budgie. I'm not bothered about that. I can ask Mum and Dad those sorts of things and they're really good about photo albums. I already told you about the scrapbook. No, I mean really big stuff.'

'Give me an example of "really big stuff".'

'How to walk again. My legs weren't damaged in the accident. Neither was my spine. It's just that my brain forgot how to make my legs work. Adam remembers, though. It's these kinds of practical things I could really use from Adam.'

'What's stopping Adam coming "home"?'

He pondered for a moment. 'Partly a no-room-at-the-inn thing, partly a too-many-cooks thing. My new soul has one way of thinking and I suppose that wouldn't necessarily be the same way as Adam's. Stands to reason, doesn't it? After all, they grew up separately.'

Doctor Sally swallowed audibly. 'Are you sure you won't have a coffee, Colin?'

He nodded.

'What do you think about Adam's predicament?'

'Well I, the new me, isn't sure what to think. Sometimes I do feel sorry for Adam. This set-up isn't his fault. And the new me is doing okay. I muddle along. Eating without choking. Not shitting my pants. I've taken up Scrabble. I may be crippled, but I pass for fixed, apart from hearing voices. Who could ask for more?' He let out a dry laugh. 'Maybe it'd be better if Adam just disappeared, because having him around makes me act like a nutcase. I know my parents wish he wasn't here. They look really uncomfortable when I talk about him. I can see them cringing.' He pulled a face, to which Doctor Sally gave no reaction. 'The thing is, though, Adam does have those memories that I'd like back. The walking memories, I mean. So, other times I think I do need Adam inside my head. It's hard to find a word to describe how I feel.'

'$S_1.P_4.L_1.I_1.T_1.$'

'What do you believe would actually happen if Adam and… um… "new you" decided to share your headspace?'

'I've given that a lot of thought, you know. Like I said before, we just don't see how that could work out. It's really, really difficult to explain.'

'I would really, really like to understand, Colin. Please try to go on.'

Struggling to express himself in a way that would make any sense, he scanned the room until his eyes fell upon her wall calendar: *A Quilt for Every Season*. 'You could say that letting Adam back in my head would be like trying to smooth down a blanket over an occupied bed. There would be obvious lumps.'

He noticed Doctor Sally smile at this analogy. But only with her mouth, not with her eyes. He continued, 'I've even considered whether a kind of time-share option might work. Like on those new holiday programmes about Spain, where a flat's got several owners, but they take it in turns to live in it and enjoy the sea view. I've wondered whether Adam could come back in, just for a bit, while my new soul went away until swap-back time. But this couldn't really work either. I mean, went away where? Buggered off into the same just-over-my-shoulder place that Adam haunts right now?'

'$B_3.O_1.N_1.K_5.E_1.R_1.S_1.$'

At this point, Doctor Sally leaned back from her desk, face turned up towards the ceiling, and had a bit of a swivel. He got the impression she was trying to digest everything he'd said. Perhaps she normally found swivelling helpful. He chewed his nails, allowing her time to gather her thoughts.

Using her toes as brakes, she brought her chair to a standstill directly opposite his. Placing her elbows on the looked-like-leather armrests, bringing her fingertips together to make a church steeple, she continued to contemplate. Clearly, she'd formulated her opinion of his story and now she was choosing her words carefully. He waited with bated breath. What would she say? Those words he longed to hear? 'I get it! Thank you, Colin. This all makes perfect sense.' What's that expression Mum uses? *'The scales have fallen from my eyes.'*

But Doctor Sally didn't say any of those things. Instead she fired her killer question: 'Are you happy with how things are, Colin?'

'No.' His eyes suddenly filled with tears.

'$A_1.W_4.K_5.W_4.A_1.R_1.D_2.$'

He desperately wanted to hide his face, but Doctor Sally's office was too small to allow him to manoeuvre his wheelchair. He had to make do with twisting his torso to escape her gaze. She pulled a couple of tissues from the box on her desk and handed them to him, apparently unsure whether he needed any help to dab away his shame. An uncomfortable pause followed, made more uncomfortable when he caught Doctor Sally glancing at her gold wristwatch.

'What have the doctors said to you about your condition?'

'The doctors say that Adam is not real. That I am psychotic.' Seeing that she had taken up her pen again, he continued, 'That's spelled $P_3.S_1.Y_4.C_3.H_4.O_1.T_1.I_1.C_3$. Twenty-one points in Scrabble. The Ys and Hs score highly.'

'$S_1.H_4.O_1.W_4. O_1.F_4.F_4$.'

'Very good. I'm impressed. Do you know what that word means?'

'Yes, I heard the doctor explaining it to Mum and Dad. I remember what everyone said to everyone else, pretty much word for word:

'"Colin's brain injuries have caused a profound abnormality of mind, which manifests itself as psychotic episodes," said the doctor. I know that profound means deep, by the way.

'Then Mum said, "What do you mean, *psychotic*?" and burst into tears.

'Then Dad said, "Calm down, Ursula!"

'Then the doctor said, "*Psychosis* is a term we use for mental health problems that cause people to interpret things differently from those around them."

'Then Dad said, "What makes you think my boy's a psychopath?"

'Then the doctor said, "Not psychopathic. I said *psychotic*. Colin is experiencing hallucinations."

'Then I said, "Adam says he can $H_4.E_1.A_1.R_1$. you."

'Then the doctor said, "*Adam* is an hallucination."'

Doctor Sally didn't say anything.

He too paused before asking, 'Do *you* believe Adam is real, Doctor Sally?'

'It's not about what *I* believe, Colin. It's about what *you* believe.'

This was pretty much the answer he'd expected all along. His heart sank. He could tell from her face her misgivings had crept in early on, probably around her second sip of coffee.

'Did the doctor have a plan to help you, Colin?'

'He said Adam would stop pestering me if I took pills.'

'And has he stopped pestering you?'

'$N_1.O_1.$'

'Are you taking the pills?'

That was when he decided to stop talking.

'Okay, Colin. If you don't wish to talk to me anymore, that's fine. You can just listen. But what I have to say to you now is important, so please listen carefully.'

Doctor Sally leaned forward in her chair and stared really hard into his face with what looked like genuine concern. 'Whether or not Adam is real or, let's say, whether or not Adam stays or goes, depends entirely on you. Not on the doctors, not on what I say, not on any pills. *You* are the one who holds the key to your future, and to Adam's. You must be prepared to recognise when it's time to let go. Think about this, Colin.'

The interview ended there.

Colin is so, so tired of the whole thing.

Ursula is as quick as she can be at the shop. She's always nervous about leaving her son on his own. And now she has to face the fact that this Pauline Dollimore business has set him off again. As she scurries homewards, she considers whether to give the head clinic people another ring when she gets in. But why bother? They've explained so many times before about what to expect for Colin:

'The cells of the brain, Mr and Mrs Peabody, aren't like those in other parts of the body. Unfortunately, when a brain is damaged it can't mend in the way that, say, a cut finger heals up. It's just not that straightforward, I'm afraid. But of course that doesn't mean people with head injuries *never* get any better. You know yourselves the wonderful progress Colin has made since his accident.'

'Yes, wonderful.'

'This progress has been possible because the brain is a very clever organ. Although it can't re-grow parts that have been lost, it can reorganise itself so undamaged areas take over the activities of the damaged bits. We call this brain "plasticity".

Because of this plasticity, if you work as hard as Colin has, and if you're darned lucky, a brain-damaged person can regain many of their original abilities. He or she may not *remember* how they did everything before an accident, but they can *re-learn* a substantial range of skills after the event.'

'What skills? How long will it take Colin to get better?'

'All kinds of skills. But what these are and how long they take to achieve depends on the extent of the injury and the effectiveness of rehabilitation. Improvements don't happen overnight. That's just not how it goes. It can take months, years even, until a patient gets to be as good as they can be. Colin had an extensive injury. Give him time, Mr and Mrs Peabody. Time and physiotherapy. He may still walk again. I have a hunch if he's able to get up and about, the hallucinations will subside.'

Ursula hastens along the pavement, clutching her purchases in one hand and the knot of her headscarf, tight under her chin, in the other. She keeps her head down and her feet moving, fast. The strength of conflicted emotions rising in her chest threatens to bring tears to her eyes. She can almost taste the anger. And the guilt. A salty cocktail, welling up in the back of her throat. Anger, because she and Nigel *have* given Colin time. Three years of time. Yet he still can't walk, and the wretched hallucinations haven't subsided. Here she is, practically running down the street to return to a son who, by rights, is more than old enough to be left by himself for the whole day, never mind just a few minutes; panicking that he's sliding a little further into lunacy with every second she's away. Guilt, because she wonders if she and Nigel are expecting too much. Isn't it enough that their son is alive and doing as well as he is? He's coping with the wheelchair, back at school, catching up nicely with his lessons. Perhaps he is 'as good as he can be'? Never mind Colin's crazy imaginings. She and his dad should be grateful.

Ursula has wished, many times over, she could accept Adam as a sort of imaginary friend of Colin's. After all, don't lots of children have one of those? But in spite of her best efforts to shrink the significance of Adam, to explain him away, it's impossible to dismiss him. Who are we kidding? How many self-respecting six-year-olds still have imaginary friends, let alone twelve-year-old boys? Ursula knows Adam represents something far more real and far more corrosive to their son than some invisible rabbit, and she dearly wishes she knew how to send him packing.

She remembers how the neighbours looked at her son when he first came home from the hospital. Eyeing his wheelchair, trying not to be noticed as they were noticing. Common curiosity, she could accept. She and Nigel have even got used to it. Colin was hit by a bus, now he can't walk. Simple cause and effect. So what? Let them look. After all, people still *said* the right things, like 'Aren't sprouts dear in the market?' and 'Nigel's done you proud with his window boxes', never mentioning buses or brains or devastated lives.

What Ursula cannot brush off, however, is neighbours' reactions when Colin started his ramblings about spooked souls, for then they looked away and said nothing. Their tacit mortification had compounded her own. Only the other day, Deirdre O'Reilly the vicar's wife had popped round, collecting for the church jumble, and Colin set off telling her 'Adam-and-I-this and Adam-and-I-that' as if it was the most normal thing in the world. The look on the woman's face had said it all. To have a disabled child is sad. To have a mad child is bad.

So, there's another emotion she cradles in her belly, the bitterest of all, which she fights especially hard to conceal. Shame. Ursula is ashamed, and because of this, she sickens herself. She keeps the shame shoved down deep, hiding it behind her fussing and faffing over Colin's physical needs, burying it still deeper with bucketsful of sunshine positivity. Her heart and face ache from smiling. But the shame lingers as resolutely as Adam.

Arriving back from the shop less than twenty minutes after she left home, Ursula swings through the garden gate, twists her key in the front lock and, with the chintzy, chintzy cheeriness that defines her poetryless life, calls out, 'I'm home, sweetheart!

Sorry I left you on your own so long. Did you get the Scrabble board set up?'

Colin hasn't minded being left alone, with Adam. Not one bit. In fact, he quickly dismissed his frustrations about the psychology sessions and allowed, instead, the wondrous events of that morning to flood his thoughts. He is filled with hope. Hope and excitement. Pauline Dollimore has died. But not just died. It's *so* much better than that:

According to what he overheard the postman tell the milkman, she's 'only gone and topped herself'.

According to his mother, this 'topping' act has dispatched her soul to a 'better place'.

According to Doctor Sally, he 'must be prepared to recognise when it's time to let go'.

This is a perfect alignment of happenstances. Now he understands. Now *is* the time to 'let go'!

According to Colin, Pauline Dollimore could be his golden ticket to freedom. At this moment, there's a soul-shaped vacancy in her head, same as there was in his when *he* died. What if one of his supernumerary souls could fill it? Not permanently, of course – that would make no sense at all – but perhaps, just *maybe*, Pauline Dollimore could be a temporary 'transitional' residence; the glorious ark that takes either Adam or the newly invented Colin from this world to the next. A reasonable enough plan, surely? All he has to do now is work out how to execute it.

'$Q_{10}.E_1.D_2$.'

Six nights later, as the Peabodys lie sleeping in their beds, the phone rings. And rings. It eventually wakes Ursula. Still groggy, she tugs on her dressing gown, totters to the landing and lifts the receiver.

'Hello?' she whispers uncertainly, plucking at her hairnet as if the person on the other end might somehow be able to detect her state of disarray.

'Ursula, it's Frank,' crackles the caller faintly.

'Frank? Is that you? Goodness! How lovely to hear your voice. But are you all right? Sandra and the kids?' she gushes excitedly, suddenly wide awake.

'Yes, yes, yes, we're all perfectly fine. Does there have to be an emergency for your big brother to give you a call?'

'Of course not, Frank, but you've muddled the time difference again. It's past midnight with us. I couldn't think who on earth was calling at this hour, unless something bad's happened.'

'Sorry, Sis. I've worked the clocks out wrong. It's seven in the morning down under. I didn't mean to get you out of bed. Apologise to Nige for me. Actually, I'm phoning with some good news.'

'What's that then?'

'I'm coming back to England. Just for a few days, mind you. Work wants me to check out a new factory in Kilburn so they're sending me, all expenses paid. It'll be me on my own, I'm afraid. Sandie's staying at home this time because Jolene's baby is due so soon. She's fretting she might miss the arrival of our first grandchild—'

'Frank!' she interrupts him. 'I can't believe it. You haven't been back here since… when was it? Your Jo-Jo was still a teenager, never mind a mum-to-be. And our Colin was, well, just a little lad. You'll hardly know him now, Frank. Really you won't.'

'It's been way too long, Sis. But I was wondering, can I stay with you?'

'What a daft question! I *insist* you stay with us. When are you coming?' she asks eagerly.

'In a fortnight. Can't wait to see you all.'

'We can't wait to see you either.'

Ursula pauses. 'Frank. I was thinking of dropping you a line, as it happens. There was something I thought I should mention…' She falls silent, wary about how to continue.

'What is it?'

'It's Pauline Dollimore...' she ventures. 'She's died. Well, committed suicide, sorry to say.'

'Oh?' He hesitates slightly before adding, 'That certainly is sad.'

Ursula can tell it was a struggle for him to find the correct response. She fears she's been insensitive in the way she's broken the news. 'I know, Frank. But I thought... I thought *you* would want to know.'

'I appreciate that, Ursula. Very thoughtful.' He's swift to change the subject. 'And how are things in the Peabody household?'

'Great. Good. Well, you know. We've so much to be grateful for, haven't we? You'll see for yourself when you come.

'Yes, I will. Listen, you get yourself back to bed now. I'll ring you with my flight times. We can talk properly soon.'

'All right. Have a good day, Frank.'

'Sleep well, Ursula.'

Frank replaces the receiver and stands by the hall table. He scratches his head. Pauline... Pauline... Pauline? Who on earth is, or rather *was*, Pauline Dolly-Wotsit? He has to think about this during the whole of his shower, breakfast and drive to work before it comes to him. Pauline *Dollimore*! She was his secretary way back when. Must have been twenty years ago. At least! Before he emigrated. She was a nice, efficient girl. They even went on a few dates, as he now recalls, but they lost touch when the old firm moved premises. He'd quite forgotten her parents lived a few doors down from Ursula and Nigel. To think, on his last visit to London, Pauline was still kicking around, and he never bumped into her once. He sighs to himself. Well, well, well, so she's dead. A sharp reminder of one's own mortality. And suicide? What a shame for her mum.

The days following Pauline's death fly by for Colin. He's got quite a project on his hands. First and foremost, he has to work out how to transfer a soul into empty Pauline before her body is buried or cremated. He wonders if there's actually a written series of instructions for how to do this, which churchgoers, for example, might somehow know about. His instincts tell him not to trouble the vicar. Colin's pretty sure his mother has already asked Reverend O'Reilly *never* to talk to him about anything to do with souls. When he's at school, however, Colin has a stroke of good fortune in the shape of his RE teacher, Miss Wilmslow, who doesn't seem to have been tipped off by any family members. It turns out she did her master's degree on primitive religions and the afterlife, and she's a positive fount of knowledge. Although he's initially a bit concerned she'd want to know why he's asking so many questions, his worries prove groundless. She's more than happy to chat with such an enthusiastic young student.

'Lovely to see a budding theologian, Colin. A-plus for effort.'

'A_1. for $A_1.R_1.S_1.E_1.L_1.I_1.C_3.K_5$.'

Second, Colin needs to keep track of dead Pauline's whereabouts and any funeral arrangements. Tricky, because he has to get most of this information from his parents and he can tell they are rattled.

'Where's the body now, Mum? Is it in a morgue or a chapel of rest or something? What do undertakers do? Do they take out the brains? Dad, do you think she's being kept in a fridge to stop rotting? Can we see inside the coffin? Will she be buried or burned? Do people have to be invited to funerals or can they just turn up?'

'Do stop *going on*, Colin. There's a good boy.'

Finally, he has to give some serious thought to who should go and who should stay. Adam or the new Colin?

Thanks to his helpful conversations with Miss Wilmslow, Colin decides that the ancient Egyptians knew a thing or two about sending souls to paradise. She described how they'd performed funeral rituals to help souls pick up their lives in 'the Other World', and there was one particular ceremony, the Opening of the Mouth, to which he's particularly drawn. This involved purification of the dead person with water and incense. They would be presented with various offerings to symbolise what they needed in the afterlife. Stuff such as loaves of bread, beer, fruit and meat. Priests recited special words, a bit like chanting prayers, and touched the mummy or its sarcophagus with tools to represent opening the mouth and eyes. This made sure the dead person, or their soul, would be able to eat and see again.

So many aspects of this custom appeal to him. He's pleased it wasn't exclusively for special people like pharaohs. It should be okay for lesser mortals too, such as Adam or Colin. Crucially, it can be done over a coffin, avoiding the need for him to access Pauline's body; something he's been fretting about. The fact the Egyptians had stuck to the Opening of the Mouth for hundreds and hundreds of years gives him confidence. They must've really thought it worked. He also likes the way they used utensils and symbols to enhance its potency. Yes! With some simple tweaks, Colin's sure this ceremony can be adapted to serve his own purposes.

Regarding Pauline's remains, Colin learns they 'rested' in the morgue for thirty-six hours hours before dispatch to Urquhart and Daughters, undertakers. He sees in the local paper that an inquest, necessary because Pauline died suddenly, has swiftly concluded she did indeed take her own life. The coroner explains how he worked this out from the GP's evidence that fat Pauline was being treated for depression, Pauline's handwritten note, and an autopsy that found 'significantly raised levels of barbiturates in her vital organs'. And, if he was still in any doubt after all that, just for good measure the vicar's wife had voiced her tuppence ha'penny about 'how miserable the poor woman had seemed'.

'Enough pills in her body to kill a horse!' his father whistles on reading the local news, clearly impressed.

To Colin's relief, after further cross-examination of his father, he figures the medical examiners probably haven't sucked out her brains to deduce this. They simply removed her spleen or something. It's important to him that the contents of her head aren't violated.

Now the body has been released for burial, the funeral will take place in two Saturdays' time, at St Francis's Church, followed by committal in the graveyard.

When it comes to choosing which soul should stay and which should go, Colin is completely unfixed. One moment he thinks that Adam should go; the next, definitely the new Colin. He puts this decision to one side, trusting he will know the right thing to do on the day.

'$E_1.E_1.N_1.Y_4.\ldots\ M_3.E_1.E_1.N_1.Y_4.\ldots\ M_3.I_1.N_1.Y_4.\ldots\ M_3.O_1.E_1.$'

Satisfied with the outline of his divine scheme, Colin devotes all his spare time to working out the details. This requires little physical activity but a great deal of intense thought. After school each day, he and Adam withdraw to his bedroom to ruminate alone, together. After some days of silent contemplation, his concentrated efforts pay off. With still a week until the funeral, the arrangements are taking shape nicely in his mind. There are, however, two very big flies in the unguent. His parents.

Ursula and Nigel notice that in the short time since Pauline Dollimore's death, their son has become increasingly preoccupied. Since the inquest, he's even paler and stranger than usual. He rarely speaks to them at all, and when he does, he only has one topic of conversation. And on this matter, they are equally resolute.

'If you think we're taking you to Pauline Dollimore's funeral, you can think again!'

Frank is shocked when he first meets Colin again. He heard all about what had happened, of course. He was expecting the wheelchair, and Ursula sends photos at birthdays and Christmas. But still this hadn't really prepared him. Last time he saw his nephew in the flesh, he was a cheeky little boy. Running this way and that. Getting under his parents' feet. Their long-awaited only child, lighting up their lives. Now this scallywag is nowhere to be seen. In his place Frank finds a feeble, thin adolescent. His life spark dimmed, there's something haunting, or even haunted, about his whole demeanour.

Each evening during his stay, when Frank returns from his business meetings, he, Ursula, Nigel and Colin sit down together for supper. Nigel opens two bottles of beer for the menfolk. Ursula dishes up, all the while prattling on about the dinner, and the wonders of Pyrex ovenware, and the weather and the traffic on the high street. She barely allows a gap in the conversation, as if afraid to let anyone else speak.

'How was your day, Colin?' Frank ventures between mouthfuls.

Colin carries on chewing, in silence.

'More gravy, Frank? These faggots can be a bit dry.'

'Yes please, Ursula.' He tries again with Colin. 'Get up to anything interesting?'

Again, his sister interrupts before Colin can answer. 'Nige, why don't you get Frank another drink? Do tuck in, Frank. It'll get cold.'

'You look very lost in thought, lad. Got something on your mind?' Then, correcting himself in a teasing tone, 'Or perhaps it's a some*one*?'

'Frank!' Ursula practically shouts. 'We'd love to hear about your meeting. What's the new factory like? Will you be coming back to England for more trips? Perhaps the girls can come with you next time?'

Frank gives up bothering Colin and lets him eat in peace, but he does wonder. Apart from going to and from school, in that special ambulance that picks him up and drops him off on weekdays, does his nephew ever go anywhere? Frank doesn't count the hospital visits. Does he have any friends? Frank's noticed he occasionally mentions someone called Adam. A school mate? But this Adam hasn't come over to see Colin once since he arrived. He gets the impression Ursula and Nigel aren't too keen on Adam anyway. They always seem to change the subject when Colin brings up his name. Colin's certainly very good at Scrabble, but he only plays with Ursula. What *does* that boy do for fun?

*

In spite of his parents' determination to avoid the whole subject of Pauline Dollimore's death and their adamant refusal to attend her burial, Colin forges ahead with his preparations. Isn't his mother always going on about only crossing bridges when you come to them? Well, he's taken a leaf out of her book. As to how he'll get to the funeral, that's another problem he'll have to iron out later. He has faith that a solution will present itself. After all, this whole plan is defined by his faith. It was born from his absolute belief in the reality of Adam, and it's been given wings by an equally powerful conviction that it will succeed, simply because he believes it will.

In the meantime, and in private, Colin focuses on practical arrangements. He assembles a series of items – his 'bag of tricks' – to take along for the ceremony. Although he has to limit himself to bits and pieces he can find around the house that are within his physical reach, still he puts a lot of thought into his choices. With great care, he selects objects he feels carry sufficient import but at the same time are not too weird to be unworkable. He has to be pragmatic, weighing up symbolism against feasibility. Clearly, he won't be able to carry large items into the church, and some things – like proper incense and ox blood – are obviously unattainable. In the end, he settles on the following sacred goods:

A letter opener in the shape of a dagger and a small, flat butter knife. The former has *MOROCCO* written on its shaft – Colin is pleased when he checks a map of Africa and finds this place is only three countries away from Egypt. The latter is stainless steel rather than silver, but it does have a yellowish ivory handle that makes it feel nice and old. These will be the ceremonial tools needed to open the mouth and eyes of Pauline's corpse.

Three stock cubes – beef, chicken and vegetable – to represent sacrificial oxen, geese and papyrus. There's something about their foil wrappings that imbues a sense of precious metal.

The little lead cruise ship from his Monopoly set. He's read that some pharaohs were buried with their own boats, and the connotation of a soul making a journey is particularly apt.

A palmful of Scrabble letters. An O_1., an R_1., two I_1.s and two S_1.s, to spell out a name, '$O_1.S_1.I_1.R_1.I_1.S_1$.', the mythical father of the first great pharaoh, murdered by his brother but restored to an afterlife by his wife, through sacraments that became the basis for *all* forms of the Opening of the Mouth. Colin's inspiration.

He arranges this whole collection on a clean tea towel and uses his mother's turkey baster to sprinkle everything with a few drops of aftershave. The name, Old Spice, seems appropriate. And he knows his father won't miss it. Mum never lets Dad wear it anyway.

The anointing of the sacrificial goods thus completed, he puts them all into an old football sock from his pre-accident life and stows them away in the bottom of his wardrobe.

As the end of his visit draws nearer, Frank finds himself curiously unsettled at the thought of leaving. It's as if he has unfinished business. Not at work, but within his sister's family — a gloomy little trio if ever there was one. He has to fly home on the Sunday. God knows when he'll be back this side of the globe again. It occurs to him that he's running out of chances to connect with his only nephew. Frank regrets that Colin's refused all invitations to play Scrabble with him. Sad kid. If ever a boy needed taking out of himself, it's this one.

Resolved to make some kind of amends, when he next encounters Colin alone on a rare foray out of his bedroom, Frank seizes the opportunity to spring a surprise. 'I'll tell you what, Col, how about a day trip? A treat. Tomorrow. Just you and me, anywhere you like.'

Visibly astonished by this suggestion, and apparently rather confused, for a moment Colin simply stares at him. Although Frank's sure he's always been friendly towards Colin, effusively jocular at times, it seems the lad had no idea his uncle could be interested in spending any real time together. Perhaps Colin thinks he's only making this offer now because he feels sorry for him? Frank flushes, acknowledging privately that the poor kid is not entirely wrong.

Eventually Colin speaks. 'Tomorrow?' he asks slowly. 'You mean *this* Saturday?'

'Yup.'

'And you'll take me *anywhere* I like?' A hint of colour rises in Colin's cheeks.

'As long as it's not the flying trapeze,' laughs Frank. 'I'm bad with heights!'

'Well, there *is* something I really want to do, but…' Colin falters before continuing, 'Mum and Dad aren't keen. They're not sure it's appropriate for me.'

'Why wouldn't it be appropriate for you?'

'Because of how the accident affected me…' Colin's voice trails off.

Frank swallows hard. He manages not to show his indignation in front of his nephew. Just. But he's seething inwardly. What a bitterly disappointing insight into his sister's and brother-in-law's attitude. In fact, a crying shame. Just because the boy's on wheels doesn't mean he can't choose the odd outing. He'd be more than glad to take his lonely nephew to the pictures – the circus, even – if it'll help to bring him out of his shell. Frank has noticed Colin often has his nose in a fat book, *The Pharaohs of Ancient Egypt*. The British Museum might amuse him. Perhaps they could invite this Adam along too? Frank feels more determined than ever to make sure they have a really good jaunt.

'Tell you what, Colin. I'm going to ask you three questions about whatever this thing is you want to do. If the answers are a "yes" then a "no" and then a "no", in that order, I'll take you myself, *and* I'll take the flak from Mum and Dad into the bargain. Deal?'

'Deal!' replies Colin, eagerly. This is the most animated that Frank has ever seen him.

'Okay. First question: is it legal?'

'Yes.'

'Second question: will it cost me a lot of money?'

'No. Actually, it's free.'

'Final question: is it dangerous?'

'No, Uncle Frank, you'll be perfectly safe. And that makes one "yes" and two "no"s!'

'Well, champ. I guess a deal's a deal,' chuckles Frank. 'So where are you taking me?'

'Pauline Dollimore's funeral!'

Later that evening, Number 34 Atbara Avenue is cowering under the wrath of Ursula Peabody.

'What were you *thinking*, Frank?' she wails. 'You should've checked with us before you made *any* promises to Colin. Really you should. Now look what's happened!'

'I'm sorry, but when I suggested he pick an outing for us both I'd no idea he would choose that,' says Frank, shocked at the force of his sister's reaction. 'You could've knocked me down with a feather—'

'And have you asked him *why* he wants to go to this funeral, Frank? Have you?' she continues, hysteria rising in her voice.

'Yes, I—'

'And what did he say?' she interrupts furiously. 'How did Colin convince you that his burning desire to see some despairingly suicidal neighbour buried is, somehow, okay? That it is, in any shape or form, a normal thing for an adolescent boy to want to do? That's what I'd like to know, Frank.' Ursula sinks down onto a kitchen chair, buries her face in a tea towel and sobs.

'Come on now, love,' says Nigel, patting his wife's shoulder in an effort to calm things down, 'I'm sure Frank only had Colin's interests at heart. Perhaps there's no real harm in it.'

'What do you mean "no real harm"?' she shouts back at him, angrily brushing his hand away. 'Of course there's ruddy harm in it! He's already half daft as it is, Colin and his accursed lost soul, without taking him to some death-fest. If this doesn't send him completely round the bend, I don't know what will!'

For several minutes the three adults say no more. The kitchen falls silent, bar sporadic hiccoughing blubs from Ursula and the sound of Nigel cracking open two fresh bottles of beer. At last, Ursula blows her nose, and this pulls the room to order. She speaks again, but now her voice is level and quiet.

'I'm sorry, Frank, for losing my temper.'

'No, it's me who should apologise—'

'Please, let me finish. I can see you're trying to do right by Colin. Nigel and I can both see that, and, God knows, it isn't always easy to know what the "right thing" is. But if there's one thing Mum and Dad taught us, Frank, a promise is a promise. You must remember that.'

Frank nods.

'We may not understand why Colin wants to go to Pauline's funeral,' continues Ursula, 'but you've given him your word that you'll take him. I do know it wouldn't be right to let him down now. Just promise me one thing.'

'What's that?'

'Promise you won't let him do anything to show himself up.'

Frank takes a deep swig of Irish stout. 'I promise.'

'I'll dig out my black tie for you,' says Nigel.

'$S_1.H_1.O_1.W_4.\ldots T_1.I_1.M_3.E_1.$'

On the eve of Pauline Dollimore's funeral, Colin's mother parks his chair as close to the sink as its cumbersome wheels will allow. She kicks on its brakes and proceeds to run a basin of hot water, adding cold and then testing the temperature with her elbow, like she used to do when bathing him as a baby.

'Honestly, Mum. I can do this.'

'I know you can, sweetheart. Arms up!' she orders brusquely as she tugs off his jumper, then his T-shirt, then his vest.

'*Please*, Mum.'

'We'll be all done soon,' she clucks, squirting a short worm of red-and-white-striped paste onto his toothbrush. 'Now, open wide!'

'For God's sake!' he snaps. 'Let me get washed on my own.'

'Oh, go on then,' she says, with a frustrated sigh. She wrings out a wet flannel and drops it into his hands. 'But mind you do behind your ears.'

As his mother retreats from the crowded little downstairs cloakroom, Colin notices her tired, sad face. 'Sorry, Mum,' he calls after her, regretting his tetchiness. 'I just want five minutes. To myself.'

'Give me a shout when you need drying off.' She closes the door behind her but evidently thinks better of it, as it immediately re-opens, just a crack. Colin can tell she's still lingering outside. He wants to ask her to go away but is afraid of bruising her feelings any more than he already has done. Mercifully, his father unknowingly comes to his rescue.

'Ursula. Where's my good shirt? I want to let Frank have it for church tomorrow.'

'Just one second, Nigel. I'll fetch it down for him,' she replies, 'but its collar could do with starching.' And to Colin's relief, she heads off.

He leans forward in his chair to inspect his reflection in the mirror. His face is, as always, pale. The shadows under his eyes make him look permanently exhausted. He *is* permanently exhausted. He flexes his biceps. There's some strength in his upper arms, from when he's had to manoeuvre himself around the place. But he has the flat, a-muscular chest of a nine-year-old. Like a pathetic shrunken *wimp*. Running a hand through his hair, he fingers the large scar where the doctors stitched him up. His mum has got a special way of parting his hair so that it doesn't show. Well, not unless it's windy. The long line of evenly spaced lumps feels like a secret zip, sewn into the top of his head. For a moment he imagines how great that would be: re-sealable access to his brain. With one quick *thrrrrrrip*, he could unzip his scalp and skull, reconfigure the contents of his messed-up consciousness, and then simply *thrrrrrrip* it back up again. There'd be no need for a fucking wheelchair, or pity, or elaborate burial rites that may or may not work.

Colin turns his head, double-checking that his mother is out of earshot, and hears reassuring sounds from the direction of the airing cupboard, upstairs. He grabs his chance.

'Adam,' he whispers. Then, a little more loudly, 'Adam, are you there?'

He's tried summoning Adam before, but never successfully. Adam only turns up for a chat when it suits Adam. God knows that's often enough, and usually at the worst moment. But this evening, Colin really wants the two of them to at least attempt a conversation. He feels the situation calls for it.

'Adam,' he tries again. 'You don't have to answer, but I know you can always hear me. So I'm just going to say what I have to say, and you can butt in whenever. Okay?'

No response.

Colin continues. 'Tomorrow's a big day, isn't it? Well, *the* big day. And I'm getting kind of nervous about... how things might go. I know you get what I mean. Adam?'

Nothing.

'I'm not just doing this for me, remember. I'm doing it for *us*. You and I both need things to go according to plan. And if people around me think I'm away with the fairies during the ceremony, there'll be trouble. Tomorrow, I need to seem "normal". So, if you could possibly let me run things by myself, just this once, I'd appreciate it. You do understand, don't you?'

He wipes the steamed-up mirror and peers into the misty glass. Once again, the cruelly altered version of Colin Peabody stares back.

'$O_1.K_5.$'

By half past ten that night, everyone in Number 34 Atbara Avenue is in bed. Everyone except $C_3.O_1.L_1.I_1.N_1$. He's taken a sheet of paper from his mother's just-for-best writing set. It's thicker and crisper than the stuff in his school exercise books and feels suitably weighty to bear the ceremonial script. Now, by the light of his bedside lamp, using Dad's fountain pen and his neatest handwriting, he carefully copies the ancient words – the ones recited by noble priests of the mighty Egyptian kingdoms for all those centuries before Christ was born – of the spell for the Opening of the Mouth, transcribed from *The Book of the Dead*.

It takes him ages. When he's finished, Colin uses felt pens to decorate the borders with blue and yellow hieroglyphs. Once he's certain the ink is dry, he wraps the paper around a pencil, rolling it into a scroll. He fastens this with an elastic band, places it under his pillow and switches off the light. He closes his eyes and prays harder than he's ever done before. To God and all the gods. When, at last, deep sleep comes, he dreams of scarab beetles, crocodiles and the endlessly flowing waters of the Nile.

Although the funeral isn't until mid-morning, Colin is up at the crack of dawn. His mother hardly says a word to him as she helps him wash and dress, and all through breakfast she keeps casting him sad, sideways looks. Colin doesn't care. He can't wait to get going. It's all he can do to contain his excitement while he waits for his uncle to get ready. His father gives him a shilling.

'Something for the collection plate, Son. Don't lose it.'

Colin tucks this into the inside pocket of his new school blazer, the smartest item of clothing he possesses, in which he's already secreted the sock-bag of tricks. Just as he and Uncle Frank are, at last, about to set off for St Francis's, his mother kneels in front of him. As she tugs tight his laces, on shoes still pristine as the day they left the shop, she looks up at him.

'*Please* watch your step today, sweetheart.'

'Will do, Mum,' he replies brusquely, steering his chair towards the front door.

She sees them off from the garden gate, dabbing tears from her eyes.

Frank waves back at her, mouthing the word 'Sorry'.

When they arrive at St Francis's, apart from themselves, there's barely more than a half-dozen attendees.

'We needn't have worried about getting a seat, then,' Uncle Frank whispers as he wheels Colin down the aisle.

Colin recognises Mr Chen the pharmacist and an elderly man – some neighbour with a foreign-sounding name Colin can't pronounce – who lives in a house called The Laurels. There's a middle-aged chap who also looks familiar. Because he's dressed in a shiny navy suit rather than his habitual brown canvas apron, it takes Colin a moment to register it's the ironmonger. A whiff of creosote gives the game away. The young doctor, with whom Colin is all too well acquainted, is in the row behind. He seems to have brought along his girlfriend. For what? Moral support or, maybe, a date? The vicar, Reverend O'Reilly, is already standing in his pulpit, thumbing through a thin pile of handwritten flash cards, checking his watch, sweating. Mrs O'Reilly sits at the piano, smoothing and re-smoothing her tweed skirt over her knees, waiting with eyes shut as if in prayer. Hovering right at the back, a sallow, drippy-looking girl is handing out bibles.

Colin isn't sure how long funerals are supposed to take, but it seems to him this little ragbag of people sits around for quite some time before the church doors finally open. The creak of their hinges is evidently a cue. The vicar turns and nods sharply at his wife. Mrs O'Reilly, whose eyes are now wide open, immediately straightens her back, poises her arched hands over the keyboard, and brings them bashing down on the ivories with such vigour that the meagre crowd springs to its feet. Even Colin feels compelled to sit to attention. To the plunking tones of 'Amazing Grace', down the aisle sails Pauline Dollimore. She's in a simple pinewood casket, teetering upon the shoulders of six undertakers, two of whom are women. Colin is struck by how similar the orangey colour of the coffin is to his mother's new kitchen units. The size of the congregation has doubled. With the aid of two walking sticks, Mrs Dollimore follows behind.

Dressed from top to toe in black, she's wearing a long, sequin-encrusted evening gown, a fox-fur stole, complete with head, draped over her shoulders, and elbow-length satin gloves. Their tiny mother-of-pearl buttons shimmer in the holy half-light afforded by St Francis's stained-glass windows. Even Colin, who never normally observes such things, reckons she has on an awful lot of makeup for an old lady. It's obvious that she's too fat for her outfit. He isn't sure, but he thinks he hears Uncle Frank actually gasp when he catches sight of her.

The procession stops, and the old woman sits down abruptly, right next to Colin. He has to be at the front of the church because of his wheelchair – something to do with fire regulations. It seems that Pauline's mother has to be at the front too. Colin assumes this is something to do with her being the chief mourner – although she doesn't look all that sad. He notices she smells funny. A mixture of mothballs and cake batter.

The undertakers unload Pauline's coffin onto a table in front of the altar. They make a show of reversing away from it, heads bowed, as if being dismissed by royalty. There are no flowers.

'Pl*eee*ase be seated,' begins Reverend O'Reilly. 'We are gathered here today to celebrate the life of Pauline Vincentina Dollimore. A dear and precious daughter. A quiet and well-thought-of neighbour, who always kept herself to herself. *Eee*ternal Father, in the midst of our pain we remember the joy that she brought us...'

Colin has no interest in this part of the proceedings. He doesn't know either of the chosen songs. They aren't hymns but remind him of tunes he's heard on his dad's *Music Hall Medley* record. Like the rest of the congregation, he makes a half-hearted job of mouthing the words, but Mrs Dollimore sings along loudly. He finds Reverend O'Reilly terribly boring. He wonders if he's deliberately elongating his vowels to make his limited material about Pauline stretch further.

Distracted, Colin can't help looking at Mrs Dollimore. Throughout the service, she pulls strange faces. At first, he assumed she was crying, but then he realises she's nibbling her way through a packet of peanuts. A little pile of shells collects between her feet. She keeps opening and closing her handbag with audible 'clunk-clicks', fishing out a lipstick to reapply a crimson smear in the general vicinity of her mouth. She doesn't seem too bothered about what the vicar's saying. But then again, neither is Colin.

$C_3.O_1.L_1.I_1.N_1.$ and Adam just want to get to the burial bit.

The only person giving any thought to Pauline in her pine box is Frank. Right up until this moment, he's been entirely focused on placating his sister and getting Colin out of the house and into the church without too much fuss. He hasn't given a second's consideration to Pauline, the woman he knew, albeit briefly, all those years ago. But now he finds he's strangely curious about her. The sketchy eulogy, delivered by the vicar, gives him no insight. Apparently, she was '*deee*voted' to her father. Apparently, she bore her depression with '*foor*titude'. Apparently caring for her mother was her 'voc*aaa*tion'. But what else? Apparently, she was so bloody miserable, she killed herself.

He wonders what she'd think of him being at her funeral. Would she have even remembered him after all this time? Probably not. With a cotton handkerchief loaned to him by Ursula, Frank quickly dismisses a tear.

'Gracious God, comfort, we pray, your servant to *whooo*m this trial has come. Be with Muriel. Be her stay, her strength and her shield. Grant that she might be touched by your Spirit and hear your voice. Lighten her darkness and bring her out of all distress. Oh God, touch all our hearts with your love in this hour, that the springs of compassion may flow. Lead us in the paths of quietness and hope through Christ Jesus our Lord, He who taught us to pray together as one family, saying… OUR FATHER, who art in Heaven, hallowed be Thy name… forever and ever, *Aaaaaaaa*men.' Reverend O'Reilly raises his head, opens his eyes and smiles. 'Family and friends are now invited to follow Pauline and Muriel into the churchyard for the committal.'

'$T_1.H_4.A_1.N_1.K_5…. G_2.O_1.D_2.$'

*

Everybody files out of the church and gathers in the car park. Colin wonders what's supposed to happen next. No one speaks to anyone else, not even the people who know each other. They just shuffle about waiting to be told what to do. Colin uses this lull in the action to make a surreptitious check on his cargo. Leaving the sacrificial goods tucked away in the sock, itself tucked under his trouser belt, for ease of access he re-stows the ceremonial tools in the inside pocket of his blazer, along with the scroll.

'This way *pleee*ase.'

Reverend O'Reilly sets off across the churchyard, followed by Pauline, perched upon her posse of undertakers. Mrs Dollimore comes next. All the others shuffle along after them, and Colin and Frank take up the rear.

It's been raining – not hard, just a shower – but the drizzle makes the long grass wet enough to snag in the wheels of Colin's chair. He can't manage to move it by himself, so Frank has to half push, half drag him to Pauline's graveside. Although it's only a few hundred yards away, this is a slow and exhausting process, made slower by having to navigate around tombstones and vases of weather-bleached plastic flowers. By the time they catch up with the rest of the party, his uncle is completely out of breath and has a face shiny with sweat.

'Sorry, mate,' Frank puffs to the vicar. 'Didn't mean to hold up the proceedings. Do go on.'

The undertakers decant Pauline's coffin onto a bright green rug of fake turf beside the open grave. A series of straps is positioned directly underneath the coffin, in readiness for lowering it into the ground. The grave itself is narrow but deep. A puddle of red muddy water has collected in the bottom. The motley crowd gathers around in a loose semicircle and waits for the reverend to continue. Colin doesn't let him get the chance.

'Vicar,' he says calmly, 'I would like to read out a poem, please. I brought it with me specially. It's a very important, very old, very traditional poem. Like a psalm.'

Colin can see he's caught the vicar completely off guard – and the man clearly can't think of any immediate reason to refuse. He sees him turn towards Mrs Dollimore, looking for guidance, but she's oblivious, busily poking around in her handbag.

'Well,' says Reverend O'Reilly, 'I suppose, if no one has any objection?'

Silence.

'Then you may go ahead.'

Colin reaches inside his blazer and withdraws the scroll. He carefully unfurls it, holding it up and at arm's length in the manner of a town crier about to announce a royal birth. He arranges his face into a picture of solemnity, lowers his voice to a tone matching the gravity of the occasion, and begins to recite:

'My mouth is opened by Ptah,
'My mouth's bonds are loosed by my city-god.
'Thoth has come fully equipped with spells,
'He loosens the bonds of Seth from my mouth.
'Atum has given me my hands,
'They are placed as guardians.
'My mouth is given to me,
'My mouth is opened by Ptah,
'With that chisel of metal
'With which he opened the mouth of the gods.
'I am Sekhmet-Wadjet who dwells in the west of Heaven,
'I am Sahyt among the souls of On.'

No one interrupts him, but everyone looks very confused, the vicar most of all. Reverend O'Reilly doesn't appear to know the reading, but he's clearly recognised it isn't from the Bible or anything by Keats.

Undeterred, Colin whips out the butter knife and the letter opener. Continuing to recite, he waves one, then the other, in the air, which he feels adds greatly to the sense of theatre. Only when he sees the vicar signal to Frank, as if inviting him to intervene, does Colin draw the incantation to a close. With a final flourish, he throws the tools into the depths of the open grave. They disappear with a *plop*, *plop*.

At first the congregation shows no reaction. They seem stunned. He isn't sure if they are embarrassed or impressed. Pauline's mother mutters something under her breath, but then she starts to clap, very slowly. Taking this as their lead, the rest of the congregation politely follows her example.

'Er… thank you, young man. Very touching,' says Reverend O'Reilly, clearing his throat. 'So, moving on to the committal… We, as Christians—'

'I haven't quite finished. I—' Colin interjects, but his uncle, who's turned the colour of beetroot, steps in.

'That's enough, Colin! Let the reverend get on with his job.'

Colin falls into a sullen silence. Brooding to himself, he realises he'll have to bide his time. But he isn't too worried. As long as the sock goes into the grave with the coffin, all will be well. He decides not to make his next move until the vicar – who is suddenly keeping his vowels as short as possible – has said his piece.

'We now commend into God's keeping our sister, Pauline, here departed. We commit her body to the ground. Earth to earth, ashes to ashes, dust to dust, trusting in God's great mercy by which we have been born anew to a living hope through the resurrection of Jesus Christ from the dead.'

As the reverend speaks, the undertakers regroup themselves, three either side of the coffin. They take hold of the straps and begin to lower Pauline into the grave. This is Colin's critical moment.

'Uncle Frank,' he whispers. 'Please will you push me a bit nearer? I have some other things I need to put into the grave.'

'That is *not* going to happen!' Frank whispers back through clenched teeth. 'I'm taking you home.'

'Uncle Frank,' Colin whines. 'You promised!'

But this pleading is to no avail. His uncle has plainly had enough. With as much dignity as the man can muster, given the cling of the wet grass, he begins to pull Colin's wheelchair back towards the church.

'Your mum's going to *kill* me when she finds out about this.'

Colin is desperate. It's now or never. He and Adam haven't come this far to fail now. He has to get those items buried with Pauline. He retrieves the sock of grave goods from his trouser belt and, to keep his hands free, clenches the end between his teeth. He grabs the armrests of his wheelchair and pushes down with all his might. As he'd hoped, he manages to pitch himself upwards and forwards just enough to overbalance, tipping himself out of the chair. With a colossal *splat*, he lands face first, sprawled out on the muddy ground no more than six feet from the open grave. Easily close enough to throw in the sock. But, to his horror, he realises it's gone! The shock of the fall winded him, making him gasp. He's released his bite on the sock and it's flown from his mouth, coming to rest… where? Where? *Where?*

The congregation looks aghast. For a split second, time stands still. Paralysed by surprise, no one moves. Then all at once Frank, the doctor and the vicar rush forwards to pick him up.

'Don't touch me! I have to find my sock. Please, please help me find it,' he wails. 'It's really important.'

He becomes frantic, flailing his arms about, hitting out at his helpers. In spite of his squirming, the three men eventually manage to lift him back into his wheelchair. He drops into his seat, panting. Cuckoo spits of foam form in the corners of his mouth, as if he's had a fit.

'You're still wearing your socks, and your shoes, lad. You're not making any sense.' His uncle sounds dismayed.

'Not *these* socks. The sock with the special things in. It's lost!'

'I think you'd better get the boy home,' says Reverend O'Reilly. 'This is causing upset to the family.' He's apparently chosen not to notice that ever since Colin fell out of his chair, Pauline's mother has been quietly laughing to herself.

'I won't go!' cries Colin. 'And you can't make me.'

It's at this moment that he sees it. A soggy little sack, teetering on the lip of the grave. Caught on a clump of plant roots sticking out of the claggy earth.

'Please. There it is! I *must* get it.'

'Leave it!' snarls Frank. With that, he and the doctor lift Colin up, chair and all, and begin to cart him away.

Colin starts screaming. The same weird, animal screams he let out when the bus hit him; the same sounds that carried Adam out of his head, thirty-five and a half months ago.

Colin's screams reverberate through the graveyard, scattering songbirds and frightening the rest of the congregation. Everyone stares, open-mouthed, at the spectacle unfolding before them. Everyone except Pauline's mother. She's gazing upon something else. A sock.

This, old Muriel Dollimore realises, must be the thing the bizarre boy has been raving about. It doesn't look like much to her. But that is not the point. She can see that it obviously means a very great deal to him. In fact, he wants this thing so desperately, he's prepared to make an unbelievable public display of himself. So much so, he's succeeded in completely upstaging *Dolores*. He's stolen *her* show!

'Well there's no way the stupid little bastard is having it.'

With a swift, mean little kick, Muriel sends the sock into Pauline's grave.

No one else sees.

Frank and the doctor manage no more than ten yards before they have to put the chair down and rest. As soon as the wheels touch the ground, Colin stops screaming. Suddenly, he feels an overwhelming sense of peace.

'Uncle Frank,' he asks calmly, 'would you please help me up?'

'For Christ's sake, Colin. It's time to quit this now.'

'No. That's just it. Now is the time to try. Please,' he begs, 'please help me up.'

To Colin's great relief, there must have been something about the way he spoke these words, the way he looked up into Frank's eyes, which makes it impossible for his uncle to refuse him. Frank looks at the doctor. The doctor looks at Frank. Without saying anything, each takes a firm hold of Colin's elbows. As he did before, Colin places his palms flat on the armrests of his wheelchair. Once again, he pushes down with all his might, pitching himself forwards. This time, though, he doesn't fall to the ground. He stands up.

'Now let go!'

Frank and the doctor let go. Colin wobbles, wavers and lurches forward. Colin walks.

'$R_1.I_1.P_3.$'

3

The Hands That Feed Us

From a distance, Elspeth Shepherd is so ethereal, colourless and remarkably unremarkable to look at, she's practically invisible. While other women in their early twenties might resent being perpetually overlooked, Elspeth appreciates that unobtrusiveness is her greatest asset. Unbeknownst to the scanty congregation of St Francis's, she's been living in their church for several weeks, and not one person has questioned her near-constant presence amongst the pews. When the Reverend O'Reilly did notice her, on her third day, he thought little of it. He's assuming the solemn young newcomer is a particularly zealous member of the local college's Christian union, who've recently taken an interest in fundraising activities on behalf of St Francis's. The members of the union became aware of Elspeth at about the same time as he did. They're assuming the thin, beige girl is some drippy loser whom the kind-hearted O'Reilly has taken under his wing, him being such a sucker for waifs and strays. But while they're right that he's been quick to welcome her into his sparse flock, when he voiced his hopes that she'll 'soon feel quite at home here', no one had any idea his wish was being so literally granted.

Although she makes no effort to hide herself, Elspeth's never had to explain why she's in church so much of the time. She's made sure her actions are explanation enough. She's always there and always busy; removing dead flower arrangements and replacing them with seasonal stems from the churchyard;

reorganising the small library of religious reading matter at the back of the north aisle; polishing brassware; saying her prayers. Elspeth barely speaks to anyone, choosing to work in silence. She keeps her head down and her hands occupied. The assured way she sets about these tasks is sufficient confirmation to any rare spectators that she must belong in this, her borrowed habitat. Each evening she secretes herself in the vestry, a stowaway amongst the choristers' cassocks, until she's satisfied everyone's left. She listens for the heavy *kerplunk* of Reverend O'Reilly's keys in the front-door lock. A solid sound that reassures her she has the place to herself for the night.

As the commotion at Pauline Dollimore's graveside draws to a close, Elspeth, who deliberately stayed behind, is once again alone in church. She quietly collects up the bibles before checking to see if the funeral party has left anything worth keeping. Apart from two dropped paper hankies and a forgotten glove, she finds nothing. Disappointed, she's just about to leave when, to her surprise, she spots a heap of discarded nutshells under the front pew and, even better, the remains of a few uneaten kernels still nestling inside them. Treasure. She carefully picks up every little bit. Thus equipped with all she needs for her next mission, she pulls on her cloak and sets off outside.

She's pleased to find Atbara Park almost empty. Although it's a mild afternoon, earlier showers have kept the usual throngs of visitors away. She swiftly makes her way past the playground with its riderless iron horse and deserted sandpit, past the municipal drinking fountain and the tennis courts, past the garishly planted flowerbeds with their regimented rows of dahlias, only stopping when she reaches the shrubberies at the farthest end of the gardens. With a quick glance to her right and left to make absolutely sure no one else is around, she steps over the low metal rail separating the path from the bushes, and crawls her way into a dense stand of rhododendrons. Satisfied she's completely hidden from view, she crouches down amidst their trunks.

From her vantage point she sees, only a few feet away from her on the other side of the shrubbery, an old man sitting on a bench. He has his back to her and, to her relief, doesn't appear to have noticed her arrival. In fact, he gives the impression he isn't paying attention to anything going on around him. He seems oblivious to a solitary pigeon pecking hopefully at the earth between his feet. The bird is very scrawny, limping about on deformed, crimson peg-legs. One of its feet is completely missing.

Elspeth watches and waits. For the next ten minutes the old man remains unmoved. The pigeon continues its fruitless pecking. Eventually, in a long, slow, purposeful movement, she leans forward, bending so low her chest is scarcely a hair's breadth from the ground. Very, very cautiously, she stretches out her arm until her clenched fist just peeps, knuckle side down, beneath the hem of her verdant hideaway. In position at last, she gradually unfurls her fingers to reveal a palmful of crushed nuts. Rigidly still, again she watches and waits. She holds her breath, a statue amid the detritus of discarded cider cans.

At first the pigeon takes no notice, but then, quite suddenly, it catches sight of the food. It lifts its head then cocks it sharply to one side; a quizzical pose, as if weighing up the offering. There's barely a moment's further deliberation before sixty staccato steps carry it across the scrubby lawn towards her open hand. As it bows its head to pick a morsel, in a single movement Elspeth lurches forward, snatches the bird up and draws it inside her cloak. She scrambles backwards out of the den, jumps upright and hastens back towards the gates of Atbara Park, her arms clasped to her bosom.

Mr Gabriel Nowakowski has been sitting on the bench by the round pond for more than an hour – a wealthy widower, adjourning to the park to ponder the years gone by. With his distinguished frame swallowed up under the weight of an astrakhan coat and his eyes as rheumy as raw oysters, he looks far more timeworn than his three score years and ten. These days, he feels the cold. Old Gabe has the bearing of a man who has both feet firmly in the past and the cares of the world on his shoulders.

A rustling in the bushes behind him rouses him from his brown study. 'The breeze has picked up,' he thinks. 'Perhaps I should be getting home?'

He gropes around in his pocket. After a bit of fumbling, he fishes out a handkerchief to dab at the drip formed on the end of his beaky nose. He looks down into his lap and observes his hands lying there; the creeping ravages of arthritis are nakedly plain to see. He feels dissociated from them, as if they're some other man's hands.

'Useless paddles! You're getting old, Nowakowski,' he reflects, but then corrects himself. 'You've *gotten* old, Gabe. You are an old man sitting on a damp park bench.'

His twisted fingers are too stiff to hold on to his hanky. Caught by another little gust of wind, it slips easily from his crooked grasp and dances off amongst a flurry of fallen leaves. He makes no attempt to retrieve it, but watches it pirouette away. He remembers wistfully that this was the last of his good cotton handkerchiefs. A favourite, prettily embroidered by a daughter of his dearest and longest-standing friend, Aleksy Wozniak.

He thinks about their meeting, earlier this morning. He and Aleksy had shared a jug of coffee at the Kardomah café, a weekly ritual honoured for over twenty years. Gabriel cherishes these opportunities to reminisce about their common pasts, to hear and speak his native tongue. Both he and Aleksy understand what it means to lose loved ones, to be hungry, to live displaced from one's roots. Although they didn't actually meet until they were grown men, in fact when he himself was in his forties, Gabriel feels as if they've known each other all their lives.

It often strikes Gabriel how serendipitous their first encounter was. It was just after the war, when he and Irena had opened their first, modest, delicatessen. Aleksy was newly wed to Doreen. One day, as a treat for her husband, Doreen came in and bought some freshly made Polish pancakes. A taste of his mother country. The very next afternoon, Aleksy visited the delicatessen, introduced himself to Gabriel, and they've been firm friends ever since.

Gabriel sighs. He thinks of his beautiful Irena. Although their marriage was childless, they were so happy. He misses her as deeply today as he ever did. Aleksy is now a widower too, but his wife bore him three fine girls and, later in life, one son… born here… in England. Gabriel's spirits lift as he pictures Polly, Jean, Susan and little Feliks – his godson – when they were small. He and Irena saw these children as blessings for themselves as much as they were for their own parents. In many ways they were – still are – the offspring he never had. As his business grew from that one local shop to several, scattered throughout the increasingly chic neighbourhoods of west London, and his fortunes prospered, he enjoyed being a generous benefactor to all four of them. Willingly he showed his avuncular affection, with gifts and sponsorship Doreen and Aleksy could not afford. He loved them then, and loves them now, as surely as if they were his own flesh and blood.

To this day, Gabriel shares his friend's pride in his children's achievements and his worries when life throws difficulties in their way. And Feliks is a worry. While the Wozniak girls are married with homes and little ones of their own, the boy is still living with Aleksy. Gabriel knows why this is. The baby of the family, just a teenager when he lost his mother, Feliks was indulged as a child. Not only by his parents, but by Gabriel and Irena too. Feliks has grown up to become, though it pains Gabriel to admit it even to himself, a spoiled and lazy young man. It makes Gabriel wince to see how he takes from his father without a second thought, or an iota of gratitude in return.

Gabriel reflects that it was only natural, during this morning's rendezvous, for Aleksy to turn to him for help and advice, as he has so often in the past. When they sat down at their usual table, ordered their usual coffee and custard cakes and, as usual, Aleksy started to confide his concerns about the feckless Feliks, Gabriel had been expecting it. Well, some of it.

'I tell you, Nowakowski, the boy is completely without direction,' Aleksy began, shaking his head sadly. 'All day he sleeps in his room. We don't talk. We don't eat together. Then he is out all night. He doesn't return until dawn. You know, I think he is drinking. But where does he even find the money for this drinking? He has no work and doesn't look for any. This worries me very much, you can imagine.'

'Of course it does, Wozniak. I know that it does.' Gabriel too shook his head, in sympathy.

'And yet today I have to tell you so much more,' said Aleksy, lowering his voice. 'The *police* have come to my house, looking for Feliks.'

'The police!' Gabriel was taken aback. He's used to hearing about Feliks's indolence, but this was something new. 'This can't be so. What did they want with our boy?'

'Two officers. "We would like to speak to your son about a number of recent thefts in this neighbourhood." That is what they said. "We believe he may be able to help us with our enquiries." Stealing, Nowakowski. *Stealing!*' Aleksy buried his face in his hands.

'Stealing what?'

'I don't know what,' moaned Aleksy. 'They didn't say. But that is not the worst of it. What happened next is far more terrible.' Aleksy drew closer to him, leaning in across the table, whispering in even quieter tones. 'I went up to Feliks's bedroom to ask him to come downstairs. "The police are here," I called through his door, "they need to talk to you." As usual, no answer. "Feliks, this is your father. Please come down now and explain yourself." Still nothing. I knocked hard and then harder. I was on the landing, banging on his locked door while the police waited at the bottom of the stairs, watching me trying to get him to come out. But he would not.' Aleksy stopped talking, slumped back in his seat, and looked away.

His friend's shame at the memory of this scene was palpable. 'Disobeying you in front of these officers of the law! Has he no respect?'

'No. I fear he has none. Absolutely none! Can you imagine if we had spoken to our fathers like this?'

Gabriel could not. 'Tata would have scolded me with his belt, never mind his tongue! That I know.' Both men fell silent, thinking of their fathers and their brothers, all gone. In due course, Gabriel asked, 'How did it go on?'

'Well, one of the policemen called out to me, "May we offer some assistance, sir?" I think he meant to come upstairs and break down the door. "No. I am fine, thank you. He will come directly," I replied... and then I said such a stupid thing: "He must be sleeping".' Aleksy let out a dry laugh. 'Sleeping? With me hitting at his door as if to wake the dead? What a fool I am... I hardly know how to tell you what happened next...'

'You must!'

So Aleksy soldiered on with the rest of his sorry tale. 'Suddenly, Feliks's door flew wide open. He was in such a fury. His face all screwed up, for a second I did not know him. He screamed at me, right into my face: "Leave me alone! You stupid old man. Leave me alone." Then I think he raised his arm and—'

'Raised his arm?' This was the revelation that particularly appalled Gabriel.

'Not to hit me, Nowakowski... I know that he would not hit me.'

'Of course not, Wozniak.' And then, after a pause, he added because he felt he must, 'We *both* know that.'

'But he did raise his arm, and this startled me. I stepped backwards. I lost my footing and stumbled a little. I was at the top of the stairs... but I grabbed the banister rail and as you can see I was not hurt, Nowakowski. I am not hurt at all, Gabriel. Not at all.'

Gabriel was stunned. Lost for words. He became aware that Aleksy was studying his face, looking for a reaction. Willing him to speak.

'It was an accident, Nowakowski. I know that it was.'

'Yes. I understand…' he said as decisively as he could, struggling to reconcile his disgust at Feliks's behaviour with his desire to reassure his friend.

'But the policemen at the foot of the stairs, *they* saw. They saw, and they *mis*understood. They ran upstairs, got a hold of Feliks, spinning him around and throwing him to the floor. Face down. They said they would arrest him there and then for "common assault".'

Aleksy's voice faltered. He shifted his gaze from his friend's face and stared into his cup of coffee. 'It was terrible, Gabriel, just terrible. Feliks pinned to the floor, a big policeman kneeling on his back, another shouting that it was a criminal offence to hit old men and that he would be in "real trouble now".'

'What did you do?' he asked, as gently and evenly as he could.

'I begged with them. I *pleaded*. There was nothing else for me to do. "Your eyes deceive you, gentlemen. My son would not strike me. I am not hurt. *Please* don't take him!"' As Aleksy repeated these words, he clasped his hands together as if in prayer, so tightly that his knuckles whitened. 'And, praise God,' he sighed, slowly relaxing his hands, 'they set him free.'

'That is some good news, at least!' At this point in their conversation, Gabriel leaned back in his seat and breathed a deep sigh of relief, believing Feliks had, as always, escaped the consequences of his actions.

But Aleksy had more to say. 'Oh, Nowakowski, these were not the police's last words on the matter, though. They said that since I was not prepared to press charges they would have to let it go "this time". But I could see from their faces that they did not believe that it *was* an accident. They think I am the one who is foolish and blind.'

Gabriel looked across the table at his old friend, stooped and somehow shrunken, literally bowed down by the burden of his woes. 'And what about the stolen things?'

'I don't know. The police made a big show of searching Feliks's room, top and bottom. Whatever they were looking for, they did not find it. But, just as they were leaving, one of them turned to Feliks and, looking right into his face, he said, "Remember that we know where to find you."' By now, Aleksy was close to tears.

Gabriel didn't know what to say, what comfort or wisdom to offer, so he said nothing.

'What am I to do now?' Aleksy sighed. 'Life at home with Feliks was not easy before. Now it has become impossible. I am his father. I want to help him earn his place, to be a good man, but I don't have the means. What can I do, Gabriel? What *can* I do?'

Cocooned there in the fug of the coffee shop, Gabriel remained at a loss for an answer. The two men finished their drinks without further conversation. He knows that during that silence, each of them was playing the incident at the top of the stairs over and over in his own mind, trying to rescript the actions of the young man so that they appeared in a better light. But whatever the angle, whatever the lighting, this was to no avail. They embraced as they parted.

Gabriel had promised to think things over. Now, sitting on the damp park bench, Aleksy's words: 'to earn his place' ringing in his ears, a solution comes to him.

'That's it! Feliks needs to *work*. With this work will come a purpose in life, the means to support himself and, in turn, self-respect.' And Gabriel knows just what this work can be. He is a rich man and he has a big house; so big, it's the only one on Atbara Avenue to have its own name, 'The Laurels'. He and Irena once hoped to fill it with their children but, of course, that wasn't to be. However, since her death, he hasn't always lived there alone. When he first sold his businesses and retired, he moved downstairs, letting out the upstairs rooms of his grand villa as bedsits. Gabriel recalls how much he liked the companionship of other people around him; how sorry he was when, in recent years, he had to give up the rentals. He didn't have much choice back then. Even the smallest maintenance jobs had become too difficult for him. But now, thanks to his idea, things can take a new turn.

'Perhaps *I* can no longer cope with blocked drains and blown light bulbs, but surely *Feliks* could easily do these little tasks?'

He sits for a bit longer, allowing the plan to properly formulate in his mind. He will be a landlord as before, with Feliks his live-in caretaker. He will give Feliks the smaller of the upstairs rooms at no cost but let a larger one to a new tenant. This tenant will not only be the source of odd jobs, but their rent can also provide Feliks with a small wage. Feliks will have a fresh roof over his head, enforced independence and a clearly signposted road to redemption.

'Yes,' thinks Gabriel, 'this is a very good plan.'

He reaches for his walking cane and, planting it firmly between his knees, pushes himself up to a standing position. Chin up, head back, he walks with purpose towards the park gates, resolved on this course of action to help his friend. As if to reward his clear thinking, on his way out he notices his stray handkerchief snagged on a rose bush. He tugs it free from its thorny hook. Again, he inspects his hands. Pleased with himself that he's avoided any scratches, he stuffs the wayward scrap of fabric back into the folds of his coat pocket and makes haste homewards to The Laurels.

Gabriel wastes little time in sharing his scheme with Aleksy who, in turn, is keen to get things moving. The very next evening, when Feliks comes downstairs to his father's kitchen to help himself to toast and jam, both men are waiting for him.

Gabriel does the talking, explaining how he and Aleksy only wish the best for him, how it's time that he took some responsibility for his own affairs, and how this modest role as caretaker will be a stepping stone to independence and self-respect.

Feliks says little, asking only for confirmation that he will be sleeping in Gabriel's house and will no longer have to live under his father's roof. With this assurance, he leaves the room at once and goes to assemble his possessions.

The two old friends shake hands, sealing the deal, before sitting down to share a glass of vodka.

As they savour their drinks, Gabriel awards himself a private pat on the back. He's delighted by the young man's unexpectedly compliant reaction. He recalls how, as a small boy, Feliks was such an engaging little fellow, often wishing to please his elders. Gabriel sees this willingness to cooperate now as at least some sign that his impiety is not as ingrained as he feared.

Aleksy conceals a heavy sigh. He remembers all the other occasions that Gabriel's good counsel... and money... have helped him in the past. Now he owes his friend another debt he will never be able to repay.

Alone upstairs, as he prepares to leave for the fresh pastures of Atbara Avenue, Feliks remembers what that policeman said to him the other day. He grins defiantly. 'They won't be able to find me so easily next time.'

Elspeth is very pleased with the pigeon's progress. She's fed, watered and sheltered it from the outside world and she's gratified by how quickly it has improved. Only rarely does it struggle to free itself now. She gathered it barely twenty-four hours ago and already the flailing and flapping are subsiding. Its thrumming and cooing have stopped completely. She hasn't yet taken the lid off its hatbox home – safely hidden with the rest of her makeshift coops in the vestry store cupboard – but she's sure that when the time comes, it won't even try to escape.

'It's happy to be with me. Naturally. And it's truly thankful.'

On the seventh night into Gabriel Nowakowski's grand plan, a full moon hangs in the navy blue heavens above Atbara Avenue, yet the church is in complete darkness. Feliks the thief approaches through the graveyard and slides around the side of the building. He's come prepared to force an entry but, to his surprise, finds a small sash window has been left slightly open. The gap at the top is just wide enough for him to squeeze in his fingers and push down the upper pane. It's very stiff. He winces at the piercingly loud paint-on-wood squeals of resistance. As soon as he's achieved an opening adequate for his skinny frame, he wastes no time in pulling himself through.

Tumbling inside, head first and hands down, Feliks picks himself up from the linoleum-covered floor and stands for a moment, waiting for his eyes to adjust to the gloom. Judging by the window's frosted glass, he expected to land in St Francis's privy, but he now sees this isn't the case. Gradually he makes out to his left an empty coat rack; next to this some trestle tables folded and stacked against the wall; to his right a large store cupboard, padlocked shut; straight ahead, what looks like a heap of laundry piled up against the nave door. He holds his breath and listens. Satisfied he's alone, he investigates the padlock. He yanks at it a few times, but it doesn't give. He opts to go in search of easier pickings.

He passes swiftly through the vestry and, almost tripping over the laundry pile, enters the body of the church. High above his head, thin streams of moonlight penetrate the stained glass, casting dappled puddles of green and blue onto the ceiling and walls. The air is laden with creeping dampness and the smell of old plaster and candle wax. Feliks has a vague sense of being underwater. He walks straight up the nave.

Just inside the church's main entrance, he finds what he came for. The collection box. Made of wood, and clearly of some antiquity, it's delicately carved to resemble a pair of hands cupping a bowl. He picks it up and shakes it. It rattles. Feliks raises it above his head and dashes it to the floor, sending splinters of wood and loose change skedaddling across the flagstones. Annoyed to see there aren't any paper notes, with nimble fingers he hurriedly harvests the higher-value coins. Anything less than a thru'penny bit, he ignores. Collecting pennies and halfpennies costs time. Job done, he turns to retrace his steps.

As he approaches the altar he stops, noticing for the first time a candlestick at the foot of the crucifix. In his pocket, his fingers play with the stolen coins.

'Ten shillings,' he thinks, 'tops.' Slim pickings.

He lifts up the candlestick. No more than six inches long, yet pleasingly heavy, it has the weight of something worth real money. He takes the glove off his right hand and runs his fingers over the candlestick's base. He can feel that it's elaborately patterned, although it's too dark to make out the design. Without further deliberation, he stuffs it inside his jacket, makes his way back through the vestry and slithers out the same way he slithered in.

Seen yet unseen, Elspeth continues to live in St Francis's. But although she remains unchallenged, to her annoyance the church is becoming a less comfortable place. Her shelves are filled to capacity, and it's getting more and more difficult to keep everyone safe. Discovery draws dangerously close when the vicar's wife turns up in search of space to stow her collection of cast-offs for some jumble sale or other. Barely acknowledging Elspeth, Mrs O'Reilly makes a beeline for the vestry store cupboard. Finding it padlocked, she summons her husband to come and open it.

'What I can't understand, Desmond,' the woman blusters, 'is why you locked it in the first place.'

'I don't know who locked it,' answers her bemused husband, 'but it was not I. Hence, the key is not in my possession. However, what with the charity money going missing, perhaps a little more consciousness *vis-à-vis* security is no bad thing?'

'Never mind about that now! I'm far too busy for any fussing about,' she tuts, jangling the padlock fiercely as if it might somehow pop open at her command. 'Why won't the blasted thing undo? Haven't you a crowbar or something to force it?'

Elspeth can tell the vicar's wife normally prefers to vault life's little obstacles rather than pussyfoot around them, so she's relieved when Reverend O'Reilly rejects such a violent approach.

'Regretfully I have neither crowbar nor axe about my person,' he replies, nonetheless patting his cassock with an involuntary checking movement. 'But even if I did, I'd prefer to seek a more considered means of entry. I shall hunt down the elusive key.'

'Oh, all right then, Desmond,' sighs Mrs O'Reilly. 'Shilly-shally if you must. I suppose I can cram this load of stuff in our spare room… for now. But I *will* be back later. Remember: time, tide and piles of tat wait for no man. Not even you!'

To Elspeth's disquiet, the vicar is only granted 'a day or two' to mount a search, before his wife intends to keep her promise 'to get into that blasted cupboard even if I have to chew through the lock myself'. As Mrs O'Reilly swings off, she makes an unkind – and worrying – comment about the vestry 'smelling like a zoo'.

Deirdre O'Reilly is certainly a darkening cloud on Elspeth's horizon, but she isn't her only concern. Much more disconcerting was the thief in the night. He'd come too close by far. Almost treading on her in passing, he'd also stolen her only means of income. Elspeth considers it a lucky thing she'd already taken most of the money from the charity box before he came. What if he returns? He could come even closer. Elspeth understands that, once more, the time has come to find a new home for her family.

Gabriel is settled in his sitting-room armchair when the doorbell rings. He wonders who it could be. Bob-a-job boy scouts? Jehovah's Witnesses? Surely not the indomitable O'Reilly woman, badgering him to let her dig his flowerbeds? He's about to go and answer it when he checks himself. 'Feliks is here. This is one of his jobs – as is the gardening.'

He leans back into the cushions and waits for the sound of his godson crossing the hallway to attend to it. The bell rings again.

'Feliks! We have a visitor.'

No response. The boy must have popped out.

The bell has chimed four times before Gabriel finally reaches his front door. Through its thick glass panels, he sees the caller is preparing to press for a fifth time. The liquid silhouette withdraws its hand and waits while Gabriel struggles with the bolt. After some difficulty he opens the door as far as its security chain will allow, and peers through the gap to find a strange girl standing on his step. She's slender, with straight dark hair and homely, understated features. No hint of the flashy makeup so many young people plaster on these days, and no hint of the immodest clothing that seems to be all the rage. In fact, to his surprise given the mild weather, she's almost completely shrouded in a heavy woollen cloak. Incongruously, her feet are bare, save for a pair of simple leather sandals. He doesn't know her but, perhaps, he does recognise her from somewhere?

'Yes,' he thinks, 'I'm sure I've come across her before,' although he can't remember the circumstances. To his frustration, these days he often finds himself confusing names, dates, faces – but manners prevent him from asking out loud what he's thinking. 'Do I know you?' He stares blankly at the girl, trying to place where he's seen her... wondering why she's come to call.

As if reading his mind, she speaks. 'I've come about the room.' Her voice is quiet, measured. Almost monotone.

'The room?'

'The room to rent. I saw your card on the noticeboard outside St Francis's.'

St Francis's! *That's* where he's seen her before. At Miss Dollimore's funeral. Gabriel is relieved to have retrieved some sensible recollection from the ether. Funerals are the only times he attends church – apart from Remembrance Day, that is. And now he thinks of it, he's sure this girl was handing out the prayer books. Or was it the collection plate? Lest we forget!

Gabriel makes haste to appear less muddled. 'Oh yes. The room. Of course. Please forgive me – I'm afraid you caught me dozing. I am still a little asleep.' He closes the door, frees its chain, then opens it wide. 'Please, my dear, please come in.'

The girl slides into his hallway. He wonders if she might even be a nun, but as she steps over the threshold he glimpses a split-second flash of iridescent turquoise – the satin lining of her cloak. This catches him by surprise. A drab little moth with such a startling under-wing, he muses. Certainly not a cloth for The Cloth! Pleased with this private joke, he smiles. 'My caretaker is not at home just now, so I will show you the room myself.'

Slowly and deliberately, leaning heavily on the banister rail, Gabriel leads the way upstairs. The girl follows him in silence.

The room hasn't been occupied for some time. Years, in fact. Its high walls have recently received a careless layer of fresh paint, but Feliks's slapdash application of 'Plum Blossom' to the tatty woodchip paper has done little to touch up the mood.

Gabriel's solid furniture is of good quality, but dated. A single bed, with a tarnished brass frame, is covered by a thin candlewick spread. Cheerless trinkets, undusted, sit about the surfaces. Apart from a pair of Indian rugs, the dark oak floorboards are bare. The ceiling light's glass shade, an upturned bowl with an art deco design, cradles a collection of dead flies. The tiled Edwardian fireplace is handsome, but the little electric heater occupying the hearth diminishes its dignity to all but nothing. Gabriel kicks a plug switch above the grubby skirting board, and the heater hums into life – its plastic embers glowing alternately red, then orange, then red, to simulate the effect of burning coal. A faint smell of singed dust fills the room.

Gabriel points out the room's various aspects. 'The view from up here is good, I think. This is a nice street and the neighbours are quiet. You will have seen my house is set back from the road here, so we are really quite private. The window is large, but you will not find it draughty. My wife always insisted on thick linings for our curtains. The things you see in this room were all collected by her. She had such an eye for the decorative. Her "treasures", that is what Irena used to call them. "My little treasures."'

He shuffles about the room picking things up, caressing each one with his crooked fingers, telling its tale before returning it to its footprint in the dust. Thus preoccupied, he forgets about the girl. Lost in the flood of memories evoked by each revisited object, he's no longer talking to her but to himself.

'Irena decorated this,' he sighs, running his hand over a bedside lamp encrusted with shells. 'She collected these periwinkles on our holidays to the seaside. So clever with her hands.'

He points at a faded colour photograph, in a frame embellished with stuck-on plastic flowers. It depicts Aleksy's and Doreen's three girls, each in a straw hat, sundress and white ankle socks, squinting in the promising post-war sunshine. 'Taken on one of our picnics in Atbara Park.'

'And *this*,' he explains, carefully selecting a plaster figurine of a misshapen woman, naked from the waist up, wielding a sword that has lost its tip, 'is *Syrenka*. The little Polish mermaid.'

At last Gabriel's eye falls upon an object he doesn't recognise – an exquisite silver candlestick, placed in the centre of the mantelpiece. It is truly beautiful. His reverie interrupted, his attention returns to his visitor. Clearly not listening to him, she's closely inspecting the interior of a large mahogany wardrobe. He's surprised such a plainly attired girl should show any interest in where she might hang her clothes.

'If it is storage space you're looking for, let me show you something.' Avoiding the further exertion required to walk across the room, he waves his stick towards the opposite wall. 'See that door over there, to the left of the fireplace? You open that.'

The girl says nothing but does as instructed. She has to tug quite hard on its grimy wooden handle before the door jerks open to reveal a built-in cupboard with eight shelves. As deep as the chimney breast and stretching from the floor almost to full ceiling height, its capacity is generous. She peers inside. On the back wall of the cupboard is a panel of block-printed wallpaper, a remnant from the day when house was very first decorated. Protected from daylight, its original colours are still vibrant. It depicts a garden trellis, supporting a climbing rose. The blooms are a subtle shade of chestnut. Not showy hothouse flowers, but something far lovelier in their unforced simplicity. Clinging to the trellis, in amongst the flowers and thorns, is a small blue bird. As if in a trance, the girl reaches inside the cupboard and runs her hand over the surface of the paper, carefully tracing the outline of the bluebird with her fingertip.

'Irena always appreciated the space we had in this big old house, you know. Even though it was just the two of us here, she would say to me, "Gabriel, good storage space is always a godsend," and I would say to her—'

'I think this place will suit me very well,' says the girl. 'I'll take it.'

He's taken aback. He wasn't expecting such an abrupt decision. He hasn't even shown her the bathroom and kitchenette across the landing – or explained the rent and house rules. 'Well, well, my dear. Well, well. This is good news. Are you sure that you don't need a little time to consider?'

'Quite sure, thank you, this is just fine. In fact, I would like to move in straight away.'

Forced into making a quick appraisal of the situation, Gabriel looks at the peculiar girl standing before him. His considerations are as follows: for his strategy to work, he needs to rent the room. This appears to be a meek young woman who, if somewhat enigmatic in behaviour, certainly does not look the type to hold loud parties or entertain male callers. It's a fact that he does not know anything about her habits, but having seen her in church, surely it's safe to assume she is decent, clean and reliable? If he hesitates now and puts her off, she will look for another room and he may not be so lucky with his next prospective tenant.

'Let us shake on it, then.'

As the girl crosses the room to take his outstretched hand, a floorboard moves beneath her feet. This stops her in her tracks. She looks down and, deliberately placing one foot on the loose plank, she plays with it as it gives, making it creak as she pushes it up and down.

Suddenly worried she might change her mind about the room as hastily as she made it up, Gabriel catches her hand and squeezes it hard. 'A simple nail will fix that,' he says firmly. 'Rent is due each Saturday. No smoking and no pets.'

When the girl slides off to collect her things, Gabriel makes a mental note that he must add the loose floorboard to his list of jobs for Feliks.

Feliks has not 'popped out' anywhere. Annoyed by the disturbance across the landing, he turns over in bed and reaches out for his watch. Seeing that it isn't even midday yet, he buries back down under the blankets to re-join his dreams.

It takes Elspeth several trips to move all her belongings from the vestry to her upstairs room in The Laurels. She is at pains to go unseen each time she enters and leaves St Francis's, and each time she enters her new home with any of her containers.

The pigeon's hatbox, she places on the top shelf of the fireside cupboard, along with those of her other birds. The mice, in their biscuit tins, she puts on the middle shelves. The toads and frogs, in jam jars, she arranges on the bottom shelf. As she hoped, the loose floorboard lifts very easily, so she releases the hedgehogs directly into the space beneath.

On her final trip from St Francis's, she comes back with a small suitcase. This contains her most precious burden. The foundling she's kept the longest and cares for the most. She quickly steals upstairs. Having gently laid the case down flat on the floor, Elspeth locks the door behind her and then checks the windows are firmly secured. She returns to the case and kneels down beside it, listening for any sounds from within. She hears nothing. She pokes at the case's canvas top a couple of times. Still nothing. She tugs at the zip, peeling back one corner of the case top as if opening a tin of sardines, and bends down to look inside.

In a split second a young fox explodes from the case and bolts across the room. Scrabbling desperately to gain a foothold on the bare floorboards, it skids about, colliding with thick, hard furniture legs, disturbing the dust and sending the seashell lamp crashing to the floor. In its blind panic, it then launches itself at the closed window. With a sickening thud, it finally comes to a halt. Stunned, its mouth and nose bleeding, it slinks under the bed.

Calmly lifting up the fringes of the candlewick pane, Elspeth looks at the terrified animal, wild-eyed, cowering in a growing puddle of its own urine. It will have to be retrieved and returned to its case. She lies down beside the bed, flat on her stomach with her arm at full stretch, straining her fingertips to catch hold of any part of the fox she can reach. She almost has it by a hind leg when it snaps out.

Surprised, Elspeth withdraws her hand and inspects the bite mark. The cub's sharp little milk teeth have left a neat row of puncture holes in the skin of her forearm. She squeezes the wound and it begins to ooze blood. For a second time, Elspeth reaches under the bed. She catches the creature by its tail, drags it out and, with a swift, silent twist, snaps its neck.

Feliks is not amused. Uncle Gabriel is constantly bothering him with irritating little jobs, but today's chore really takes the piss. For the past week, the old man has been obsessing about noises, which he claims are coming from inside his bedroom ceiling. Feliks has been summoned downstairs more than once and made to stand around for a good half-hour each time, to listen out for these wretched sounds. He hasn't heard a thing, but the senile coot is absolutely insistent that there must be rats somewhere in the house.

'I hear them above my head, scratching and chewing,' whines old Gabriel. 'They're worst at night. Disgusting things, they could gnaw through the wiring and cause a fire. It is no good, my boy. You must go to the ironmonger's and buy poison. Put it out around the dustbins. I cannot expect the young lady upstairs to pay rent to stay in an infested house.'

To Feliks's mind, the dingy little piece of a 'young lady upstairs' doesn't look as if she would care tuppence if the house were alive with vermin as long as she has a hook on which to hang her moth-eaten cloak. He's had a gutful of attending to pointless tasks for the sake of the pallid, unattractive girl whom he's barely seen, let alone spoken to.

Nevertheless, this evening he finds himself crawling about the filthy dustbins, scattering kitchen scraps laced generously with freshly purchased ratsbane.

From the day she moved in, Elspeth has been secretly monitoring the feral young man from across the hall. Drawn to his feline shiftiness, she's fascinated by him. Although she and Feliks ostensibly share the upstairs kitchenette, she's never seen him in there, and she's found no evidence he ever goes in, even to make himself a cup of tea. Neither have they ever spoken. She's observed that he's more or less nocturnal in his habits: in daylight hours, he only emerges from his room when ferreted out by her landlord to run some errand, but by night he seems to come alive. She knows that he, like she, feeds himself by raiding Mr Nowakowski's pantry, sneaking downstairs and then returning with dried sausage or fruit. Nevertheless, he's extremely thin.

Spying on him now from her bathroom window, Elspeth can make out his bony shoulder blades through his tie-dye T-shirt as he moves in and out of the shadows, the wide flares of his frayed jeans emphasising the leanness of his legs.

'I see you there, Feliks. My panther in the dark. Spreading your own meagre rations around the rubbish sacks for the rats and mice to share.'

The following morning, Deirdre O'Reilly arrives at The Laurels, equipped with everything she needs to complete her mission: thick gloves, trowel and a bucketful of well-rotted resolve. After ringing the bell several times, yet still no one answers, she's perplexed. She's come at the time she and Gabriel agreed they'd tackle his herbaceous border together; it's not like him to miss an appointment.

Stepping back from the door, she peers up at the front elevation of the imposing house, checking for signs of life. As she does so, she glimpses something – a movement in one of the upstairs windows. For no reason Deirdre can divine, the back of her neck tingles. She feels as if she's being watched. Lifting her hand to shield her eyes from the sun's glare, she looks more closely. There's no one there. Just a cerclage of little house martins, high overhead, flitting to and fro. Their mud-pie nests are tucked up all in a row below the lofty eaves. It must have been the birds' reflections she saw, darting across the windowpane. Of course. She scolds herself for being so easily spooked. Why ever would someone be lurking about indoors, ignoring her summons? The very idea! And she has an equally simple explanation for why Mr Nowakowski doesn't hear her: he's no doubt already in his garden, getting stuck into the weeding. Without her! Discovering the side gate unlocked, she determines to slip round to the back and join him.

Just as she rounds the corner of the house, she finds that Gabriel is, indeed, out on his terrace, but he's not alone. He's with another, much younger, man. She guesses the latter must be his godson, recently taken on as caretaker. Long and lanky, leaning on a rake, he's uninterestedly staring at the ground, while Gabriel is doing all the talking. Although much of what's being said sounds like Polish, it's pretty obvious he's delivering a reprimand. Neither of them notice her. Unsure what to do, she withdraws, but carries on watching, waiting for a polite moment to interrupt.

'So,' she ponders, '*that's* the famous Feliks.' Deirdre remembers Gabriel mentioning, proudly, that he'd soon have family living with him. Based on the warmth of his words, she'd pictured someone strong, willing and able to help with everything and anything. Now, peeking out from behind a dustbin, uncomfortably close to the corpse of a rat... and that of an emaciated fox cub... she appraises the figure standing before her and quickly finds him wanting. She spots a rainbow of beaded bracelets on his wrist, the kind she's seen for sale in the market – Indian love beads, she thinks they're called. His T-shirt, emblazoned with the CND symbol on its back.

'All very flip-flops and flower power, I must say,' she mutters under her breath.

The young man's body language, however, suggests a less than serene character. There's something surly about the way he tosses his head each time his greasy, shoulder-length locks flop over his face. There's a truculence in his stance. His baggy denims, like his hair, look as if they could do with a good wash and, even from several yards away, she can see the first two fingers of his right hand are heavily nicotine-stained. If her son Christopher had ever presented himself in such a sloppy state… well… she and Desmond would have been absolutely *appalled*.

Realising she's called at a bad time, Deirdre decides to cut her losses and come back another day. She gropes through the pockets of her gardening jacket, finds a scrap of paper and a pencil, and scrawls a message to the effect she's sorry to have missed Gabriel and she'll telephone him later. She beats a furtive retreat, retracing her steps to the front of the house. However, as she goes to post her note through his letterbox, she's shocked to tread upon an unpleasant, earthy mess, right in the middle of the coconut coir doormat. It's as if someone's tipped out the contents of a dried-up flowerpot, in the very spot she was standing less than five minutes earlier. She looks around her, curious as to where it's come from, but there's no empty planter, and no person, to be seen. She snaps a twig from a nearby bush and gives the pile a firm poke. As she loosens bits of soil and bird droppings and feathers from the concretion, a sad realisation dawns. It's a martin's nest, somehow dislodged and fallen from above. Much more gently, she completes her inspection, afraid she'll uncover an abandoned brood of chicks, but to her relief there's nothing, alive or dead, to be found.

Intending to shake off the worst of the nest's remnants before they get walked into the house, Deirdre picks up the doormat and turns towards a flowerbed. Just as she does so, to her utter astonishment, she finds herself face to face with a girl. 'Good Lord!' exclaims Deirdre, jumping backwards, scattering dust and debris all over herself. 'Wherever did you spring from?'

The girl – or, more accurately, young woman – apparently unmoved by their abrupt meeting, doesn't offer any answer. Dressed from head to toe in a cloak, holding the prop for a washing line like a staff in her right hand, her appearance is bizarre. The expression on her face is impossible to fathom as she slowly looks down at the mat, then at Deirdre, and then back down at the mat. But somehow, her uncanny stillness speaks volumes. The tingling Deirdre felt earlier has another, deeper gnaw into the back of her neck. It occurs to her that this stranger bears a resemblance to the Mona Lisa. Something to do with her generally vapid demeanour? Or perhaps her lack of eyebrows? Whatever the case, it's a painting Deirdre's always thought greatly overrated. And she cannot for the life of her work out why the young woman should be toting about an eight-foot-long pole. Positively eerie.

'Well, well, well,' she tuts, bending over to brush herself off as best she can. 'I don't blame you for staring… I almost jumped out of my skin! But no harm done. As my mother would say, worse things happen at sea. Not that she ever went to sea, as far as I'm aware…' Straightening up, Deirdre notices that the young woman has a cardboard egg carton tucked under her other arm. Lid closed. 'If you've come to rescue the baby ones,' Deirdre continues, 'we're both too late. Fledged and flown, or else Mrs Dollimore's naughty ginger tom has beaten us to it.'

A curious little smile creeps across the young woman's lips before, at last, she speaks. 'Shall I let Mr Nowakowski know that you were here?' Her voice is quiet, her tone flat.

'Er… thank you… yes,' stammers Deirdre. 'If you could just tell him Mrs—'

'Oh, I know who you are, Mrs O'Reilly. From church. Goodbye.' And with these few dismissive words, their conversation comes to an end. The young woman drops the pole, pushes open The Laurels' front door and swiftly disappears inside.

Just as she glides past, for a fleeting second Deirdre thinks she hears a faint cheeping sound. Surely not? For the second time in one day, she curses her overactive imagination.

Although he can never find Feliks when he needs him, Gabriel notes that the boy makes himself available enough on paydays – another disappointing behaviour that adds to Gabriel's mounting frustration. It's obvious Feliks takes no pride in keeping the house, or garden, up to scratch. He shows no initiative, doing nothing at all unless cajoled into action. Even then, jobs are either put off or so badly executed, Gabriel may as well have called in a tradesman to get things sorted.

'Is the boy determined to waste this opportunity to improve his lot?' he ponders sadly as he watches slimy, half-rotten azalea heads sidle across the unswept back terrace.

Gabriel has also noticed food is going missing from his kitchen. 'Am I being harsh, to begrudge him a free supper?' he wonders. Perhaps. Although Feliks should at least *ask* before he helps himself. Where is the respect for his elders?

But he can't allow himself to believe Feliks is, after all, a complete good-for-nothing. He's given his word to Aleksy. Gabriel is too proud to admit defeat, and too troubled by the thought of disappointing his friend. More than that, if he doesn't see his plan through, he won't only be letting down Aleksy, but Feliks as well. Ingrate that his godson certainly is, the boy so beloved by Aleksy, Doreen and sweet Irena, must still have one more chance to prove himself.

But what sanction can he impose to motivate the layabout? Should he dock his wages for each uncompleted chore? Forbid him access to the kitchen cupboards, day and night? Surely not! But he has to think of *something*. He's determined to remind Feliks that the consequences of failure go far beyond the walls of The Laurels.

As soon as the Reverend O'Reilly enters the vicarage kitchen, he can tell his wife is out of sorts. She's shelling a basin of broad beans and, although she has her back to him, the tension in her shoulders is unmistakable. When she went out, earlier that afternoon, she was in good spirits, merry at the prospect of getting her hands on Gabriel Nowakowski's unruly flowerbeds. Yet since she got back, earlier than expected, she's been uncharacteristically quiet. 'Hello, my love,' he ventures cautiously, moving to join her by the draining board.

'Desmond, you startled me!' she gasps, sending a stray bean skittling under the refrigerator. 'My nerves will be in shreds at this rate.'

'Sorry. I thought you heard me come in.' Kneeling on the stone floor tiles, he uses the handle of a wooden spoon to attempt a retrieval, but quickly gives up. 'That's *more* food for the mice,' he sighs, rising to his feet. 'Tell me, how was your gardening assignation with old Gabe?'

'As it happens, I didn't get to do any digging,' she grumbles, popping open another pod. 'He was otherwise engaged.'

'A wasted trip, then,' he commiserates.

'I wouldn't say that. I did meet his two cohabitees. Although perhaps "meet" is over-egging things a bit. I caught sight of one, back view, and had a near head-on with the other!'

'Gosh. News indeed,' he whistles, amazed that Deirdre seems so subdued after getting to see their newest neighbours. He knows she's been busting with curiosity about them, ever since Mr Nowakowski first mentioned his plans. And Desmond's not uninterested himself. 'Come on then... *Spill the beans*!' he chuckles, chuffed with his pun. 'What are your first impressions?'

'Quite honestly?'

'From you, I expect nothing less.'

'The boy's a beatnik, and the girl... she's...' Deirdre pauses. 'I hardly know how to describe her. Picture La Gioconda, but on a very off day!'

'Harsh!'

'Maybe, but there it is. Do you know, I've met her before? So have you for that matter. It occurs to me now, she's that odd little madam from Christian union who keeps messing up my floral altar arrangements.'

The vicar ponders for a moment but can't place whom she means.

'Anyway,' his wife carries on, 'I really don't like the look of the godson or the lodger.'

'One mustn't judge a book—'

'I knew you'd say that!' she interrupts irritably. 'But call it animal instinct, *I* wouldn't trust him, or her, as far as I could fling them. In fact, the whole atmosphere at The Laurels felt thoroughly wrong today. It gave me the heebie-jeebies.' Deirdre wipes her hands on a tea towel and stares into the middle distance, as if trying to work out for her own benefit, as much as for his, what's unsettled her. After a moment's contemplation, she shrugs her shoulders in defeat. 'Oh, ignore me. I'm seeing things and hearing things. Something and nothing.' She shakes her head reflectively. 'I just hope Gabriel hasn't bitten off more than he can chew, renting out rooms, trying to help his friend's wayward son…'

'Well, I commend him for it. Think of Luke, chapter fifteen, verse six: "Rejoice with me; I have found my lost sheep".'

Deirdre casts him a teasing smile, and he can see her spirits are beginning to be restored. 'Honestly, Desmond! Vicars and their Bible quotes! Need I remind *you* of Matthew, chapter seven, verse fifteen?' She makes a silly snarling noise as she recites, "They come to you looking gentle like sheep, but they are really dangerous like wolves".'

While Desmond chases Deirdre around the kitchen table, baaing like an amorous ram, both of them howl with laughter.

*

Elspeth is very disappointed with her latest acquisitions. They won't eat. The rest of her birds gulp down every morsel of their bread and water, but of the four nestlings that survived the fall, two have already starved themselves to death. Stupid things. She takes another look inside the egg box. As soon as she lifts its lid, the remaining chicks throw back their heads, beaks agape. Although they're screeching to be fed, she knows another attempt to get them to swallow her rolled-up pellets of stale granary will be futile. She'll have to find something different, even more special, to give them instead.

As Elspeth slips on her cloak, preparing to go foraging, she hears raised voices coming from the landing. Not wanting to draw attention to her presence, she tiptoes to her bedroom door and presses her face to a crack in one of its panels. She spies Mr Nowakowski and Feliks standing just on the other side, arguing. When she first moved in, such quarrels only happened occasionally. Of late, though, they've become more frequent and – at least on the younger man's part – more heated. The gist of tonight's spat sounds much like the others.

Her landlord calls Feliks 'lazy', 'disrespectful' and 'aimless'. He expects him to 'work harder' and 'be grateful'.

Feliks shouts back at her landlord, calling him 'uptight' and 'uncool', telling him to 'get off my back, dude!'

Indifferent, Elspeth is about to turn away and wait for another opportunity to slip out unnoticed, when things suddenly get interesting. Feliks reaches forwards and pushes Mr Nowakowski in the chest. Not very hard. But firmly enough to make him take a step backwards. The shouting immediately stops, as if both men are shocked by what has just happened. However, while Feliks still appears intractable, Elspeth sees a marked shift in the countenance of Mr Nowakowski. His body stiffens. His fists clench. For an intoxicating second she wonders if he's actually going to try and thump his godson back.

To Elspeth's surprise, it turns out the old man has a much more powerful blow to deliver. Pulling himself up straight, he looks Feliks directly in the eye. He reduces his voice to a growl. 'That is fine, my son. Perfectly fine. You hit me if you want to, just like you hit Aleksy – *twój ojciec*. But remember, if anything happens to me, we *both* know you will be the first person the police will want to talk to.'

Feliks says nothing but looks up to return his godfather's gaze.

'You may believe I'm making your life hard,' persists Mr Nowakowski, 'but the law has the power to take away your freedom permanently. Think about that.'

These words have an abrupt effect. Feliks steps back, albeit with a sneer, and slowly sets about sweeping the landing as he's been asked to do a dozen times before. Head down, back bent – Feliks the night leopard, cowed in an instant! Elspeth registers this reaction... and bottles it for later use.

She stays for a while, hidden, watching Feliks; listening until she's sure Mr Nowakowski has gone. Glad to hear the slam of his sitting-room door, she flits downstairs to his vacant kitchen to collect more supplies, before hastily returning to her own room. Feliks ignores her both times she passes him – so close she can smell his sweat.

Sitting on her bed, she re-opens the egg box, and is confronted by the inevitable wide-mouthed pleading. She empties her pockets and selects a Garibaldi biscuit from her latest haul. Breaking it in half, she uses her fingernails to pinch out two hard, dry currants. With precise aim, she drops one straight into the centre of each blood-red throat. Silenced, the mouths snap shut. She observes the chicks intently, anticipating some sign of swallowing. Still blind, no larger than two grapes, their pinkish-grey skin is so translucent she can make out the organs packed inside their tiny bodies; the flutter of their heartbeats, the bubbles of air in their empty guts, and the currants lodged in their crops. All of a sudden, first one chick, then the other, makes a retching movement. The precious food summarily ejected, the ear-splitting begging resumes. Disgusted by the little birds' ingratitude, she shuts the egg box, this time securing it with a rubber band. As she stuffs it to the back of her cupboard, Elspeth decides it is time to focus her efforts on a much more deserving specimen.

Each night, on the dot of ten o'clock, Elspeth places some food on the floor outside Feliks's bedroom door. She knows he won't show up any earlier. Returning to her room, she switches off all the lights and takes up watch through the crack in her own door. Still and quiet, she waits attentively for him to take the offering.

The first time she does this, when Feliks finally emerges to find a small pile of pink wafer biscuits on the landing, he seems confused. He opens his door just wide enough to peer around the edge. He looks down at the food, then peeks his head out to look right and left, clearly wondering where it came from. Perhaps he thinks it's a peace gesture from the old man? He hesitates before snatching up the saucer and disappearing back into his room.

The next evening his reaction is much the same, but by the end of one week he's obviously got used to the food being there. Eventually, she sees that not only has he come to expect the food, he's even begun to look forward to its arrival. Appearing at just five past the hour, he takes a bite before he's completely closed his door.

Elspeth sees all this, and is pleased.

Frustrated, Gabriel puts down his novel. He has re-read the same paragraph four times, yet still can't follow the story. He seems unable to concentrate on anything these days. His mind is occupied, constantly twisting and turning things over. All these confrontations with Feliks are unsettling. Not only that, he's exhausted. He never seems to get a decent night's sleep. The rat poison hasn't stopped the nocturnal scratching noises. Nothing is going as he hoped. Even with Feliks and the young woman both staying under his roof, he feels just as alone in the big house as he did before. Feliks hasn't taken to his role as caretaker. If anything, his attitude is worse and he's ruder and more unappreciative than ever.

Although Gabriel has told Aleksy about the rows with Feliks, he hasn't let him know about his growing unease about the girl. Gabriel reflects on why this is so and concludes it's because he finds it much harder to put his finger on what it is about her that bothers him. She does pay the rent on time, but always in copper coins with only the occasional ten-shilling note. She's polite enough to acknowledge him if they pass in the hall, but she never makes any small talk. Sometimes – he feels foolish admitting this even to himself – he has the sense that he's being 'watched', but he's never caught her hiding in a cupboard or peeping through a keyhole. As if! This is surely his own paranoia, no doubt brought about by his tiredness. Nevertheless, he's uneasy about challenging her, especially as she's come to him through the church. Sort of. Perhaps he was too hasty, agreeing to let her have the room without even asking for references? But isn't *God* her referee? He resolves to ask Deirdre O'Reilly about her when the good woman next comes calling. In the meantime, he's hardly in a position to judge Miss Shepherd too harshly. Not when there's vermin in the building. The infestation can't have escaped her notice, any more than it's escaped his. This pricks his conscience. He must do the decent thing and reassure her of his steps to get it sorted.

With Feliks, however, he must be more resolute. It's time for an ultimatum. Sort out the rat problem once and for all, or move out. Gabriel realises he might have to admit not just to Aleksy, but also to himself, that his designs to save Feliks have failed.

Elspeth is out in the back garden, using one of her landlord's silver spoons to dig for worms, when Mr Nowakowski himself appears at the French windows.

'Miss Shepherd,' he calls, 'I wonder if I may have a word?'

She ignores him, feigning deafness. She lets him repeat his polite summons twice more, concealing her writhing catch in her handkerchief before finally turning to acknowledge him. 'You wish to speak to me?' she answers serenely.

The old man picks his way down the steps from the terrace to join her on the lawn. 'I am sorry to interrupt your gardening. It's a pleasure to see you taking an interest in the flowerbeds. My wife, Irena, she planted those roses. I only wish my godso—'

'How may I help you?'

'Oh… yes… I apologise. I am wandering from the point.' With apparent apprehension, he clears his throat, before continuing. 'I have been unsure whether to raise this with you, Miss Shepherd, but on reflection I believe it is only right that I do. You see, I have some concerns about…' He pauses again, choosing to rephrase his sentence. 'I have some little issues regarding…' he seems embarrassed to finish his sentence, but persists, 'regarding some uninvited guests in our house.'

'I have had no callers at all, Mr Nowakowski.'

'Sadly, I am referring to visitors of the four-legged kind,' he flushes. 'I fear there are *rats* living in The Laurels.'

'Rats, Mr Nowakowski?' she asks cautiously. 'What makes you think there are rats?'

'The noises. I may be wrong about it being rats, of course. I suppose it could be mice. Or even squirrels… Surely you must hear them too? I am convinced you know what I am talking about.'

'Why are you telling me this?' she asks lightly. Although deeply uneasy, Elspeth, the mistress of dispassion, doesn't allow one squeak of trepidation to betray itself in her voice.

'Because I am your landlord. Naturally, I want you to understand that I am aware of the, er…' his gaze settles upon the dessert spoon, still half buried in the rose bed, '… problem.'

In spite of her cool exterior, inside, Elspeth's thoughts are racing. Does he know about her family? It certainly sounds like it. In fact, hasn't he just said as much? This is a very troubling development. The worst kind. She needs to know his intentions. 'What, may I ask, are you planning to do about this "problem"?'

'Rest assured,' says Mr Nowakowski clearly, 'I will take every necessary step to eradicate it. I will not sleep until every one of the filthy pests is gone. You need have no doubt about that!'

And there it was. The inevitable threat of extermination, albeit delivered in the most civil of tones. 'I see,' sighs Elspeth. Although she hoped to stay longer at The Laurels, it comes as no surprise that she has to leave. After all, she's never lived in one place for more than a few weeks. Sometimes it's only been a matter of days before she's been unearthed and sent packing. So, she's done quite well. And it makes a change that, for once, she's received a warning before having to up sticks. It's given her a chance to prepare her next move.

'Thank you for your frankness, Mr Nowakowski,' she says sweetly, her contempt immaculately hidden beneath one of her best otherworldly smiles. She turns on her heels and heads back to the house.

Once again the time has come for Elspeth – and the most treasured of her collection of outcasts – to relocate.

At one minute past ten, Feliks opens his door to collect his supper, only to find the creepy-looking girl from across the landing standing in front of him. He jumps back in surprise.

'What the *hell* do you want?' he snaps, trying to conceal the fact she's given him a fright.

'I wanted to let you know I've been watching you and I know what you've been up to.'

He looks her up and down, waiting for her say something else, but she just stands there, staring back at him.

'Watching me where?' he asks nervously. The urge to turn his head – to check the ottoman housing his growing cache of altar-ware is firmly shut – is almost overwhelming. But he resists.

The girl pauses, before answering matter-of-factly, 'I first saw you in St Francis's Church.'

This rattles him further. 'When, exactly?'

'A month ago.'

'Have you told anyone else about this?'

'No, of course not, I would never do that… and then I saw what you were doing by the dustbins. I watched you in the night, and I understood.' She smiles a weird, thin-lipped smile.

'What I was doing by the dustbins?' He's very unsure where this conversation is going. 'What the *fuck* do you mean, "I understood"?'

'I understood that you too look for God's creatures, to bring them salvation.'

Based on appearance alone, Feliks suspected this girl to be a fruitcake. And now his suspicions are being completely borne out. He marshals his thoughts, which are in danger of running away with him, and asks, 'Is there some reason why you feel the need to share your loony ramblings, or are you just having a bad trip?'

'I have been sent to save you,' replies the girl.

'Save me?'

'Naturally.'

Feliks is in disbelief. '*I* am *not* the one who needs help around here!' he mocks.

Undeterred, she continues. 'I heard how your godfather spoke to you. He threatened to take away your freedom, and I saw that made you afraid. I can see that you don't want to be in this place.'

'You're not wrong about that last part,' he mutters wryly.

'Gabriel Nowakowski has threatened me too. If I stay here, he has vowed to destroy all the things I care for. Just like you, I need to keep moving. So, I wanted to let you know I'm leaving tomorrow morning.'

'Well, so long. Have a nice life,' he says brightly, more than a little relieved that this will be the first and last time they'll ever converse.

Until now the girl's face has shown little expression and her voice has held an even, flat tone. As if she were stating the obvious. However, it seems his last response confused her. Her brow furrows. 'I wanted to let you know that I am leaving tomorrow,' she repeats more slowly, 'so that you have time to get ready.'

'Ready?'

'Yes. Ready,' she repeats. 'Ready for when we leave together.'

He's had enough now. This really is too much. Throwing back his head, he laughs out loud. 'Seriously! You think I'm about to go anywhere with *you*? I don't know what you saw in the church, but you can't prove anything. As for the dustbins, that had fuck all to do with salvation. I don't give a toss what you think you saw, or what you think you know about me. You're nothing but a Bible-bashing loony. If ever it was your word against mine, I know who people would believe.'

The girl looks incredulous. 'But I'm the one who has been bringing you food,' she stammers.

'If I'd known it was from you I wouldn't have touched it with a barge-pole! You give me the willies! Creeping about the place. And look at the state of you, wrapped up in your miserable hessian sack! Why don't you piss off back to the woods or wherever the *hell* else you crawled out from, and leave me alone?' With that, he slams the door in her face.

Elspeth is astounded. This is not the reaction she was expecting at all. She returns to her room and collects her thoughts. It takes her about an hour to decide what to do.

Having flushed the dead house martins down the lavatory, she opens her window and, one by one, lets the other birds go free. They disappear like phantoms in the night sky, without so much as a backward glance at her. The hedgehogs and frogs she releases at the bottom of Mr Nowakowski's long, overgrown garden; the mice, under the sink in the kitchenette. She packs her few remaining things in the canvas case, makes the bed and inspects the room. Apart from the broken lamp, it's just as she found it. She sits on top of her case and waits patiently for dawn to come.

*

Gabriel rises early the next morning. He shaves meticulously and irons his shirt, taking extra care to dress in his suit and tie for his weekly date with Aleksy. Before setting off, however, he must speak to Feliks. He gathers his resolve. With hardened heart and leaden legs, he mounts the stairs and very slowly climbs his way up to the top landing. He turns to knock on the boy's bedroom door, but his knuckles never meet the wood.

Elspeth strikes just once, but the blow is easily enough to smash open the old man's skull. In the few short seconds it takes his body to tumble its way back down to the bottom step, he's already died. She picks up her case, places the bloodied candlestick beside Feliks Wozniak's door, and slips unseen into the late-summer sunshine.

Aleksy knows that only something really serious would keep his friend from their engagement. After his repeated calls to Gabriel from the public phone box outside the Kardomah café go unanswered, he dials 999. He hails a black cab, but by the time he arrives at The Laurels the police have beaten him there. A trio of blue and white panda cars awaits him, pulled up higgledy-piggledy on the crazy-paved drive.

Having forced entry, straight away the officers discovered the old man, deceased, in a pool of blood at the bottom of the stairs. Their search of the house revealed its only other occupant, caretaker Feliks, sleeping in his room. The fact he'd returned to bed and slept after committing such a heinous crime is particularly shocking, but the cold-heartedness of this young murderer comes as no surprise to one policeman, who witnessed his treatment of his own father just a few weeks before.

Handcuffed and flanked by two officers, Feliks is fighting like a mad thing. Screaming about a girl, and rat poison and stealing from a church, protesting his innocence of this murder.

'Tell them, Dad. Tell them that you know I couldn't have done this thing!'

Heartsick but resolute, convinced of the truth, Aleksy turns away.
Amen.

4

Sticking to the Rules

From a distance, it's easy to mistake Reginald and Richard Pyles for the same man. Same height, same weight, same voice, same gait, both have their late mother's watercress eyes and their late father's brick-dust hair. There's a suggestion of mischief in Richard's smile – he likes to be called Dicky – which is absent from his brother's. Reginald – always known as Reginald – is certainly the smarter dresser. But apart from the giveaway feature of Dicky's wild, red beard versus Reginald's conscientiously clean-shaven chin, the twins are strikingly similar to look at. They always have been.

They grew up on Atbara Avenue, where they were raised by their devoted parents. In the same way that, as newborns, the brothers were swaddled in a single cot blanket, Ethel and Norman Pyles never did split their affections down the middle. Love was always given undivided, to both boys simultaneously. Not *two* twins, but *one* brace. Ethel proudly referred to them as her 'brood', wrapping her arms about their shoulders, pulling them in unison to her bosom. When they were small children, Reginald and Dicky were so identical, even their parents muddled them up.

'Tea's ready!' Ethel would call, and one or other child would trot to the table, only to be greeted with the wrong name. 'That's a good boy, Reginald. Get stuck in to your sardines on toast while they're still hot.'

'Mum! I'm *Dicky*.'

'Of course you are,' Ethel would reply without troubling herself to make any further inspection. It made very little difference to her who was who, so why split hairs? She had two splendid sons, she loved them equally, and sardines aren't nearly so good eaten cold.

As Reginald and Dicky got older, if anything they became still further alike in appearance. Their temperaments, however, diverged sharply. Reginald emerged as a highly controlled personality. Such a stickler for correctness that his twin, perhaps as a reaction, became evermore laidback. In the eyes of their parents, their boys' polar opposite personal habits perfectly countered one another. Neat Reginald, messy Dicky. Funny Dicky, sourpuss Reginald. The best of both worlds in one fell swoop. They simply loved them all the more.

From a distance it's also easy to assume the Pyles twins are loving brothers, but as much as Ethel and Norman doted upon Reginald and Dicky, the siblings detest one another. Perhaps because they're physically identical, each strives to be remarkable in some other way. Since childhood, Reginald has needed to be better than Dicky. Dicky has needed to be better than Reginald. Life has always been defined by bitter rivalry – an unending series of competitions in which the hard-fought-for prize was ever the same. Individuality.

'Look, Dad! *I* am the one who's best at spelling [Reginald], *I* am the one with the tidiest room [Reginald], *I* am the one with the fewest fillings [Reginald], the loudest singing voice [Dicky], the most complicated Meccano [Dicky]. There are four "s"s in Mississippi and thirteen thirteenses makes a hundred and sixty-nine. Surely you can recognise me now?'

'Those boys!' Ethel would sigh. 'Even carrying them, I felt them kicking each other inside my belly.'

'And just which one of them will be first to leave home to start a life of his own? That's what I'd like to know,' Norman sighed back.

In that particular contest, however, there has been no winner. Time's rolled by. The boys are middle-aged men, yet neither has flown the nest. They've never even tried. Norman used to tell Ethel their reluctance to spread their wings was because no other woman could beat her cooking. Ethel laughed at this, reminding her husband which side of the family their sons' competitive streak came from. But the truth was, and still is, that each man is far too afraid to abandon his slot lest his sibling should claim it as his own.

After decades of loving companionship, childhood sweethearts Norman and Ethel died within a few days of each other. She of a stroke, he of a broken heart. Both passed away in the home they'd shared since the twins were schoolboys, leaving it and all their worldly goods to their warring sons. Although young to retire, Reginald immediately gave up his role as a senior ticket inspector on the London Underground so that he could properly oversee his due inheritance. Dicky followed suit, putting his odd-job business on the back burner to spend more time in his half of home.

That was ten, very long, years ago. With no resident referees to moderate the twins' jealousy, and no outside occupations to divert their energies, Number 3 Atbara Avenue has since slid into a full-blown battleground. Today, orphans Reginald and Dicky cannot stand each other's presence for a single minute without exchanging cross words. Things have got so bad, Reginald has drawn the line, quite literally, as follows:

Outside, Dicky is allotted the right-hand side of the garden, including the shed, so he can have a 'den' to house his pottery wheel and kiln. Reginald has taken the left-hand side of the garden, including the rockery. Reginald went to a lot of time and trouble to ensure a fair bisection, calculating to the nearest square inch the area of the whole garden (432,000 inches^2) and dividing this by two. A nylon washing line, which stretches the length of the garden from the back door of the house to the back gate at the far end of the lawn, now marks the border between the two halves. Reginald has arranged the line with great precision to make sure that each of them has *exactly* half of the available ground. Indoors, Reginald's divisions are just as meticulous, 'and, Richard, just as fair'. He claims the three upstairs bedrooms as his living space, the smallest of them used as his 'studio'. This is where he keeps his books on engineering, his large drafting table and his tools. As he's pointed out to Dicky, these are *precision* instruments. There is no question about *these* living in a shed. Dicky is allocated the downstairs sitting room – where he sleeps – the scullery and the dining room.

Reginald grudgingly accepts that the kitchen and bathroom have to serve as communal spaces. A far from ideal situation, mitigated as far as possible by setting down strict daily schedules for times of use. These he has pinned on a cork noticeboard in the hallway of the house. The latter, serving as the only thoroughfare for both men, is No Man's Land. Here stand two large, well-stocked trophy cabinets and an atmosphere you could cut with a knife. To Reginald's annoyance, Dicky has added a *No Trespassing* sign to the pinboard.

'You may jest, Richard, but this is how it needs to be.'

Early one November morning, Reginald is standing in the window of the first-floor landing, surveying the back garden, and he does *not* like what he sees. In his mind, domains are sacrosanct, so he monitors his borders closely. He's explained to his brother, on numerous occasions, the only way for them to cohabit with even a semblance of civilisation is to be completely clear about personal boundaries. Even small contraventions cause him huge irritation, and at this moment he is hugely irritated. He's just paced the length of the lawn five times and now he's come inside to view the scene from above, he is absolutely certain that *someone* has moved the washing line to the left – by a good six inches. It's pretty easy to assess the degree of transgression by eye, given the stark contrast between the manicured green velour of the left side of the lawn and the un-mown meadowlands of the right. Still, he goes in search of a ruler to measure exactly how far Dicky has overstepped the mark.

*

Dicky Pyles observes his twin with a considerable degree of satisfaction. He chuckles so heartily that he spits crumbs of toast into his whiskers. Watching old Reg marching up and down the garden in the cold was funny enough, but now the man's returned with a geometry set and a notebook. This is too much! Dicky opens the kitchen window and calls out merrily, 'Morning, Reggie! Is there a problem?'

'You know bloody well there's a problem. We *agreed*, Richard.'

'No, Reggie, you *decided*, and I didn't *dis*agree.'

'Look at the state of your side of the lawn, Dicky! It's like a paddock. Only fit for livestock.'

'You know what, Reggers, I think you're on to something there. How about I get a goat?'

While the Pyles brothers enjoy a bitter argument about Dicky's grazing rights, shafts of pale yellow sunshine flood the vicarage breakfast room, bestowing gilded blessings upon the Bavarian cuckoo clock, the willow-patterned butter dish, the second-best crockery and the faded Face of Christ. The gas fire sputters, the fat cat purrs, and twinkling galaxies of unapologetic dust dance in the comfortable air. Out in the frost-kissed shrubbery, the blackbirds have spoken. Inside, Deirdre O'Reilly is in full flow.

'In all the years that we've known the Dollimores, I never believed Pauline would actually kill herself. Her poor mother. Although Muriel does seem to be taking it remarkably well. If anything, she's looking sprightlier than she has done in ages. Do you think I should call in on her again, just to check she's not suffering from delayed shock or something?'

'Whatever you think best,' mumbles the vicar, face buried in his latest edition of *The Innovative Churchman*.

'Mind you, Pauline was obviously a very unhappy woman. She didn't look well, did she? I suppose I should have seen it coming. But there we are. Everyone missed the signs.' She sighs. 'Nevertheless, one can't help blaming oneself. And then what should happen but a *murder*! Not in my wildest dreams did I imagine we'd see such a thing in this neck of the woods. What *is* the world coming to? A lovely man like Gabriel Nowakowski, done in by a boy as dear to him as a son. Beggars belief. But at least we'll get the church's candlestick back, so I suppose that's something. Mind you, it'll need a good polish. That reminds me, I must add Silvo to my shopping list...'

'Whatever you think best,' Desmond mumbles again, still preoccupied by his reading matter.

'Funny thing is,' she continues, between loud slurps of hot, muddy Darjeeling, 'I'd been starting to think that peculiar girl from the Christian union... the quiet lass who was always creeping around... might've been the one pinching things. Just goes to show how you can be *so* dreadfully wrong about people. I wonder where's she's staying, now the police have got The Laurels all taped off. Who knows. But if I see her again, I should apologise.'

'Whatever you think b—'

'Have you listened to a word I've been saying?' interrupts Deirdre crossly, annoyed she's wasted so much useful breath. She spends her frustration by swiftly decapitating a soft-boiled egg.

The vicar looks up from his periodical. 'I'm sorry. I was distracted by this article.' He folds the magazine open and passes it across to her. 'Have a read for yourself.' He jabs the marmalade spoon at a photograph of a tiny Norman church with a very large tree embedded in its tower.

'Golly!' whistles Deirdre.

'Brought down by lightning, it was.'

'An act of God then?' She chuckles.

'At times you do overstep the threshold between humour and cynicism,' scolds her husband. 'That horse chestnut,' he goes on, 'caused serious problems for St Ignatius's. A bell-ringer was concussed, a resident colony of bats abandoned ship, and it sent the already astronomical church restoration costs quite literally through the roof. Local residents were very displeased, regular worshippers or not. Ignatius's roosting bats are mentioned in the Domesday Book, you know.'

'But what's the relevance of all this to us?'

'Well, the story is really about the value of community projects in restoring morale. Even though mood was low, the presiding vicar decided to enter his church in a national Graveyards in Bloom competition. He rallied the troops: local gardening groups, the boy scouts, etcetera. Got them to pull together, digging and pruning, to put on a good show. He must be a pretty dynamic chap, don't you think?' His voice trails off in wistful admiration.

'Please could you get to the point?' Deirdre feels her gaze begin to stray towards the next article, 'What Makes a Dutiful Church Wife'.

'The long and short of it is they ended up being runners-up.'

'I presume the tree must have been removed before judging?'

'I don't know. It doesn't say. But "the point" is that since the contest, spirits are greatly improved. The congregation of St Ignatius's is happier, and larger, than ever. I believe organising something similar here would be a healthy step for St Francis's flock.'

'No!' cries Deirdre, replacing her cup in its saucer so abruptly that a dollop of tea escapes onto the freshly laundered, already stained, whitish tablecloth. 'Pauline Dollimore and Gabriel Nowakowski are barely cold in their graves and you're considering St Francis's as the focus of some sort of Chelsea Flower Show. Hardly tactful. Besides, it's practically winter. Nothing's out. That's *two* very good reasons why it's the wrong time to even think of such a thing.'

'On the contrary. This is exactly the time. When did we last have a really good good-news story in this parish?'

'When the Peabody boy got his legs back,' she answers without hesitation. 'How did you manage to forget that?'

'Yes, well, of course,' splutters the vicar, '*that* was indeed something of a miracle.' He pauses, removes his reading glasses, and allows his eyes to roll upwards towards the heavens for a moment. 'However, I still think our neighbourhood would benefit from some shared, positive activity. I hesitate to contradict you,' he says nervously, 'but I'm determined this is something we should do.'

'You're being very forceful,' teases Deirdre.

'I apologise for sounding assertive,' says her husband with a blush, 'and I agree a flower show won't work, but there must be some other event that would fit the bill?'

'Yes, there must. Let's put on our thinking caps and see what distils from the ether.'

For the next ten minutes the vicarage breakfast room falls quiet, apart from the stereo sound of two sets of teeth chomping through Deirdre's very crusty homemade granary loaf.

Desmond eventually breaks the silence. 'I have an idea! A very "*constructive*" one,' he adds with great deliberation. 'You see, I believe our church should be the venue of…' he pauses, tapping his fingertips on the table to give the effect of a drum roll, '… St Francis's first annual Arts and Crafts Competition! What do you think? Not too William Morris?'

'It's inspired!'

'People could enter whatever they like, as long as they made it themselves. There are bound to be unsung painters and potters and what have you who'd be interested in taking part. We can make a real occasion out of the judging: decorate the church hall, serve teas, give it a village-fête-type feel.'

'Wonderful! We'll have to come up with a few rules to keep people on track, though. Set a deadline for entries and so on.'

'Of course,' says the vicar. He leans back in his chair and lets out a satisfied sigh. 'There's nothing like a little friendly competition to bring out the best in people, is there?'

At this last remark, Deirdre O'Reilly looks across at her husband. She knows his tendency to assume the heavenly in every character is thoroughly offset by her own awareness of the more down-to-earth aspects of common human nature. Smiling gently, she reaches over the breakfast table, takes his hand and gives it a hard squeeze.

Reginald Pyles, long-standing member of the Guild of Matchstick Modellers, is very excited when he sees Deirdre O'Reilly's poster in the post office window: *WANTED – LOCAL ARTS AND CRAFTERS. Are you a knitter? A baker? A candlestick maker? St Francis is hosting its first annual Competition of Creative Talents. Whatever your skill, come and share it with us on Saturday, 7 December. Entries to church hall by 11 a.m. Winners announced at 3 p.m. (Rules available – please ring the vicarage.)*

Eager to make a start on his entry, he rushes home, stopping only briefly to buy extra glue. As soon as he gets back to Number 3, he goes straight upstairs to his studio. He swiftly removes his jacket, taking care to arrange it on a hanger before tidying it away in the wardrobe. He dons a starchy white lab coat that's been waiting in stiff obedience on its hook by the door, and then stands in front of the wardrobe mirror as he fastens his buttons. From a stack of shelves that completely covers one wall of the room, Reginald lifts down a box labelled *ADHESIVES*. He opens its lid, counts the contents, adds his recent purchases to the five other tubes already nesting within, and replaces the lid. He returns the box to its allotted space on the shelf, in between (but not touching) a box labelled *MATCHSTICKS [1½ inch]* and a box labelled *LABELS*. From the *GEOMETRY SET* box, he selects a thin metal ruler, a compass and a protractor, which he places on a wide drafting table that stands proud beneath the window. The drafting table, with its weighty steel top and uncompromising, machine-tooled edges, is the epicentre of Reginald's perfectly balanced universe.

He retrieves a pencil from the breast pocket of his lab coat. Holding it at arm's length, he squints to inspect its graphite tip. Fetching down a box labelled *BLADES*, he unearths a Stanley knife. With consummate proficiency, he whittles the end of the pencil into a clean grey spike, making sure that every bit of debris lands in the wastepaper basket. Reginald blows on the newly sharpened point, tapping it with his index finger to satisfy himself of its clinical precision. Rather than tear a sheet of graph paper from the pad he keeps underneath the table, he chooses another knife to slice it from the spine, thus avoiding any frayed borders. He then puts the *BLADES* back on their shelf, in between (but not touching) *TWEEZERS* and *MATCHSTICKS [1¼ inch]*. He spreads the graph paper out on the work surface, smooths it flat with the back of his forearm and puts small lead weights on each corner to hold it in place. He repositions these several times to ensure they're quite square.

Reginald perches himself on a high stool in front of the drafting table, closes his eyes, bows his head and thinks. As he cogitates, he strokes his chin. He quickly dismisses the idea of an artesian well. He made one of those three years ago. As for Tower Bridge, that seems a bit dull. He could always do the Eiffel Tower, but there are no moving parts. Far too easy. Think, man, think!

More minutes pass. He suddenly opens his eyes and smiles. Got it! He leans forwards to adjust the head of an Anglepoise lamp, flooding his little quiver of implements in a harsh pool of light and casting the rest of the room into comparative shade. At last, just as a surgeon must make his first incision, with a steady hand Reginald takes up his pencil and makes his first mark on the paper.

Dicky Pyles, proud holder of the coveted Plasticine and Clay Sculptors' Award for Excellence, comes across the poster thirty minutes after his brother did. He too hurries straight back to Number 3, fired up with enthusiasm and full of good ideas.

He enters by the front door, but without stopping to remove his duffle coat or announce his arrival to Reg, he sweeps down the hallway, passes through the kitchen and exits by the back door. He scurries down the garden path to reach the potting shed. When he flicks on the light – a single bare bulb suspended from the timbers of the roof – it reveals a world of disarray.

Most of the room is stacked to the ceiling with various gardening paraphernalia, all lumped together in a single impenetrable heap. Shovels lie upon hoes that lie upon rakes, like a crazy game of pick-up-sticks. Strata of damp seed catalogues fester under a thicker deposit of damp newspapers. Tall, curving towers of flowerpots lean this way and that, threatening to topple at any moment. Trowels, forks, sieves, hosepipes, all entombed and forgotten. Only a lawnmower stands apart from the mound as if, in embarrassment, it has deliberately stepped to one side. Oiled, clean and as close as possible to the shed door, it's the one sane inmate in an asylum of confusion.

All the rest of the space is occupied, in tight proximity, by a gas heater, an armchair, a filthy wooden workbench, several bulky sacks of clay and another kind of chaos: an army of little figurines. Each no more than six inches high, they sit, stand and lie amongst discarded biscuit packets and mugs of cold tea. There are dozens of them, all different, but all perfectly formed of clay. Some are arranged in groups; others singly or in pairs. Their intricately sculpted costumes – from loincloths and codpieces, to chain mail, togas and top hats – denote a disparate range of historical eras, and the fine details of their tiny faces express myriad human emotions, from ecstasy to boredom.

Dicky addresses his people. 'Ladies and gentlemen, I bring great news. Our terracotta Lilliput is, once again, to swell in ranks. So I'm sorry, but we're going to have to clear the decks a bit. I need elbow room while I'm working.' With that, he begins to gather up his creations one by one, and put them away. In spite of the disorder, Dicky takes great care, painstakingly wrapping every character in straw, speaking to each in turn before consigning him or her to storage.

'Abraham Lincoln, sir, sleep well. You too, Anthony and Cleopatra. Harry Houdini, none of your escapology tricks, now. I expect you to stay put in this flowerpot.'

He stows his collection of American presidents in an empty compost bag. Great naval captains have to share their seed tray with the Romanovs, but Jack the Ripper gets a wellington boot all to himself.

Once all are safely packed away, Dicky drags a hefty sack into the middle of the room. He pushes up his right sleeve, plunges his hand into the sack and withdraws a generous fistful of claggy, wet clay. He squeezes it tight, chuckling to himself as red, sticky water runs down his forearm and drips onto his trouser legs. He's ready to begin.

With five days to go until the competition, Deirdre O'Reilly is firmly focused on the task in hand. Having scoured the vicarage in search of her husband, she eventually finds him, in spite of the chilly weather, at the far end of the back garden, snoozing in his favourite deckchair. Clad in knitted bobble hat and scarf, he's tucked up in a tartan rug, beneath the bare boughs of a wantonly overgrown rose bush.

'So this is where you're hiding,' she puffs. 'I've been looking high and low. Didn't you hear me calling?'

'Alas, no,' replies the vicar, sitting upright and rubbing his eyes.

'We need to discuss the arts and crafters. We're getting telephone calls from potential entrants,' she says, using her thumb and forefinger to pinch off a withered rose hip, 'and one thing they all ask about is the prizes.'

'Prizes?' He looks puzzled.

Deirdre often wonders whether her husband is quite of this world. 'What kind of a competition would it be without prizes for the winners?' She deftly severs another couple of dead heads and stuffs them in her cardigan pocket.

'Hmm. I hadn't even thought. I don't suppose you have a suggestion as to what award would suit?'

Deirdre knows her husband supposes perfectly well that she has an excellent suggestion she's bursting to share. 'Well,' she says excitedly. 'I think people would like to take home a trophy for their mantelpiece. A commemorative cup.'

'I'm not sure Church funds will run to anything that *actually* glisters, gold or otherwise.'

'And that's where my brilliant idea comes in. If I were to dig out Christopher's old sports trophies from his school days, we could re-use them. How about that?'

'What if our son should want his trophies back?' her husband replies doubtfully. 'It'll take a bit of explaining that we've given them away for best-beadwork-in-show or whatever. Perhaps a little wanting in the parental pride department?'

'Really, Desmond,' says Deirdre, no longer managing to conceal her impatience, 'your sentimentality does you credit, but he left home more than a decade ago. I doubt he's still losing sleep over the under elevens' swimming gala, and neither is his wife.'

'Whatever you think best,' sighs the vicar, clearly resigned. 'By all means proceed.' He slides back down into his deckchair and closes his eyes.

'Thank you, Desmond. Now, let me find you the secateurs.'

It's four days before the contest when a cry of, 'Morning, oh brother of mine!' heralds Dicky's abrupt entrance into the back bedroom.

Reginald is taken so unawares that he drops his tweezers. 'For God's sake, Richard. What the hell are you doing in *my* studio? You've no business up here, and well you know it,' he mutters testily, retrieving the tweezers from the floor and swabbing their tips with surgical spirit before replacing them on his drafting table, tutting and sighing as he does so.

'Just thought I'd pop over and see what you're at,' replies Dicky, nonchalantly.

'If you must know, I'm "at" my entry for the arts and crafts competition, and,' he adds with a sniff, 'I choose to work without company.'

Dicky makes no move to leave, but steps closer to get a better look. 'What are you making? Another one of your Twiglet mountains, I see,' he remarks dismissively.

'What's it to you, Richard? Are you genuinely interested in my latest project, which I happen to be taking very seriously, or are you just here to get in the way?'

'I'm most interested, Reggie. Most interested indeed. Since I plan to enter and, no doubt win, the very same contest.'

'*You? Win?* What makes you so sure about that?'

'Oh, nothing. Or… well, just a *feeling*.' Dicky helps himself to a handful of discarded stick ends from the wastepaper basket and lets them fall through his fingers. They rain down onto Reginald's fastidiously tidy tabletop like gummy grains of rice. 'I mean, *matchsticks*? I ask you! Hardly the medium of choice for a real artist, are they? Who knows if they're even allowed in the competition. I, on the other hand, will be working in clay. A classic, traditional material and,' he jokes, 'no risk of the judges getting splinters.'

'Sod off to your revolting mud pile, Richard, and get out of my hair!'

Dicky cheerfully departs, singing one of his favourite tunes. *'Oh, what a beautiful morning, Oh, what a beautiful day, I've got a wonderful feeling, Everything's going* my *way.'*

His brother slams the door behind him.

Not for the first time, Reginald finds himself wishing he'd put a lock on his studio door. Richard's little interruptions are exceedingly annoying. Reginald is, of course, quite sure a competition entry made of matchsticks will be perfectly acceptable, but he decides it won't do any harm to ring the vicarage and check. Just to be on the safe side.

It's the vicar's wife who answers. 'Hello. This is the vicarage. To whom am I speaking?'

'Reginald Pyles here, Mrs O'Reilly. I trust this is a convenient time to call?'

'Good morning, Mr Pyles. Yes, yes. More than convenient. I was just trying to scrub away the inscription from our

Christopher's old badminton cup. Actually, it's proving difficult to shift. I'm glad to put down my scouring pad for a moment.'

'Try 320 grit sandpaper then buff up with a shammy leather. That should do the trick.'

'Oh, wonderful! How helpful you are. Was it me or my husband you were wishing to talk to, Mr Pyles?'

'Well, either. I have something about the art contest I'd like cleared up.'

'Cleared up?'

'I mean I have a query about what *is* allowed and what is *not*.'

'A question about competition rules? Excellent! The reverend and I did come up with a list of rules to keep us all on the straight and narrow. I'm so pleased it's going to be useful. I think there are just five dos and don'ts, but I will just check. Just a tick, Mr Pyles – I need to go and find that list. It's somewhere on Desmond's desk.'

There's a loud clunk in Reginald's ear as Deirdre O'Reilly drops the telephone receiver onto the hall table. He hears the sound of her shoes' sensibly flat soles clippety-clop away, followed by fainter, more distant sounds of rustling papers. He also hears her shout, 'Where *is* that list, Desmond?' and a bit more rustling before her soles clippety-clop back across the hall floor. She picks up the receiver again.

'Got it, Mr Pyles. Now, what's your query?'

'Well, I was wondering if there are any restrictions on an artist's choice of material. Are all media acceptable?'

'Yes, I can't think why not. What is it you're planning to use?'

'Matchsticks, *but...*' he continues hastily, 'not just the burnt-out ones from lighting cigarettes. These are actual art ones I buy from the craft stall at the market.'

'Oh. That sounds fine. Let me read the relevant rule out to you.' Another loud clunk and a pause. 'Hello, Mr Pyles. Are you still there?'

'Ready and waiting, Mrs O'Reilly.'

'I have it here. Rule number three clearly states *"Any and all materials of a kind suitable for home crafts or cookery are permissible, providing they pose no hazard to human health"*. Does that help?'

'Yes, thank you, madam. Matchsticks it is!'

'Perfect.'

Three days before the competition, when Dicky returns to the potting shed after his regular Wednesday pie and a pint at the Brown Cow, he's surprised to find his brother inside, leaning over his workbench, carefully examining the clutch of half-finished figures he's been so lovingly crafting.

'What's going on in here, then?' scoffs Reginald, before Dicky can speak.

'What does it look like?' he replies irritably, removing his flat cap and hanging it on a nail above the shed door.

'The Mad Hatter's tea party, that's *what*,' retorts Reginald, looking around the cramped shed with an expression of undisguised disdain. 'How you manage to do anything in the eye of such chaos is beyond me.'

'Since you find it so uncomfortable in here, you know what you can do.'

'I'll stay for a bit, Richard, if you don't mind.'

'I do mind,' huffs Dicky, elbowing his way past his brother to reach his precious flock.

'Who are these supposed to be?' asks Reginald, casually picking up two of the models. 'Alice and the White Rabbit?'

'In your right hand is Gregor Mendel and, in your left, Louis Pasteur. Now, would you please put them down.'

Reginald does not put the figures down, but instead makes a show of passing them between his hands, to and fro, feigning to almost let one drop. 'Whoops! That was a close one. I can be so clumsy.'

'If any harm comes to them, I *swear* I'll punch you so hard…' hisses Dicky furiously.

'All right, all right. Cool down!' Reginald laughs as he at

last replaces the little people on the workbench. 'But who the Dickens *are* these Tweedledum and Tweedledee characters when they're at home?'

'Gregor Mendel was the father of genetics and Louis Pasteur invented the pasteurisation process. They are distinguished members of my soon-to-be-prize-winning diorama, *Giants of Science*.' Warming to his subject, Dicky begins to point out other figures. 'This is Antonie van Leeuwenhoek, here's Copernicus, Archimedes, and here, of course, we have—'

'Tiniest giants I've ever come across,' Reginald interrupts again.

'Don't be so bloody literal. They're "giants" in the sense of their intellects.'

'I know. I get it. It doesn't take a "genius" to work that one out,' snorts Reginald. 'You're just so easy to wind up, that's your trouble. Now,' he asks as he helps himself to another figurine, 'why don't you introduce me to this little fellow?'

'That is no "little fellow". That, I'll have you know, is Marie Curie.'

'Marie *who*?'

'Marie *Curie*.'

Reginald turns the model upside down. 'Whoever she is,' he says, raising one eyebrow suggestively, 'I'm glad to see you've gone to the trouble of giving her pantaloons.'

Dicky snatches back the model and gently lays her down on the bench, whispering to her soothingly. 'There, there… Pay no attention… The man's an imbecile.' He turns to face Reg. 'That, you oaf, was the greatest woman scientist of our century, so kindly show some respect! She won not just one, but *two*, Nobel Prizes.'

'Did she now? Isn't that clever?' Reginald pauses before adding in a casual tone, 'Though I've never heard of her myself, of course.'

'*Everyone's* heard of Marie Curie,' blusters Dicky.

'Clearly, Richard, that last statement is untrue, as *I* have *not* heard of her, nor of any of her pint-sized pals for that matter, and I'll bet you that most people round here won't have heard of them either. Do you know what I think?'

'No. And I'm not really interested,' answers Dicky tetchily.

'I think you should have gone for someone English,' Reginald continues, undeterred. 'Heroes. People who are properly famous, like Churchill. Not some scrum of obscure foreigners. But I suppose it's too late now.' He trails off back towards the house, leaving Dicky alone with his claycropolis and his thoughts.

At first, Dicky doesn't let his brother's remarks rile him. But, as the day wears on, he begins to turn them over in his mind. Reginald has planted seeds of doubt and, as always, they've started to grow. What if there's a grain of truth in what the ignorant clown said? What if that vicar and his wife *were* put off by his inspiration being un-English? What if this was even against their rules? There wouldn't be any harm in checking. He thinks he'd better give the vicarage a bell. Send his niggling worries packing.

'Good afternoon, Reverend O. Dicky Pyles speaking.'

'Good afternoon to you, Mr Pyles,' replies the reverend cheerfully. 'How may I be of service?'

'I've a quick question about the arts and crafts shindig. I was wondering—'

'Ah! The competition,' interrupts the reverend. 'As a matter of fact, that's on my mind too. Even as you telephoned, I was drafting a few lines to the editor of *The Innovative Churchman*. I think readers will be most interested to hear about our little community initiative, don't you agree?'

'Um, yes. Anyway, I wanted to ask you whether there's anything in Mrs O's rules about subject matter?'

'I'm sorry, Mr Pyles, I don't quite follow.'

'I mean, are there any "no-go" areas regarding who or what an artist chooses to use as his, er, muse?'

'Well, obviously nothing lewd, Mr Pyles. My wife and I *never* entertain that sort of thing. That's rule number two. "*All entries must be original and of a content/design suitable for a universal audience.*"

Perhaps if you were to give me a hint of what you're planning, then maybe I could provide you with some more reassurance that you're on track?'

'I'm working on a series of clay figurines.'

'How charming.'

'The thing is, one's a woman, and she's someone famous but she's *French*. Or she was. She's dead now. I assure you she's not in the nude or anything like that,' he adds hastily, coughing slightly. 'Her name was Marie—'

'Careful not to give too much away!' interjects the reverend. 'Let it be *une surprise merveilleuse*. As far as rule number two goes, it all sounds completely appropriate. I think Deirdre and I are in for a treat.'

'Well I don't know about that, but I'll try my best. Thank you, Rev.'

'Goodbye, Mr Pyles.'

With just forty-eight hours until the contest, Dicky feels restless. It's damp in his potting shed, even in summer, but today the chill of winter seems to seep right to the marrow of his bones. His mind wanders to Reginald up in the backroom, all nice and warm, fiddling about with his stupid bits of stick. It's time for Dicky to pay him another of his special visits. He carefully covers Da Vinci with a wet cloth to prevent him drying out. 'See you anon, Leo. I'll be back later to finish your beard. Old Dicky's fabrication skills are needed elsewhere.' With cheerful purpose, he makes his way into the house and up the stairs, to the door of Reginald's studio.

Dicky knocks hard but enters without waiting for any invitation. 'Hello, hello, hello. I just thought I'd check on your progress in woodwork for beginners.'

'Barge on in, *again*, why don't you?' answers his brother angrily, spinning round from his drafting table with such force that his brass-capped professional-grade drawing pins tremble in their jam jar.

'Such sarcasm, anyone would think you weren't pleased to see me,' snorts Dicky.

'*Anyone* would be right,' snarls Reginald.

Dicky leans forwards and peers intently at an intricately constructed tower of matchsticks growing out from the centre of Reginald's workspace. 'What's this all about?' he asks, screwing up his eyes as if struggling to work out what he's seeing. He makes a move to poke it with his finger, but with lightning speed his brother smacks his hand away.

'Since you ask, I am making a guillotine,' retorts Reginald, 'and you'd do well to keep your filthy paws to yourself.'

'A *guillotine*, is it?' Dicky rummages in his trouser pocket and takes out a pair of thick-rimmed spectacles. He makes a show of wiping their grubby lenses on the end of his even grubbier tie before putting them on. He leans further forwards until his nose almost touches the tower and, with a carefully affected air of doubt, he closely re-inspects the tower. As he does so, Dicky slowly shakes his head from side to side, making sure that no sliver of scepticism can possibly go unnoticed.

'Well, Reggie, you're certainly ambitious. I'll give you that. How many matchsticks will that take?'

'Seven thousand, four hundred and sixty-four. Roughly. So,' Reginald continues with a highly strained pretence at politeness, 'if you wouldn't mind, I'd like to—'

'That many, eh? It's not going to be a *small* guillotine, then?'

'It'll be an accurate, working, scale model,' his brother replies through gritted teeth.

'But quite *big*?' Dicky waves his open arms in the air, stretching them tall and wide, as if defining the dimensions of a large, loose and structurally unsound colossus.

'As big as it needs to be,' rumbles Reginald. In a tacit attempt to dismiss Dicky from the room, he pointedly turns his back and, with now shaking hands, picks up his tools and resumes his labours.

'Did you know that your ears turn pink when you're annoyed?' teases Dicky.

'That's enough, do you hear me? Enough! Now just bugger off and let me get on.' Reginald's ears are practically purple.

Dicky smiles. 'Well, Reggie, much as I would love to stand here chatting all day, I'm afraid I have other things to get on with. I bid you a fond farewell. For now.' Pleased with his mischief-making, as he heads downstairs he whistles 'La Marseillaise', very loudly.

It's Deirdre O'Reilly who takes Reginald's call.

'Hello. This is Reginald Pyles again. Hope I'm not interrupting anything.'

'Not really. Just getting the decorations ready for… you know…' she pauses before adding meaningfully, *'The Day of Judgement.'*

'Pardon?'

'Sorry. My silly play on words. Desmond has requested bunting to cheer up the church hall for Saturday's competition, but I've found it was put away in a right old bird's nest. I'll be untangling until teatime. But it's nothing that won't wait, Mr Pyles – how may I help you?'

'Actually, it's the competition I'm phoning about. According to the rules, is there a size limit for an entry?'

'How big are we talking, Mr Pyles?'

'Allow for three feet high, two feet and one three-quarter inch wide, and eleven inches deep. How does that shape up, Mrs O'Reilly?'

'Oh, I expect we can cope with that. Let me double-check for you, though. I have the rules on the telephone table in front of me. Ah, yes, I shall read rule number five to you in full. Here goes: *"Any shape or size of entry is acceptable as long as the maximum dimensions of any given single entry do not exceed the surface area of one trestle tabletop – these dimensions being three feet long by eighteen inches wide."* So that works out at… um…'

'Four and one-half square feet.'

'Yes. Exactly. I'm sure you're right. Does that help?'

'Sounds ideal. Good afternoon.'

'Good afternoon to you too, Mr Pyles.'

The day before the competition, when Dicky emerges from his shed, he finds Reginald waiting for him in the kitchen. 'What are you doing here? It's not your time for another half-hour. You should check your blasted rota. *I'm* first with the kettle on Fridays, and *you're* second.'

'Well, it's funny you should say that,' replies his brother, slowly stirring his freshly brewed coffee, 'because I'm not so sure that it's *always* good to be first at everything.'

'What?' Dicky gasps, unable to conceal his astonishment. 'N-n-not good to be the winner?' he stammers. 'Impossible. You're the one who says, "The person who comes second is the first of the losers".'

'Yes, and under normal circumstances I'd stand by that. But you see, Richard, as things stack up at the moment, I don't believe you *are* labouring under normal circumstances. Shame, really, when you're so dead set on bagging the prize in the competition.'

'What on earth can you possibly mean by that?'

'I suppose I *could* explain myself, Richard, but I'm a very busy man. Perhaps another time?' Reginald takes a sip of his drink and makes towards the kitchen door.

Dicky steps in front of him, blocking his exit. 'You wait right there, damn it! You can't blurt a thing like that and then just slide off. Out with it. Now!'

Reginald smirks, clearly revelling in the angst he's so easily provoked. 'Oh, all right. Since you ask so nicely.' He perches himself on a corner of the kitchen table and kicks out a chair towards Dicky, gesturing for him to sit opposite him. 'Please, take a seat.'

Dicky says nothing and remains standing.

'As you wish.' Reginald clears his throat before continuing in a solemn tone, 'Here are my concerns. Lately, I've been giving some serious thought to competitions and the people who enter them. I've been thinking about the people who always win, the people who always lose and, Richard, I've been thinking about the *Church*.' He raises his eyes heavenwards and crosses his chest in mock reverence.

'I'm not following.' Dicky is confused.

'Okay, Richard, who won the biggest marrow prize in the garden produce show?'

'I did,' replies Dicky.

'And who was the judge?' asks Reginald, casually inspecting his own fingernails.

'The vicar.'

'Who won best homemade chutney in the church fête?' Reginald pulls another face, as if attempting to swallow a particularly unsavoury mouthful.

'I did, and you didn't. *Ha ha ha.*' Dicky's aware that his laugh is a little too shrill and much too hollow.

'And your rosette was presented by?'

'The vicar,' Dicky replies again, uncomfortably.

'Who won most original hat in the Easter bonnet parade?'

'You know *I* did, idiot.'

'Yes, *you* did, Dick. And the book token was handed over by...?' Reginald goes on, pretending to stifle a false yawn.

'O'Reilly. He pinned it on my lapel himself. This is a stupid game.'

'Do you really not see what I'm getting at yet?' Reginald pushes up his shirt cuff to check the time on his wristwatch.

Dicky shakes his head. 'No, I don't. I win a lot of prizes. But,' he adds grudgingly, 'you've won the odd thing here and there yourself, over the years. Quizzes and crossword puzzles. Best-kept allotment.'

'All quite true, thank you. However, there's a crucial difference. The Church knows all about your wins but next to nothing about mine. The vicar has never pinned anything on me, sunshine.'

'So what?'

'Well, I must say you are being uncommonly thick, even for

you. The point is, Richard, in the eyes of the vicar, *you* are a person who *always* wins. Not *me*. He must be sick of the sight of you, crawling up onto the stage to gobble up yet another award. Always showing off. Not very humble. Or fair. If there's a rule about monopolising prizes in this arts and crafts contest, well, I wouldn't be surprised if you were disqualified. Stands to reason in my book.'

'Well, your rule book has nothing to do with anything,' Dicky retorts furiously. 'It's the vicar's rule book that counts. And I'll bet you anything there's no rule about winners being winners. And you know what else, Reginald? You'll always be a loser in my book.'

'Whatever.'

'Whatever!'

Reginald stands up and calmly leaves the kitchen, quietly closing the door behind him.

Reverend O'Reilly feels it necessary to spend the evening before the competition taking his ease in the vicarage sitting room. Gathering strength, knowing not what the morrow may bring. He pores over the *Telegraph* crossword while his wife works off her mounting anticipation by rustling up a steamed pudding.

'Deirdre!' he calls to her from his armchair, 'I'm stuck on twenty-six across.'

'Read it out to me!' she calls back from the kitchen.

'Clue is: "Sounds like there was a lot at stake when he killed his brother".'

'How many letters?'

'Four.'

'Have you got any of them?'

'Yes. Seventeen down, "STOIC", gives me a "C" and nineteen down, "ALIBI", gives me an "I". So, it's "C" – something – "I" – something—' He's interrupted by the telephone.

'Could you answer that, Desmond? I'm up to my elbows in suet.'

'Will do.' He pads dutifully into the hall and lifts the receiver. 'Hello. O'Reilly at your service.'

'Evening, Reverend. Dicky Pyles again. May I clear up one more small matter about the competition rules?'

'By all means.'

'Well, as you know, I've enjoyed a good deal of success in recent years regarding the size of my courgettes – and my cauliflowers too, come to mention it.'

'Yes, indeed, Mr Pyles. Your contributions to the harvest festival suppers have *not* gone unnoticed.'

'You see, that's what's worrying me. The fact that I'm already what one might call "a recognised local champion", does that affect me winning the arts and crafts competition?'

The vicar's unsure. 'Um, I can't think it would, but I'll just check. Hang on, please.' He cups his hand over the phone's mouthpiece. 'Deirdre! What do our rules say about previous winners?'

'Nothing,' she answers at once. 'How could they? This is the first arts and crafts one we've ever done. The rules are on the telephone table if you want to see exactly how they're worded.'

'Ah yes. Found them. Mr Pyles?'

'Yes?'

'As always, my wife has been able to straighten things out perfectly. Rule number four clearly states: "*There are no restrictions to eligibility as long as: the entrant has been resident in the parish of St Francis for at least the previous twelve months; the entrant has made the entry him-stroke-her-self; the entry has never been entered in any other similar competition before; the entry is an entirely original piece*".'

'Thank you, vicar. See you tomorrow.'

'We look forward to it. Goodbye.'

Just as the vicar replaces the receiver, Deirdre emerges from the kitchen, brushing crumbs of raw pastry from her apron but leaving streaks of white flour dust on her forehead. 'Who was that on the phone?'

'Pyles-with-a-y.'

'Again? What did he want?'

'Another question about the rules,' he says vaguely, returning to his crossword.

'Got it,' replies his wife. 'It's "CAIN"!'

The day of the competition dawns, clear and bright and dry. Beneath a blameless blue sky, the lime trees of Atbara Avenue stand proud, their nakedness made starker by their fiercely pollarded tops. In front and back gardens, almost nothing remains of the frills and spills of autumn. Its russet reds and golden ochres have been swept up and put away, replaced by the leafless parsimonies of winter. Although there's warmth in the sunshine, pockets of ground frost linger here and there, hidden in the cold creases of the streetscape: below privet bushes, in the shadow of a birdbath, and on the rhomboid of lawn that shivers in the lee of Dicky's shed.

Dicky addresses his party. 'Men and women. My *beloved* and *most* distinguished delegation. Today is a marvellous day, for it is the day we shall claim as our own. Singly, each of you embodies greatness. When you stand together, this greatness is magnified. With my own hands I have formed you, united you, made your faithful likenesses to show the world. By celebrating your achievements, your ambitions, in this small way I have sought to realise my own. Today, I…' he pauses to correct himself, '*we* will win.' With these rousing words, Dicky closes his eyes and bows his head several times, as if receiving a silent but sustained chorus of applause. 'Thank you. Thank you. I thank you.'

Dicky wraps each figurine in newspaper and places them lovingly into a couple of shoeboxes, lying them head to toe to ensure a snug fit. 'Don't want you lot jostling around too much in my bike basket.'

Reginald rises earlier than his brother. He set his alarm to wake him well before sunrise, to allow plenty of time for final adjustments to the guillotine. Prior to setting off for the church hall, he gives his tour de force three test chops – with a carrot, a cake of soap and another carrot – to satisfy himself all is in working order. Chock-full of gratification at his own cleverness, he washes, shaves and breakfasts. He's on the doorstep of Number 3 at 8.26 sharp, to meet the taxi he booked days before. It may only be 800 yards to the end of the road, but he considers the fare of one shilling and sixpence a small price to pay to ensure safe passage to his destination.

'What time do you call this?' he rebukes, when his cab pulls up at half past the hour.

'Sorry, governor,' answers the driver, cheerfully ignoring Reginald's angry griping. 'Got stuck behind the rag-and-bone man's horse and cart.'

'Well you're here now, so we'd best get on. I need a hand getting my things downstairs.'

'Nobody said nothing about no luggage,' the cabbie grumbles. He stubs out his half-smoked cigarette and pockets the dog-end, before rolling up his sleeves and following Reginald into the house.

A few minutes later the two men emerge, carrying between them the form of the guillotine, mounted on a heavy plywood base, its angles and corners loosely shrouded within a mackintosh sheet. The taxi driver, who has to walk backwards, misses a step.

'Watch out, man!' barks Reginald. 'Pick up your feet.'

'What have you got under here? The flamin' crown jewels?'

Under Reginald's precise instruction, they gradually manoeuvre it onto the front seat of the taxi. 'An inch this way. No, you've gone too far. Three quarters of an inch back to me… and… towards you. That's it. She's there!'

It's a tight fit. The top of the guillotine is a hair's breadth from the roof of the cab and its base presses against the dashboard. Reginald leans into the vehicle, fussing with the corners of the mackintosh sheet, folding and tucking them underneath, before fastening, unfastening and then refastening the seatbelt across his masterpiece.

'The meter's still running, y'know,' mutters the driver under his breath. While he waits for Reginald to finish his adjustments and get into the car, he sits down on the garden wall, relights the remains of his cigarette and puffs smoke rings up towards the cloudless sky.

Just as the taxi finally drives off, Dicky appears at the front door with a shoebox under each arm. 'Oi, Reggie!' he calls out merrily. 'Going my way?'

'Want me to stop, boss?' the driver asks, slowing down and making to pull to the side of the road. 'There's plenty of room for one more.'

'Certainly not. Drive on!' barks Reginald. 'But,' he adds firmly, 'take it steady. No bumps.'

The Reverend O'Reilly and his wife have barely nailed up their first swathe of bunting when Reginald Pyles and his taxi driver arrive at the church hall.

'Oh, Mr Pyles,' says Deirdre, 'you *are* loaded up. We shall have to have *both* doors wide open to get you inside. Hang on a moment while I summon Desmond.'

'Be quick, lady,' puffs the driver. 'This thing's bloody awkward.'

With a degree of choreographed posturing, the vicar, the cabbie and Reginald carry Reginald's show entry, still under its shroud, through the double doors. Under the excitable directions of Deirdre, they slowly lower it onto the nearest trestle table, which bows stoically as it receives the weight.

'Well, well, well, Reginald. What have you got for us here?' gushes Deirdre.

'Ah well,' says Reginald, encouraged by the impressed tone in her voice, 'if everyone will just give me a bit more space, all will be revealed.'

His little audience complies, in unison shuffling three or four paces backwards.

'Okay. That's far enough. Ready?'

They nod.

'Then allow me!' With these words, he takes hold of one

corner of the mackintosh sheet and, in a single, swift flourish, whips it clean away.

For a moment, everyone stands in silence. The vicar raises his eyebrows, expressions of puzzlement and surprise fighting for position on his furrowed brow. The taxi driver removes his cap and strokes his chin thoughtfully. Deirdre O'Reilly looks down at the parquet floor, notices it needs sweeping, and looks back up again at Reginald. His gaze is fixed on the huge matchstick tower, tears of pride welling in his eyes.

'My *word*,' breathes Deirdre, conscious that someone has to say something, 'that *is* interesting. I don't think any of us were expecting that, were we, Desmond?' She glances towards her husband for some kind of confirmation. On getting no immediate reaction, she continues. 'Now, let me get you an entry card, Mr Pyles, so that you can fill in your address and give your… er… exhibit its proper title.' She hesitates, blushing a little. 'I'm sure it must be obvious to everyone else, so *do* forgive me for asking, Mr Pyles, but is that what I think it is?'

'Depends what you *think* it is, dear lady.'

Before she can answer, the driver breaks in. 'Some kind of fancy veg slicer, I reckon. Not very practical, mind you. Just how big is that thing? A good yard high?'

'Actually,' begins Reginald, 'I think you'll find that's thirty-two and one-half inches. But she's not a—'

'I believe it's a *humidor*,' interjects the vicar confidently.

'Er, no, Reverend,' says Reginald, with unconcealed surprise. 'What is a humidor?'

'One of those bladed gadgets for trimming cigars.'

'I knew that,' says the cabbie.

'Well *I* think it's a guillotine,' says Deirdre.

Reginald beams with satisfaction. 'She is indeed, Mrs O'Reilly. And she really works.'

Dicky decides to push his bike, slowly, along the pavement rather than pedal down the avenue. It's a pleasant walk, and it wouldn't do to hit a pothole. By the time he arrives at St Francis's church hall, a short queue of people has already gathered at the entrance. He locks his bike to the iron railings and, cradling his shoeboxes in his arms, joins the back of the line. He recognises the very fat lady in front of him as his neighbour, Trixie Cartwright. She's carrying a string quartet of stuffed canaries. Ahead of her is a woman with an elaborate arrangement of dried flowers; then a little girl with a slackly crocheted, lime green loo roll cover in the shape of a flamenco dancer.

'Quite a turnout,' he comments cheerfully.

'You can say that again,' replies the fat, stuffed-bird lady. 'There's *everso* many more than I was expecting.'

'Not half,' says the dried-flower lady. 'I don't envy them judges, having to choose.'

'Well,' Dicky says with a wink, 'let's just hope *the best man wins*.' Both ladies sniff and turn to face away again. The girl draws her loo roll cover a bit more tightly into her chest. The next entrant enters the hall and they all shuffle forwards.

When Dicky reaches the door, he's greeted by a business-like Deirdre O'Reilly, armed with a clipboard and a someone-has-to-keep-things-organised-around-here tone to her voice.

'Name, please?' she pipes, eyes down, pencil raised.

'Pyles. That's spelled P, *Y*, L, E, S.'

'Good morning, Dicky!' she cries, looking up from her registration sheet. 'You've come along too. How lovely. Are you here to offer some moral support to that brother of yours?'

'Pardon?'

'You know, cheer Reginald on.'

'Why would I do that? I mean, no. I'm here to register an exhibit.'

'*You've* come to register? Oh, Dicky! If I'd known that earlier, I could have saved you the bother of queuing. Reginald has already registered the exhibit for you.'

'Reginald has? That's not possible, Mrs O.'

'I assure you it is. I was here when he brought it in. And

quite a piece of work it is. You can't miss it, can you?' She waves across the room. 'Oh, look! Reginald is waving back at us.' She hands her clipboard to Dicky, pointing at her own neatly formed handwriting. 'See, here's the entry down on my list: Name: *Pyles, R.* Address: *3 Atbara Avenue, London W5.* Title of exhibit: *Guillotine. C18*th. *Scale model (working).*'

'But I have my entry with me now, in here,' Dicky chuckles, giving his shoeboxes a gentle shake. 'You're talking about *Reggie's* offering, not *mine*. Another thing entirely.' Unfazed, he passes the clipboard back to Deirdre, who seems rather nervous as she watches him put the boxes on the floor, open a lid and pull out one of the little newspaper parcels. 'Feast your eyes on this!' He unwraps it just enough to provide her with a glimpse of the figurine nestled inside. 'Say hello, or rather *bonjour*, to Marie. But then I'm sure *you* recognise a famous Frenchwoman when you see one.'

'No. Well, yes. Indeed.' She pauses before continuing. 'So, just to get this straight, you're saying that you *also* wish to enter something in the competition?'

'Yes, of course. Why wouldn't I?' Dicky asks carelessly, concentrating on rewrapping the figure. 'I've been on the vicarage blower about the competition. A couple of times, as it happens.'

'*You* have? *You've* been on the telephone. More than once?'

'That's what I just said.'

'But I don't recall any of these chats. I did hear from Reginald, of course, but not from you, Dicky.'

'Correct. And that's because *I* spoke to your husband. Twice. He put me nice and straight over all the rules.'

'Oh dear!' Deirdre O'Reilly flushes deeply, her neck, cheeks and décolletage turning a mottled dark pink. 'I'm afraid there's been a mix-up.'

'What sort of a mix-up?'

'A serious one, Dicky.'

'Just how serious, exactly?' he asks, slowly, sensing that the growing blotchiness of the woman's cleavage is unlikely to portend good news.

'Very serious. You see, the thing is...' she begins, but then stops herself. 'This is awkward. I don't think that Desmond... I don't think that Desmond *or* I... can have quite covered *all* the rules.'

'I don't get your meaning.'

The vicar's wife's hands start to tremble. She drops her clipboard, picks it up, but in her flustered state, immediately drops her pencil. 'I think we had better call over the vicar, and let's call your brother too, to help explain.' With that, she gives a shrill shout across the busy hall. 'Desmond! Reginald! A quick word.'

Reginald, who is inspecting the cups on the judges' table, and Reverend O'Reilly, who is adding his finishing touches to his prize-giving speech, both down tools and make their way over.

'Isn't it a beautiful day, Reggie?' chimes Dicky brightly.

'We'll see,' says Reginald, with a smug grin.

'What can we do for you?' asks the vicar.

'Am I right in thinking that you've taken a couple of calls from Mr Pyles about the competition rules?' blurts Deirdre.

'Guilty as charged,' replies her husband evenly. 'We *both* did, if I'm not mistaken.'

'Oh, Desmond, you are *not* mistaken. But then again you *are*. We *both* are, or were, rather. The thing is, you spoke to *Dicky* Pyles. I spoke to *Reginald*. And neither of us realised. And neither did they. And now Reginald and Dicky have *both* presented us with lovely pieces for the crafts show.'

The vicar looks at his wife, then at Dicky, then at Reginald... and he bursts out laughing. 'Well, if that's not funny then I don't know what is.' He slaps each of the brothers, who are mirror images of confusion, heartily on the back. 'A comedy of errors worthy of Shakespeare, don't you think, Deirdre?'

'No I do not!' she snaps. She stares hard at her husband and, with a meaningful look, adds under her breath, 'You're forgetting rule number one.'

'And what is rule number one?' ask Dicky and Reginald in unison.

'Yes, do remind me,' says the vicar, still laughing.

The vicar's wife sighs heavily. She reaches inside her pinafore pocket and salvages a tired-looking sheet of lined paper that is the list of rules. 'I'll read it out: *Rule number one: Strictly one entry per household.*' These words silence the vicar like a round of buckshot.

Now it's Reginald who starts to laugh. 'So, Dicky. I guess that's hard cheese for you, isn't it? I got here first. I'm in and you're out.'

'To *hell* with that. What a bloody stupid rule,' shouts Dicky. 'Why the Devil didn't anyone mention this before?'

'Is "Devil" a swearing word?' asks a small boy holding an Airfix Spitfire.

'Shh!' replies the boy's father.

'Steady on!' exclaims the vicar. Dicky's raised tones are pricking the interest of people in the queue behind. Their impatience is giving way to curiosity, and necks crane to get a good view of the scene as it threatens to unfold. Reverend O'Reilly turns to his wife. 'Surely we could make an allowance for Dicky?'

'If only it were that simple.' She's almost in tears. 'But I've already limited other families to just one thing. The Briskets have five children, in fact it may even be six, and I was firm with them. It wouldn't be fair to bend the rules now. Especially not for adults.'

The vicar addresses Dicky and Reginald. 'Listen, gentlemen,' he says, uncharacteristically decisively. 'You two must resolve this together. Quietly. In my experience, with a little calm discussion and some clever thinking, there is no problem that cannot be overcome.' Taking each twin by the arm, he steers them, gently but firmly, towards the trestle table bearing Reginald's guillotine. Dicky puts up no resistance, and neither does his brother. 'Now, I shall leave you to it.'

Reverend O'Reilly pats both men on the shoulder before retreating to his wife's side.

Reginald and Dicky wait until the vicar is out of earshot before continuing their altercation. They keep their voices low and speak through gritted teeth.

'Open and shut case as far as I'm concerned,' spits Reginald. 'My name is in the register and yours is not.'

'Technically, Reggie, it could be either of us on that register,' Dicky spits back. 'It says "Pyles, R.", remember. Who's to say what the "R" stands for?'

'It stands for "Reginald".'

'It could just as easily stand for "Richard".'

Dicky hastily unwraps his figures, fumbling with the paper as he shakes with rage, and begins to line them up on the table, in front of Reginald's guillotine. As fast as he arranges them, Reginald knocks them down.

Dicky elbows his brother out of the way. 'Don't you touch them, bastard!'

'And what are you going to do about it?'

'I'm warning you, Reginald, break off so much as a toe and I'll—'

'You'll what, Richard? Punch me on the nose? I'd like to see you try!'

Dicky leans into Reginald's face, so close that their foreheads are touching, and snarls, 'If you make a mess of any one of my people, *I* will make a mess of you.'

'Really? We'll see about that.'

The sequence of events that follows is over before either man can blink: Reginald takes a step away from his brother and flicks his thumb and forefinger against the side of the guillotine. A matchstick snaps. The trigger is released. The blade drops. Marie Curie, Nobel Prize winner, the most cherished of Dicky's daughters, loses her head.

At first Dicky doesn't react. He stands in stunned silence, staring open-mouthed at the speed and cruelty of the guillotine's progress, trying to take in the irreversibility of its action. Reginald smiles. A slow, wide, triumphant smile. Then tears well in Dicky's eyes. He bends down and, on hands and knees, rummages around under the trestle table to retrieve the little head. Raising it to his lips, he gently blows off the dust before placing it, with great reverence, next to its decapitated corpse. Dicky turns to face Reginald, his fists clenched so hard that his knuckles turn white. His arms twitch, and Reginald prepares to duck, but to Reginald's surprise, his brother doesn't follow through.

'Not going to take a swing at me, then?' Reginald goads.

'No,' Dicky answers calmly. 'I'm not.' As suddenly as it came, the tension in his body melts away. He relaxes his hands and they fall limp at his sides. 'But you were warned, Reginald. You were warned.' He turns to leave.

'That's right. You skulk off somewhere to lick your wounds, loser!' murmurs Reginald. 'I know a good place. That shitty shed of yours. *Ha ha ha.*'

'I know a better place,' Dicky growls back at him. 'Your shitty studio. *Ha ha ha.*'

Dicky walks out of the hall, jumps on his bike, and pedals for home. He's hotly pursued by Reginald, on foot.

Reverend O'Reilly stands on a chair and waits for the crowd to notice him. When this doesn't happen, his wife claps her hands and shouts. 'Our vicar wishes to speak.' Straight away the room falls silent.

'Thank you, my dear. Yes, I wish to announce that registration for the arts and crafts competition has formally closed. I therefore ask that you clear the church hall to allow the judges to complete their work. Deirdre and I look forward to welcoming you all back here at three o'clock, when the winners will be revealed.'

Thus dismissed, the good folk of Atbara Avenue shamble off to the scout hut in search of tea urns and cake.

When Dicky gets back to Number 3, Reginald is still some way behind, puffing and panting to catch up. Dicky runs straight to his shed and grabs a rubber bucket of clay slurry. He immediately returns to the house, moving through the kitchen and up the stairs as fast as his heavy load allows. As soon as he reaches his brother's studio, he flings open the door and swings the bucket into the room. Its contents fly everywhere. In this one, explosive instant, all Reginald's order is undone. Wet red muck covers the floor, runs down the walls, and soaks into the pristine seams of his snowy white lab coat. Dicky stands in the doorway, shoulders heaving with the effort of lugging the bucket.

'You bastard!' he screams into the room.

With a *fizz* and a *phut*, the bulb in Reginald's Anglepoise lamp blows.

Having left their judgement of the Pyleses' entry until last of all, the vicar and his wife circle the trestle table, carefully appraising the aftermath of Reginald and Dicky's handiwork.

'What have we here?' ponders the reverend.

'I'm not sure,' replies Deirdre, scrutinising the scattering of figurines lying over and around the matchstick guillotine, 'but it does look as if they've made a most vigorous attempt to combine their efforts. Look, Dicky's little people are all carefully arranged on Reginald's chopper, and they're just the right size to make sense of the thing. One of them's even lost its head on the block. How clever!'

'How so?'

'If they have, as I say, "combined their efforts", then technically this is now just a single competition entry. That means neither needs to be disqualified. They can be judged as one.'

'Now, that *is* clever. I knew they'd come up with something sensible once they calmed down,' the vicar says sagely. 'To have found such an harmonious solution is very much to their credit.'

'And I'll tell you what else, too: I don't think this is just any old execution scene.'

'It isn't?'

'This is the execution of a *queen*.'

Desmond O'Reilly continues to stare at the guillotine and the bodies, stroking his chin and musing. He continues to look blank.

'Are you honestly not seeing it, Desmond?'

He shakes his head apologetically.

Deirdre continues, 'Who liked to dispatch their royals with a guillotine? The French, that's who. And I'll tell you another thing: this morning Dicky said one of these characters is supposed to be a famous Frenchwoman called "Marie". Ringing any bells?'

'Actually, yes,' replies Desmond thoughtfully. 'On reflection, I'm pretty sure he *did* mention something about making a model of a Marie person when he rang earlier in the week. But I still don't absolutely get the connection.'

Deirdre lets out an exasperated sigh. 'Okay. Here's a clue.' She takes a deep breath, spreads her arms wide, and in the most imperious tone she can muster, proclaims, 'Let zem eeeet cek!'

'You mean Marie *Antoinette*?'

'Of course!'

'She never actually said that, you know. Historians think it came from Princess Marie-Thérèse of Spain. Married Louis the *fourteenth* rather than Louis the *sixteenth*, of course, and interestingly enough—'

'The point is, the Pyles brothers have pulled off a masterstroke. They've merged their two, seemingly unrelated creations into a vignette of the execution of Marie Antoinette. Look!' Deirdre picks up the two halves of the figure lying on the block. 'This poor creature minus her noggin is Marie Anne herself. These others... well... they must be various courtiers, lined up for the same fate.'

'Why are they all lying down?'

'I expect they fainted.'

'One of them looks a bit like Einstein,' chuckles the vicar.

'Don't be such a philistine. I doubt you or I could do any better with a lump of wet clay.'

'Right as always, Deirdre. Right as always.'

Reginald mounts the stairs, following a trail of muddy footprints.

'Back already, Reggie?' Dicky calls from the studio, voice laden with sarcasm.

'Don't think you can leave this mess on the carpet, Dicky, and expect me to clean it up!' Reginald shouts back, as he continues to climb. 'And you'd better not be in my studio... and...' he puffs, 'I'm telling you now that I'm not letting you get away with wrecking my chances of winning the craft competition.'

'Well you *murdered* my chances. You were warned.'

'Where are you, you son of a bitch?'

'I'm in here!' replies Dicky in sing-song tones. 'And if *I* am a son of a bitch, dear brother, what does that make *you*?'

Reginald reaches the studio door. It's closed. Silence. But he can sense his twin on the other side.

'I know you're in there, Dicky, and you're for it!' He seizes the door handle and tears into the room.

Dicky never gets the chance to hit Reggie. Or to break his fall. The instant Reggie's foot meets the wet mud he's sent flying... up into the air... smack down to the floor. He lands heavily. Face up.

Deirdre O'Reilly is all for giving the Pyles brothers first place, but her husband vetoes it.

'A guillotine is an apparatus designed for killing. I think we should go for something more homespun.'

'Actually, do you know, for once I completely agree with you. Two grown men squabbling like naughty children. Don't you just wish you could bang their heads together?'

So, it comes to pass, later that afternoon, the vicar finds himself announcing to the reassembled crowd: 'I am delighted to award first prize to Colin Peabody, for his papier-mâché replica of the Sphinx.'

Dicky Pyles steps out from behind the studio door and bends over Reginald's motionless body. Seeing his twin all dressed up in his best suit, lying there in a puddle of mud, he finds his own anger is completely spent.

'Reggie,' he laughs, offering his hand to help him up off the floor, 'get back on your feet and we can shake on it!'

No response.

'Come on, Reginald. Stop messing around.'

He looks at Reggie's chest, waiting for it to rise and fall. Nothing.

Dicky takes up a pencil (*GRAPHITE [3H]*) and, very gingerly, gives his brother a sharp jab in the side of his cheek. Still no reaction, but Reggie's head rolls to one side. And that's when Dicky finally sees it. The deep, dark, perfectly formed gash where Reggie's skull must have hit the cold, exacting, metal corner of his draftsman's table. A copious river of warm red blood begins to spill, gradually mingling with the mud and the matchsticks and Dicky's open-mouthed astonishment. The mess is spectacular.

Since neither Pyles brother is present at the awards ceremony, a few days later Deirdre O'Reilly takes their runners-up medal round to Number 3.

Dicky doesn't hear the doorbell on first ring as he's digging in the back garden. 'Just getting the ground ready for my broad beans. An especially deep trench.'

'Well, I shall look forward to some prize-winning vegetables in next year's produce show. Anyway, congratulations again, Dicky,' she says, shaking his hand firmly as she turns to leave. 'Do tell Reginald that I'm sorry to have missed him. I hope he enjoys his world cruise.'

'Will do. Good afternoon, Mrs O.'

'Goodbye, Mr Pyles.'

5

Mixed Messages

From a distance, it's easy to mistake ex-school dinner lady Miss Trixie Cartwright for a totally fulfilled person. As round and red-faced as a cherry Chupa Chups, she'd smile benevolently at all the boys and girls as she dished up their fish fingers. Bless all the chicks, clucked the red hen. Her neighbours, at least the women of Atbara Avenue, do sometimes wonder if she's sorry to have no brood of her own. But then again, Trixie never comes across as incomplete. Enviably confident in her own skin, she has a full-bodied buoyancy that seems to carry her through life. She's always busy with this and that. The Women's Institute, church choir, her dancing classes. And thanks to the sale of her late father's successful meat-packing business, she's now a woman of independent means. She has no one to please but herself, and she appears to be very good at doing just that.

On Saturday afternoon, as she waddles homewards, it's all Trixie can do to avoid glancing at her substantial reflection in the shop windows. She's *everso* pleased with her new perm. Her curls are so blonde and pert and high on her head, she feels positively girlish. She's been to her regular salon, but Anthea, who usually does her, was off with her veins, so a different stylist saw to her this time. This 'Mandy' – or was it Mindy? – said it would be better to use bigger rollers, or set it for longer, or something. Trixie hadn't quite followed. Mandy-Mindy had explained, but she was shuffling a line of hairpins around between her lips while she was talking. Well, whatever the girl did, she's bouffed her up a treat. Trixie also likes the shade of polish she picked out for her nails. 'Nearly Nude'. A cross between 'Sunset Harem' and 'Blizzard', apparently. One of their most enticing lines.

Trixie decides she'll definitely ask for Mandy-Mindy next time she makes an appointment, whenever the big day comes.

As soon as she opens the front door of Number 5 Atbara Avenue, she's met by a very fluffy Pekinese, yapping in wild delight at her mistress's return. 'Yes, yes, Puffball. Mummy's back.' Trixie staggers into the kitchen, closely followed by the pudgy little dog, and drops her shopping bags onto the worktop. She flops down heavily into the nearest chair and her pet flops down heavily at her feet. Both pant at their exertions.

'Dear me, Puffy. That was quite an expedition.'

Trixie waits until she's composed herself, a full five minutes, before she turns her attention to her purchases. She wants to savour them properly.

She opens a medium-sized cardboard box first, its lid embossed with Belle's Boutique in gold lettering, and lifts out a large, flesh-coloured bra. It's of a sturdy construction with a reassuring amount of wire reinforcement stitched into its seams. She carefully inspects the detailing sewn onto the front, running her fingertip across tiny clusters of ribbon rosebuds. She sighs at how pretty they are. Gorgeous workmanship. So delicate. She deliberates for a moment, then takes hold of the bra by its wings and gives it a couple of firm tugs – just to be on the safe side. It creaks a bit, but that's all. She's satisfied it'll be fit for purpose. She resolves that when she's next out, she'll go back for the matching knickers.

Next, she unwraps her new kaftan. Covered in bold, abstract blocks of colour, it is a cacophony of orange and blue. Holding it up to the light, she realises it's a tad see-through. How naughty. She slightly regrets going for trendy polyester rather than good old-fashioned silk – but only slightly. It feels silky enough to the touch.

The ensuing bits and pieces comprise scented candles, which she bought from the hippy-ish Import Emporium recently arrived on the high street, an orange liqueur chosen because she liked the fancy glass bottle, and a box of Cuban cigars.

Carefully, she stows all these things away in her place in the bottom of the larder, before looking at her final acquisition. She's saved the most extravagant item until last. From a large paper bag with fat cords for handles, she retrieves a shoebox. She swiftly removes its lid to reveal a dainty pair of sandals cowering within a nest of pale blue tissue paper. They are a confection of gold leather straps and turquoise beads. Trixie gasps at their beauty. Never mind about that shop assistant. 'Would madame prefer something more sophisticated?' Indeed! There's no rule book saying forty-something ladies can't wear kitten heels. And what would that skinny young woman know about *real* feminine allure?

Tingling with excitement, Trixie kicks off her well-worn court shoes and slips the sandals on over her tights. They are a very snug fit. She's not worried, though. Her feet have no doubt got a bit bloated, traipsing round the shops. She'll just have to wear them in for a few days, that's all. She examines her toes, which she's always considered her very best feature, tightly crammed into the new sandals, and gives them a wriggle. She's cheered by their loveliness. Yes. A couple of coats of 'Nearly Nude' will set them off nicely.

Trixie is delighted with everything she's bought so far. Things are shaping up nicely for the special evening she's planning, alone with her own *ever so* special Mr Pyles.

Puffball turns her frying-pan face to look up at her mistress, rolls her bulging black eyes and licks her chops expectantly.

'I know, I know,' clucks Trixie. 'You're a hungry girl.' She hauls herself to her feet and teeters to the larder. She opens a tin of salmon and empties its entire contents onto a bone china dish. Using a silver fork with mother-of-pearl handle, she flakes up the flesh before placing it in the middle of the table. She scoops up Puffball and plonks her down beside the dish. No sooner have the Pekinese's paws met the Chantilly lace cloth than she begins to eat, wolfing down every morsel in wheezy, appreciative gulps. Trixie pats her affectionately on the rump and lifts her back down to the floor.

'Now, how about I make us both a drink to wash that down?'

Trixie sways her way over to the sink. Looking out of the window as the kettle fills, she glimpses the top of someone's head moving around on the other side of the garden fence. Immediately, she turns off the tap and totters out of the back door, her dog at her heels. 'Dicky!' she calls. 'Is that you I spy?'

No one answers, but she hears a faint rustling, as if somebody is tiptoeing across fallen leaves. She tries again. 'I was wondering if we could have another of our little chats,' she coos hopefully.

Still no one answers. Puffball snuffles at the air, as if catching a scent. Trixie bends down, puts her face to the fence and squints through a split between two posts. 'Dicky,' she chuckles, 'I know you're there. I can see your muddy wellingtons. Why don't you come on over? Puffers and I were just about to put the kettle on… and I've been to the baker's.'

There's a long pause, then a groan. 'Oh, all right then.'

'Terrific!' Trixie claps her hands and totters back inside.

Ten minutes later, Dicky Pyles shuffles across the threshold of Number 5 to re-enter the suffocatingly comely realm of Trixie Cartwright's kitchen.

'I'm *everso* pleased I caught you,' his hostess says, passing him a very flowery, very full cup of tea. 'It seems ages since you brought me up to date with Reginald's "Grand Tour". How long is it since he left?'

'I'm not sure exactly.' His cup rattles loudly in its saucer as he attempts to balance it on his knee. 'A couple of months, give or take.'

'Actually, now I think of it, I believe it's been twelve weeks and two days.' Trixie puckers her lipsticky lips, cocks a podgy finger and takes a long, wet suck from her drink. 'I imagine you're really missing him.'

He helps himself to three lumps of sugar. 'I'm managing just fine.'

'Well, so you say, Dicky – and would you please use the tongs – but I find that hard to believe. I'm sure your home feels empty without Reginald to keep you company. All on your own when you're so used to having him there. And you're certainly not on top of the gardening. In spite of *all* those hours you spend tinkering around out there. We both know Reginald likes to keep his lawn so nice. He's not going to be best pleased when he gets back to find a rainforest in his yard.'

Dicky doesn't reply but extracts a custard tart from a plate of cakes and pastries set before him on the kitchen table.

'Where's Reginald now?' continues Trixie, biting down hard on a cream horn.

Dicky gives his answer some thought. He finishes the tart. 'Timbuktu,' he says at last, licking crumbs from his fingers. 'May I have that éclair?'

'Be my guest. How do you know he's in Timbuktu?'

'He sent me a postcard.'

'A postcard! I don't suppose you'd pop home and fetch it?' asks Trixie eagerly.

'Sorry. No can do. It was a while ago. I chucked it away.'

'Dicky,' she scolds, 'you are *so* mean. You must know how much I would've liked to see it. Promise that next time you hear from him you'll keep the card.'

He takes a loud slurp of tea.

'Is he still in Timbuktu?'

'Dunno.'

'When's he coming back?'

'Dunno. Not for ages.'

'How long is "ages", Dicky? Another week? A month? Phileas Fogg would be back by now.'

'I wouldn't hold your breath.' He reaches down to pat Puffball, who's dozing beside Trixie's chair. Without opening her eyes or raising her head she curls her lip and growls. Dicky quickly withdraws his hand.

'Manners, Puffball!' tuts Trixie, tugging a corner from an apple turnover and pushing it into the dog's mouth. 'But that's your one and only piece, or you'll set off your sicky tum.'

Puffball makes a retching sound as she swallows. Slowly, she gets to her feet, wanders across the room and begins scuffing at the back door.

'All right. Off you go for a widdle,' giggles Trixie, releasing her whimpering pet into the garden, 'but keep away from the fence, you rascal.'

For the next few minutes Trixie and Dicky sit quietly, concentrating on their cakes. When they've polished off the last of them, Trixie leans back in her chair.

'Dicky,' she says pensively, eyeing Dicky up and down. 'I do think it's awfully odd your brother never mentioned to *me* that he was planning to go away, and that he hasn't sent *me* a postcard. Nor a Christmas card, for that matter. On February the fourteenth, I waited in all day for the postman… but he never came.'

Once again Dicky considers before answering. 'Well,' he says eventually, 'I think it's "awfully odd" Reggie never mentioned to *me* that you and he were… whatever you and he were.' He blushes burgundy.

'Whatever we *are*, Dicky. I told you before,' Trixie exclaims triumphantly, 'Reginald and I are *lovers*!' She laughs. So heartily that her entire upper body shakes.

Dicky blushes still deeper. He looks away, only for his gaze to land upon Trixie's newly purchased bra peeking threateningly from its box. Trixie follows his gaze, permitting his embarrassment to linger a few seconds longer before she reaches over and closes the lid.

'Reginald is a passionate man, Dicky. *Ever so* passionate. And before he left on his cruise he gave me no indication his feelings had waned. If anything, they'd grown. Let's just say,' she continues, re-checking her perm in her reflection in the oven door, 'he gave me cause to hope that, in time, you and I would become much more to each other than just neighbours; we would, one day, be brother- and sister-in-law. So, it's only natural that I'm disappointed.' She falls silent and her expression becomes reflective, as if distracted by private memories of Dicky's covertly hot-blooded brother.

Dicky observes the mountainous form of his next-door neighbour as she slowly stirs her tea, and he tries to see her through Reginald's eyes. The thick coat of fat covering her body simplifies her outline into a succession of rolling curves. Her breasts, her belly, her hips, thighs and calves, all run together as if she's been carved from a single slab of lard. The only suggestion of Trixie's skeletal scaffold, enveloped somewhere deep inside, are the dimples in her elbows and the dents in her knees. All that roundness makes her easy to look at. Not one harsh angle to jar the eye. There's no doubting that she's a fine figure of a woman. A very fine figure. Dicky peels back the sleeve of his grubby sweater and inspects his own thin, wiry forearm, so meanly made by comparison. Just like Reginald's. A man – a very intrepid man – could truly lose himself in the folds of her embrace. There's something mesmerising about the heavy rise and fall of her bosom, even in repose; the way her neck trembles when she laughs. And she laughs a lot. Beyond her evident physical plenitude, he's learned to his cost that she's doggedly loyal. Were these the qualities that drew Reggie to her? And who was this fervent, fearless, tender man, so adored by Trixie, who bears no resemblance to the uptight sibling he was raised with? Such are the questions that must forever remain unanswered.

Trixie rests the teaspoon in her saucer. 'I *do* wonder what made him pick Timbuktu,' she says, ponderously.

'Completely random choice,' he answers decisively, before adding, 'I imagine. Probably a spur-of-the-moment thing.'

Trixie lets out a long, wistful sigh. Dicky says nothing but picks at a loose thread in a crocheted doily.

'Well,' Trixie goes on lightly, 'please don't fiddle – I suppose you of *all* people would know if there was anything to prevent Reginald from coming back to me.'

'I'm sure I don't know what you mean.' Dicky raises his cup to take a mouthful of tea, but finds he's already drained it.

'Oh, Dicky!' Trixie lets out another peal of laughter. 'Why do you look so nervous? You're squirming around like a hooked worm. I'm talking about that special telepathic bond twins have between them. You know… if one of you has a heart attack, the other feels a pain in his chest too… That sort of thing? You see, you've gone pale just at the very thought of it.'

Dicky stands up abruptly. 'You're absolutely right. I do feel a bit queasy. Must be all that cake. I think I'll make tracks.'

'That *is* a shame.' Trixie hoists herself to her feet and opens the door for Puffball, who pitter-patters purposefully back into the kitchen. 'Remember to let me know when you next hear from Reginald. I just wish he'd drop *me* a line.'

'Will do,' Dicky Pyles calls back over his shoulder. 'I'll see myself out.'

Puffball snaps at his ankles as he bids his hasty retreat.

Dicky lurches back into the sanctuary of Number 3, slamming the door behind him. He leans against the hallway wall, his heart drumming in his chest.

'Infuriating woman,' he groans aloud, then straightens up, checking himself. What if she's listening on the other side of the brickwork? He wouldn't put it past her. This is the umpteenth time Trixie Cartwright has grilled him about the whereabouts of his brother. She started on at him almost as soon as Reginald 'set sail'. With each encounter, her questions have become more probing and his responses, necessarily, more evasive.

At first, she simply asked in passing, with apparently no more than neighbourly interest, where Reginald had 'got to'.

Dicky told her he was 'having a little holiday'.

A couple of days later she called round at Number 3 'with a teensy gift'. It was a plant for the garden. 'I hoped you might find a nook for this in your rockery, seeing as you've been giving it a makeover and, by the way, how *is* Reginald's jaunt going?'

'Fine. Now if you'll excuse me, I'd best get on.'

Trixie's next visit was precipitated by a conversation she'd had with the vicar's wife, who'd let slip about a 'round-the-world trip'. Thank you so much, Mrs Deirdre-blabbermouth-O'Reilly! This piece of information greatly upset Trixie. She wanted to know why Reginald had left on such an ambitious journey 'so all-of-a-sudden, without so much as a word?'

Dicky had offered up what he thought would be an innocent enough explanation, that 'perhaps old Reg had been hankering to get away from it all?' So he was greatly shocked at the strength of Trixie's reaction. It was as if his words hit her like a hail of bullets. She let out a wail and burst into floods of tears. Blubbering away like there was no tomorrow.

'Why would he want to get away from it all?' she sobbed. 'He has everything a man could ever want right here. He's always saying so.' That was when she dropped the bombshell about their secret affair. How she was sure her heart would break at this abrupt, and completely unexpected separation from her 'darling Reginald'. Her only consolation, she explained, as she finally blew her nose, was that Dicky would be there to keep her 'abreast of Reginald's adventure until he returns'.

True to her word, since that day, Trixie has hounded him for details. Summoning him into her lair to quiz him about intentions, destinations, dates. And every time she gets him to open his mouth, things seem to become just a bit more complicated than they already were.

The very idea of a Trixie–Reginald scenario has set Dicky's planet spinning. Although he and Reginald were never close, like it or not, it was a fact that as twins they were eternally united by unseen but inerasable biological bonds. Bonds far more visceral than simple parentage. They'd grown together in the womb, simultaneously, swimming in one sac, attached to one and the same placenta. Whether they loved or hated each other, from the moment of their conception until the day that Dicky accidentally dispatched Reginald to the hereafter, they'd existed in an exclusive, conjoined universe that contained no outsiders. Or so Dicky believed, until Trixie's doorstep revelations about a clandestine affair.

Now, as his brother's 'lady love', she represents a second soul on the surface of this earth who has a claim on Reginald's personage, and she isn't about to give it up. Although Dicky tries to avoid her, she and that bloody dog of hers have a knack of sniffing him out. There's no getting away from it, Trixie Cartwright has become a thorn in his side. He thinks about her now, just the other side of the wall, fussing about with her terrifying lacy undies. Watching, listening, waiting to pounce. He knows she won't leave him alone unless he can somehow convince her that Reginald is alive, well and definitely not, under *any* circumstances, coming home. Trixie is a fearsome meddler, and Dicky has decided it's high time to draw a line. So, she wants to hear from Reginald, does she? Then her wish shall be granted.

This is his plan: he will compose a series of letters to Trixie, supposedly from Reginald. 'Reginald' will tell her he's fine. He'll imply he'll be back, but won't commit to exactly when. Then, after perhaps the third or fourth letter, 'Reginald' will begin to cut his ties; make mention of wishing to stay away a bit longer. Then a lot longer. Eventually he'll write that, despite what she still means to him, he's choosing to sail the seven seas for the rest of his life. As a bachelor. It's too much to ask any woman – even one as magnificent as Trixie – to live like that, and so he bids his one true love farewell.

It takes Dicky several days to find the tools he needs to carry out his scheme. He searches the house from top to bottom, but ever since he's had the place to himself, it's become so untidy it's practically impossible to keep track of where things are. In the end, he stumbles across his quarry quite by chance. He's lying on his brother's bed, eating lunch, when he drops a grape. In the process of retrieving it – waste not, want not – there under the bed he finds a dusty suitcase. His curiosity piqued, he drags it out, rummages inside and, bingo! Reginald's thick, leather-bound stamp album. Just as Dicky had hoped, not only is the collection comprehensive, it's also meticulously catalogued. Bookish bore! He quickly identifies a stamp from Timbuktu. It pictures a swarthy man, some ruins and a camel. Dicky scuttles into Reginald's studio, takes a pad of airmail paper from the desk and a pen from a beaker marked *PENS*, then settles down to compose his first dispatch.

For the next hour, Dicky simply sits and stares at the blank page. He's never been much of a one for letter writing, and the fact he isn't privy to the exact nature of Trixie and Reginald's relationship makes it even more difficult. It's going to be hard to phrase things with any authenticity. But find words he must.

At last he begins: '*Dear Trixie,*' but he immediately falters. Did Reginald even call her 'Trixie'? He was so correct that for all he, Dicky, knows he'd probably called her 'Miss Cartwright'. Dicky had never heard his brother refer to her as anything else. But then again, their romance was conducted in secret. Perhaps they had pet names for each other, a private joke to share just between themselves?

Cursing aloud, he rips up this first attempt, gets a fresh sheet of paper and tries again. '*Greetings to you from Timbuktu.*' This, he feels, reads better. It's almost poetic. And it avoids addressing her directly. '*I hope this letter finds you well,*' he continues. '*I am well too. The weather is fine. I hope the weather is fine in London.*' Christ, this is dull. But Reginald had, in Dicky's opinion, been a very dull man. Still, the letter would need more than this to be anything like convincing. Dicky chews away at the end of his Biro, and thinks, thinks, thinks. What sort of thing would've interested Reginald if he were visiting a new place? '*I have seen fifteen different types of bird today. I have taken thorough notes on their beak lengths and plumages. I expect you would like me to tell you all about them when I get back, although I cannot say when that will be.*'

Perfect. Now what? An appalling realisation strikes him. Trixie says that she and Reginald were lovers. Perhaps she'll expect a letter from him to mention… sex! This was a side to Reginald he knows nothing about. Much to Dicky's horror, an image of his brother and Trixie Cartwright in flagrante delicto suddenly pops into his mind. He makes an involuntary movement to cover his eyes. *'I must keep this letter short and sweet as I have a camel ride planned for this afternoon, but I wanted you to know you have no need to worry about me. Love from your sweetheart, R. Pyles. PS. I wonder if Richard has dug over the rockery like I planned? He didn't want to do it, but I insisted.'*

He slips the finished letter into an airmail envelope. He writes Trixie's address on the front, in block capitals, remembering to include 'GREAT BRITAIN' at the bottom. On the back, he scrawls 'S.W.A.L.K.' He isn't entirely sure what it means, but it's an acronym he understands ladies in love are supposed to appreciate. He selects a tube of gum from the box labelled *ADHESIVES* and carefully sticks the stamp to the envelope. Partly by accident, partly by design, he achieves a makeshift postmark with a simple ink smudge. To give the effect that the letter has travelled thousands of miles to reach its intended recipient, Dicky distresses it a little by dropping it on the floor and treading on it.

Satisfied with his work, he waits until Trixie goes out the following morning before nudging it through her letterbox.

A week passes without any further interference from Trixie. Dicky begins to believe Reg's letter might actually have done enough to get her off his back. But on Sunday afternoon, as he relaxes in his front room with a can of beer and a copy of the weekend's *Sports News*, he hears the unmistakable tickety-tackety sounds of Trixie's improbably refined footwear progressing up his short front path. He jumps up and makes a dash for the privacy of his kitchen, but he's barely out of his armchair before she reaches his door. Has she spotted him? She's much faster than she looks.

'Dicky, it's me!' she calls from his front step, without trying the bell. 'I have wonderful news. Reginald's written to me.'

'You don't say,' Dicky mutters under his breath.

'Oh good. You're in. May I show you his letter? I'd really value your opinion.'

Dicky pauses before answering. 'What, *now*?'

'Yes please. I've been wanting to show you for days, but you never seem to hear me ring.'

Dicky pauses a bit longer. 'Well, all right, but you can only come in as far as the hall.' With leaden steps Dicky emerges from the cupboard under the stairs and opens the door.

'It's a *terrible* mess in here,' Trixie gasps as she steps inside. 'Why are there sheets of newspaper covering the floor?'

'I spilled something.'

'So I see. You've trailed it all the way from the top of your stairs to the kitchen door! And it looks like it's dried in. Shall I pop back later with bleach and a mop? It'd be no trouble. This place is screaming out for a woman's touch.'

'Just show me what he sent you, if you would,' Dicky says flatly.

'Oh. Yes.' She reaches into her cleavage, withdraws the crumpled letter and pushes it into his hand.

It feels warm, and a heady waft of perfume rolls over him like a blousy, unstoppable tidal wave. He unfurls the paper and makes a show of carefully reading its contents before handing it back to Trixie. 'Very nice.'

'Oh, I *am* relieved to hear you say that,' she gushes. 'When I first saw it, I was over the moon with it too. All fluttery inside, I was. I mean, just look at the stamp. It's so deliciously exotic. And the envelope's so ruggedly grubby. It's had more than a few scrapes winging its way over the oceans to reach me, that's for sure.' She presses it against her lips and kisses it, where, she must be supposing, Reginald had kissed. 'What a sweet touch to add, all for little me. Do you know, I'm almost ashamed to admit it now, but over the last few days I'd started to get some very *silly* ideas about it. So you saying it's "nice", when you know dear

Reginald as well as you do, is *everso* reassuring.' Trixie clasps the paper to her bosom and smiles a wide, dreamy smile.

'What kind of silly ideas?' he asks, slowly.

'Well, it's a terribly short letter and...' Trixie hesitates. 'I'm *everso* sorry to say this, it's also terribly banal. You know, lacking in passion. Not at all like my Reginald. And he didn't use my pet name "Twinkletoes", either. Marty and Antoine said if it wasn't for the S.W.A.L.K. they'd be worried.'

'Who are Marty and Antoine?'

'Oh, just the boys at the dog-grooming studio,' says Trixie matter-of-factly. 'I showed them last week and they agreed with the others.'

'Others? Who else has seen Reginald's letter?' Dicky is becoming apprehensive.

'Practically no one, except the girls at the salon, the gang at Belle's Boutique, the WI ladies, a few of my closest neighbours. Ursula, Sharon, Nesta—'

Dicky interrupts her. 'I see.'

'And I *may* have mentioned it to Deirdre O'Reilly. Otherwise, I haven't breathed a word. I simply daren't. Not with Reginald being so sensitive about secrecy.'

'Well *that's* a relief,' says Dicky.

Trixie, who seems oblivious to the undisguised sarcasm in his voice, carries on. 'Anyway, Antoine, Marty, the ladies and I, we'd *all* started to think Reginald might not be...' she hesitates again, '... quite *himself*. Do you know, Dicky, I was even beginning to feel very cross with him for sending such a thin, dull letter after all but deserting me? Some women would not take it kindly; being left, just like that. Not kindly at all.' Trixie's face begins to colour as these sentiments pass her lips, but she quickly recovers. 'Thank God he chose to go to Timbuktu, that's all I can say. At least I can draw comfort from that.'

'You can?' Dicky is baffled.

'Absolutely. I know you think when Reginald set off he just stuck a pin in a map, as it were, but I'm not so sure. You see, that's one of our little sayings: "*I'll love you to Timbuktu and back again*". In fact, I'm convinced his destination is a hidden message to me. Reginald still *adores* me, and he'll be coming home. It's obvious.'

'It is?' Dicky is aghast.

'Oh, yes. I feel so much better now that we've talked this through. You're an absolute brick.' She turns to leave. 'I suppose I mustn't take up any more of your time.'

Dicky stops her. 'Trixie, would you mind if I were to ask you a personal question?'

'Of course not. We're practically family, aren't we?' she says warmly.

'Thank you. Well…' he wavers, struggling to phrase his next sentence.

'Don't be shy, Dicky,' coaxes Trixie, giving his hand a squeeze. 'I'm not easily embarrassed.'

'All right then. The thing is, I don't understand why it had to be a secret that you and Reginald were' – he quickly corrects himself – '*are* courting.'

'That's simple,' laughs Trixie. 'It's Reginald who's dead set on being so hush-hush. If it was up to me I'd have been shouting it from the rooftops months ago. "Trixabella Cartwright is Reginald Pyles's paramour!" But no. Your brother is determined to keep it under wraps. Or, rather, he *was*…' Trixie's voice trails off. She looks very intently into Dicky's eyes.

'What do you mean "was"?' he asks cautiously, meeting Trixie's gaze with equal intensity.

'Well it's not secret any more, is it? I've told you.'

Dicky exhales with relief. 'Oh, is that all? You've told me and a dozen other people. Not a catastrophe, surely?'

'Well, that's just it. You see, *you* are the one person he wanted to keep it from. The rest don't matter. You, Dicky, are the sole reason why Reginald and I have been hiding our love away. He said, for as long as he can remember, you and he have been in competition. As if life is a race and each of you is determined to get to the finish line first. He thought if you knew he and I were seeing each other, then you'd be bound to "stick your beak in" and try to win my heart. As if,' she scoffs. 'I know it sounds *everso* childish now I say it, but that's the simple truth of it. Reginald wants all of me *all* to himself.'

Dicky stands in silence, mulling over her words.

Trixie suddenly looks concerned. 'Oh dear. I've made you uncomfortable. I do hope I haven't spoiled things between you and me, now I've let the cat out of the bag.'

'No. It's okay. I appreciate your honesty, all things considered.'

'Oh, what a sweet thing to say,' titters Trixie. She leans forward and, much to his confusion, plants a hearty kiss on his unsuspecting cheek. 'Let me know if you change your mind about the mop.'

Before he has time to react, she spins on her kitten heels and begins to pick her unsteady way home.

No sooner has she departed than Dicky scuttles out to his potting shed – the space where he so often retreated to escape his brother, in those days when territory mattered. He needs to think. He sits amongst the sacks of dried-up clay, which he's all but abandoned since Reginald 'left', and picks up one of his terracotta figurines.

'Who do we have here, then?' he grumbles, rubbing a bloom of mould from its face with the ball of his thumb. 'Aha! Old Bill Shakespeare. How ironic. You'd never have got into such an almighty muddle writing just one letter.' As he speaks these words, the tiny statue crumbles in his hand. 'Sod it!'

He thinks of Reginald, of all the battles fought and lost, and all the battles fought and won. Somehow his creative juices haven't flowed in quite the same way now there isn't anyone to vie with. Does he miss the bastard? Never. But it's true that without his brother to kick against, life has lost a good deal of purpose.

Trixie's explanation as to why Reginald kept his love affair secret makes perfect sense. In fact, it's the only thing she's revealed about their relationship that 100 per cent smacks of the Reginald he knew.

Dicky finds himself gloating. So Reggie feared me as a love rival, did he? That was such a pleasing thing to learn. Perhaps Dicky *should* make a play for the woman, just to prove he'd win? He imagines what it would feel like to secure the trophy Reginald coveted above any other. Trixie's heart. He feels a quickening, like a rising head of sap, as reawakened competitive spirits course through his veins. The idea of this final victory makes him snort out loud. But he curbs himself. Think of the consequences: Trixie Cartwright in his bed? The last laugh would definitely be on him.

Dicky pulls himself together and tries to focus on how to move forwards. His initial plan isn't quite unfolding as he envisaged. If anything, it's taking on a direction all of its own. Because of his disastrously unlucky choice for Reginald's whereabouts, Trixie is still confident he loves her and will, at some point, return to her side. Dicky cannot for the life of him understand why he blurted out Timbuktu. Of all the place names on the surface of this earth, what the *Devil* made him pick the bullseye of ruddy lovesick Reggie's stupid motto? And then Trixie pitched that second curveball: she'd shown his letter to other people. He's annoyed with himself he didn't see that coming. But thanks to her uncanny knack for muddying already muddy waters, a growing audience now shares Trixie's expectation that Reginald will eventually come home.

He resolves that the next time he writes, he'll make sure Reg's intentions are clearer.

The second letter, from Morocco – its stamp depicting cacti, buildings and more hot sunshine – reads as follows: *'Dear Twinkletoes. I've travelled north, to Casablanca. I find I like it here, very much. I'm not sure when I'll next be moving on, but my trip is far from over, of that you may be absolutely certain. There's so much more of the world to see. Hope you're finding time to enjoy yourself too. Here's looking at you, kid. That's all for now. Reginald. XXX.'*

In the days following its stealthy delivery to Number 5, Trixie fails to intercept Dicky, and Dicky does his best to banish his dead sibling and his fat neighbour from his mind. But this proves difficult. Every time he sets foot out of his house, some acquaintance of Trixie's stops him in the street to ask, 'Where's that brother of yours got to now?' People who barely passed the time of day with him before, apparently now consider themselves on friendly waving terms.

'Let us know when he drops you a postcard from Egypt,' hails Nigel Peabody brightly. 'Colin would be chuffed if you'd let him have the stamp.'

After a fortnight of unsolicited interest in Reginald's progress – and, worse, good wishes for his safe return – Dicky has had enough. To improve his chances of spotting and avoiding approaching neighbours, he sets about hacking down the overgrown privet hedge at the front of Number 3. However, he's barely got started when he spies Deirdre O'Reilly making a beeline for him from the end of the avenue. He drops his shears and quickly retreats to his back garden, only to discover Puffball snuffling around in the wilderness of his flowerbeds. Much to his annoyance, the feisty creature refuses to come to him, and only after a spirited chase does he manage to snatch her up.

Hot and angry, Dicky wastes no time in returning her to her owner. He yanks twice on his neighbour's bell-pull, sending a tuneful peal of 'Oranges and Lemons' to muster Trixie from her sett. He hears the distinctive trip-trap of her trotters approaching from within, but she doesn't open the door. He becomes aware she's scrutinising him from the other side of her security spyhole.

'Who is it?' she quavers.

'Me,' he says, his voice almost drowned out by Puffball's snarling.

'Oh, Dicky. Just a second.' She fumbles to unfasten what sounds like a complicated arrangement of locks and chains. 'Sorry for the delay. Everyone looks like an axe murderer when you peer at them through that little lens. Reginald *insisted* I had it put in. He didn't want anyone to come and steal me away.'

The door is barely open before the dog, which he's restrained under one arm, squirms free and disappears into the house, her whole body wagging unrepentantly. 'She dug through. Again.'

'The minx. I don't know what it is about your garden. She's so determined to get at it. I could almost believe there was a bit of terrier in her if I didn't know she's a pure-bred bitch.'

'Yes. Well. No harm done.' He shuffles from foot to foot, grasping for an excuse to leave. He's too slow.

Trixie looks him up and down and smiles coquettishly. 'As it happens, now that you're here, I wonder if I could trouble you to take a look at something. You see, I've had more news from Reginald. And I do have cocktail snacks,' she adds temptingly, opening the door a little wider.

'Well…' says Dicky cautiously, reversing away.

'Wonderful. Let's be proper for a change and eat in the parlour, *as the spider said to the fly*,' Trixie warbles cheerily, giving him a wink. 'You go through while I fetch us a tray.'

Dicky's been into Trixie's house more times in the last couple of months than he ever has in the past ten years, but until this day she's never invited him beyond her kitchen. Their tête-à-têtes always unsettle him, but, for some reason, as he pushes open the parlour door, he feels especially nervous. As if he were crossing an unmarked boundary to enter a sanctum open only to a chosen few. Uncharted territory. Here be dragons.

Trixie's parlour is so softly lit, it takes him a moment for his eyes to adjust. The large bay window is dressed on each side by swags of heavy brocade, and net curtains so thick only the bravest of sunbeams dare infiltrate. A tall lamp, standing apologetically in the corner, might cast a more penetrating light, were its shade not swathed in a richly embroidered, tasselled shawl. The room is brimful of belongings. No inch of wall lacks a picture; no inch of floor, a rug. Whatnots, fruit bowls and plastic flowers, all are bathed in a dim apricot glow. Dicky feels as if he is Jonah in the stomach of the whale. Then he realises he's not alone. Right in the middle of the room, curled up on a red velvet cushion, lies Puffball. Sleeping.

Trixie hobbles into the room carrying a tray laden with glasses, plates and napkins. 'It's never too early for a soupçon of sherry, is it?' she declares conspiratorially, using her foot to sweep a stack of *Bridal Monthly* magazines off the top of the coffee table. The cut-glass flutes tinkle merrily as she sets down her burden. 'There are some lovely spring collections this season. I'll have to let you have a gander some time. Now, grab a pew. Why not squeeze in next to me?' she suggests breathlessly as she lowers herself, a bit at a time, onto a satin-upholstered chaise longue.

'I'll be all right here,' he says quickly, choosing a large armchair.

'Oh yes. Much more manly. That's Reginald's favourite perch too. Seeing you sat there is making me do a double-take. You'd be one and the same man, if it wasn't for your beard. And the clothes, of course. He's *eversuch* a dapper man, your brother. Anyway, as I was saying about those wedding dresses, Antoine says that organza is *in* and naturally *I* won't be wearing boring old white.'

Dicky has several handfuls of peanuts ('May I pass you a serviette?') and quaffs his generous measure of Amontillado. All the while, Trixie chatters away, apparently content to listen to her own aspirations of romantic wedded bliss. She seems to have forgotten about the letter. Dicky rests his feet on a tapestry footstool, leans back in Reginald's chair and lets her words flow over him. He finds it all unexpectedly soothing. He gazes at the sleeping form of Puffball, who appears blissfully unconcerned by their recent fracas in his back garden. He hopes he wasn't too rough, manhandling her off the rockery. Very cautiously, he reaches out to give her a pat. To his amazement, she doesn't growl. In fact, she doesn't even stir. He carries on caressing her, quietly gratified that the stupid animal is getting used to him. At last. She spends enough time on his side of the fence. It strikes him she must really trust him, lying there so completely and utterly still while he runs his fingers over her velveteen ears, her funny flat snout... Dicky abruptly withdraws his hand.

'Trixie! There's something wrong with Puffball. She's not breathing!'

'What do you mean?' asks Trixie lightly, breaking off from her soliloquy. 'She's fine. I've shut her in the kitchen to keep her out of mischief.' She gives Dicky an appraising stare.

He's aware that his face must be a picture of confusion, his shaky hand still hovering over the dog on the cushion.

'Oh, Dicky!' she cries, bursting into laughter. 'That's not Puffball. *That's* Pom-Pom, her sister. Isn't she a poppet? She passed away last year. It was all so sudden, we couldn't bear to be parted from her.'

'You had her *stuffed*?' He's aghast.

'Oh, dear me *no*,' rejoins Trixie, plainly horrified. 'I stuffed her myself.'

Dicky's incredulous. 'How ever did you manage it?'

'Funnily enough, it wasn't as hard as you'd think. In fact, I was pleasantly surprised. There's a trick to getting the eyes right, which I couldn't quite master. That's why they're stitched shut. But apart from that, I think I did a very tidy job. Of course, one's upbringing helps,' she continues cheerfully. 'You must know Daddy was Bernie Cartwright of Cartwright and Cartwright's Butchers? Mummy was a gifted seamstress. And Cartwright women are very resourceful, Mr Pyles,' she adds with a sparkle. 'We tend to achieve whatever we put our minds to.'

Dicky shakes his head and closes his gaping mouth.

Trixie doesn't seem to notice his thunderstruck state. As she's been speaking, she's been rifling through a cavernous carpet bag that's hooked over the arm of her chaise longue.

'Aha!' she exclaims at last, whipping out a tortoiseshell comb. She leans forwards and drags it brusquely through the dead dog's fur. 'I know it's not quite the same as having Pommers with us in person, but it's so much better than giving her up completely, or just sticking her in a hole in the garden, don't you think? Every time I look at her it's as if she's still here,' she continues longingly. 'It's rather as I feel when I see you, Dicky. I just have to clap eyes on you to sense Reginald's presence close by.' She offers him the comb. 'Would you like a go?'

'No thank you,' he says, firmly changing the subject. 'How about we have a look at that letter now?'

'Quite right! The letter.' Trixie heaves herself to her feet. Taking care as she navigates her way around the obstacle course of occasional tables, she retrieves the envelope from the centre of the mantelpiece where it has pride of place amongst her collection of miniature china Pekes. She passes it to him.

Dicky casts an eye over it, nodding sagely. 'Yes, well. It's very brief, but it's also very clear. He gives the impression that he's pretty settled in Morocco. Definitely no plans for an imminent return, I'd say. And there isn't much of a show of romance or any of that nonsense.'

'Well, I did notice there wasn't any S.W.A.L.K. this time. Just "ex ex ex",' Trixie sighs. 'Oh, Dicky. If only your brother were a straightforward man like you, then perhaps I too could take his words at face value. But I'm finding that impossible.' She has another rummage in her bag, this time retrieving a lace handkerchief with which she dabs her moistening eyes.

'You've lost me, Trixie.'

'You know how I said his last port of call was a hidden sign to me?'

He nods.

'He's done it again! You see, the one and only proper "date" Reginald and I have ever had, when we went out of the house together, was to the cinema. He thought it would be all right as it was dark in the Odeon, so we wouldn't be recognised. We held hands… and…' For several, very awkward seconds Trixie's voice trails off before she continues. 'Anyway, the film was *Casablanca*. Don't you see? By choosing to actually go there, he's telling me that he remembers that evening and although he won't – or can't – say when he'll be back, he wants me to wait for him.'

'Seriously?' says Dicky acerbically.

'Why do you sound so grumpy? Aren't you pleased that he's planning to come home?'

'Yes. Naturally,' he stammers. 'I'm just amazed at how you can read so much into so very, very little.'

'I am a woman in love, Dicky. I can read between the lines however closely they may be spaced.' She takes the letter from his hand, carefully refolds it and returns it to the mantelpiece.

At that moment Dicky becomes aware of muted gagging noises coming from another room.

'Oh no! Not again,' groans Trixie. 'Mummy's coming!' she calls, exiting the parlour as quickly as her frivolous shoes allow.

Dicky follows. Putting his head round the kitchen door, he sees Trixie slip a copy of *Bridal Monthly* in front of Puffball just in time to catch a tidy little pile of puke before it lands on the spotless lino.

'Honestly, Puffers, what *have* you been eating this time?'

Once again, Dicky sees himself out.

That night, Dicky has trouble sleeping. He lies on his bed, chewing over his last conversation with Trixie, trying to sort out his feelings about her taxidermy project. Recent personal experience has taught him that dealing with a dead body is a nasty, messy business all round. Even for a man... even if he's just burying it. It's quite something for a woman to proudly admit to skinning and gutting a corpse. Her actions seem, somehow, less than feminine. All that gristle and bone. The fact that she dissected her own lap-dog, rather than a human body, doesn't really daintify her actions. An uncomfortable image keeps bouncing about in his mind: Trixie in her kitchen, wearing a butcher's apron, rubber boots and a polka-dot shower cap covering her stiff curls; Pom-Pom stretched out before her, tummy-side up, her stocky little limbs nailed to the tabletop; *The Archer*s playing in the background... scones rising in the oven... Trixie deftly wielding a melon scoop.

He considers it a wonder that his hygiene-fixated brother wasn't put off by Trixie's 'interests'. Dicky shudders. He decides it's best not to dwell on this any further. And he'll have more chance of dropping off if he turns his thoughts to a different topic. Reginald's letter. Once again, he curses himself. 'What the *hell* made me choose fucking *Casablanca*?'

Dicky keeps his next message so short it would hardly have been worth the postage, had it been real. Supposedly from Mexico, its stamp depicts the profile of a Mayan statue with very exaggerated features. He can't tell if it's a man or a woman, but he finds it quite an ugly face. The big, fat nose reminds him of Trixie's. In the hope that increasing the interval between communications will add to the impression that Reginald's ardour is on the wane, he waits three weeks before 'mailing' this one. As he makes his next sneak-delivery to Number 5, Dicky is reasonably confident that this handiwork will do the trick.

He's therefore more than a little disappointed at how swiftly this belief is swept away. Just twenty-four hours later Trixie is on his doorstep, so flustered that he has to help her inside.

'Whatever do you think of *this* little billet-doux, then?' she asks excitedly, thrusting Reginald's letter into his hand. 'It may be brief but it's dripping with meaning. *Everyone* agrees with me. Antoine says it's the next best thing to a proposal!'

Dicky uncrumples the obviously well-read paper and scans his own words, '*Hello again, old girl, I have just arrived in Acapulco. My room has a lovely view, right out over the bay. Best regards. Reginald*', then passes it back to her. 'Trixie. There are no more than two sentences here. I'm afraid I'm at a complete loss to see—'

'He's in Acapulco, Dicky, near the *bay*. Don't you recognise it?' she pants. 'He's quoting from that Frank Sinatra song. I just know he is.'

Dicky racks his brains. At first the only lyric that comes into his mind is 'I did it my way'. An arch smile plays across his lips, but he quickly wipes it away with the back of his sleeve. Then it comes to him. 'You mean the one about "exotic booze"?'

'Yes. That's it. It's called "Come Fly with Me". Do you think he's hinting at me joining him out there? Us getting married on the beach?'

'Good Lord, no!' Dicky blurts, astonished. 'Wherever did you get that notion?'

'That's *our* song. Reginald's and mine. He *croons* it for me, when we're alone and he's "holding me so near". Better than old blue eyes himself. Just listen!' Trixie clasps her hands together, raises them to her ample breast, and begins a fervid rendition of her own. By the end of the first verse, however, she's too choked up to continue. 'I wish I had the strength to give you the full version. It's got a line about "flying honeymoons" and being "together" and *everything*. I suppose… I thought… maybe…' Tears spill down her cheeks, dragging rivulets of blush-pink powder in their wake. 'Oh, Dicky!' All at once Trixie buries her face in his chest and weeps.

Feeling highly uncomfortable, Dicky rests an arm around her heaving shoulders. 'You have a lovely singing voice,' he mumbles awkwardly, struggling to know what else to say.

She burrows her face in a little deeper and lets out a stifled, 'Thank you.'

He looks down at the top of Trixie's head, her absurd straw-coloured curls quivering as she sobs. 'There, there now,' he says, patting her gingerly on the back. 'It's not as bad as all that.' But she continues to make howling noises. She looks so crestfallen, for the first time in this whole frustrating saga Dicky feels a sentiment that approximates to guilt. He realises that while his letters have maintained an illusion that Reginald is alive, they've done nothing to reduce her attachment to him. If anything, they've strengthened it. In all his planning to deceive, he never factored in the lumpish Trixie's actual *feelings*. These, he decides, are not something he wants to monkey around with any longer. He resolves, there and then, to draw things to a swift conclusion before anyone gets seriously hurt.

'Trixie,' he says, slowly, 'I don't think I've been as straight with you as I could have been about Reginald's letters.'

'How do you mean?' she asks, her face still buried in his chest.

Dicky continues to pat her back. 'When you asked me what I thought of them, you probably noticed I've been a bit vague in my answers.' He feels her head move as if she's nodding. 'Well,' he goes on, 'that's because… fact is… they've never struck me as the work of a man in love.'

'They haven't?'

'Nope. Never.'

'Not even the last one? How can you be so cruel?'

'I'm sorry to speak so plainly, but *especially* the last one. You've over-interpreted it, massively, just as you have the others. There *is* no clever hidden reference to a song lyric. I believe it's no more than what it seems: a short, badly written letter from someone you used to know. Answer me honestly, Trixie: do you really feel that Reginald's letters are everything a devoted lover would send to his best girl?'

Trixie stiffens in his arms.

He perseveres. 'The Reginald you were in love with is well and truly gone. I am quite certain of it. He's been replaced by a selfish man, filled with wanderlust, who has no thoughts of settling down with you. Mark my words, Trixie, neither you nor I will be hearing from him again.'

Trixie raises her head and steps back. To Dicky's great surprise, he sees that while her face is very red, her eyes are dry.

'And what would you know about that?' she asks breezily.

She doesn't look sad, or shocked, or hurt. It's hard for him to put his finger on exactly how she does look. Perhaps the closest description is 'smug'.

'Nothing,' he splutters. 'I mean I'm guessing. That twins' instinct thing you were talking about the other week.'

Trixie draws herself to her full four-foot-eleven-inch height, pushing her shoulders back and her huge chest out. She cups her hand and pats the hem of her perm, plumping it up. Calling her assets to order. 'Oh, dear,' she tuts, looking at Dicky's shirt front, 'I seem to have got a speck of rouge on your collar.' She tugs a tissue from her sleeve, spits on it, and rubs at the mark until it turns into a vivid red smear. 'Oops. I've made it worse. Oh well. It's nothing a hot wash won't shift. Now, if you'll excuse me,' she says perfectly evenly, 'I'm going to take myself off home. Poor Puffball will be wondering where I've got to.'

'Yes. Of course. But are you sure you're all right?' Dicky asks, completely mystified by her reactions.

'Never better,' she answers sweetly. 'Goodbye.'

Dicky closes the door behind her then listens until he's quite sure she's returned to her own house. Satisfied, he makes straight for his pantry to ferret out a bottle of beer. He takes a deep draught and wipes his mouth on the back of his hand. To his annoyance, he can smell Trixie's perfume on his skin. A blonde hair clings to his russet beard. He goes to the sink and splashes his face with cold water. 'Bloody madwoman,' he mutters, drying himself roughly with a tea towel. It should be a weight off his mind, managing as he has to bring the Reginald–Trixie love story to its dénouement. But, to his disquiet, he isn't experiencing the sense of relief he expected to feel. He shrugs away his unease. As much as Trixie may puff and blow, surely she must have got the message by now?

That afternoon, Dicky puts away Reginald's stamp collection, nails a sheet of chicken wire over the gap under the fence and even makes a tentative start at cleaning Reginald's blood off the stair carpet. Apart from the usual yapping noises on the other side of their adjoining walls, he hears and sees nothing of Trixie or her dog. With each passing hour he becomes more and more confident that both his brother and Trixie are well and truly out of his life.

So, the next morning, when he goes to fetch his pint of milk from the front step and finds her waiting for him, he's utterly unprimed. Trixie is not only restored to her breathlessly animated self, she looks a bit wild. He seriously contemplates not letting her in.

'Richard Pyles, prepare to eat your words! I have another letter. And,' she cries, elbowing her way into his hallway without waiting to be invited, 'you'll never guess who it's from.'

A shiver passes up and down his spine. 'Who?' he asks, with considerable trepidation.

'Reginald!' she gushes.

He hardly knows how to react. 'It can't be,' he stammers. 'It's simply not possible.'

'Why ever not? Who *else* would this be from?' Trixie laughs, wafting a sheet of airmail paper in front of his face.

Dicky is speechless.

'Would you like to read it?'

He shakes his head.

'No? Well, let me read it for you then.' Trixie clears her throat and begins. '*My darling Twinkletoes.*' She pauses and reflects. 'Isn't it nice, Dicky, the way Reginald likes to use my pet name?'

Dicky nods dumbly.

She continues: '*Please forgive the cool tones of my first letters. I hardly know why I have been so distant in my manner. I hope that you haven't found them wanting. Please be reassured my feelings for you have not faltered since my untimely departure, and that I remain completely yours.*' Trixie pauses again, fanning herself with her hand as if fighting back tears of joy at such sweetly expressed sentiments. 'It's enough to make you weep, isn't it?'

He nods again.

'There's more: *I have grown tired of my travels and plan to return to your side, just as soon as I can book my passage. However, since I am already in France it shouldn't take too long to get home. Expect me soon and be ready for me, my darling girl. Yours forever and ever and ever and ever. Reginald   XOXOXOXOXOXOXOXOXOXOXOXOXOXOOO.* And do look! There's a S.W.A.L.K. too.'

Trixie pauses. She studies Dicky's face. He knows she expects him to respond somehow, but words fail him.

She speaks again. 'Such a good letter, isn't it? *Everso* much better than the ones *you* wrote.'

He feels the blood drain from his face. Afraid his legs might give way beneath him, he sinks down on the bottom step of his staircase. 'You knew?' he mouths.

'For God's sake, Dicky. Of course I knew.' The scorn in her voice is undisguised. 'Reginald was the last person who'd be writing to me from all corners of the globe. We weren't even particularly good friends, let alone lovers. I wanted to be,' she says, affecting a sulky pout, 'but he just wasn't interested. Said I was "ridiculous".' She tweaks the neckline of her blouse, exposing several square inches of trembling cleavage. 'But that's his loss, wouldn't you say?'

Dicky says nothing and puts his head between his knees.

'You see, I am a highly sexual woman. I am simply not designed to live without a man in my life. So, whatever Reginald's…' She thinks for a few seconds, choosing her words before continuing, 'Let's call them "current circumstances", I'm still prepared to give him a second chance. In fact, I'm throwing a special welcome-home supper for him this very evening. And I'm counting on you to make sure that he turns up.'

Dicky's mouth is bone dry. 'I can't do that. I just can't.'

Trixie slowly shakes her head. 'Oh, Dicky, Dicky, Dicky,' she smiles, wagging a fat pink index finger at him, 'I think we both know that you can. If I'm perfectly honest, I realised some time ago that the Reginald I knew, albeit only in passing, would never be coming back. But you are so *very* much like him, I'm sure you can think of *some* way of making this work. You owe me that much, surely?'

'I don't owe you anything,' slurs Dicky, barely able to make himself coherent.

Trixie leans forwards to whisper directly into his ear. 'You, Dicky Pyles, owe me *everything*. Unlike you or your anal-retentive brother, I have plenty of friends. And as you know, I have been more than free in sharing Reginald's oh-so-touching letters with each and every one of them. So, thanks to me, half the neighbourhood are of the firm belief your brother is in rude health. As long as they continue to believe as much,' she adds emphatically, 'you're safe. However, one word from me could change all that.' She reaches into her pocket and pulls out a little silk purse. She pops it open and empties its contents into Dicky's sweaty hands. 'Cast your eyes over that lot, sunshine!'

Dicky stares, nonplussed, at a crusty assortment of odds and ends lying in his palms.

'Don't you recognise them?' Trixie goads him. 'Go on. Have a proper look.'

Dicky inspects them more closely. There's a jacket button made of knotted leather, a tie pin, an enamel badge bearing the words 'One Hundred Years of Allotmenteering'. He thinks he's actually going to vomit. 'Where did you get these?'

'From Puffball. Ever since you started work on your rockery, she's been bringing things up all over the place. Some of them are a bit grimy-looking, which is hardly surprising given what they've been through. Or perhaps I should say "who"?' she adds with a deep, throaty laugh. 'Honestly, my Chinese rug will never be the same again.'

Dicky's mind is spinning, frantically replaying all his past conversations with Trixie Cartwright, trying to reassemble what was said; what he knows; what *she* knows; what others could yet learn. He closes his fist around Puffball's assemblage of trophies, so tightly that the tie pin pricks his thumb.

'Please feel free to hang on to those,' says Trixie, 'I've got a whole jam jar full of similar mementos at home. The little poppet even brought home one of his ears... but I let her keep that.'

'Oh Christ!' moans Dicky.

'Whatever,' says Trixie dismissively. 'So, as I said, I'm expecting Reginald to call this evening. Shall we say six o'clock? It's your job to see he's not late. I'm off for my hair appointment, and I can hardly *wait* to tell the girls at the salon. I wonder if Reginald's thought to bring me a present from Paris. Isn't this just *too* romantic? Now don't forget to bring in your milk, or the tits will have the cream.'

For the rest of that day Dicky remains on the bottom step of his staircase, paralysed by misery. His options parade through his brain – marching into his consciousness, each one to be inspected and then dismissed.

He could call her bluff and stand her up tonight? If anyone asks about the letters, he could just deny he wrote them – say he genuinely believed they were from Reginald. Or he could say she wrote the letters to herself?

But whichever way Dicky tries to escape Trixie's snare, he keeps coming back to one thing. If he doesn't dance to her tune, she'll tell people about the rockery, and there is no doubting the meaning of what they'd find under there.

What if he scarpered? Got as far away from Atbara Avenue as possible? But then he'd have to spend the rest of his life on the run. Dicky regrets that he didn't act more definitively right from the start. Why didn't he dig a deeper hole? Why didn't he mend the fence? Why didn't he send a telegram 'from Calcutta' or some other arbitrary shithole, saying Reggie'd been carried off on a tide of dysentery? He could even have made a show of scattering his brother's ashes at the allotments. That would've got Reggie's runner beans running.

But now it's all too late. Defeated, his heart fills with revulsion and dread as he contemplates what Trixie has planned for him. Is he to become Reginald, her lover, forever? 'What about *me*?'

Wretched and alone he sits until, at last, the shadows in the hallway begin to lengthen. Only then, resigned to his fate and with the leaden tread of a dead man walking, does he drag himself upstairs. Dicky goes into Reginald's bathroom, opens the metal over-sink cabinet and finds his brother's razor and shaving brush. He lathers up his face and slowly, slowly, slowly, he scrapes off his beloved beard. He goes to his brother's bedroom. He takes Reginald's dinner jacket and a clean, ironed shirt from the wardrobe and puts them on. He selects a tie, a black one, and stands before the mirror as he ties the knot. He stares at his reflection. Gone is Dicky. Reginald is back.

And it is at this moment that he has an epiphany!

He looks at his watch. Half past four. Not long left to act! He races downstairs and bursts out onto the avenue. There are only a few people around. Dammit! Hurrying off towards the high street, he makes a point of greeting as many neighbours as he can along the way.

'Nesta! Nice to see you again, too. Yes, the Bahamas were lovely.'

'Mrs Dollimore, as I live and breathe. Don't you look well!'

He is particularly glad to run into Deirdre O'Reilly.

'Why, Reginald Pyles! When did you get back? Wait till I tell *all* the—'

'Mrs O'Reilly. If only I could stop and chat. Sadly, I must get to the ironmonger's before he closes. But please *do* pass on my greetings to the ladies of the parish.'

'Long time no see!' exclaims the ironmonger, warmly shaking Dicky's hand. 'And what can I get you today, Reginald?'

'A claw hammer, please.'

'A *claw hammer*?'

'Yes please.'

'What size?'

'Something good and sturdy.'

'Perhaps a twenty-ounce steel model? With a curved hook?'

'A curved hook sounds just the ticket. You know how I always like to have just the right tool for the job… and a non-slip handle if possible.'

'Would you like me to wrap it up?'

'No thank you. I'll take it just as it is.'

Dicky's next stop is the florist's. 'Two dozen red roses please.'

'Are these for the lucky lady?' the saleswoman giggles knowingly.

'Mistress Trixie Cartwright and none other!' says Dicky, adjusting the knot of his tie.

He makes it back to Atbara Avenue just in time to hear the church clock strike six. As he stands on the front step of Number 5, Dicky salutes to a couple of passing boy scouts. He buffs up the toes of his shoes on the backs of his trouser legs, straightens his jacket collar, and is about to ring the bell when he discovers the door is already ajar. He hears a gramophone playing somewhere inside the house.

'*Strangers in the night, exchanging glances…*'

'It's open!' calls Trixie, her voice coming from the same direction as the music.

'*… Something in your eyes, was so inviting…*'

Dicky enters Trixie's parlour quietly, closing the door behind him.

The air is so thick with the waxy aroma of scented candles, it catches at the back of Dicky's throat. Their flame-lights dance upon the clusters of knick-knackery adorning every surface of the room, setting them a-twinkle like a thousand flickering fireflies. Trixie lies, recumbent, upon her chaise longue. She's sheathed in a voluminous kaftan, so sheer he can see the rolling mass of her bare body slithering around inside it. There's a half-empty box of Turkish delight at her elbow. Puffball is at her feet. Both the woman and her dog have traces of icing sugar around their lips.

'Oh, Reginald,' she murmurs. 'Come a little closer so that we may kiss at last.'

'Okay, Trixie. You can cut the crap now!' snaps Dicky. He gives the arm of the record player a sharp smack, sending the needle skating across the vinyl.

'What are you doing? You've scratched our special Frank Sinatra!' She scolds him as if speaking to a naughty child. 'That wasn't a very nice thing to do.'

'Well, I'm not very nice, am I? In all your planning and plotting that's the one detail you seem to have forgotten. I'm really very nasty.'

'I know you are. But so long as you behave yourself,' she

breathes seductively, pulling at her kaftan to reveal yet more cleavage, 'that will stay our little secret. Puffball and I won't tell if you don't. So why not just settle down and make yourself comfortable? Help yourself to a liqueur, or a nice, juicy cigar?'

'No thank you.'

'Well, in that case, you might as well give me *your* present, Reginald,' she simpers, nodding at the bunch of flowers he's still holding in front of him.

Dicky moves closer to the chaise longue. 'As a matter of fact, I do have a surprise for you,' he says calmly, 'but I doubt it's the one you're expecting.' He reaches inside the bouquet, withdraws the claw hammer and tosses the roses straight at Trixie's face.

Since the day Dicky met her, this is the first time he's ever seen Trixie look genuinely shocked. Letting out a startled whine, Puffball takes shelter under the chaise longue.

'What are you doing, Dicky?' asks Trixie, uncertainty rising in her voice.

'Nothing,' he says, 'but then I'm not Dicky. I'm Reginald, remember! *Reginald* is the man coming to call on you tonight, back from his travels to be reunited with his one and only true love. That's what you've told all your friends and neighbours. They were *everso* pleased to see him earlier this evening, when he went shopping. He bought you these flowers… and he also acquired this little beauty too,' he laughs as he uses the hammer's claw to send a couple of china Pekes crashing to the floor. 'You're always saying he's a jealous man, afraid his brother would come and steal you away. Well, just *imagine* how such a passionate and impulsive chap is going to react now he's discovered you've been spending so much time with his brother while his back was turned. Enjoying all those cups of tea, intimate little chats – and we can only guess what else – with tricky Dicky!' He watches the fear creep into every crease of her stupid, fat face as she finally seems to understand her fate.

Trixie hauls herself unsteadily to her feet. 'You won't get away with it,' she stammers.

'Of course I will. All I have to do is change my clothes and grow back my chin-fluff to make murderous Reginald disappear, never to be seen again. Perhaps he'll go abroad again? You know *him*,' he adds, wryly, 'here one moment, gone the next.' With those words, he swings the hammer above his head and draws himself up, poised to bring it down with all his might into Trixie's crown of freshly set curls.

Puffball shoots out from her hiding place and dashes at Dicky's ankles. He kicks out at her, staggers a little and, as he does so, Trixie steps towards him in a last-ditch attempt to knock the weapon from his hand. Trixie lunges… she grabs… she misses.

Trixie isn't quite certain what causes her to trip, but she's fairly sure it's those *darned* kitten heels. They probably caught in the hem of the kaftan. Whatever it was, she topples forwards like a felled tree. With no time to put out her arms to break her fall, she crashes down so heavily that the room shakes. For the next few seconds she lies still, eyes screwed shut, waiting for the impact of the hammer on the back of her head. But it never comes.

When she landed, she'd felt something 'pop' beneath her. Now, as she gathers her senses, she becomes aware of a muffled hissing noise, like the sound of a deflating tyre, coming from somewhere buried under her own body. With considerable effort, she rolls over and slowly opens her eyes. It's then that she realises she's just heard Dicky Pyles exhale his last breath.

Gradually, she takes in the scene. Dicky, pale and lifeless, spreadeagled on the parlour floor, his expression one of open-mouthed surprise. The splintered remains of an occasional table sticking out behind his legs. Did he, too, trip? Stumble backwards? He must have done. But that fall alone surely couldn't have been fatal? As she stares at his motionless body, a thick, gloopy trickle of blood oozes from his nose. Puffball, who's been cowering in the corner, suddenly reappears, tail wagging, and begins to lick it off his face. 'No, no, no, little missy,' whispers Trixie, scooping her into her arms. For a terrible moment, she thinks the sheer weight of her frame must have squashed Dicky to death, flattening him like a fly. Feeling fat and ungainly, she colours at her own embarrassment. She gives Puffball a comforting squeeze. Trixie is relieved when she finally sees that it was far more likely to have been the claw hammer, protruding from the side of Dicky's neck, that killed him.

Desmond O'Reilly puts down his knife and fork and looks across at his wife, sitting at the opposite end of the vicarage dining table. She appears lost in thought.

'This schnitzel is delicious, Deirdre.'

'It's always better with veal than pork,' she answers, roused from her daydream. 'And we have Trixie Cartwright to thank for that. Her freezer's overflowing with offcuts, so she kindly gave us a bagful. Mind you, the recipe is from my Austrian cookbook.'

'What were you thinking about just then?'

She smiles. 'Oh, that little weather-house we had when Christopher was small.'

'What weather-house?'

'You know the thing I mean. It was on your study windowsill for years and years. It looked like a miniature log cabin, with tiny wooden roof tiles and painted-on shutters. My cousin brought it back from Salzburg. A little alpine couple made out of plastic lived inside it, and they'd pop in and out of its two front doors, depending on the weather. The man came out when it rained, but he'd have to swing back inside again if it got sunny, because that was when his wife appeared instead. Christopher loved it.'

'You mean the hygrometer?'

'... and that *weather-house* made me think of Dicky and Reginald Pyles.'

'I'm not following you.'

'The point is that you'd never see both Mr and Mrs Weather-house at the same time. And *that's* how it is with the Pyleses. No sooner has Reginald returned to our midst than Dicky evaporates into thin air.'

'Now you mention it,' says the vicar indifferently, 'I haven't seen him out and about for a while. I wonder where's he gone?'

'Guess!' teases his wife.

'Timbuktu!' he teases back.

Deirdre gasps. 'Who told you?'

'No one,' says Desmond, surprised. 'That was a completely random answer.'

'Well, as it happens, you're right,' sighs Deirdre, obviously deflated that he's spoiled her news. 'Dicky's taken off on an extended trip of his own. Trixie Cartwright was telling me all about it. Apparently, when he heard what a wonderful time his brother had travelling the world, he got itchy feet too. Trixie and Reginald have been getting lots of postcards from him telling them all about his adventures.'

'And how is Reginald? He's been keeping a pretty low profile himself.'

'Never better, according to Trixie. I caught sight of him the other day through her bay window, sitting in the parlour. I gave him a wave, but when he didn't wave back I spotted that he was *fast* asleep. Must be the jet lag. More veal, dear?'

6

Sightseers

From a distance, it's easy to mistake Robert Watts for a young man with a clear conscience. Although below average height, in his polo shirt and loafers he walks tall enough. Most of the time. He's well-groomed, and polite to his elders. He has a beefy physique, with particularly muscular forearms, like Popeye. Robert also has a tattoo; not an anchor, but an acorn. He has surprisingly powerful hands. Those who know him best call him Bobbo.

It's 8.30 in the morning, and Robert has a spring in his step. Passing Number 5, he doffs his hat at wan-faced Reginald Pyles and risks a cheeky wink at pink-cheeked Trixie Cartwright, who throws him back a flirtatious little smile. He is not, however, quite so poised in front of other Atbara Avenue residents. When he sees the vicar's wife approaching, he bends down to pet a cat. Not that he's an animal lover. He just doesn't choose to look the woman, or her husband, in the eye. As soon as she's gone by, he quickly straightens up, and whistling a careless tune, he continues on his way to Number 47 – his parents' house. He likes to pop in now and then for breakfast, or dinner, or a bath. It's something to do while he doesn't have a steady job. Or a steady girl. Or any girl at all. It makes a change from his grotty flat and his even grottier housemates. Besides, Mum and Dad like to see him, don't they. And some of his stuff is still there for safe-keeping. It's good to return to his old stomping ground every so often, to make sure everything is where he left it.

Gay Marris

*

At the same time that Mrs Peggy Watts places a plate of scrambled eggs in front of her adult son, in a sleepy campsite somewhere outside London, one couple's morning is only just beginning. As it happens, they are tourists, from an alpine district of Germany – where the cuckoo clocks come from. That's why the man, who prides himself on being fit for his sixty years, is short-sighted; the result of a life's work creating intricate timepieces. At home, he and his wife live close to lakes, mountains and the sky, so they're used to a thin atmosphere and long winters. However, since retirement, they've spent the summer months travelling. Every July they load up their camper wagon, shut up their house and set off to explore new pastures. They've been to Italy many times and France twice, but their current expedition is to be their one and only trip to England. So far, they've been enjoying it very much.

This is the final day of their motoring adventure. They're packing up especially early. With efficiency honed by years of practice, they make short work of stowing their foldaway bunks. Not wishing to disturb neighbouring campers, they dress in silent synchronicity. Shorts, T-shirts, socks, sandals. The woman is thinking about the day that lies before them; where they will go, the sights they'll see. Her husband, a particularly gregarious fellow, is wondering about the characters they'll bump into along the way. He tops up the wagon's radiator while she boils a pan of water, half of which they use to make hot drinks and half for their washbasin. Two glugs of chicory coffee, a quick wipe-down with flannel and soap, and they are on the road ahead of schedule. Unbeknownst to either of them, the man who so enjoys making new friends is about to encounter an English girl who will change his life forever.

When she was last seen by her mother, Lesley Bonnard was a vivacious teenager, born and bred in the suburbs of London. Back in those days, she had little curiosity about any world wider than her own home, her friends and the pop charts. The furthest she'd ever been from Atbara Avenue was a week spent on the sands of Slapton Lea. She'd never seen a proper mountain and wouldn't have been able to point out where Bavaria is on a map. Sporty and funny, occasionally a little unruly, she was popular at school. Neither an exceptional student nor a dunce, she expected to pass her O levels. There'd have been no more exams after that, though. Lesley was dead set on getting a job in a beauty salon. She was certainly a very pretty girl. At five feet and one-half inches in height, she was small for her sixteen years. Lesley had thick blonde hair, which she wore in plaits, and freckles, but it was her smile that people noticed most of all; the smile that shone from a thousand posters that once adorned off-licence windows and lampposts across five boroughs. Police at the time she went missing described it as 'infectious'.

But that was five years ago, so Lesley Bonnard has been waiting a long time to meet a Bavarian horologist.

A pedant when it comes to planning, the man has worked out his route in meticulous detail, poring over Ordnance Survey maps to make sure he and his wife will take in as many sights as possible in the short time they have left. His exacting itinerary includes a thirteenth-century monastery, Roman ruins and a riverside picnic, but he's saved the best until last. After lunch, his course takes them over the South Downs. With rolling hills and the promise of spectacular views, these should be a special treat.

Although they've both looked forward to it, the drive turns out to be tiresome. By mid-afternoon, the sweltering main roads are jammed with holiday traffic. Mirages quiver above the baking tarmac, which in places has melted into tacky liquorice puddles. The camper wagon is like an oven. It's a relief when they turn off to begin their snaking ascent of Chalk Hill.

Flat, yellow fields of stubble are soon behind them, giving way to the welcome shade of lush woodland. As the byroad winds higher, it becomes narrower. Its tall banks are so heavily overgrown that the vegetation on one side of the road arches over their heads to meet the vegetation on the other. Enveloped in this cool, green corridor, they continue to wend their way upwards. It would be easy to lose track of how high they've climbed, but every so often they pass unexpected openings in the hedgerows; a fallen branch, a telegraph pole, things like these allow tantalising, arrow-slit glimpses of a dazzling, sunlit vista awaiting them just the other side of the tunnel wall.

'*Halt! Was für eine malerische Aussicht.*' The woman wants her husband to stop somewhere so she can get a proper look, but he's determined.

'Not yet, *Liebchen*.' They must press on.

Lesley, who has already seen the view, is still waiting.

While the sightseers continue their journey, Atbara Avenue languishes in the fuggy heat of suburban high summer. In some back garden, under the shade of a lilac tree, children play in a paddling pool. Splashing and jumping, their shrill squeals of delight rise up, like starlings, flocking in glad circles in the air outside the windows of Number 49.

The bedroom curtains sway slightly, as if wafted by a host of invisible wing beats. Sharon Bonnard gets up from her rocking chair, closes the window and draws the curtains shut. In the now-darkened space, stiff, automaton paces carry her to the side of the single empty bed. She runs her hands over its patchwork quilt... up and down, this way and that, smoothing it perfectly flat. She picks up a cushion resting against the bedhead and, for a moment, buries her face in its slippery pink satin cover, inhaling deeply. She gently re-plumps the cushion before replacing it, with exquisite care, in the exact position from where she lifted it.

With the tip of a finger, she nudges up one corner of a framed portrait of Elvis Presley. Straightening it just so. She pulls the cuff of her cardigan down over her clenched fist and uses her makeshift duster to buff up his puppy-dog face. Sharon Bonnard turns up the volume of her transistor radio by two notches and returns to once more sit in her chair. Careless of the airlessness of her self-imposed twilight, she concentrates on remembering to breathe in and out, in and out, in and out. Rocking herself. Pretending she still minds whether she lives or dies.

At last the camper wagon pulls off the road. It bumps across the dry, gravelly lay-by, kicking up plumes of dust as the German man brings it to a crunchy halt.

'*Endlich hier*, Sabine!' he declares to his wife.

'*Hurra!*' Sabine cheers with relief. She sticks her head out of her open window, keen to absorb her surroundings. Several other vehicles are already parked up, their occupants ambling around in the sunshine, taking in the prospect. Everyone is smiling, happy to behold the stunning natural wonder laid out before them. An ice-cream van is enjoying brisk trade. There's a bus-load of Americans… other Germans too, by the sound of it… and day trippers, no doubt escaping the big smoke to gulp some lungsful of their own English air.

'Just look at that *view*, Günter!' she breathes. She hastily unfastens her seatbelt and reaches to open the wagon door, but her husband stops her.

'*Nein*, Sabine. *Warten Sie!*' he insists, selecting a guidebook from the thick stash of maps and pamphlets that fill the glove compartment. 'You must first allow me to tell you about this place.'

Sabine sighs. 'It will feel so good to stretch our legs,' she says hopefully as she leans back in her seat, making ready to be educated.

Günter clears his throat and in his very best English accent, he begins to read aloud: '*A naturally formed platform perched on the south side of Chalk Hill, just a few yards from its summit (elevation 950 feet), this popular lay-by affords magnificent, uninterrupted views across the Downs. Guaranteed to "take… your… breath… away"…*' He stops for a moment. 'I don't know this last expression. Remind me to look it up.' He reads on, '*If you are lucky enough to visit on a clear day, look around you. You may see as far as fifty miles in any direction.* Okay, my love, that's eighty kilometres to the right, eighty kilometres to the left and eighty kilometres straight ahead. *Look down, if you dare, and you will notice that the drop is not completely sheer, but characterised by a series of flat outcrops at various intervals between cliff-top and bottom. It is from these shelf-like projections that the rock face derives its ancient name "The Giant's Dresser". In total, there are fifty "shelves".'*

Sabine gazes longingly at a melting cornet as it disappears into the mouth of a leather-clad biker. Günter nudges her with his elbow. 'We must count these shelves, Sabine. *The smallest is no more than six inches wide; the largest three feet.* Listen to this next bit: *According to folklore, if a man throws an acorn from the roof of The Dresser and it lands on a shelf, he will have good luck for the rest of his life.* That is the nut from *ein Eichenbaum*. An *"oak tree"*. *However, visitors are asked not to put this legend to the test, since it is dangerous to drop even small items from this height. Enjoy your visit. Fertig!'*

Günter passes the guidebook to Sabine to let her look at the pictures, while he gets out of the camper wagon. He removes his cap and mops his glistening scalp with a handkerchief, replaces his cap, then, tipping his head back, he stretches his arms wide and inhales extravagantly. His nostrils flare. He doesn't immediately exhale but for a moment holds this stance. Masterful, triumphant, he almost looks as if he might begin to pound his chest. Instead, quite abruptly, he lets his arms drop to his sides. Facing dead ahead, with a series of highly exaggerated knee lifts, he makes a short show of running on the spot. The gingery hairs of his bare forearms and calves twinkle in the sunshine.

Knowing her husband would perform this ritual, because he always does when they arrive somewhere worth seeing, Sabine waits until he has quite finished before she too alights.

Together, hand in hand, they stroll to the edge of the lay-by.

Back on Atbara Avenue, Deirdre O'Reilly isn't going to allow the heat of the day to deter her from her duty. She taps on the door of her husband's study, but thrusts it open wide before he's finished his call of 'Enter!'

'I'm going out, Desmond,' she trills, cheerfully stuffing empty carrier bags into the pockets of her voluminous cotton smock.

'Anywhere interesting?' enquires the vicar, peering at her over the top of his spectacles.

'Just collecting jumble. I'm doing the odd house numbers today. I'll cross over to the even ones next week.'

'Systematic as ever. Do you need a hand getting your "wheels" out?'

'No thanks,' she calls back over her shoulder, already halfway to the cupboard under the stairs. 'I can manage.'

'All right. Happy hunting.'

Trying, but failing, to avoid scuffing the already scuffed hall skirting, Deirdre lugs their grown-up son's baby carriage into the front garden. With her heart filled with holy determination, and the creaking suspension of her doughty chariot heralding her mission, the good reverend's better half bursts through the vicarage gates and trundles off down the avenue.

She makes good progress, but when she reaches Number 49 she sees the upstairs curtains are closed. Her finger hovers over the doorbell before she decides against pressing it. She continues on her way, taking care to close the gate quietly behind her.

The perimeter of the lay-by is defined by a low stone wall. Scabs of yellow lichen encrust its top. Tiny, pink, pom-pom flowers, in tight little bunches, grow in between the cracks. Sabine's husband instructs his wife to sit on the wall so that he can take her photograph with the South Downs in the background. She happily complies.

He takes his time composing the shot. Meanwhile, she peers tentatively downwards, over the edge, and sees at once the so-called 'shelves'. She expected them to be bare rock, but to her surprise, each one is covered by a variety of plant life. Like little floating gardens. She doesn't even try to count them. She imagines 'The Giant', standing at the foot of his dresser, arranging ornaments. *'On this little shelf, I put my bird's nest and some dandelions. On this wider one, perhaps a gorse bush or two. And if I stand on tiptoe, yes, I can manage to place a buddleia on the very top shelf. It will bring the butterflies.'*

'Don't look down, Sabine. It will make you dizzy. Look at me. That's it. Move just a little this way. *Nein, zu weit!* A little that way. *Wunderbar.* Say "cheese"!' *Click-click.* '*Sehr gut.* Definitely one for the album. Come, take my picture now!'

Now it's his turn. It's he who must sit on the wall, while Sabine has to operate the camera. He shuffles around a bit, eventually striking a pose to his satisfaction. One leg bent to his chest, one leg hanging over the edge of the wall, right hand raised to his brow, as if surveying all that lies before him. She takes the shot.

Then he begins to readjust himself. Swapping legs. This one bent, that one hanging.

'*Achtung*, Günter!' tuts Sabine.

'But remember, my dear, *I* am an alpinist,' Günter reassures her. 'Take another, with me waving.'

She's just about to bring the shutter down for a second time when his glasses slip from his nose. The expensive prescription spectacles he bought especially for driving. He makes a grab to catch them. His reach is instinctive. A knee-jerk lunge forwards.

He's scarcely airborne when his flight comes to its abrupt conclusion. Before Sabine can even form her scream, the man lands – with a sickening thud – on a narrow ledge, sixty feet below.

Günter's hot, fleshy body crashes down upon his sunglasses, and a sapling oak tree, and the bleached skeletal remains of a dead girl. The impact, which shatters her bones, breaks his neck.

When the police come to speak to Sharon Bonnard, she's sitting in her daughter's bedroom, just as she has done every day since the disappearance. She has the radio on, as always tuned to the news broadcasts, listening for those five words that will end her vigil. 'Lesley Bonnard has been found.' Yet, on this warm summer evening, when she looks out of the window and sees three men coming up her front path, the vicar and two police officers – in uniform but helmets in hands – she recoils, terrified of ushering in the news she's longed for… and dreaded… for five years. She creeps downstairs and waits in the hallway, willing them to go away.

They ring the bell a few times, and knock repeatedly, but she doesn't answer. Standing motionless in her dressing gown, she knows they know she's there. After a few minutes, one of the policemen kneels on the doorstep, opens the letterbox and peers inside. She catches sight of his grey eyes and his bristly moustache.

'Good evening, Mrs Bonnard,' he says, speaking loudly and clearly into the mouth of the letterbox. 'Please forgive our calling unannounced, but we need to talk to you as a matter of urgency.'

'Not today, thank you,' she replies brusquely.

'It's important, Mrs Bonnard. If you'd be so good as to let us in, then we can explain what it's all about.'

She greets this request with stony silence.

'Please, Mrs Bonnard. It's very important.'

'No. Leave me alone!' she snaps. 'I've my laundry to do.'

'I'm afraid we can't be going anywhere until we've spoken to you.'

Once again, the policeman looks through the letterbox. She feels him watching her, taking in her thin, pale frame, sensing her weakening resolve. She thinks for a moment, considering what to do.

'Go on, Mrs Bonnard,' he appeals to her, 'let us in. I think you know it's for the best.'

'Will it take long?' she asks hesitantly. 'Only I *am* very busy just now.'

'We'll try not to outstay our welcome.'

'Well, I suppose, if you promise to be quick.'

The policeman lets the letterbox snap shut and no sooner has she opened the front door, all three men step swiftly into the darkness of her unlit house. They don't allow her a moment to change her mind. She closes the door behind them but remains, standing, in her hallway.

'Shall we go into the kitchen, Mrs Bonnard?' asks the second policeman. He's younger than the first, and clean-shaven, but no less laden with professional determination.

'I'm perfectly fine as I am,' she says, blinking uncontrollably.

'I think we should all go and sit down,' he suggests.

'I'd prefer it if you'd just say what you've come to say, if you wouldn't mind.'

'At least let me get you a chair,' offers Reverend O'Reilly.

Sharon Bonnard puts her hands over her ears and squeezes her eyes almost, but not quite, shut, as if anticipating a loud bang. 'Please, just spit it out!' she whines.

Through the slits of her eyes she sees the men look at one another. Then the vicar nods at the policeman with the moustache, evidently indicating he should continue.

'As you wish, Mrs Bonnard.' He clears his throat. 'Madam, we have come to tell you that a body has been found. It is the body of a young girl, who has been dead for some time. We regret to inform you, Mrs Bonnard—'

'Call me Sharon,' she wails in a high-pitched half-scream, clamping her hands even more tightly against the sides of her head.

'We very much regret to inform you, Sharon, that we have reason to believe we have found the body of your daughter, Lesley. We must also tell you, Sharon, that we have reason to believe Lesley did not come to harm by accident. We have reason to believe she was murdered.'

Sharon Bonnard re-opens her eyes and removes her hands from her ears. She lets her arms drop down by her sides and stands in rigid silence.

'Would you like me to put the kettle on, Sharon?' the vicar asks her gently. 'Or I could telephone Deirdre to come and be with you?'

'No. I'm fine.'

'Are you sure?'

'Yes, thank you. Absolutely fine,' she answers calmly. 'I understand you mean well, keeping me up to date with your discoveries, but clearly it isn't Lesley you've found. Obviously it's some other missing girl, which is a shame for her family, but it's not Lesley, because Lesley is *not* dead. And I'll tell you another thing: my Lesley *cannot* have been murdered. So, I'm fine.' She smiles politely and gestures towards the front door, as if to show her visitors out.

None of them moves.

'We know it *is* Lesley,' says the clean-shaven policeman. In a clear, steady voice he goes on, 'Although the condition of the remains... the condition of Lesley's body... means a formal identification may take some weeks, we have good evidence that we have found your daughter.'

'What good evidence is that?' she asks scornfully.

'A roller skate, Sharon.'

'How do you know it's *her* skate?' she scoffs. 'You're just guessing. It could just as easily belong to some other missing, skating, girl.'

'It is an exact match for the size, colour and make of Lesley's roller skates. It's a size five. We have retrieved part of the white leather strapping. The metal wheels and eyelets, which are distinctive, are still intact.'

'Where's the other one, then? Lesley went off with *two* skates. So, you see, it's *not* her.'

'We are confident dental records will confirm your daughter is no longer missing. Sharon,' he pauses before repeating, with a tone of firm finality, 'Lesley Bonnard *has* been found.'

Once again, Sharon Bonnard falls silent. But there they were. Those five words. She studies the faces of the policemen and the vicar, slowly taking in the unmistakable truth waving at her from their sympathy-filled eyes. She straightens up, tightening the cord of her dressing gown at her waist. Pulling herself together.

'Well, gentlemen, thank you all for coming to tell me,' she says breezily. 'It's such a lovely evening, I'm sure you must have other things to be getting on with. I'm just glad her father didn't live to see this day. I honestly believe the shock would have killed him.' Then, stabbed by the irony of her own words, she begins to laugh.

'Sharon,' Reverend O'Reilly says to her gently, blinking back tears, 'I can't tell you how sorry I am.'

Quite suddenly, Sharon Bonnard feels her legs fold beneath her. Reverend O'Reilly catches her in his arms and, as he does so, her laughter dissolves into wrenching sobs.

'Rest assured, Sharon,' says the policeman with the moustache, 'we will leave no stone unturned in our search for the person who took Lesley's life. We are confident that those responsible for this terrible crime will not go unpunished.'

'Now,' begins Reverend O'Reilly, still supporting the caved-in leftovers of Lesley's mother in his arms, 'let us pray together…'

The events surrounding the German tourist's death quickly come to the attention of the press. *'Finally Snapped'*, reads the headline in the *Evening News*. *'Last Moments Caught on Camera'*. There's a photograph of him, waving, squinting in the sunshine, blissfully ignorant of his imminent swan dive. Robert Watts buys a copy of the paper on his way to the job centre, but pays little attention to the front pages, turning instead to the sports section.

Twenty-four hours later, the news that Lesley's body has also been discovered is made public. *'Beauty Spot'*, reads her headline. *'Missing Teenager Found Dead'*. There's a photograph of Lesley wearing a party frock, standing under a twinkling mirror-ball, taken at her school's end-of-year dance. Next to it is the view from the top of The Giant's Dresser. Bobbo feels the hairs on the back of his neck stand on end.

Robert knows his mother's planning to give him an evening meal tonight. He decides he'd better show up for it. However, when he arrives at Number 47 he's relieved to find she's too preoccupied with supper preparations to engage in conversation.

'Mind if I have a bath, Mum?'

'Go ahead. Leave your shirt on the landing and I'll give it a wash. You can borrow a clean one of Dad's.'

He slips upstairs and runs himself a deep bath. Lying back in the water, he can no longer hold back the surge of bottled-up memories, now uncorked and rocketing around in his head. Until today, he's seldom felt it necessary to revisit the private little details of the Sunday morning when he changed from ordinary boy to murderer. But now she's been found, things have changed. It's time for him to share his own secrets with himself. Closing his eyes, he flicks through them like a film, one frame at a time:

The day had started much like any other, but a funfair had come to Atbara Park and he wanted to earn extra pocket money to spend at the stalls. Keen to make a good impression on Mum and Dad, he started his chores especially early. Taking care not to disturb his sleeping parents, he crept downstairs before 6 o'clock and collected the car keys from their little china dish on the hall table. As quietly as possible, he let himself out of the front door of Number 47, closing it gently behind him. Blinking in the sunlight, he breathed in the promise of a beautiful summer's day. He strolled to the end of the street, turned the corner and then turned again, to walk down the alleyway running between the back-to-back exteriors of Atbara Avenue and the next row of properties.

Arriving at the rear of his house, he dragged open the heavy garage doors. He unlocked Dad's pride and joy, a plum-coloured Rover, and slid into its driver's seat. Without switching on the motor, he released the handbrake, and the car rolled, almost silently, into the waiting sunshine. Having filled a battered rubber bucket from an outside tap, he added a couple of squirts of detergent to the water before popping open the bonnet to top up the windscreen wash.

'Give her a rinse down too, Son, and I'll throw in an extra shilling,' his dad had said.

He was sponging a wheel hub when he caught sight of a movement out of the corner of his eye. He swung round in time to see the wooden fence of Number 49 shudder violently. In the next second, Lesley's head and shoulders appeared, like a jack-in-the-box, above its lip. With what he recognised as practised efficiency, she swung first one leg, then the other, over the top of the fence, before she dropped down, feet first, into the alleyway. Thighs together, knees bent, she achieved a tidy landing.

Now, lying in the bath, he evokes her slim, lithe little body as the film show in his head plays on.

Lesley hadn't immediately sprung upright. She remained still, crouching down behind the fence, one eye pressed against a knothole in its wooden slats. 'Don't say anything,' she muttered under her breath, without removing her eye from the hole.

He'd been taken aback. So much that, at first, he wasn't even sure she was addressing *him*. Although he and Lesley went to the same school and had been next-door neighbours for three years, she'd never so much as acknowledged him before that moment, let alone spoken directly to him. But even in those days, he understood girls like Lesley – perfect girls – had no reason to acknowledge boys like Bobbo. He, of course, knew her.

'What are you doing?' he called out to her.

'Shh,' hissed Lesley. 'No need to wake the whole town. I'm making sure no one saw me, that's all.'

'Why?'

'Keep your voice down and I'll tell you,' she whispered.

'Okay,' he whispered back.

Apparently satisfied she'd escaped her home without detection, much to his astonishment, she jumped up and joined him by the car. He was acutely aware that this was the first time Lesley had, voluntarily, come anywhere near him. Her perfect blonde plaits, as fat and yellow as corn on the cob, had danced on her shoulders as she trotted to his side. She was so close then, he could smell the shampoo in her hair. Medicated, like pine trees. Clean. Disinfected. Perfect.

The memory of it makes Robert flush. He holds on to it, inhaling the steam from his bath, trying to recapture some sense of her. Then he returns to the show.

He'd decided to be brave. Ask her another question. 'Who are you hiding from, Lesley?'

'Mum and Dad. Well, mostly Mum, if you must know. She's such a *bitch*,' she replied casually. 'She's giving me a hard time about seeing AJ.'

'Who's AJ?' he'd asked, although he already knew the answer. Anthony Jobbins, who lived over the road at Number 64. Captain of the cricket team, the tallest in their class, and merciless tormentor of anyone less significant than himself. AJ had a special name for him: Gobshite. '*You, Robert Watts, are a gobshite!*'

'My Tony, that's who,' Lesley sighed wistfully. With some difficulty, she tugged a strip of bubble-gum from the pocket of her very tight, very short shorts. She tore off the paper wrapper with her teeth and spat it onto the ground. Her small, pert body exactly occupied her small white shorts and small white T-shirt. Blazing white, like in the soap adverts. Spotless.

'Would *you* like a bit?' she giggled. She had a satisfied smile when she saw how his hand shook as he took the piece of gum.

For a short while they'd both chewed in silence. He continued to sponge away at the car, watching her furtively from the sides of his eyes. Lesley pushed skeins of bright pink bubble-gum out between her teeth, inflating each taut little bladder until it snapped. Her perfect tongue immediately retrieved the remnants from her lips, drawing them back inside her mouth to be reassembled, chewed and burst all over again.

'Why doesn't your mum like Tony?' he eventually asked.

'Says he's only after one thing. Like all boys.' She looked at him playfully. 'Do you think that's true? Are all boys just after one thing?'

He didn't answer but registered the unmistakable mischief in her perfect blue eyes.

'What's your name again?' asked Lesley.

'It's Robert. We're in the same maths group.'

'Whatever. Sums are boring. Is this your car?' She idly ran a finger over the soapy bonnet, drawing the outline of a flower in the bubbles. Like a daisy. He noticed her skin. The rays of summer making a cinnamon blizzard of her freckles. Delicious.

'No,' he spluttered, flattered and confused. 'It's Dad's.' Did she honestly think he owned a car?

She dipped her hand in the bucket of soapy water and flicked a ball of suds at him. It landed on his forehead, like a wet kiss. He let it trickle down his cheek for a moment before wiping it away with the back of his forearm. He knew she was mocking him. But at the same time, he wondered if it was just possible that she, perfect Lesley, was flirting with him too? He wasn't sure. Yet there she stood, observing him as a cat might observe a mouse.

'AJ and I have got a date today.'

'Where are you going?'

'Guess!' she laughed, holding up a pair of roller skates by their laces. He hadn't even noticed them until then. 'There's a rink set up at the fairground. I'm meeting AJ there. He's a *dreamy* skater.'

'I bet he is,' he mumbled sarcastically. 'Anyway, isn't it way too early? The fair's not starting up for hours.'

'I know,' she said lightly. 'But if I stay home till later, Mum'll only stop me going. I've told you, she's a bitch.' In an attempt to dry her wet hands, she rubbed them down the front of her T-shirt, all the while studying his face.

'What are you going to do between now and then?'

'Hadn't really thought.' She circled him slowly, looking him up and down. 'So, Mister Whatever-your-name-is,' she continued nonchalantly, turning towards the car, 'can you drive?'

'Yes,' he answered. And it was true. Sort of. His dad had let him take the car up and down the alley at least six times. He was getting lessons for his seventeenth birthday. Next month. 'Would you like a lift?'

Lesley didn't say anything, but to his amazement she opened the front passenger door and got in. 'Well, chauffeur,' she asked with a little giggle, 'where are you taking me?'

And he replied with the only place name he knew beyond Chiswick. That place on the way to Granny and Grandpop's, where Dad said he'd take him to practise hill starts. 'The Giant's Dresser.'

He climbed into the driver's side and, with trembling fingers, fumbled the key into the ignition. It took him two attempts to start the engine and their exit from the back alley was hardly stealthy. Thanks to his bungled adjustments to the choke, the car threatened to stall several times as they lurched along Atbara Avenue towards the high street. Lesley slid down low as they passed her house, pulling faces.

'So long, *dearest* Mama,' she sniggered, gesturing a V-sign at Number 49.

He got the hang of the driving quickly enough, and soon they were bowling along nicely in the merry early-morning sunshine. Lesley leaned back, resting her feet on the dashboard, talking and giggling and chewing her gum. *Chomp, chomp, snap.*

'Go on,' she teased, 'show me how to change the gears.' So he showed her. Then, each time he put his foot on the clutch pedal he called out 'Now!' and she grabbed the stick and ground it up or down, roaring with abandoned laughter. Throwing back her head, exposing her perfect neck. He couldn't believe Lesley Bonnard was actually sitting next to *him* in his dad's Rover. But she was. They were on a secret adventure, just the two of them. Fugitives together, like Bonnie and Clyde.

Once again Robert freezes the frame. He turns on the taps and tops up his bath, savouring the memory of still-alive Lesley and not-yet-a-murderer him. In that bygone scene, *he* is the innocent – the character being led astray. *She's* the dangerous one. But, of course, the great plot twist is yet to come. Back to the action:

Gay Marris

It took them less than an hour to reach the lay-by at the top of The Giant's Dresser. The roads were empty. They met no other traffic on the ascent of Chalk Hill and when they arrived at the lay-by itself, they had the place to themselves. As soon as he pulled up, Lesley jumped out of the car – before he'd even switched off the motor. She flung her arms wide and turned her face upwards, eyes closed, offering up her smile, her perfection, to the sun and the cloudless blue sky. He watched her whirl around and around on the spot in a series of wild pirouettes. Whooping with delight.

He left her to dance her dance and walked alone to the edge of the lay-by to take in the mighty panorama stretched out in front of him. He'd seen it once before. Not with his mum and dad – forays to grandparents were strictly non-stop both ways – but on a school trip. And it was just as he remembered. A vast vista without foreground, from the top of The Giant's Dresser the rest of the world seemed only to exist far, far away and all things in it were made small. Their teacher had said that in centuries of old, kings of England rode their horses up to this dusty out-of-the-way spot to survey their realm. Now there were no longer any castles left to count. The shires were punctuated instead by new tower blocks and power station stacks. But reduced to no more than suggestions of themselves, the ugliest features of human activity appeared beautiful. Wisps of pure white cotton wool puffed harmlessly from toy-town chimneys. A train-set locomotive sped gently towards an unseen destination lost in the vague immensity of the scene. It was an infinite, benign landscape, and as far as the eye could see, all was well.

Dizzy from her exertions, Lesley staggered a little as she came to join him. 'How did you know about this place?' she asked breathlessly, shaking gravel out of her sandals.

'We came here for O level history. On a coach. Don't you remember?'

'Nope. Must've had something better to do that day.'

'I'm sure you were there. You were wearing blue ribbons in your hair.'

'Was I really?'

'Yes. And you got too hot and rolled up your school skirt to make it short. Miss Brown told you off.'

'Well, if you say so,' she sniffed.

'What do you think of the view?'

'It's all right, I suppose, if you like history,' she replied uninterestedly.

He felt he should find some fitting words to describe the scene. To impress her. 'I think it's awesome.'

Lesley blew and popped another gum bubble. *Snap*. 'I'd just as soon be getting back.'

But he didn't want to be getting back. The unbelievably perfect Lesley was out with him, just him, in that unbelievably perfect place, and he needed to keep her there for as long as possible.

'Close your eyes,' he said.

'I don't want to.'

'Go on,' he coaxed. 'I'll give you a present.'

She stood there, once again looking him up and down, making squidgy chomping noises with her gum. 'Okay then,' she giggled, shutting her eyes.

'No peeking!' Luckily, he didn't have to search the ground long before he found what he was looking for. 'Now, put out your hand.'

'It isn't anything disgusting, is it?'

'No. I told you, it's a present.'

Lesley put out her hand. He pushed a shiny brown acorn into her open palm. 'All right. Take a look.'

She opened her eyes and inspected his offering, turning it over in her hand. She had a questioning look on her face. The little furrows in her temples deepened ever so slightly.

God, she was pretty.

Clearly her default was to be utterly unimpressed. He fully expected her to throw it back in his face. Yet she asked, 'What's this for, then?'

'It's for luck. There's a story that says if you drop that over the edge of the cliff and it lands before it gets all the way to the bottom, you'll get good luck.'

'I've never heard anything so daft,' she snorted.

'Aren't you going to throw it over?'

'No, I am *not*,' she replied. But he was pleased when he saw her work the acorn into the tight, tight pocket of her shorts. She'd accepted his gift.

'Do you want to see something else that's really awesome, Lesley?'

'I want to go back and find AJ.'

'Go on. It won't take a minute. If we lean over the edge, we'll be able to see the "shelves".'

'I'm not bothered about seeing any "shelves",' she said doubtfully, 'and I'm not good with heights.'

'It's safe if you kneel down, like miss showed us. Look!' He knelt in the gravel, resting his elbows on the low stone wall.

'You'd better not be messing with me.' She hesitated, but then she too kneeled down.

'All right, on the count of three, we'll both look over the edge together. Ready?'

She nodded.

'One, two, THREE!' In a single movement, the pair of them leaned forwards and peered down the cliff face.

'Wow!' exclaimed Lesley with a gasp of surprise. 'Now *that* is awesome.'

'Told you. Those are the shelves. They look like little gardens. Each one is different—'

'What *are* you on about?' she interrupted. 'I mean down there, right at the bottom. I think that's a whole car smashed up. Do you think people were still in it when it went over the edge?'

He looked straight down, beyond the shelves, to see what she saw. At the foot of the cliff was a graveyard of twisted refuse; washing machines, mattresses, sheets of corrugated iron, bikes – and what appeared to be the wreckage of more than one rusty old car. Nothing beautiful.

Lesley nudged him with her elbow. 'Thank you for bringing me here,' she said. Her voice was soft. Sincere. She smiled at him. And that was his perfect moment. Suspended in time. Leaning over the low stone wall with perfect Lesley kneeling beside him, impressed by what he had to show her, happy to be with *him*. That was why he reached over and tried to take her hand. He was so sure she wouldn't mind – that she was feeling what he was feeling. But the second he touched her she recoiled, snatching her hand away like she'd received an electric shock.

'What d'you think you're doing?' she snapped. 'Keep your hands to yourself!'

He was stunned. He couldn't understand how he'd misread things so badly. Was she still toying with him? He reached out again, this time catching her more firmly, by both wrists. Lesley pulled back, trying to squirm free, but he didn't release his grip.

'Let me go! What the hell's wrong with you?' she shouted.

'What the hell *is* wrong with *me*, Lesley?' he shouted back at her. 'Why is Tony allowed to be with you, and touch you, while I'm not?'

'Because I fancy him. And because he's cool.' Lesley started to wail.

'He's not cool. He's a bullying shit who doesn't deserve you. *I* think you're perfect. *I* deserve you.'

'I love Tony and he loves me.'

'What a joke. People like Tony don't love anyone except themselves. Your mum's right. I bet he *is* only after one thing.'

'After it and got it and I don't care what *you* think. You're a nobody. A bloody NOTHING!'

'Shut up,' he yelled at her. 'Shut up!'

But Lesley didn't shut up. 'You're a weirdo. I don't even know who you are!' she screamed. 'Take me home! Now!' She sank her teeth, hard, into his thumb. The shock made him relax his grip and Lesley broke free. She made a frantic dash back to the car, throwing herself inside, slamming and locking the doors behind her. He followed without any particular haste. When he reached the car, he tapped on the windscreen and dangled the keys up for Lesley to see. There she was, sitting on the back seat, cradling her roller skates in her arms. Crying. Snot was streaming out of her nose. He felt quite calm as he unlocked his dad's Rover.

'Get out, please,' he instructed in an even, civil tone.

'No, no, NO!' The skate she flung at him missed its mark and he caught it by its laces.

Although she'd failed to hurt him as she intended, Lesley's sudden act of aggression irritated him. Stupid girl. Laughing and joking one minute, making all this fuss the next. 'If you won't come nicely, then I'll have to help you,' he said. He reached into the car, grabbed hold of her plaits and dragged her, kicking and screaming, from the vehicle.

'Tony will kill you when I tell him about you,' bawled Lesley, lashing out at him with her fists. 'He'll find you and he'll KILL you. Because he loves me. I know he does.' Then she spat in his face.

Suddenly, he was angrier than he'd ever been in his life. A strange, white-hot fury shot up inside him, unlike anything else he'd ever felt before. Her efforts at escape were futile. Pathetic, really. He delivered a swift punch to her face and, dazed, she fell to her knees. Propping her up against the side of the car he fumbled with the roller skate, struggling to wrap its lace around her neck before she fully recovered her senses. As he pulled the lace tighter, she clawed at her throat, trying to loosen the garrotte. But her fingers couldn't get a proper hold.

'Now I have you, Lesley Bonnard. Now you are mine.'

'Please... don't... B... B...' she gasped.

'My name is Robert Watts. Say it, Lesley! Say *Rob-ert*!'

Lesley moved her lips, trying to shape a word. 'B... B... Bobbo...' she rasped, in a barely audible rattle. 'Bobbo.'

She was turning blue. Gobbets of white spittle frothed at the corners of her mouth. Her eyes bulged wildly, red and bloodshot, like raw meat. She smelled of sick. And shit. She wasn't perfect any more. She was revolting. With all the strength he could muster, he yanked on the bootlace. He felt her body stiffen and her back arch. Then she went completely slack. He let go. Lesley folded over and slid to the ground.

There she lay, motionless at his feet. He prodded her with the toe of his shoe, expecting her life force to return. In the very next second, he was sure that healthy, ripe, pinkness would course through her body, restoring her perfection. He waited. Nothing happened. She stayed disgusting, purple-faced. Dead.

Strangely, as his fury dissipated, all his old feelings for Lesley twanged back into place, like letting go of an overstretched rubber band. Filled with tender concern, he stroked her hair. He attempted to untie the bootlace, but it was impossible. It was embedded in her neck like the wire of a blunt cheese slicer. He slid his arms under Lesley's lifeless little body and lifted it up. He carried it back to the edge of the lay-by and laid it down gently on top of the low wall. He straightened her plaits, one on each shoulder. He knelt next to her, lifted her right arm, and kissed disgusting dead Lesley once, very softly, on the palm of her hand. He closed her eyes, then his own, and with a swift, firm shove, he rolled the corpse over the cliff-top.

There was a brief whooshing sound as the body flew through the air, and a dull *thwump* when it landed. He opened his eyes and peered, gingerly, over the edge of the wall. The body was nowhere to be seen. To his surprise, dead Lesley hadn't fallen all the way down to join the other stolen, discarded things at the foot of the dresser. He realised she must have come to rest on a shelf; received by the tall green fronds of some floating garden, which closed over her as a sea anemone swallows a prawn. But he couldn't tell which one. He stared and stared, waiting for a breeze to come and show him where dead Lesley lay amongst the waving bracken. But when the wind did eventually blow, and the bracken did eventually sway, it didn't reveal its secrets. The bracken whistled, the birch trees sighed, and skylarks trilled overhead.

He looked at his watch. Eight o'clock already. 'Time flies.' Calmly, he brushed the gravel dust from his clothes, returned to the car and drove home. Watching his speed, like his father always told him. He finished washing the car and checked the oil. He knew that would please Dad too. As he closed the bonnet, he caught sight of Lesley's remaining white leather roller skate on the back seat. He took it into the garage and stuffed it into a tin trunk containing an assortment of sports equipment, burying it deep amongst the cricket pads and deflated footballs. That was when he heard his mother calling his name from their back garden.

'Oh, this is where you got to,' she said, popping her head over the top of the fence. 'You must be ready for your breakfast.' Just like he was still her precious, ordinary son.

So he replied to her, 'Yes please, Mum.' Just like he hadn't murdered anyone. He put the car away and went inside for his bacon and eggs with mushrooms, then spent the rest of the day finishing his chores.

Bobbo picks up the loofah and scrubs his back. He knows the mere thought of throttling Lesley, all intertwined with the memory of that greasy plate of bacon and eggs, should physically revolt him, but he finds the association very... ? What? Satisfying, maybe? As if he'd worked up a legitimate appetite doing something he needed to do. He wonders whether other people, other murderers even, would find it so easy to set aside the horror of that day, almost as if it never happened. Yet for him, Bobbo, this hidden callousness is something he can live with perfectly comfortably. It's a facet of his character only he and Lesley ever properly explored. He smiles to himself and, shrugging off any further self-analysis, he loads the next reel. There's a swift change of scene.

That same day, after supper, he took the two shillings from his father and went to the fair. It wasn't quite dusk – sunset yet to form itself in the pinking sky – but Atbara Park was already thronging with activity. The air was filled with the smells of fried onions and spun sugar, the flashing illuminations, the hollers of the people playing at the sideshows and riding the rides. His senses were flooded. This was the spangle-lit, razzle-dazzle evening Lesley had been looking forward to. Promising so much iniquity and hullabaloo. All in all, a much more plausible backdrop for wrongdoing than the still, quiet beauty spot on the hillside.

He wandered from stall to stall, content with his own company. He bought a toffee apple and ate it as he made his way to the roller-skating rink, where he took up position in the shadows to one side of its entrance. He didn't have to wait long until he caught sight of his target: Anthony Jobbins, at the Lucky Ducks booth, standing beneath a candy-striped canopy fringed by polythene bags of goldfish. AJ was using a bamboo cane with a hook on one end to fish rubber ducks from a swirling whirlpool of blue-stained water. He was very good at it – naturally – repeatedly hooking out victims and lining them up one after the other on the side of the stall. Yet AJ appeared distracted. Even though he was several yards away, it was obvious to Robert that he was anxious, taking nervous gulps from a can of soda, looking over his shoulder, glancing at his watch, as if he was waiting for somebody. Waiting for Lesley.

Robert flicks to the next frame.

He'd been watching the arsehole for a while, enjoying his unease, when, quite suddenly, Anthony's demeanour changed. It relaxed. Why? Because he'd seen something, or someone, at the nearby coconut shy. AJ's face broke into a slow, assured grin. He dropped the cane and blew a clear, sharp wolf whistle. Almost at once, a young girl emerged from the horde and began to walk towards him, summoned from the shadows. A girl with thick blonde hair in two fat pigtails, roller skates slung over her shoulder, who knew that wolf whistles were always meant for her.

For the next few, extraordinary seconds he, Robert, allowed himself to believe the impossible. Lesley was alive! He hadn't killed her after all. Of course, as soon as the girl stepped forward into the light, he saw it wasn't her. She was similar, but the hairline wasn't quite right. The waist was a little too thick; the lips a bit too thin. A flawed version of the perfect original.

Anthony started to talk to the girl. Whatever he said to her, it made her laugh. He offered her his fizzy drink. She took a swig, keeping her eyes fixed on his, looking up at him through her fringe. Anthony ran his hand through his hair. The girl fiddled with the cuff of her cardigan. She leaned in closer, locking into his slippery pitter-patter over the cacophony of the fair. Anthony mirrored her posture, leaning in closer to her. Now they were laughing in unison. He slipped his arm about her shoulder, drawing her in. And, just like that, Anthony Jobbins hooked the doppelganger, as quickly and easily as he'd hooked the real thing. Obviously not Lesley, but to indifferent AJ, Lesley near enough.

Even now, this recollection makes Robert angry. How could Anthony have been such a bastard? He, Bobbo Watts, loved Lesley so much that he'd killed her. Anthony hadn't even liked her enough to keep their date.

Standing there, surrounded by all the revolting fun of the fair, he was consumed by hatred. 'Hey, Jobbins!' he shouted. 'Did she stand you up then, loser?'

Anthony swung round, his face a picture of fury, but when he saw who'd called him out, this expression immediately transformed into one of disgust. 'Are you talking to me, Gobshite?'

'Too right I am. A bloke like you doesn't deserve a girl like Lesley. Guess that's why you're having to make do with second best.'

'Is that so, Gobshite?' Anthony laughed.

'You're the gobshite. You're the bloody, fucking gobshite, AJ!'

Anthony grabbed a rubber duck. 'Better catch this,' he mocked, lobbing it straight at him, 'because it's the only bird you'll ever get your hands on.'

It had plopped down on the grass at Robert's feet.

Anthony and the girl turned on their heels and slowly strolled away. He could hear them laughing as they disappeared, hand in hand, into the hurdy-gurdy candy-floss crowds.

He bent down and picked up the duck – an egg-yolk yellow fist of rubber with a brass ring screwed into the top of its hollow head. Its stumpy, lipstick-red beak puckered up as if to receive a kiss. The eyes lime green, cartoon-like, with long, painted lashes; one wide open, as if in a state of amazement; the other with lid half lowered, in a winsome cutie-pie wink. He turned it over in his hand. Printed on the flat underside, two words: *YOU LOSE*. He decided to keep it. A ticky-tacky souvenir of the moment Anthony Jobbins assassinated the memory of Lesley Bonnard. Forgotten before she'd even been missed.

Doorbell chimes shake Robert from his reverie. He realises the bathwater is cold. He pulls out the plug and wraps himself in a towel. As he begins to dry himself, he hears his mother go to the door, then muffled sounds of a conversation between her and another woman, followed by the front door closing. The visitor had evidently left without being invited in.

'Robert!' his mother shouts up the stairs. 'Come down here! I've got something to tell you.'

He detects anxiety in her voice. He wonders if the caller was from the police. *Already?* 'Can it wait? I haven't any clothes on!' he calls back.

'No. You need to hear this.'

Fighting a nasty little flutter of apprehension awakened somewhere in his stomach, he quickly gets dressed. He takes care to rinse the soap scum from his favourite bath toy – AJ's lucky duck – tucking it away at the back of the medicine cabinet before he pads down to the kitchen.

'Who was that at the door then?' he asks, as coolly as possible.

His mother seems flustered. 'The vicar's wife, after jumble, but I hadn't anything for her because I gave it all to the Methodists. I said to come back when I've had time to do another sort through, but she says she's finishing our side of the avenue today and then crossing over the road… and that's that. So I said she'd be getting nothing from us then and she said, "That's just the way it goes then." Absolutely adamant about it. Honestly. What possible difference could it make? But *no*. She always has to do things her way, that Mrs O'Reilly.'

'Is this your urgent news, Mum?'

'What? No. Of course not. It was what else she said. And she couldn't wait to get it off her chest either. It was about the Bonnard girl. She's been found, and the police are saying she was *murdered*.'

'I know she was murdered,' he says. He turns his back to her, helping himself to an orange from the fruit bowl before adding, 'I read it in the paper.'

'The police'll be back, Robert,' she blusters. 'Asking questions. Stirring it all up again.'

'I dare say they will.'

'Well, I'm not sure my nerves can take it.'

Robert pushes his thumb into the base of the orange and starts to work it under the skin. 'Mum. Do *I* seem worried?' he asks, dropping a curl of peel into the bin under the sink.

'I don't know. Turn around and look at me!' He complies, and she studies his face, trying to read his expression. 'Quite honestly, Robert,' she sighs sadly, 'I really can't tell.'

'Well, I'm not worrying. So there's no point in you, or Dad, worrying either.' He kisses her on the cheek. 'Don't bother about supper for me. I'm not staying.'

'But it's nearly ready.'

'I'm sure Dad'll be grateful for it when he gets back,' Robert calls over his shoulder, making a swift exit. He pockets another orange before heading off to the pub.

Peggy Watts watches her son leave, no doubt off for one pint too many at the Brown Cow. She turns off the gas ring under the potatoes and puts the lettuce and tomatoes that she already plated up for him back in the fridge. Knowing that her husband isn't keen on salad, she hopes that if she adds a big enough dollop of piccalilli he'll eat it anyway. She goes in search of suitable condiments, but as she picks up a jar of chutney, she sees her hand is shaking. Peggy realises she needs to pull herself together before Alf gets home. She doesn't want him to catch her in a tizzy. It'll only get him all worked up too. Reaching right to the back of the larder, she retrieves the Christmas brandy. Without bothering with a glass, she takes a swift draught straight from the bottle, then another, before returning it to its hidden niche on the top shelf.

Still a little unsteady, she sits down at the kitchen table. That's when she notices Robert's left behind his copy of the paper. Almost afraid to look, she reads the news coverage about Lesley, of which there are several lurid columns, on the front and on the inside pages too. It's all there in black and white. The girl is dead. Murdered. And has been all along.

Peggy's unsure what to feel. She knows she ought to feel deep sympathy for Sharon Bonnard. And she does. She also knows she ought to feel relief that the poor child has, at last, been found. But for some inexplicable reason, she doesn't. At this moment, her overriding sentiment is one of dread. There's no getting away from it, the news so zealously imparted by Deirdre O'Reilly has stirred up disconcerting memories; a whole book-full, starting on the Monday Lesley's parents reported her missing. She and Alf, and of course Robert, were amongst the first to hear that their next-door neighbours' daughter hadn't come home from the fair, but they weren't particularly worried for her. Not in the beginning. It seems awful to think it now, but Lesley did have something of a reputation for being 'wayward'. Not to say that she was a *bad* girl. Just a bit flighty. They also knew, through the grapevine, that the police were making house-to-house enquiries. So, when their doorbell rang that afternoon, they weren't surprised, in fact they were even a little excited to find a uniformed officer on their doorstep. They were sure Lesley would turn up soon enough, but in the meantime the prospect of being interviewed as part of the search effort had seemed quite fun.

They eagerly ushered him into the front room of Number 47. Peggy recalls how she and Alf sat on the settee, leaving their new recliner free for their guest. Robert, still in his school clothes, squatted on a pouffe while the craggy-faced constable worked through his questions.

'So, young man, did you see or speak to Lesley Bonnard at any time yesterday?'

'Yes. Early in the morning.'

'Do you know what time?'

'It was about six o'clock. I'd set my alarm to get me up for extra chores.'

'And where did you see her?'

'In the alleyway at the back of our houses. She climbed over her garden fence. She said she was escaping.'

'Escaping?' queried the constable, raising a bushy eyebrow.

'From her parents.'

The policeman's eyebrow lowered again. 'I see. What were you doing in the alleyway at that time?'

'Tinkering with Dad's car.'

The policeman turned towards her and Alf. 'I take it you can confirm this?'

Alf nodded. 'Quite true, officer.' Then, looking across at Robert, he added proudly, 'Our son's a good lad.'

'And how did Lesley seem to you, Robert?'

'She seemed fine. Excited. She told me she was going roller-skating. At the fair.'

'Did she say if she had plans to meet any one?'

'Yes. She was going to meet Tony Jobbins. He's her boyfriend.'

'Is this Mr Anthony Jobbins, your neighbour from Number Sixty-Four?' the constable asked, flicking through his notebook, obviously checking the information the Bonnards had given him.

'That's him. Some people call him AJ.'

The constable wrote that down. 'What was Lesley wearing?'

'White shorts, a white T-shirt and pink sandals. She had her hair tied back in plaits. She was chewing bubble-gum. She had her roller skates with her.'

'Thank you, Robert. Very detailed.' Flashing a peculiarly piercing glance directly into Robert's eyes, he continued, 'What happened next?'

'How do you mean?'

'I mean, what did you and Lesley do?'

'Nothing.' Peggy remembered that Robert flushed. 'She left.'

'Just like that?'

'Yup.'

'Did anyone see you with Lesley, or see her leave?'

'I don't think so.'

'Which way did she go?'

'Up the alleyway and then she turned right, as if she was heading back along Atbara Avenue.'

'Robert,' said the constable, repositioning himself in his seat, making the leather rasp, 'can you think of anyone who might wish to do harm to Lesley?'

Robert didn't answer 'yes' or 'no', but shaking his head he replied, 'I think Lesley is perfect.'

And this, Peggy reflects, was the point at which the tone of the interview altered. The change was subtle, almost imperceptible, yet it was certainly there. She sensed it in the marrow of her bones. That was why she interjected, to try to change back the tack. 'Yes, she's a really lovely girl,' she said nervously. 'Sharon and Malcolm Bonnard must be out of their minds with worry.'

'Indeed,' said the constable, without averting his gaze from Robert's. 'So, after you'd said goodbye to Lesley, how did you spend the rest of your day?'

'I finished washing down the car, had breakfast and did my other errands for Mum and Dad. In the evening, I went to the fair.' Robert paused before adding, 'And that's when I saw them, together.'

'Saw who?' asked the constable, sitting up a little straighter, pen poised over his pad.

'Tony Jobbins and Lesley. They were holding hands. Sharing a joke. I saw them by the Lucky Duck stall.'

'What time was this?'

'I don't know exactly. Around nine, or nine thirty. It wasn't dark, but the fairground lights were switched on.'

'Did you get a good look at them?'

'They mostly had their backs to me.'

'Did you speak to them?'

'Not to her, but I did say hello to Anthony Jobbins. I know he saw me.'

'Are you absolutely certain the girl was Lesley, Robert? It's important you're clear about this.'

'Well, I didn't go right up to her, but she looked very much like Lesley. She had the same hair, she was with AJ, and Lesley definitely told me she was meeting him there, at the fair. She had her skates with her. Who else would Anthony be with?' Robert smiled. 'After all, he's her steady boyfriend, isn't he? So, yes, I am certain enough it was her.'

'Thank you, Robert,' the constable said, closing his notebook and replacing his helmet. 'You've been very helpful.'

With those words he departed, leaving in his wake a strange cloud of suspicion that's never really dissipated.

Anthony's mother, Mrs Nesta Jobbins, is plumping up the sofa in Number 64's front room when she comes across her husband's copy of the *Evening News*. For some reason, it's tucked deep down between a cushion and an armrest.

'What's Ivor done that for?' she tuts to herself.

She tugs it free and is about to bin it when she reads the line '*Police vow to find monster who killed Lesley*'. Taken aback, she sits down abruptly, then realises she's landed exactly where one of the constables sat when they came to question her family, five years ago. And in that instant, it all comes flooding back.

Thirty-six hours after Lesley left home, the police arrived on their doorstep. She, her husband and Anthony sat on one side of the sitting room; two officers – one in uniform, one in plain clothes – sat on the other. After an hour of interrogation, Nesta and Ivor knew their son was in serious trouble. And so did AJ.

'All right, Anthony,' went on the constable, a gruff man with a gnarled brow, 'you admit Lesley Bonnard is your girlfriend and that you arranged a rendezvous for Sunday evening. You and she planned to go roller-skating and you were going to meet at the fair. Yes or no?'

'Yes,' Anthony muttered, avoiding his gaze.

'Look at me when I'm talking to you, please.'

Anthony complied, resentfully, rolling his eyes upwards.

'Thank you. You also admit that you kept this appointment. You waited for Lesley at one of the side stalls. The, er…' the questioning officer referred to his notes, '… "Lucky Ducks", I believe?'

'Yes,' he muttered again.

'But you're telling me Lesley never showed up?' The constable made no attempt to hide his scepticism.

'Yes. It's like I said. I waited for her, but she never came.'

'And you'd swear to that, would you?'

'Yes,' replied Anthony with rising frustration. 'I already said.'

'I'd watch your tone of voice if I were you, young man!'

Ivor clutched Anthony's arm. 'There's nothing to upset yourself about, Son. All you have to do is tell the truth.'

The officers exchanged a glance before the constable resumed his questions. 'What if I told you we have a witness who says he saw you and Lesley together, at the fair? He's certain it was you two.'

'Well, he's wrong.'

'I think that unlikely. This witness is someone who knows you and who knows Lesley. A classmate of yours, Anthony. He's quite certain it was you two he saw…' The constable referred to his notebook again. '… "sharing a joke", apparently. That's what I've got written down here.'

'I suppose you're talking about that Gobshite Watts!' shouted Anthony. 'Well he's just a *liar*.'

'I've warned you about your tone of voice.'

Ivor clutched Anthony's arm again, harder than before. 'Sorry, officer.'

'So,' the constable persisted, 'you admit you saw Robert Watts. He is accurate when he says he encountered you at the fair?'

'Yes. That's true. But he didn't see me with Lesley. I told you, she was a no-show.'

The constable paused, put down his pen and notepad, and leaned back in his chair.

His colleague, a detective inspector with a well-cut suit and chiselled jaw, leaned forward. He rested his bent elbows on the dining table, chin on knuckles. 'Okay, Anthony,' he began matter-of-factly, 'let's have it your way. Let's suppose, for the sake of argument, Lesley didn't keep her date with you. How long did you wait for her before you realised she wasn't coming?'

Anthony shrugged his shoulders. 'I don't know.'

'Surely you have some idea. Was it half an hour? An hour?' he asked lightly.

'Somewhere in between.'

'Okay. So, you waited forty-five minutes for your girlfriend. Is she usually late for your dates?'

'No. Never.' The trace of a smirk passed across his mouth.

The detective inspector smiled. 'Didn't you become concerned when she didn't show up? Didn't you wonder where she was?'

'No.'

'Not at all?'

'Not really,' Anthony sighed.

'And why not?' The detective inspector sounded no more than casually interested.

Silence from Anthony.

All at once the detective inspector's manner changed. A light-switch flip from friend to foe. 'Okay, Anthony, I'll be straight with you. This is what I think happened. I don't think you had to worry about Lesley, because I think Lesley kept her appointment with you. And after that, she disappeared.'

'I swear to you. I wasn't with her at the fair,' he whined, but then his voice dropped to a mumble. 'I *was* with someone, but it wasn't Lesley.'

'Speak up, lad. PC Ratchet and I didn't catch what you said.'

'I was with another girl.' He blushed a deep red.

'What's this?' shouted the detective inspector. 'Your girlfriend is less than an hour late for your date, so you cut your losses and take up with the next girl who comes along? Just like that?'

'Quite the Casanova,' interjected the constable.

Unable to hide their embarrassment, both Nesta and Ivor shifted awkwardly in their uncomfortable chairs. 'Really, *Anthony*!' Nesta hissed at their son. He didn't meet her gaze.

'Who was this girl, then?' the detective inspector went on doggedly. 'I presume she'll vouch for your movements yesterday evening?'

'I don't know her name.'

'Don't know because you can't remember? It was less than twenty-four hours ago, Anthony!' The man's tone was loaded with incredulity.

In a voice scarcely more than a whisper, Anthony answered, 'I don't know because I didn't ask.'

Nesta remembers putting her head in her hands. Ivor fiddled with the knot of his tie.

'Where does she live? Where is she now?'

'I've no idea. I don't think she's from round here.'

'Of course you haven't, Anthony. And I'll tell you why not. Because I don't believe this girl exists.'

'She does. She's got blonde hair. Robert Watts saw me go off with her. Ask him! Or find that girl. *She'll* tell you.' Anthony was beginning to sound desperate. Like a desperate, cornered liar. He shook his head.

The constable smacked the flat of his hand onto the table. 'Where is she, Anthony? Where's Lesley?'

That was when Ivor asked whether their son needed a solicitor.

Anthony Jobbins is on his way home from work when he sees the billboard outside the tube station. *'Lesley Bonnard Found Murdered'*. He feels sick. He decides not to go back to his flat but to head, instead, across town to his parents' house. In many ways, Atbara Avenue is the last place he wants to be at that moment. He's made a new home of his own, out of sight of Gobshite Watts, Sharon Bonnard and a hundred other pairs of censorious eyes. But he's sure his mother and father will want to see him. They'll be properly worried. And frightened. He knows it's only a matter of time before the police come looking for him. They'll have the same questions they asked him when Lesley went missing, and he'll offer back only the same answers. He wishes he could prepare for their arrival; wishes he had something more convincing to tell them. But all he has is the truth, and nothing but. God help him.

As he rounds the corner of Atbara Avenue he sees a figure heading straight towards him. A woman. Although he can't see her face he's certain it's Deirdre O'Reilly. The unmistakable *creak, creak, creak* of the laden pram gives her away. He's barely a dozen yards from his parents' front gate but he knows he won't make it before she reaches him. If it wasn't for bad luck, he thinks, he wouldn't have any luck at all. He toys with the idea of crossing the road, making it look casual, as if he were about to call in on an old neighbour. But who would he be visiting? What would they say? 'Do pop in for a coffee, AJ. It's been ages?' Hardly! He'll have to brave it out.

In ten strapping strides, the vicar's wife is upon him. 'Hello, Anthony. Just look at you in your snazzy suit. Quite the smart young man about town.'

'Evening, Mrs O'Reilly.'

'This is a surprise. I can't think when I last saw you on the avenue. Here to see Mum and Dad, I'll bet. And how *are* Nesta and Ivor?'

'Fine, thank you,' he falters, before veering the subject away from his family as swiftly as he can manage. 'I see you've got a good old pram-load there.'

'Haven't I just. Muriel Dollimore is having a clear-out and she's donated all poor Pauline's things to the church jumble.'

'Very generous, I'm sure. Now, if you'll excuse me.' He makes a move to pass on by, but Deirdre and her pram are too wide.

She makes no attempt to get out of the way. 'Yes. Once again, Mrs Dollimore is setting an example for us all. Bless her.'

Anthony jangles his keys inside his jacket pocket in the vain hope she'll take a hint and let him go, but the woman sails on. 'Will your parents be donating anything?'

'Why wouldn't they?' he retorts sourly, fighting the urge to challenge whether their cast-offs are good enough for her. 'You can come over straight away if you like. I'm sure Mum will find you a whole bag of things in the blink of an eye.'

'No need to trouble her yet. I'm on my way back to the vicarage now. I'm not even starting collections from *this* side of the avenue until tomorrow. So, no rush.'

'Well that's just fine, Mrs O'Reilly. Ideal, in fact. That means we can have a good rummage tonight and,' he continues pointedly, 'I'm sure you'll agree it's about time my family got the chance for a *proper* clear-out. Carrying around unnecessary rubbish can really weigh a household down.'

Deirdre O'Reilly blushes. 'As I say. No rush.'

'Oh, I disagree. Strike while the iron is hot. In fact, I'm going to go through my old room right now. After all, most of the unwanted junk in that house is *mine* anyway, wouldn't you say?'

'Well, I'd better let you get on then,' splutters Deirdre, struggling to manoeuvre the heavy pram out of his way.

Seeing her embarrassment and annoyed with himself for allowing her to get him rattled, Anthony helps her drag it to one side of the pavement. After all, what could the silly busybody say that could ever really hurt him? He doffs his imaginary hat as he sweeps past. 'Good day Mrs O'Reilly.'

Reverend O'Reilly warned Mrs Bonnard about the press. 'Best not look at the news for a bit, Sharon,' he said. But when the evening paper plops onto her doormat, pure habit makes her glance at the headlines. Although it takes her less than a second to remember the vicar's advice, it's still too late to prevent herself from reading '*Girl throttled with her own bootlace*'. She lets the paper drop to the floor. Slowly she re-climbs the staircase and returns to Lesley's bed.

Sharon Bonnard's world is saturated with grief. She's tried to find a place in her head, some tiny backroom, into which she can crawl away from her own misery. But it's inescapable. Now, curled in the foetal position, she hangs on to the only comforting thought she's been able to muster. That Lesley isn't alone but with her daddy.

'Is she in your arms, Malcolm? Are you keeping our baby safe?'

She thinks about the Sunday their daughter went missing. While the enormity of the loss is impossible to grasp, so many trivial details about that day are embedded in her brain. It wasn't long after she and Malcolm got up that they realised Lesley had slipped out of the house. Again. They'd been annoyed, but not overly concerned. Sharon can still remember how offhandedly she remarked to her husband, on discovering Lesley had taken her roller skates with her, 'Honestly, I could kick myself. I should have known she'd pull one of her stunts.' At that moment, she was sure Lesley had sneaked off because she'd put her maternal foot down about the Jobbins boy. And equally sure that her daughter would be back.

Sharon recalls how, over their breakfast, they were in good spirits as they discussed the sanctions they would impose when she came home. 'How about washing up for a week? Or no pocket money for a fortnight? What do you think?'

'Well, a certain young lady can kiss goodbye to any birthday trip to the pictures,' Malcolm grumbled when Lesley missed their Sunday roast. Sharon remembers him dragging his armchair into the front bay window so he could sit in comfort as he looked out for her return.

Then she winces. She recollects her own words when Lesley had still failed to show up by six. 'That lass is going to feel the back of my hand.' She put Lesley's spaghetti hoops in the oven to keep them warm.

'Mark my words,' Malcolm said to her when Lesley wasn't home by her 9 o'clock curfew, 'she'll be at that fair, larking around with her friends.' He switched on the outside light above the front door.

'Larking about with Tony Jobbins, more like,' she replied. But it was then that she pulled on her jacket. 'I'll just walk to the top of the road to catch the little madam on her way home.'

'I'll come with you.'

They reported Lesley missing at one o'clock on Monday morning, an hour after the fair shut down for the night.

In their statement to the police, she and Malcolm explained how Lesley had slipped out the previous morning, probably with the intention of going roller-skating with her boyfriend, and she'd almost certainly made her getaway via her usual route: over the back fence. The police waited until dawn, 'just to give her the benefit of the doubt,' before beginning their enquiries.

Over the hours immediately following the disappearance, officers spoke words of reassurance, clearly convinced Lesley would turn up soon. Though Sharon tried to believe them, even then her instincts were screaming something else. And as one, two, three days crawled by, the mood of the investigation became sombre. After a week, the police called at their home and quietly told them that the longer their daughter remained missing, the greater the likelihood was that she'd fallen victim to foul play.

'Foul play,' Malcolm repeated, over and over again. *'Foul play?'*

'I'm afraid so, sir. That is a possibility we all have to face.'

Sharon wanted to comfort her husband but found herself emotionally bankrupt. 'Who would hurt our girl?' she asked weakly. 'I just can't understand it.'

'We have several lines of enquiry, madam.'

'Are you saying you have a suspect?' Malcolm sounded incredulous. 'Some piece of *shit* is out there, hiding my little girl, and you're sitting in front of me, chewing the fat?'

'At this stage in the investigation it would not be helpful to name names.'

'If you know who's got her, then why can't you arrest the low-life bastard, make him tell us where she is?' Malcolm shouted.

'It's not that simple, sir.'

'Balderdash!' Malcolm roared, shaking with rage. 'There must be something you can do?'

'We will do everything in our power to find Lesley, but in the meantime I can only ask for your patience.'

Just a few months later, the burden of patience killed her husband. That, and a realisation that the police's two 'persons of interest' were their neighbours' children, classmates Robert Watts and Anthony Jobbins. Malcolm shot himself.

In an effort to feel less exposed, Sharon pulls the bedcovers right over her head. In the years since Malcolm checked out, the police have continued to visit her, bringing updates on the case. She knows AJ and Robert have been interviewed many more times, and neither has deviated from his story. Then and now, the police strongly suspect Anthony. His alibi, some mystery blonde, has never been traced, despite numerous requests to the public for her to come forward. He looks like a liar. As for Robert, he freely admits seeing Lesley on the morning she went missing. But there's not a single witness to vouch for her movements during or after that encounter. It's Robert's word against Anthony's that Lesley made it to the fair. If Watts is the liar, then he, not AJ, was the last person to be seen with her.

Throughout the intervening years, the police and, thanks to local gossip, the residents of Atbara Avenue, have remained convinced one of these boys, grown into young men, knows more than he's saying. Which young man? That's anyone's guess. There's never been a scrap of hard evidence to corroborate either version of events. And without a body, where was the proof that a crime had even taken place?

But now, at last, Lesley Bonnard *has* been found, and Sharon senses that for one 'low-life bastard', the game is about to be up.

'Give her a kiss from me, Malcolm. Give her a kiss from Mummy.'

As Bobbo takes a mouthful of his second pint, he finds himself musing on what an odd thing 'chance' is. Since the moment Lesley jumped over that fence to join him, random twists and turns of fate have carried him this way and that, yet guilty as he is, he's been delivered, unpunished, to where he is today.

On reflection, he can see some logical reasons why his crime has remained concealed. For example, it's easy enough to understand how no one noticed Lesley talking to him in the alleyway or getting into his car. After all, she herself engineered a secret escape from her home. He supposes it's reasonable no one saw them on their drive to the top of The Giant's Dresser. It was so early on a Sunday morning, they simply beat the crowds. Perhaps that fact could also just about explain how he managed to kill her in broad daylight without any witnesses. And he did make a very quick job of it.

But, Robert acknowledges, in many other respects he's been extraordinarily fortunate to escape detection. It was lucky for him that when he disposed of dead Lesley, she landed on a 'shelf'. If she'd fallen all the way to the bottom of the cliff, as he'd expected, then she'd have been quickly discovered – either by fly tippers, or by the gypsies who scavenge the wreckage for scrap metal. They've found a couple of other bodies there, victims of suicide, in the time since Lesley's death. It's very lucky that whichever shelf she landed on had enough vegetation to cover her body. And then, even perfect Lesley must have rotted.

Isn't it amazing that the smell of her decomposing body didn't arouse any suspicion? The squabbling flocks of carrion crows never piqued the curiosity of so much as *one* of the thousands of tourists who came to take in the view that long hot summer when she died. After the event, it strikes him as remarkable he was able to complete the drive and the murder and return home without his parents missing him, or the car for that matter. And what about that girl at the fair, the one he saw with Jobbins? Robert knows she was real. Yet she's conveniently vanished into thin air.

Chances were, he should have been caught on day one. But despite the stacking odds, fortune has been in his favour and he's remained a free man. Bobbo thinks about the folklore of The Giant's Dresser... about the hard, shiny, auspicious acorn squeezed into Lesley's oh-so-tight shorts as she went over the edge... still with her as her fall ended on a shelf... and he swallows another mouthful of his beer.

But what now? The police are bound to come sniffing around again. Robert must consider that his luck's about to run out.

That evening, tired out by their day's various worthy tasks, the vicar and his wife withdraw to their snug. This is their usual habit. Valuable time set aside to reflect upon the mortal state of St Francis's flock and what makes it so endlessly rewarding to serve.

'Who do you think did it, then?' asks Deirdre.

'Did what?' replies her husband, folding away his copy of the *Evening News* and placing it face down in his lap.

'Don't pretend you don't know what I'm talking about. I'm asking you who killed Lesley Bonnard. Robert Watts or Anthony Jobbins?'

'I pray it was neither,' says the vicar sadly, shaking his head.

'Well it has to be one of them. The boy next door or the boy*friend* over the road. The police never looked at anyone else when she vanished. Now that she's been discovered... murdered... they must be thinking one of them did it. Stands to reason. And,' she adds irritably, 'you don't fool me for a minute. I know you've as much natural curiosity about your fellow man as the next person has. You just keep it hidden behind loftier sentiments like compassion and forgiveness and all the rest of that clutter.'

'What about the benefit of the doubt?'

'That ship has well and truly sailed,' she snorts. 'And do you know what's always surprised me?' She marches on, knowing her husband isn't going to ask *what*. 'I think it's very strange that neither family ever moved away. Even though this reeking cloud of suspicion has hung over two households for all these years, the Wattses are still at Number Forty-Seven and the Jobbinses are still at Number Sixty-Four. Robert and Anthony keep coming and going from Atbara Avenue as if they haven't a care in the world, and all the while Sharon Bonnard is sitting alone upstairs in Number Forty-Nine, waiting.'

'What reason would they have to leave, if their children did nothing wrong?'

'No reason. But if one of them *is* guilty, his family might have decided to stay because disappearing off elsewhere would make it look like they have something to hide.'

'So, staying is a sign of innocence and staying is a sign of guilt? Ducking-stool reasoning, surely?' sighs the vicar.

'Well, I still believe the chances are that for whatever reason, one of those young men, when he was no more than a child himself, took that girl off and he strangled her. Mark my words, since her body's been found, things will finally happen to bring the right person to justice. I can feel it. And you know my instincts are never wrong.'

Ivor Jobbins sticks his head up through the loft hatch of Number 64, scanning his torch beam over mounds of accumulated junk. His son stands at the foot of the ladder.

'There's piles and piles of stuff up here, Anthony. Did Mum say what wants keeping and what wants chucking?'

'No. She just wants at least one bag of rubbish to give to the church jumble.'

Ivor climbs the last few rungs and disappears into the hot, stuffy gloom of the attic. Thudding to and fro in the darkness, he bangs his head on a low rafter as he searches for the light pull. When he eventually tugs on its frayed cord, the bare bulb flickers and threatens to fail, before it floods the loft space with light. 'Now we're in business!'

Ivor spends the next few minutes pottering about, cheerfully setting things to rights in the roof of his castle. He pushes some stray wads of lagging back up into the eaves, whistling as he tinkers. He checks the level of the hot-water tank, lifting its cover just enough to make sure there are no drowned mice. 'Good,' he says to himself, placing the palm of his hand on the bricks of the chimney stack. 'No damp.'

Procrastinations complete, he turns his attention to the task in hand. Pulling bags and cases, one at a time, from their sleeping stacks, he brushes off the dust, looking for any outward indication of their contents. He mutters and curses as he works, exasperated that he doesn't recognise most of what he finds. God knows how long it's been there. Some containers he opens briefly, just glancing inside before closing them up again, satisfied that they can stay. Christmas decorations. Definitely a 'keeper'. Others require more of a rummage-through before he makes a decision.

'This one looks like toys, Anthony,' he calls down. 'Do you want your old train set? It's pretty busted up.'

'Not really.'

'Okay then. That can be chucked.'

'What about this box of comics?'

'Get rid. I didn't even know it was there.'

'What about your—'

'Honestly, Dad,' interrupts Anthony, 'I can't think there's anything of mine up there I want to keep. No need for any more delving. Let's save both of us some time and donate the lot. That should satisfy the O'Reilly woman.'

'Good. Agreed.' He's relieved this tiresome chore will be so quickly completed.

Ivor Jobbins dangles a grubby canvas bag through the loft hatch and, much as a lumberjack lets out the warning cry, 'Timber!' when he fells a tree, he shouts, 'Below!' as he lets the bag drop.

Anthony catches it in his arms. 'It's quite heavy, Dad. I'll put it straight by the front gate. The vicar's wife is collecting in the morning, so we can save her the trouble of ringing the bell for it.'

Robert Watts waits until his mother goes shopping and his father leaves for the allotments before letting himself into their garage. The old tin trunk is waiting for him, stoically, in the oily gloom. At first he thinks it's locked, but then discovers it's simply rusted shut. He uses a car jack to prise the lid free and quickly finds what he's looking for. The roller skate. It's in good condition. He sniffs it, hoping to catch a lingering scent of Lesley, but it just smells fusty. He puts on his dad's gardening gloves and gives it a thorough wipe to clean off any fingerprints before hastily wrapping it up in a couple of sheets of newspaper.

Resolved to act as quickly and discreetly as possible, he slips out of Number 47, his bundle concealed under his jacket. He crosses the road, intending to head for Atbara Park, where there are several litter bins. Nice, anonymous, frequently emptied, council-owned ones. However, he's hardly made it twenty paces up the street when he sees a distant figure trundling towards him. It's some way off but he recognises the outline, and the sound. *Creak, creak, creak.* Shit. Just what he didn't need.

Robert knows the vicar's wife won't pass him without stopping for a chat. She, of all people, will notice his bulging jacket, the sweat forming on his top lip. If he crosses back over the road, she'll notice that too. It'll be obvious he's avoiding her. He has to think. Fast.

It's then that a way out, albeit a desperate one, offers itself to him. A lumpy canvas sack, apparently containing rubbish, lying on the pavement right in front of him. Robert looks towards Deirdre O'Reilly. She's distracted from her mission, perhaps only briefly, having encountered another neighbour. In a lightning movement he shoves the precious, poisonous package into the top of the sack and continues on his way.

'Hello, Robert!' hails Deirdre, as he passes her by.

'Morning, Mrs O'Reilly. Lovely day for it.'

Deirdre O'Reilly's recurring nightmare started happening just after the discovery of Lesley's body. It isn't about murders, but the church fundraiser. In her dream, she's always in the vestry of St Francis's, sorting donations for the jumble sale, and she's always naked. Somehow, her clothes have been put away in the store cupboard, which is inexplicably locked. Suddenly, she hears someone entering the church. This 'someone' is always the Archbishop of Canterbury, but his character is played by a variety of film stars, depending on how much cheese she's eaten for supper. Terrified of discovery, she tears frantically at sacks of bric-a-brac and old clothes in the hope of finding something to cover her embarrassment. But this is never to any avail. The sacks only contain shoes.

On every other night, luckily, just when His Grace is about to open the vestry door, Deirdre has awoken a start. She's sighed, taken a sip of water, turned her pillow cool-side up and quickly fallen back into a sleep-land of sweeter dreams.

Tonight, however, it's different. Deirdre sits up and switches on her bedside light. This time something about the dream has really unsettled her. She thinks it through, but she can't quite put her finger on what it is. It isn't anything to do with the archbishop, played by Steve McQueen, or the locked cupboard, or even the excruciating nudity. It has to be something to do with the jumble.

'But what, what, what,' she wonders, 'could *possibly* be so sinister about a pile of old slippers and flip-flops?'

Then it comes to her.

'Desmond! Wake up!' she shouts, elbowing her sleeping husband in the ribs.

'What*ever* is it?' splutters the vicar, sitting bolt upright, rubbing his eyes.

'I know who murdered Lesley Bonnard!'

At the police station, Deirdre O'Reilly swears on the Bible – although the sergeant explains this isn't necessary until the case is tried in court – that she cannot have made a mistake. An arrest swiftly follows. Sharon Bonnard watches from the bedroom window as the prisoner, handcuffed, is frogmarched to a waiting police van. He doesn't put up any resistance. With a jacket draped over his bowed head, he seems resigned to his fate. His old school pal waves from his garden gate as he's driven away.

The subsequent trial is well attended and short. Reverend O'Reilly is forceful in his assertions. His wife, being the most systematic woman on the planet, would not... could not... have got it wrong. 'If Deirdre says the jumble she picked up that morning all came from the even-numbered houses on Atbara Avenue, rather than the odd, then I haven't a shred of doubt she's correct.'

Under cross-examination, Deirdre is as impressive as she is obdurate. 'That,' she cries triumphantly, pointing directly towards the roller skate, cowering in its transparent evidence bag, 'did not come from the Wattses' household. It came from the Jobbinses'!'

It was all the assembled jury could do not to burst into a round of applause. Perhaps that would have drowned out AJ's vain protestations. Then again, probably not.

Frank doesn't live in the Australian outback exactly, but his family home is far enough from the nearest town that the post van only comes once a week. This makes it an event. He drags his favourite cane chair to the shady end of the veranda, fetches himself a cold beer and settles down to open his mail. It's a pleasant change to get a proper handwritten letter, and this one has come all the way from England. He already knows who it's from. He recognises the handwriting. Of course the postmark and the stamp give the game away too. Nevertheless, he will savour smoothing out the thin blue sheets of airmail paper and deciphering Ursula's excitable, runaway scrawl.

To his surprise, as he slices open the envelope a fragment of newspaper falls out and flutters to the floor. He picks it up and scans it. At first, he can't fathom why Ursula has sent him an advertisement for hair-restoring oil. Then it dawns on him. Younger than he is, she's always teasing him about the more obvious manifestations of their age gap. This is his cheeky sister getting in a dig about his receding hairline. He smiles to himself as he screws up the cutting and drops it into his ashtray. He begins to read.

34 Athara Ave
West London

Dear Frank,
It's so long since I put pen to paper that I hardly know where to start. Nigel's back is playing up. I blame the damp. Of course, you know about our Colin walking again. Coming on in leaps and bounds, he is. Not quite literally, but the doctors are really pleased with him. He doesn't even use a stick now. He's had his last appointment with that Dr Sally, too, which is more than a blessing, I can tell you. We're taking the caravan to Margate. We won't get the sunshine like you do, but it'll be nice to get a change of scene...

So the letter goes on. Good old Ursula. He counts no fewer than sixteen references to British weather and three to his brother-in-law's lumbago. He turns over to the last page.

But here's some news! Remember when you and your girls came over from Oz when Colin was a tot and our neighbour's daughter went missing?

I'm sure she disappeared when you were still staying with us and not after you went home. But only just, mind you. I remember you saying something like 'There but for the grace of God' to me and Nige, because Lesley who went missing was about the same age as your Jolene and Jolene was always getting into mischief with boys chasing after her back then. You and Sandra told Nige and me we were lucky having our lad Colin, because girls give their parents such a run-around. 'Eyes in the back of your head, Sis, that's what you need with daughters.' Can't have been long after that you flew back down under. Anyway, I thought you'd like to know that she turned up murdered and one of our other neighbours did it. There's been a trial and everything.

Well, I'll close now. Rain's forecast so I must get the shirts in off the line.
Love to Sandie and the girls.
Your loving sister,
Ursula

PS. Newspaper clipping enclosed. I think she's the spit of your Jo-Jo, though it never struck me at the time. Isn't life funny? xxx

Frank retrieves the cutting, blows off the flecks of ash and carefully unfolds it. This time he looks at both sides. *'Anthony Jobbins sentenced to life'*, reads the article, but it's the photograph underneath that takes his breath away. The instant he sees it, he gasps out loud. For a shocking few seconds, he thinks the girl with two blonde plaits, smiling out from the newsprint, actually *is* his own daughter. Not as she is now – a young woman with a baby of her own – but as she was five years ago, on holiday. The night she stopped late at the fair.

7

Keeping Mum

From a distance, it's easy to mistake Deirdre O'Reilly for an invincible woman with a steely resolve and a fixed itinerary. Brimful of good sense and determination, she's equally blessed with the energy needed to share these assets throughout the parish. While St Francis's flock trusts the reverend to take care of their spiritual lives, they're relieved his wife is in charge of absolutely everything else. Her dogged qualities make them feel secure, because when it comes to the messiest aspects of life, death and church fêtes, it's vital their vicar doesn't have a squeamish spouse. Deirdre understands the needs of her community. Perfectly. That's why she keeps her chin up, her brogues laced, and her own vulnerabilities well hidden in the crypts of her heart.

In that afternoon lull when it's not yet time for high tea but long past lunch, the vicarage is peaceful, as if sleeping off the beef stew and apple charlotte whose rich aromas still permeate the motionless fug. The oak wall panels of its library, the Kashmir stair runner, the thirsty parlour palm quietly dying in the hallway – all nap through the dull, postprandial hours of Saturday. They're preparing for the more stimulating eventide activities that promise to come, these being Welsh rarebit, cribbage, and *Desert Island Discs*.

Deirdre O'Reilly has spent most of the day out of the house, breathing God's air and door-knocking for the Fallen Women's

Fund. This undertaking was more protracted than expected. Thanks to her recent role as star witness in the conviction of that wicked Anthony Jobbins – Crown Court, no less! – every neighbour she met wanted to stop and congratulate her on a job well done. Although Deirdre could never be found guilty of sloth, she does find herself wrestling with perilously sinful levels of pride. Her husband, meanwhile, who chose not to join her on her rounds, has been fighting an altogether different emotion.

After dealing with morning appointments, he ate alone, his appetite quelled by lack of company and the weight of his deliberations. He then retired to his study, where he's remained until now, ensconced with his thoughts, praying for guidance. Unable to procrastinate any longer, he closes his well-worn New Testament, slips it back into his pocket, and with as much resolve as he can muster, goes in search of the indefatigable Deirdre. He soon finds her, in the kitchen.

She's sitting at their pine-topped table, her back to the door, sorting through a sizeable bag of darning. Engrossed, she doesn't seem to notice him enter the room. He feels a surge of affection as he takes in her familiar frame, bent over, busily making do and mending. Her hair is pulled back into a bun. This typically slack arrangement started the morning perched on the top of her head, but due to Deirdre's constant activity, it's worked its way loose, travelling towards the side of her face with each passing hour. As always, she's done nothing to check its progress. To glance in a mirror more than once a day is, in his wife's opinion, not only a waste of valuable seconds, it's also a warning of insurgent vanity. He watches with silent pride as she attacks her work. Practical, effective and grounded. She's the perfect counterfoil to his own ethereal nature, and so much better than the sum of her good works.

He clears his throat, preparing to speak, but she beats him to it.

'You're letting in a draught, Desmond,' she says cheerfully, without looking up. 'Come and sit beside me and tell me all your news.'

He closes the door and joins her at the table. 'Deirdre,' he begins, choosing his words with care, 'while you were out, a most unsettling visitor came to call. It was a young lady—'

'Don't tell me,' she interrupts, still concentrating on her mending. 'She was from Tottenham.' There's a hint of mischief in her voice.

'As a matter of fact, she *was*.'

Deirdre looks up abruptly, evidently taken aback. 'Really? She actually *did* come from Tottenham?'

He nods blankly.

A playful smile appears on her lips. 'And did you offer her tea?'

'Naturally I did.'

'Well I trust she didn't "rip off her knickers",' she laughs, unable to contain her mirth any longer, 'as that *would* have been unsettling.'

'What an extraordinary thing to say!' he exclaims, completely disconcerted. He feels himself flushing. 'I can assure you that Miss Blenkinsop—'

'Oh, Desmond!' cries his wife, using a threadbare sock to wipe tears from her eyes. 'It's the limerick. Surely you know the one I mean?

'There was a young lady from Tottenham,
'Her manners she must have forgotten-em,
'Having tea at the vicar's,
'She ripped off her knickers... Must I really say the whole thing...?
'And said she was far too hot-in-em! Dear, dear. I'm getting a stitch in my side.'

'Ah, yes. I get it now,' says the vicar. He also allows himself to laugh, but a good deal less heartily than his wife. He looks away, turning his gaze to the window and the view it affords over their untidy vegetable garden.

'I'm sorry,' Deirdre says at last, having taken several moments to collect herself. 'I spoiled your story.' He can tell she's detected he's ruffled. Perhaps she imagines he's smarting from her teasing. 'Please go on,' she continues in more dutiful tones. 'What made Miss Blenkinsop come all the way over from the straits of north London to the steps of our vicarage?'

'She's some sort of investigator.'

'A *police*woman?'

'Not exactly. Perhaps more of a cross between a charity worker and a private detective. She called herself a "missing persons" something or other.'

'How intriguing. But I can't think of anyone unaccounted for in these parts. Neither man nor woman. If you'd asked me a few months ago, I might have said Reggie Pyles, but he's turned up safe and well, and so did the Bonnards' girl. Although she was dead, of course—'

'The thing is,' he interjects, 'Miss Blenkinsop is following up on what she called "an historic case". And it doesn't concern a missing adult, or teenager. Deirdre, love,' he goes on, gently, 'it's about a baby.'

Deirdre's needle jabs into her thumb so hard it draws blood.

Jane Sweeting did her best to prolong her conversation with the Reverend O'Reilly, in the vain hope Mrs O'Reilly might return from her errands while she was still at the vicarage. However, after an hour of polite chit-chat interspersed with increasingly lengthy silences, there was still no sign of his wife. Eventually, she cut her losses and arranged to return on Monday when, the vicar assured her, 'Deirdre will be more than glad to help with your investigation.'

Although something in Jane's insides told her Deirdre would be anything *but* glad, she thanked him for his time and slipped out into the late-morning sunshine.

Now, as she makes her way along Atbara Avenue towards the high street, she toys with the idea of treating herself to a taxi ride back to town, but decides against it. With two clear hours until she's due to meet Bruce, she has plenty of time to use less direct means of transport. Besides, with their wedding fast approaching, it's good to avoid unnecessary expenses. She's got her eye on the perfect hat for her going-away outfit: a smart felt cloche in navy blue. An added incentive to count the pennies.

It's while she's waiting at the bus stop that needles of guilt begin to prick at her conscience. Was it very wrong of her to have given a false name? She shifts from foot to foot in an effort to shake off her unease. Even worse, to have lied to a vicar? With a modicum of mulling-over, she quickly dismisses her misgivings. Surely using Bruce's surname instead of her own isn't exactly giving a false name. After all, in a mere seven and a half weeks she will be Mrs B. Blenkinsop and the untruth will be undone. So, if not a pure white lie, at least it's only a temporary one.

Her second lie, that she's making enquiries in any kind of official capacity, is trickier to assimilate. However, since she doesn't consider herself to be an inherently duplicitous character, she decides to give herself the benefit of the doubt about that one too. While she's *implied* to the vicar she's on official business, she hasn't actually *said* she is. Not in so many words. Reverend O'Reilly assumed she was acting on behalf of some higher authority; she didn't correct him. She hardly thinks that counts as fibbing, more a failure to disclose all the facts. She chooses not to wrestle with her scruples any longer. Her mission is important. If a little subterfuge is necessary, then so be it.

By the time the number seven to Oxford Circus arrives, Jane is convinced her copy book is still sufficiently unblotted to allow her passage into Heaven in the end. With righteous steps she hops aboard and scuttles up the stairs as fast as she can, but she doesn't quite make it to the front row of the top deck – her preferred roost for longer journeys – before the bus lurches off again. She half sits, half falls into an empty seat, narrowly missing the lap of the passenger next to the window. Jane garbles her 'oopsie-daisy' apologies, he mutters his 'perfectly all right ducks' don't-mention-its, and both stare straight ahead until she gets off, twenty stops further down the line. With Selfridges in her sights, she swims through the throng of other shoppers in search of her future husband and her cloche hat.

On Sunday morning, after service, Deirdre and Desmond O'Reilly set off to Munster House. It was Deirdre's idea to go, but Desmond insisted on driving her. Although the roads are quiet, it takes them several hours to get there. They travel in silence, each lost in their own thoughts. When they arrive, Deirdre mounts the steps to the grand front door, rings the bell, and speaks briefly to the woman who answers. Refusing a polite invitation to come inside, she instead slips around the side of the house to enter its grounds. Her husband stays in the car. As always, she visits the little grave alone.

Even though no path leads to its hiding place in the farthest corner of the garden, she walks straight to it, as if the tufty grass remembers her footfall and ushers her to the right spot. The headstone, a simple granite cross no more than a foot high, is all but consumed by the encroaching shrubbery. She kneels down and tugs away handfuls of ivy tendrils. Her movements are not rough, but firm, as if she's combing the knots out of an untidy child's hair. She whispers as she works. 'Dearie me, we are in a mess… let's get you straightened out a bit… I'm sorry I haven't been to see you for so long.' At last, when the inscription is once again visible, she rests. *God Bless, Little Angel.*

Deirdre murmurs a short but heartfelt prayer before quickly returning to her waiting husband. Evensong at 5.30, and it would never do to be late.

Jane bids Bruce a fond goodnight and waves him off from the window of her flat. She knows he was angling to stay, but she's determined to stick to her resolve. Hers will be a snow-white wedding and their first night together will be their first night.

'No, Bruce,' she said firmly as she wriggled free of his slightly too ardent embrace. 'We said we would wait, and we must stay strong.' As Bruce dragged himself away, she caught him muttering something about the word 'we', which she chose to ignore.

No sooner is he out of sight than she retrieves a manila folder from her bedside table and begins to revisit its cherished contents. She wants to get her facts straight before her return visit to the vicarage. The item of chief interest to her is a trio of faded black and white photographs. She removes the paper clip holding them together and places all three directly under the beam of her brightest table lamp. Although she's pored over them many times, she hasn't tired of looking at them. She takes up her magnifying glass to make absolutely sure she hasn't missed some tiny but crucial detail.

The first shot shows a young woman, scarcely more than a girl, standing on the steps of an imposing stone-built house. Initially the potted palm trees either side of the steps made her believe the picture must have been taken abroad, somewhere hot, but she's since discovered it was nowhere more exotic than Bournemouth. Something about the lack of curtains in the huge sash windows and the presence of a fire bucket on the top step makes it obvious it's some kind of institution rather than anyone's family home. Cradled in the young woman's arms is what looks like a parcel. Closer inspection reveals it's an infant, swaddled in a blanket. She can just make out a baby's fist, protruding from the top of its woolly cocoon. Initially, she didn't recognise the youthful woman as her own mother, Catherine. But she's looked at it enough times by now to be certain that it is.

The second photograph shows a different woman, slightly older, also standing outside the same building. Tall, thin, with broad shoulders, dressed in a stiff white nurse's uniform, she's either saluting or holding her hand up to her forehead to shield her eyes from the sunlight. The name *Deirdre O* is penned on the back of this picture, in her mother's writing.

In the third picture, it's Deirdre O who's holding the blanket parcel. Sitting on the bottom step, her head is tilted forwards, her face pushed close into the bundle, her mouth pressed against the tight, chubby fist. Jane's mother is nowhere to be seen.

With great care, she reunites the photographs with their paper clip and returns them to the folder.

Next to receive her attention is her parents' marriage licence. Dated 14 March 1941 and kept folded in its original envelope, there are still a few grains of rice trapped in its creases. Jane feels sad as she puts this away again. Poor Mum and Dad. They should've had many more years together. They so wanted to see her and Bruce married. When Jane showed them her engagement ring, her mother had quipped, 'At long last! A wedding where our daughter won't be the maid of honour.' Jane gives the envelope a little shake before she slips it back into the folder, making the rice rattle. If they were alive now she could ask them about all this. But then again, how would they answer?

The final document in the folder is a birth certificate. Stained, ripped and hard to decipher, it's nevertheless clear it was Peter's. Whenever she looks at this scrappy piece of paper it makes her heart falter, and it's no different this time. It's the most tangible proof she has of his coming into the world, and the fact that it has all but disintegrated seems both ironic and poignant.

Jane sighs to herself. Although raised as an only child, when she was five or six years old, she worked out she had an older brother. Not because anyone talked about him openly. Rather the contrary. On the rare occasions her mother referred to 'baby Peter, taken from me', it was in hushed tones. Her father never mentioned him at all. She came to know of his existence because, like most unspoken family secrets, it had a thousand subtle ways of making itself heard. The funny thing was, when she *did* find out about Peter, she wasn't surprised. As far back as she could remember, Jane had a sense that something, or someone, was missing from her life. And that feeling's followed her wherever she's lived. When she was just a baby, her family upped sticks from Kent to London. She was precociously bright, and her parents later said the move was for her, so she could start school early, 'in the big city'. But she was clever enough to know otherwise. It was for her *parents*. Another attempt to distance themselves from the memory of their little lost son.

Before her parents' car accident, before their funeral, before she found the manila folder amongst their private effects, she thought she knew the whole of Peter's story, assembled from the snippets and whispers she'd collected over the years, the pitying looks exchanged between uncles and aunts, and from her mother's oceans of unshed tears: *Once upon a time, Mum and Dad had a baby boy. They named him Peter. He was a sickly baby. He died. Mum and Dad had another baby, and they called her Jane. But Mum never got over the loss. To protect Mum's feelings, no one spoke about Baby Peter. The end.*

Jane smiles wryly at the simplicity of this version of events. It was a short, sad tale, and for a long time she'd been quite satisfied with it. Until she found the folder.

She holds the birth certificate up to the light and peers at it intently through the magnifying glass. Despite its deterioration, there's no mistaking what she can see. The date: 31 December 1940. More than two months *before* her parents' wedding.

She remembers the moment when she first discovered Peter was born out of wedlock as if it were yesterday. She was clearing her parents' house. Sitting alone on the bare boards of the sitting-room floor, files and boxes spread around her, she'd been looking for a lost gas bill. It was quite by chance that she opened the folder and found the birth certificate. Comprehension had struck her like a thunderbolt.

'Now I get it!' she exclaimed aloud. '*Now* I get it.' Her brother wasn't a tragic secret. He was a shameful one. All at once she saw his shadowy presence in the family in an entirely new light. Best not mentioned for so many reasons, sympathy not being top of the list.

After the discovery that Peter's birth had been illegitimate, creeping doubts about the legitimacy of his death began to haunt her thoughts. If he hadn't been born when they said, how could she know that he'd died when they said? How could she be sure he'd died at all? She'd searched high and low and although the gas bill did eventually turn up, she never found any death certificate.

Slowly, she pieced together her disturbing new interpretation of events. If no death certificate meant no death, then the baby in the photographs, alive and well in Catherine's, her mother's, arms, could be Peter. For hours and hours, she stared in vain at the grainy pictures, hungry for a clearer impression of the baby's face, yearning for some clue to his identity. Although this eluded her, the more Jane thought about it, the more certain she became that she was looking at Peter. What other baby could it be?

So if Peter wasn't dead, what was the significance of these three photos? Mum and Dad had kept them all those years. Carefully tucked away. Never looked at, yet never thrown away. Surely they didn't show her mother, and then this random 'Deirdre O', simply taking turns to hold Peter? They *had* to be a record of something far more important. As she turned over various explanations in her mind, her mother's plaintive words, '*taken* from me', resonated more sharply. Since Peter hadn't died, she must have meant 'taken' in an alternative sense. Perhaps Peter was adopted? If he was, then did these pictures capture the moment her mother handed over her beloved baby to another woman? That theory had seemed to fit, until Jane scrutinised the expression captured on her mother's face. It was one of joy. Not the face of a woman parting with her beloved child, never to see him again. Certainly not the face of her mother on those rare, distraught occasions that she'd talked about Peter when Jane was growing up. Giving up her baby was obviously something she'd deeply regretted.

What, then, were the facts?

Number one: Peter didn't die.

Number two: Mum shared Peter with Deirdre O.

Number three: Mum was sad for the rest of her life.

Jane reconfigured her theory, over and over again, until she was able to fit the last part of her jigsaw puzzle into its place.

Her mother had Peter, and she'd handed him over to Deirdre O. That much had been captured on camera. However, Jane realised, this was never supposed to be a permanent arrangement. A fostering? A loan? A promise to look after him until her mother was ready to give him a home? Who knew. But whatever the plan, her mother hadn't been able to reclaim Peter. To her mother's eternal regret, when the time had come, as it surely must have, for her to return and get her son, Deirdre O hadn't given him back. Had Deirdre disappeared, run off with Peter to a place unknown? Or had she just point-blank refused to surrender him?

No matter what the precise details of Peter's departure were, the more time Jane has spent chewing things over, the more confident she's become about certain broad facts. She's used them to rewrite her brother's story: *Once upon a time, Mum had a baby boy. She named him Peter. He was a shameful secret. Mum wanted to keep him, but she had to give him away. When Mum got married she tried to get Peter back. But the wicked woman who took him vanished. Mum had another baby, and they called her Jane. But Mum never got over the loss. To protect Mum's reputation, no one spoke about Baby Peter. The end.*

Keen to put this new construction of events to the test, she approached her aunts and uncles, asking them to tell her what they knew. But those who would talk to her at all stuck to their guns.

Peter was an 'unfortunate' little thing, they tutted, shaking their heads and looking at their shoes. It was a mercy that he died. They clearly expected her to be satisfied with that.

But Jane was not satisfied. She's convinced her brother is still alive, and she's made it her mission to find him. And to do that, she needs to find Deirdre O.

Armed with his birth certificate and her photographs, over the past months she's been digging deeper. She knows that Peter was born in Dorset, at Munster House Mother and Baby Home. After many hours perusing old council documents and hospital records, she's identified several potential Deirdres, qualified nurses who lived and/or worked in the area in the early years of WWII: Deirdre Osmotherly, Deirdre Overgood and Deirdre Outhwaite were quickly eliminated from her list – all too old to be the woman in photograph. Misses D. Orme and D. Oldham were too young. Other candidates required greater scrutiny. Having tracked down their current addresses, mustering more guile than she'd known she had, Jane paid them personal visits. Using 'I'm an Avon lady and I appear to be lost' as her ploy, she managed to engage each one in doorstep conversation for long enough to be absolutely sure that they were not her elusive Deirdre O either.

Undeterred, her hunt has continued.

And in a logical world, it would have been Jane's systematic approach that eventually paid off. In the end, however, it looks like pure chance may be about to win the day. Last week, travelling home from yet another fruitless encounter, she picked up a copy of the *Evening News* she found discarded on the tube. The big news story that day, as it had been for many days, was the notorious 'fairground murder'. *'Anthony Jobbins Gets Life'*. On the inside pages was more coverage about the trial; about perfect, pretty Lesley; about the street where she went missing, her neighbours; about the wonderful woman who delivered the murderer into the hands of the police. This respected pillar of the community was named as Mrs Deirdre O'Reilly, incumbent of St Francis's Vicarage, West London. Apparently, the vicar and his untarnished wife have one grown-up child. A son. There was a picture of Mrs O'Reilly. And when Jane saw that, she let out an audible gasp. The resemblance to the person in her tattered old photograph was incredible.

Perhaps tomorrow, finally, she'll meet the baby-snatcher Deirdre and learn the whereabouts of long-lost Peter. She tucks the certificate back into the folder and switches out the light.

On Monday morning Deirdre launches into her housework at the crack of dawn, confronting her chores – if not her emotions

– with even more gusto than usual. It's important to her that their home looks its best for this visitor, but the physical activity is also helping to dispel the savage waves of anxiety lapping in her chest. Having seen to the kitchen and dining room, and after scrubbing the tiles in the hall, it's time to face the sitting-room chiffonier. Her nemesis.

Most of the vicarage furniture nestles patiently under at least one layer of household detritus, but this piece is particularly laden. Dark brown surfaces all but buried by a dusty huddle of knick-knackery, it's become a shrine to the saints of domestic clutter. As always, she'll have to tackle this an offering at a time. She untucks a yellow felt rag from the waistband of her apron and gives it a short, sharp flick. It cracks like a whip.

She begins with her husband's pipe rack. It's filthy. Deirdre thinks better of it. She moves on to the fruit bowl. She picks up a banana that she'd forgotten was there and gives it a squeeze. Feeling it squish within its blackening skin, she wonders about using it up in a fruit loaf recipe. Perhaps she could knock one up for the Women's Institute's tea for starving Biafrans?

She gives the banana another, harder, squeeze and a tiny fly emerges from its stalk. She drops it into the wastepaper basket. The apples pass her inspection, especially after she's given them a buff with her sleeve. A broken metronome pricks her conscience. She makes a note to self: get this fixed. She mentally files this next to note to self: get piano tuned and note to self: empty bin.

Brass candlesticks, silver sugar bowl and ebony napkin rings all respond well to her elbow grease. She carefully arranges and rearranges them in front of a framed portrait of her mother. Is *that* spotless enough for you?

Deirdre is about to confront her next quarry when she hesitates. She stays still, holding her breath, listening for any sign that her husband is nearby. Satisfied she's safe from disturbance, she lifts her mother's picture, and uses the longest of her short fingernails to prise off its back. As she does so, a sheet of writing paper drops out and floats to the floor. With a swift movement, she picks it up and slips it into her apron pocket. She hastily reseals the picture frame, holds it to her bosom for a few seconds, then gives it an extra hard rub with her waxy duster before replacing it on the chiffonier.

She moves on, resolutely steering her attention to a photograph of herself and Desmond taken not long after they met. They were in a punt, floating on the River Cam. She studies his face and hers, smiling, squinting into the camera lens. God, we look young.

She recalls those riverbank picnics. Simple food. Sausages and cheeses wrapped in greaseproof paper. Hungry, without cares or cutlery, they tore off pieces with their bare hands. They'd share a bottle of Guinness, one between two. Desmond went first, like a royal taster, checking the beer for its purity before allowing his queen to drink. Putting his mouth around the glass top, taking a full swig then passing it to her without wiping the neck; watching her as she too swallowed, her lips sipping where his lips had just sipped. He would read her D. H. Lawrence and verses from the Bible. She blushed as she recollected the urgency of his ideas, and of their lovemaking. To this day, she feels there's something abandoned, 'continental', about eating with one's fingers. 'Courting' is such a funny old word.

At that moment, standing in the half-cleaned sitting room of St Francis's Vicarage, afraid of what the next hours and days might bring, Deirdre realises that if it were possible to claw her way back in time on her hands and knees, she would. But 'the cataclysm has happened and...' How does that passage from *Lady Chatterley* end? '... We've got to live, no matter how many skies have fallen.'

She returns to her work, dismissing thoughts of amateurish sex and unforgotten letters to the furthest recesses of her mind. Heaving a heavy sigh, she grabs a bunch of dead lilies by its neck and stuffs it into the wastepaper basket to join the banana. The vase is her favourite. Blue Wedgwood, a silver wedding anniversary gift from Christopher. She knows perfectly well that their daughter-in-law, and not their son, chose it. But this makes her no less fond. Iolanthe is a good girl.

Deirdre sniffs at the liquid left in the bottom and wrinkles her nose at its rotten smell. Without further ceremony she carries the vase to the scullery, holding it at arm's length. She puts on the cold tap and leaves it running as she pours the vase's contents into the sink.

'Is that you in the kitchen?' Desmond calls from his study.

'Who else would it be?' she calls back.

'What time's lunch?'

She doesn't answer but stares out through the kitchen window at the lawn beyond. She recalls their son, playing outside when he was just a small boy, his little blond head bobbing in the sunshine. So precious. A bygone time of footballs in the flowerbeds, kites in the monkey puzzle, biscuits in the sandpit. The mixed feelings these memories evoke are more acute now than ever. They used to have lovely birthday tea parties on that terrace.

Her husband's head appears round the side of the kitchen door. 'Have you been chopping onions?'

'No. Just thinking.'

'Thinking what? Something sad?'

'It sounds silly, but I was just thinking that you never know when you're cutting the crusts off a Marmite sandwich for the last time.' She swallows hard, in an audible attempt to hide her misery.

Her husband takes her in his arms. 'Deirdre,' he says kindly, 'Christopher is a grown man. That's what children do. They grow up, spread their wings and fly away. No one could have asked for a better mother, but children are *God*'s possessions. Only on loan to their parents, remember. Not for keeps.'

These words of comfort, so tenderly spoken, hurt Deirdre more than her husband could ever know.

Half an hour before she's due to arrive at the vicarage, Jane turns in to the end of Atbara Avenue. Not wanting to be spotted loitering in the street, she chooses to wait in nearby Atbara Park. She enters through its iron gates and strolls down towards the duck pond. It's 3 o'clock. The end of the junior school day. The spring weather is mild and there are lots of people, mostly women and children in little packs, enjoying the open space and sunshine. Finding an empty bench, she sits down to take in the unfettered sounds of happiness coming from the boys and girls playing on the nearby swings.

This place, she supposes, must be where *she* pushed Peter out in his pram. He must have swung on those swings, slid down that slide. Jane smiles wryly. Perhaps Deirdre O'Reilly even sat on this very bench, when she stopped to chat with the other 'mothers'?

These evocations unsettle her. In fact, to her surprise, the butterflies of excitement which awoke her early that morning have disappeared. They've been replaced by a woozy sensation that feels less like anticipation and more like dread.

She cautions herself. Come on, Jane! Miss Blenkinsop has a brother to find.

Acting at once upon her inner rallying cry, she jumps to her feet and marches herself directly to her appointment.

Deirdre has locked herself in the bathroom. She turns on the taps as if drawing a bath, yet remains dressed. She closes the lid of the lavatory, sits down on its wooden seat and retrieves the letter from her apron pocket. She uses a flannel to wipe the steam from her bifocals, perches them on the end of her nose and begins to read.

Godalming, Surrey
March 1941

Didi,
Dreams come true! Douglas is alive! Separated from his patrol, wounded behind enemy lines, a blessed French family sheltered him till he recovered

and could find a way home. After all this time, he is safe and I am saved, for we are married! I wanted to let you know at once. Just a small registry do, but the knot is tied. You, of all people, know what this means to me. I so wish you could have been there, but naturally you are busy with baby.

Oh, Didi, you'll have to excuse my scrawl. My hand is shaking with joy as I write my next few lines. We are about to take a house. Not round here. In Kent. Dougie will decorate the nursery. I've chosen the colour. The pram is already bought. It's a brand-new one, too. No scrimping. War or no war, as man and wife, Dougie and I are in a position to be the parents we could not have been before. We are more than ready. Every day I remember how it felt to hold my own baby in my arms. I ACHE to feel that way again. Didi, be assured that our little one will want for nothing. I promise to be the best mother I can be. I SWEAR it.

When can we meet? I can't wait to take my precious baby with me to a new home. Please telephone. I'll come to Munster H. whenever you say… just say…
Your affectionate and eternally beholden friend,
Cat Sweeting (Mrs!)

When Jane reaches the vicarage, she finds the Reverend O'Reilly waiting for her at the gate. He greets her with the same air of earnest disorientation he displayed at their first meeting, taking the time to point out various flowering shrubs, cracks in the crazy paving, and a parade of tulips and daffodils with which he seems especially pleased, as he slowly steers her up the sunny garden path, over the threshold and into the relative gloom of the capacious interior. Relieving her of her hat and coat but not her folder, he ushers her into the sitting room, instead of his study where they met just two days earlier. Slightly disconcerted by so much informality, Jane stands in awkward silence while he goes in search of his wife.

She sees that a table has been set out with cups, saucers and a plate of buttered malt loaf. A fat, long-haired cat sits at the foot of the table, licking its paw.

'Looks like just you and me for tea, puss-puss,' she whispers, offering her outstretched hand. The creature ignores this gesture of solidarity. It gives first her, and then the buttery malt loaf, an inscrutable stare, before it saunters out of the room.

Jane is just beginning to wonder whether her hosts have likewise taken their opportunity to tiptoe out of the back door rather than answer any difficult questions about stolen babies, when the vicar returns. The woman at his side is tall and full-figured. Handsome rather than homely, she has an open, intelligent face and very untidy hair. All at once the niggling doubts Jane was still harbouring evaporate. Much to her private satisfaction it's plain that Deirdre O'Reilly is indeed the Deirdre O captured in the photos, snapped so many years ago.

'Miss Blenkinsop,' the vicar says proudly, 'please allow me to introduce my better half, Deirdre.' Turning to his wife, he adds, 'This, of course, is Miss Blenkinsop.'

Deirdre O'Reilly grabs her hand and shakes it warmly. 'I do apologise for keeping you waiting. I was in the kitchen and I didn't hear you arrive. Please take a seat — no need to stand on ceremony here.'

Jane complies, obediently making herself as comfortable as the overworked springs of a small wingback chair will allow. Deirdre O'Reilly drops down into the loose-covered depths of an even saggier sofa on the opposite side of the room.

Once Jane has settled herself, the vicar enquires most pointedly if her journey from *Tottenham* was a smooth one. As he does so, he looks towards his wife, apparently expecting some kind of retort. He gets none. Mrs O'Reilly remains unmoved. Although she continues to smile politely, and has gushed such a hearty welcome, Jane can see the woman has been crying.

'You have a lovely home,' says Jane brightly. 'You must have a gem of a cleaner.'

'I do indeed,' smiles the reverend, again looking towards his wife. Again, he gets no reaction. Jane glimpses a small but unmistakable flicker of concern appear on his face. As if responding to a silent cue, he crosses the room to join his wife on the sofa. When he sits down, she takes his hand. Jane notices how firmly Mrs O'Reilly clutches his fingers, and how firmly he clutches hers. The room falls quiet.

Deciding her time has come to bite the bullet, Jane is the first to speak again. 'Mrs O'Reilly, I expect your husband has explained that I'm investigating a missing person's case. It dates back to the war. A baby, born at Munster House, was taken from its mother when no more than a few weeks old.'

'Yes, Desmond did tell me all that,' she replies evenly. Jane spots the vicar's grip on his wife's hand tighten.

Jane continues. 'The reason why I've been so desperate…' She quickly corrects herself. '… I mean, *keen* to speak with you personally, is that I believe you have, shall we say, intimate knowledge of this baby and can tell me more about what happened. You must by now realise I'm talking about the missing infant Peter Smith.'

'Peter Smith?' repeats Deirdre O'Reilly. 'You're here about *Peter Smith*?' There's a nuance in her voice, which sounds like… what? Surprise? Or is it closer to relief?

'Why didn't you say so on Saturday?' asks the reverend.

Before Jane has a chance to reply, his wife cuts in. 'Yes, well, yes. Of *course* you're here to talk about Peter. And you're quite right, I did know him, and his mother. As a matter of fact,' she goes on, looking towards her husband as if seeking reassurance, 'I was with her on the day he was born.'

'My wife was a midwife prior to our marriage.'

At this qualification, Deirdre casts her husband another sideways glance, but doesn't contradict him.

'I see, Reverend. Thank you.'

The vicar goes on, 'The thing is, Peter isn't missing—'

'Would you like to see a picture of Peter?' interrupts his wife.

'Very much!' exclaims Jane, surprised by such a forthcoming offer. She's also surprised the reverend so freely admits that he knows Peter's current whereabouts. She expected to fight far harder to unearth the truth.

Mrs O'Reilly gestures towards a mahogany writing desk in the corner of the room. 'Desmond, would you fetch me my locket? It's in the top drawer of my bureau.'

He readily obeys, passing his wife a little silver pendant on a long silver chain. Without looking at it, she passes it straight to Jane.

Jane pops the locket open. In one side is a photograph of a newborn baby, his face screwed up like a walnut, eyes tight shut; in the other side is a lock of gingery brown hair. She's disappointed. 'This is lovely, but I would much rather see a picture of Peter as he is now.'

The vicar stares at her, uncomprehending. Deirdre O'Reilly appears equally baffled. 'As he is now?' she repeats slowly. 'I'm sorry, Miss Blenkinsop, but I really don't follow. And as you can see, neither does my husband.'

'I mean snaps of Peter as an adult.' Jane tries not to let her frustration show in her voice. 'You must have plenty of them. Albums and albums of him as he is now, and when he was growing up. Schoolboy, teenager—'

Mrs O'Reilly cuts her short. 'I'm afraid I must stop you there. I am very sorry to have to tell you, but Peter isn't *missing*. He's dead. He died in infancy. At Munster House. I thought you would know that,' she adds, 'in your *official* capacity.'

Jane almost blushes, but aware of the need to keep her composure, she manages to remain calm. 'According to my own extensive research, although I do have Peter's birth records safely filed, accounts of his death were…' She hesitates. 'Sorry, *are* "anecdotal".'

'Miss Blenkinsop,' says the vicar, 'whatever you may have heard to the contrary, I can assure you Peter is certainly dead. I could have told you that at our first meeting and saved you the trouble of making a return visit to speak to my wife and—'

Again, his wife interrupts him. Much more forcefully than

before. 'It's all right, Desmond. I'm happy to talk to Miss Blenkinsop if it helps her case.'

Although it's clear the reverend is reluctant for the conversation to go any further, he resettles himself in his seat. Deirdre O'Reilly turns to Jane. 'Would you like me to tell you *exactly* what happened to Peter?' she asks. She has a strange look in her eyes that makes Jane's heart rate rise still further.

'That would be great, Mrs O'Reilly. That's why I'm here, after all,' she replies, fighting to maintain her poise.

'Then tell it I shall. If I must, I must. But please, let me speak without interruption. This applies to both of you,' she adds, throwing a loaded look in her husband's direction. 'I think the unbroken facts would be best.'

Jane and the vicar nod in agreement.

'All right then. Bear with me while I take a moment to collect myself.' Deirdre O'Reilly leans back and closes her eyes. She presses her palms together, raising the tips of her fingers up until they sink into the soft underside of her chin. Her expression is solemn, her stance like that of a woman in silent prayer. Jane has the impression she's trying to summon her memories from the heavens, preparing the right words to give them shape and form. Is she planning to tell the truth, wonders Jane, or is she working out how to organise her lies?

Deirdre O'Reilly opens her eyes and clears her throat. 'Are you sitting comfortably?'

Jane and the vicar nod again.

'Then I shall begin: I hadn't been at Munster House very long when I first met Catherine. Such a lovely girl. So unspoiled.' Pausing for a moment, she looks sharply at Jane before continuing archly. 'Oh, I know what you may think, Miss Blenkinsop. I can spot a raised eyebrow from a hundred paces. You may think that by their very circumstances, the residents of Munster House were as spoiled and soiled as could be. But that's simply not true. Catherine "Smith", as she was in those days, was a sweet, innocent girl. I was immediately drawn to her. When she talked about her life, I instantly recognised the difficulties she'd had growing up.

'Now, you mustn't misunderstand me. Catherine and I both came from good families. Homes that were, in many ways, very happy. But they were strict. There was a right way and a wrong way of doing things, which never could be questioned, even during a war. When Catherine's fiancé, Douglas, went missing in action, there was no way keeping his child was an option. As a mother now, I find it hard to understand the amount of importance anyone can place on appearances... Even the most loving mother in the world.'

She pauses once more and looks across the room. Jane follows her gaze and sees that it falls upon a framed portrait of a stern-looking woman, not dissimilar to Deirdre O'Reilly. Delicate watercolour brushstrokes have failed to dilute the subject's distinctly judgemental air. The features are strong. Prominent, even. Jane catches herself reaching up to touch her own nose.

Deirdre O'Reilly returns to her tale. 'Poor Catherine. In her efforts to hide her condition from her family, she'd all but starved herself. Of course, while her arms and legs reduced to scarcely more than skin and bone, her middle grew ripe enough for all to see. And once her parents realised she was expecting a baby, they sent her away. It was they who dropped her off at the steps of Munster House as unceremoniously as if they were delivering coal. They didn't abandon her, but they made it clear she'd only be welcomed home if she returned empty-handed. That was the respectable way for her to behave.' She lets out a long, sad sigh. 'All those babies... swept under the carpet like dust.

'As I'm sure you are aware, Peter was born in the early hours of New Year's Eve. My friend had a very difficult time with her labour. It was long and complicated. Because she hadn't been looked after in those first months of pregnancy, she had no strength. She endured contractions for almost two days before she finally pushed him out. I was with her the whole time. How she struggled to bring that child into the world, and how she struggled to keep him here. He was so tiny.' Tears well in the woman's eyes. 'Forgive me becoming so emotional. There's something about the pain of losing a baby… it never fades with time.'

'That I know *is* true,' says Jane.

'No interruptions, remember?' Deirdre O'Reilly sniffs. 'Well, the next few weeks were terrible. Such a mixture of joy and sadness. Peter was a beautiful little thing, but he never looked right. He never *was* right. When he first arrived, the doctors didn't expect him to last twenty-four hours. But against all the odds, somehow, he did.' A broad smile lights up Deirdre O'Reilly's face. 'Oh, Catherine and I were so happy. We thought her baby had fought his battle and won. That he would live…' Her voice trails away, as if she's lost in bitter-sweet memories. The smile fades. 'But then the doctors came and spoke to Catherine. "Yes," they said, "Peter might live." But he'd never walk, or talk, or see.

'This news hit Catherine like a ton of bricks. She collapsed to the floor. Beside herself with grief, she couldn't bring herself to believe that so many afflictions could be meted out upon her brave little son.

'I helped Catherine as much as I could, but every day, Peter seemed to slip a bit further from her. He wouldn't suckle. Day and night she tried, but it was no use. How it pained me to watch them suffer, Catherine and her beautiful, blameless child.

'On his last night, totally exhausted, she placed him into my arms. "Didi," she said, "take him while I sleep. If I can rest, I'll have the strength to feed him better." So, as Catherine slept in her bed, I sat beside her, cradling her baby… I was the last to hold her baby…'

Suddenly, Deirdre O'Reilly closes her eyes again. Smiling a strange, faraway smile, she draws her arms firmly into her chest, perhaps imagining she's once again holding that fragile scrap of life to her bosom in a final, tight embrace. For a full minute she holds this pose, rocking, squeezing the memory with all her might lest it should slip away. Jane and the vicar say nothing, watching, afraid to rouse her.

Very quietly, still smiling, she begins to hum. It's a lullaby.

'Go to sleep,
'Go to sleep,
'Go to sleep… My dear baby.
'Lullaby,
'And goodnight,
'Bright angels beside you abide…'

All at once, Deirdre O'Reilly's eyes snap open and she looks directly at Jane. Her glare is penetrating, as if she means to burn her next sentences into her listener's core. 'Miss Blenkinsop, if the strength of Catherine Smith's love for her son could have kept him alive, Peter would still be with us to this day. But the next morning, when she awoke, he was cold in my arms. Taken from us…'

On hearing these last three words, so often muttered by her heartbroken mother, a shiver passes down Jane's spine. She barely manages to hold her tongue.

Deirdre straightens up. Pulling herself together, she heaves a heavy sigh. 'It was terribly sad. Just before Catherine went home, we had a little funeral for him, in the grounds of Munster House. She planted snowdrops on his grave.' She adds, wistfully, 'They're at their best in January, you know.'

Jane can contain herself no longer. 'Dear God in Heaven, never mind about blasted snowdrops!'

'Miss Blenkinsop!' cries the vicar. 'I must ask you to moderate your language.'

Jane's incredulous. 'You're asking me to believe that Catherine Smith had a baby boy. A real, living, breathing baby boy. And then, one night, he died. So, just like that, he was stuffed in the ground as if he was never here at all, and his mother skipped off home? End of?'

'I can tell this is hard for you to hear!' retorts Deirdre O'Reilly, emotion once again rising in her voice. 'But in those days, and in that place, life was not always valued as it should have been; not seen as the priceless gift it is, whatever form it takes. When babies died, sometimes the staff thought it was for the best. That's what they thought when Peter died. I know they did. What future did he have? When prospective adoptive parents visited the home – came to choose a baby from so many little outcasts lined up like stray puppies – who would have wanted Peter? He had so many needs, so many problems, he had to struggle for every breath he took.'

The tears Deirdre O'Reilly had been fighting to keep at bay are now taking hold. She swipes them away with the backs of her hands, but sobs snag at her words as she continues. 'And what about my friend Catherine? What of *her* future? She couldn't take Peter home. Her parents had made that more than clear. But neither would she ever have left him behind. Not ever. When Peter died, God forgive me, *I* too believed it was for the best. But,' she adds angrily, 'don't you think for one moment that Catherine Smith, or I, didn't value Peter, or didn't love him. Because we did. His death left scars on both of us that could never heal. Please forgive me,' she gulps, 'I didn't mean to come so unravelled. Not after all these years. Perhaps I'd better go and wash my face.'

The woman lurches out of the room, her face buried in her husband's handkerchief. The reverend rises to follow, but she waves him away, closing the door behind her.

At first, neither Jane nor the vicar speak. Jane is perplexed. When Deirdre O'Reilly had begun to talk, Jane was convinced she was telling the truth. Her descriptions of how she and Catherine had met at Munster House, the circumstances of Catherine's arrival, Peter's birth – all these concur with what Jane herself already knew. What Jane didn't expect was the story about Peter's death. Not that she believes it. After all, she has the photographs to prove he was handed over to Deirdre O, alive and kicking. But to hear such a vivid account was unsettling. What a graphic lie, delivered with a truly Oscar-winning show of grief. She hardly knows what to make of it.

Clearly displeased, the vicar strides across the room, selects a pipe from its rack and fills it with a generous pinch of tobacco. Striking a match so brusquely that its head breaks off, he mutters a less than saintly word and thrusts the unlit pipe into his top pocket. He sinks back into the sofa before addressing her.

'I trust you are satisfied, Miss Blenkinsop. If your mission was to thoroughly upset my wife, you have succeeded.'

Jane chooses to ignore this rebuke. 'Sometimes it's necessary to be tenacious in order to get the whole truth.'

'The whole truth?' he echoes. 'Forgive me for asking, Miss Blenkinsop. I'm sure you must have told me, but would you be so good as to remind me who sent you? I neglected to write it down when we first met.'

'I'm a *private* investigator, Reverend. I'm not prepared to reveal my client's name.'

'Well, it seems you hold the entire deck. My wife must reveal everything, her aces *and* her knaves, while you may play your cards as close to your chest as you please. Perhaps you can at least explain why your mysterious client is so interested in the unfortunate Peter Smith?'

'As I said, they believe him to be missing,' she replies curtly. 'They wish to find him.'

'Indeed. And now that you've spoken to Deirdre and myself, you can have no doubt he's dead. If you wish, I can take you to Peter's grave, if that would bring your client closure. Whatever the case, it seems to me that your investigation has reached its natural conclusion.'

'So, if I understand your wife correctly,' says Jane, without acknowledging his suggestion, 'Peter Smith died when he was just a few weeks old.'

'Three weeks and four days, to be exact.'

'He was never adopted? Or given away?'

'Adopted? No. Why would you say such a thing?'

Before Jane has a chance to answer, Deirdre O'Reilly returns. She bursts back into the room, apparently re-galvanised, with a laden tray and bloodshot eyes. 'Good strong tea, that's what we need,' she blusters, resting teapot, milk jug and sugar bowl beside the malt loaf.

'Excellent!' exclaims the vicar with obviously strained enthusiasm. 'You sit down, Deirdre. *I* shall be Mother.'

Jane shifts in her chair.

Deirdre O'Reilly must have sensed her discomfort. 'Miss Blenkinsop. You clearly have more on your mind. If you have anything to say, I do wish you'd spit it out.'

The vicar coughs, loudly, but Jane will not be put off. 'Okay then,' she says defiantly. 'I will. I've listened to everything you've had to say, Mrs O'Reilly, and frankly, I'm far from satisfied. You've put forward such a pick-and-mix of fiction and fact, it's hard to know where the truth ends and the lies begin. I believe you all right, when you say that you and Catherine both loved Peter. I think you *adored* him. And I believe you when you say Catherine would never have given him up. But I don't believe Peter died. I think Peter was "taken".' Her hand shakes with indignation as she points an accusatory finger straight at Deirdre O'Reilly. 'I think he was taken by *you*!'

Jane's actions have an instant and dramatic effect on their target. The blood drains from Deirdre O'Reilly's face. She visibly recoils.

The vicar jumps to his feet. 'Young lady, may I say that your tone is both highly unprofessional and extremely offensive. I cannot think your client would expect you to speak to people in that manner. I don't know what you've been told, or by whom, but my wife is a woman of great integrity. She does *not* lie.'

'Well, maybe not,' Jane flushes scarlet, 'but even the most honest people on the planet can be guilty of withholding aspects of the whole truth.'

'Balderdash! That counts as lying too.'

'Please, both of you. Stop this unpleasantness at once!' cries Deirdre O'Reilly. 'It is neither necessary nor civilised.'

'Yes. Quite right,' blusters the vicar, straightening his tie, pulling himself to order. 'It was wrong of me to raise my voice. But where my wife is concerned,' he splutters, 'I will not brook any slurs on her decency.'

Jane feels herself flush even deeper, like a scolded child.

The vicar returns to his seat, pulling a series of grimaces until he finally achieves a facial expression more fitting for a man of the Church.

Deirdre O'Reilly turns to Jane. 'Miss Blenkinsop,' she asks calmly, 'may I ask what reason you have to doubt what I'm saying?'

Jane swallows. This is her big moment. The dénouement when she will expose Deirdre O for the woman she is. She withdraws the manila folder from her briefcase, whips out the photographs and smacks them down on the coffee table. 'This reason!' she exclaims triumphantly.

The teacups rattle in their saucers but, for a few seconds, neither the vicar nor his wife give any discernible reaction. It's Reverend O'Reilly who eventually reaches forward and picks up the pictures. He inspects each in turn, with no more of a sense of urgency than if he were looking at a series of holiday snaps.

'Go on!' challenges Jane fiercely. 'Tell me what you see!'

'I see my wife as a younger woman, looking as fine then as she does now, I might add. I see another lady, whom I surmise is a resident of Munster House, as I'm quite sure that is where these shots were taken,' he goes on, apparently nonplussed. 'And each of the ladies takes a turn at fussing over what appears to be a babe in arms. I see absolutely nothing mysterious about—'

The vicar stops abruptly. Jane hears him gulp. As he passes the photographs to his wife, Jane sees them exchange glances. The man's eyes are laden with sympathy, imploring even. The look in the woman's eyes, when she too examines the photos, is more like terror. As if she's seen a ghost. 'Where did she get these, Desmond?' she stammers. 'Why does *she* have *these*?'

The vicar puts a protective arm about his wife's shoulders. 'Deirdre, there's no need for you to continue this conversation.

Miss Blenkinsop came to find out about Peter Smith, nothing else. In my view you've set her completely straight on that matter. Whether or not she chooses to believe you, you couldn't have been more frank.'

'But, Desmond? I've come this far…'

'It's up to you, of course,' he sighs. 'You must do whatever you think best.'

Deirdre O'Reilly pulls a small sheet of paper from her cardigan pocket and pushes it into Jane's hand. 'Before I continue, I think you should read this.'

Jane unfolds the letter and quickly reads its brief contents. The hope-filled words of her mother, newly wed, un-disgraced and ready to be the parent *she could not be before*, and her beseeching tone as she describes how she *aches* to hold Peter again, shake her very foundations. Jane feels jubilant. And vindicated. At last she has the confirmation she needed that her mother Catherine left her baby with Deirdre O. More than that, here's written proof that she tried to reclaim him and bring him to her marital home. 'You never made any appointment with Catherine Smith, did you, Mrs O'Reilly? Because by the time she wrote this, you and Peter were long gone. Busy playing happy families as a vicar's wife with your lovely new addition.'

Deirdre O'Reilly stares blankly at Jane. When she finally answers, her voice is low, her tone resigned. 'I assure you I *did* meet Catherine again. At Munster House, on the twenty-second of March 1941. A Saturday. That's when these pictures were taken. But you've misunderstood the letter. When Catherine Sweeting penned it, she wasn't writing about Peter. Peter was dead. She was writing about *my* baby. The rendezvous she was so eager to arrange was the day on which I would hand *my* baby over to *her*. The day she, in return, gifted me her most treasured memento. Her locket. It's true I was a midwife before my marriage, and when I was at Munster House, I did what I could to help. There was a war on. I even wore my uniform. Hung it up when it got too tight; put it straight back on again once I was fit to resume work. But I was never officially employed there, in spite of what my husband gallantly implied. Just like Catherine, I lived there. As the Luftwaffe blitzed Coventry, Miss Deirdre Ormeroid was sent to Munster House in disgrace. I gave birth not long after Peter died. Re-examine the letter, Miss Blenkinsop. I'm sure you'll interpret it differently on second reading.'

Jane is stunned. She looks back at the note, trying to fathom its true meaning, but the words just seem to swim about on the paper. 'Why would you do such a thing?' she stammers. 'Give away your child? Why would Catherine take him?'

'Please don't judge me, or Catherine too harshly, Miss Blenkinsop. What were my options? I didn't believe I would ever be allowed to keep my baby. Neither did Catherine. But we dared to share a dream. If *I* couldn't raise my child, perhaps, one day, in a kinder universe, *she* could, rather than some stranger I'd never met. Catherine and I went through so much together; there was no person I trusted more. We didn't really think that day would come, though. As I said, it was our dream. But then the miracle happened. Not long after she left Munster House. As the letter explains, Peter's father came back from the dead and, like a fairy tale, he and Catherine were married. They'd take my baby… give it a loving home…' Deirdre O'Reilly pauses and picks up one of the photographs. The one of herself kissing the baby. 'So, you were right when you said the photos capture the moment a mother held her precious… precious… child for the last time before she handed it over to another woman. You just got the mothers the wrong way around. And of course, my baby was a girl.'

'You had a baby *girl*?' Jane asks thickly, the enormity of these revelations hitting her like a steamroller. 'A *daughter* who was raised by Catherine Sweeting?'

Deirdre O'Reilly at last succumbs to her distress. 'I didn't know I'd meet Desmond,' she wails. 'I didn't know… I didn't know…'

'Of course not, my love. You did nothing wrong.'

'I honestly believed I was doing the right thing. I was sparing my family...' She breaks free from her husband's arms and staggers out of the room. This time she doesn't return.

Jane scarcely knows how she managed to get home. The vicar had to help her into a taxi. Just as she was leaving, he pressed an envelope into her hand. He was most insistent that she should take it.

'Here, Miss Blenkinsop. I think this should clear things up once and for all. It's Peter Smith's death certificate.'

'You've had this all along?' Her voice was faltering.

'My wife has. Not that I've read it, but at the risk of repeating myself, if you'd told me at our first meeting you were looking for Peter Smith, I could've set you straight at once.'

'But why do you, or rather your wife, have Peter's death certificate? Why not his family? Why not my... my *client*?'

'I assume Deirdre simply held it in safekeeping for her friend, to spare Catherine the pain of seeing it. Quite frankly, you've subjected my wife to more than enough questions, so let's leave it at that. Whatever her reasons, I hardly think they matter now. You take the damnable certificate. File it in your records. Case closed.'

She stuffed the envelope into her manila folder, mumbled her thanks, and collapsed into the back seat of the cab. It was all she could do not to vomit as it bore her away.

When Deirdre eventually comes downstairs, she finds her husband in the sitting room, in repose by the fireside.

'Did Miss Blenkinsop get off all right?' she asks gently, placing her hand on his shoulder.

'Yes. You mustn't worry about her. Come and sit with me.' He pats the cushion beside him on the sofa. 'You look done in.'

Deirdre complies. She rests her head against his. 'I'm sorry I crawled off like that. I should have been there when you saw her out.'

'Saw her *off*, more like,' rejoins the vicar. 'She was a dogged young person, wasn't she? Very persistent in her beliefs, in spite of the facts before her. Such determination is a quality I usually admire in a woman, but she really was quite something. Raking up all that stuff about… well, things that couldn't possibly have had any relevance to her case. I believe even *she* realised she'd gone too far in the end. She was ashen when she left. I had to help her into a taxi.'

Deirdre nuzzles in a bit further. 'Why *did* you marry me, Desmond? After you knew I'd had another man's child. Worse than that. Given her away?'

'Come on, now. I know a true gem when I see one. I've never regretted it for one moment. One of the things I treasure most in our marriage is that we have no secrets from one another. Besides, I can't think of anything you could ever do, or have ever done in the past,' he pauses to plant a kiss on her forehead, 'that would change my mind. Miss Blenkinsop got what she came for. She's gone back to her office or wherever she came from. End of.'

'Yes, darling,' mumbles Deirdre quietly. 'End of.'

Jane is still shaking when she reaches the door of her flat. She stumbles inside and immediately rings Bruce. While she waits for him to arrive, she sits on the kitchen floor, swigging cooking sherry straight from the bottle.

She never goes back to the vicarage, to see her mother. She makes no further contact, and never tells the O'Reillys who she is. She does visit Munster House, though. Now a care home for the elderly, the staff are kind enough to show her to the little grave. It's January and the snowdrops are out.

Only years later, when she and Bruce and their two small children are moving house, does she re-open the manila folder. That's when she looks at the death certificate for the first time.

Cause of Death: Asphyxiation

8

The Final Curtain

From a distance, it's easy to mistake Micky Milestone for a new resident of Atbara Avenue. Given the amount of time he's been spending there recently, it's a perfectly reasonable assumption. And it's true he's renting locally, if not on the avenue itself. He's taken a little bedsit on the high street. The one above the baker's. It's nothing fancy: a dingy room, with a pull-out bed, and a stove and sink in the corner, tucked away behind a shabby curtain. Its bathroom is tiny, with an ancient pink rubber shower attachment for the taps. The windowsill is barely broad enough to take a pot of geraniums. All in all, a bit of a hole, although he's stayed in much worse. But it doesn't really matter to him. He simply needs a place to lay his head and a good view of passing game. So now that he's ditched the geraniums, the bedsit, with its grubby window facing the busiest parade of shops, serves its purpose well enough. Anyway, it's only a short-term thing, just while money's tight. Just while he needs to be in the area. Just while he's being Micky Milestone. Last month, he was Matty Black; the month before that, Sir St John Barclay-Pratt. And next month? Well, he hasn't decided yet. It depends how it goes. If he does hang around a bit longer, though, he's not too sure he'll stick with the Micky Milestone moniker. He doesn't feel he looks like a 'Micky'. Even with his blond toupee and matching moustache, the name smacks as too young for a man in his forties. And he's slightly worried he's used 'Milestone' once before. But he's not losing any sleep over it. A better handle will no doubt come to him when the moment's right.

Old Mrs Dollimore shuffles out of Woolworths, dragging her canvas shopping trolley behind her. Managing that, her handbag, her sticks and the jostling crowds on the busy high street is almost too much for her. As is her wont, she showers passers-by with vitriolic, *sotto voce* curses. These go unheard. When her useless lump of a daughter was still around, Muriel seldom had to venture any further than the corner shop, but now Pauline isn't available to run errands, she has to make regular trips to the butcher's and the baker's – *'it'll be the bloody candlestick maker's next'* – to pick up the bits and pieces she needs to keep herself going. Not only is this exhausting, it's playing havoc with her bunions. She's nudged this way and that by faceless shoppers intent on making her progress even slower and more tiresome than it already is. Today it almost feels as if people have been bumping into her on purpose.

Even though her larder's stocks are running dangerously low, Muriel decides to abandon her plan to visit the grocer's. It's time to call it quits. If she can carve a reasonably clear corridor through the throng, she may just make it home for her favourite TV show. She takes her usual route, bellyaching away to herself as she picks her way back to calmer waters. As she passes the vicarage garden, Deirdre O'Reilly, who's hacking at a rose bush, signals with a merry wave. Muriel completely ignores her and ploughs on. It's a relief when she at last staggers over her own threshold.

She locks up behind her, making sure to keep the outside world firmly out, before sitting down heavily on a hall chair. With a lot of effort, she unlaces her shoes, kicking them to one side. Then she tugs off her headscarf and her gloves, which she stuffs into the top of her handbag. Finally, she climbs out of her tweed coat, but when she reaches up to hang it on the nearest peg, something about it strikes her as odd. It lacks weight. The usual bulge in its right-hand pocket is missing. A quick rummage confirms her fears. Her *sodding* purse is gone. She flops back onto the chair and mentally retraces her steps. What did she buy? A pound of tripe at the butcher's, a packet of Epsom salts at the chemist's, two ounces of wine gums in Woollies… Yes! That was it! The last place she spent any money was at the pick-and-mix counter. She must have left it there. Spitting expletives, Muriel begins the arduous process of re-cladding herself in her outdoor clothes to set off back to the high street.

She's interrupted by a loud knock at her front door.

If that's the vicar's wife come to rattle my cage, she can piss off.

Although Micky Milestone has had Muriel Grace Dollimore, OCCUPATION: *singer (retired)*, under surveillance for a while, this is about to be their primary encounter. He's prepared for this moment, having rehearsed it several times, given that first impressions are so important. She hasn't answered his initial knock (he's found people often don't), but he knows she's in. He can hear her shuffling about inside. Besides, he followed her home. He straightens his back, smooths down his hair and, just for luck, gives his gold cufflinks (recently acquired by Matty Black) a little rub. He knocks again. The sounds change. She's moving towards the door. He adjusts his Balliol College tie (courtesy of a charity shop), tweaks his makeshift buttonhole (freshly appropriated from the vicarage offcuts), and slides his best smile into place – one broad enough to suggest he has nothing to hide, but tight enough not to let any insincerity leak out. With a rattle and a clank, the front door opens just as much as its security chain will allow, and the face of his latest target appears before him.

'I am very sorry to disturb you, madam, but is this Number Seventeen?'

The old lady mutters something he doesn't quite catch.

'Well in that case,' he continues, just as if she'd confirmed the address, 'do I have the pleasure of meeting Mrs Muriel Dollimore?' He offers his outstretched hand.

The old woman recoils, muttering something else.

'Please don't be alarmed,' he says quickly, before she has time to slam the door in his face. 'I just wanted to return a possession to its rightful owner, and I believe that must be you.' He reaches inside his breast pocket and withdraws a fat leather purse. As he passes it towards her she snatches it away, immediately popping it open to examine the contents. While she probes around in its various creases, she casts him nasty, accusatory glances.

He continues to smile his best smile. 'You are very wise to check as you are doing. Who knows *what* type could have had hold of your purse before I recovered it. One can't be too careful. Please, reassure me. Is all in order?'

'Where did you find it?' she snaps, ignoring his question.

'I was getting out of a taxi, on the high street – on the way to an appointment with my business associate, as it happens – when I spotted it lying on the pavement. So I made my excuses to Bernard. "Bernie," I said, "my accounts will just have to wait. The good lady to whom this belongs will no doubt have become aware of her loss and started to fret. I must return it to her forthwith." And without further ado, I beat a path directly to your door.'

'How did you know where I live? Or that it's *my* purse?' Her wariness seems to be mounting.

'Luckily for me,' he says, holding out a small, blue, very dog-eared slip of card, 'I came across this tucked in the lining.'

'Give me that!' She seizes it out of his hand. 'How dare you go through my things!'

'I assure you it was purely in my efforts to discover the purse's ownership that I ventured to look inside it. Although I do confess, when I found your old National Registration ID, it brought a smile to my face. My own dad still carries his, you see. I'm forever teasing him about it. "Dad," I say, "we're not at war now." And he comes back at me, quick as you like, "Mark my words, Son, it's always handy to know *exactly* who's who."'

'Well,' Mrs Dollimore grumbles, 'don't be thinking I'll be giving you any kind of reward.'

Although she still looks defiantly ungrateful, his practised ear detects a very slight softening in her tone. 'Oh, no, indeed. It's reward enough for me to know you've not been robbed blind.' He risks cranking up his smile one notch wider before continuing. 'I hope you don't mind me mentioning this, but I couldn't help noticing from the card that you used to be on the stage.' He makes sure she can't miss the calculated note of admiration in his voice. 'Of course, now that I meet you in person, that makes perfect sense. Please don't think me impertinent, but you have a certain *presence*. No,' he corrects himself, 'an *aura*, about you, Mrs Dollimore, which is quite unmistakable. That's another thing Dad likes to say: "True stars never lose their shine."'

'Does he now?' she whispers. Muriel Dollimore visibly relaxes, and the blush fighting to show itself on her powder-caked cheek tells Micky Milestone everything else he needs to know. He has her exactly where he wants her.

'Well,' he says, with an air of finality, 'I have troubled you long enough. Lovely as this has been, I must go and find Bernard. I bid you good day.' He gives her a short, sharp, closing bow and makes to leave.

'No, wait!' The old woman shuts the door, removes the chain, then opens it wide. 'Won't you come in?'

'Alas, commitments prevent me from lingering.'

'I've got a home-baked batch of macaroons.'

'Well, that certainly sounds tempting, but I promised Bernard lunch. My treat. I've booked my usual table at the Café Royale. I hate to let a pal down.'

'Another time, then?'

'Perhaps. Really, madam, you mustn't feel under any obligation to—'

'I'll dig out pictures of me on stage. I have plenty.'

'Now that *is* an offer I find very hard to refuse.' He makes a show of hesitating, stroking his moustache as if weighing up the propriety of accepting her invitation. 'If you're *sure* I wouldn't be inconveniencing you?'

'Come on Saturday, three o'clock, and I'll get out my albums.' Her mouth splits into an unsightly grin.

'In that case, dear lady, you have well and truly twisted my arm. *Au revoir* until then.' He nods again and turns towards the garden gate.

'Just a minute, young man,' she calls after him. 'I don't know your name.'

For a fleeting second Micky Milestone is caught off guard. He just isn't comfortable with the 'Micky', or the 'Milestone', but he must say *something*, right now, or he'll lose her confidence. As he scrambles to find a better name, he glances down at his hastily assembled buttonhole. It's already beginning to wilt. Turning back to face Mrs Dollimore, he takes her hand and gives it a firm shake. 'It's Greenleaf, madam. Vernon Greenleaf Esquire at your service.'

'Do you know, Desmond,' ponders Deirdre O'Reilly, dolloping a ladleful of tepid kedgeree onto her husband's waiting lunch plate, 'I saw Muriel Dollimore on her way back from the shops this morning and she looked absolutely *done in*. Too tired to even throw me a wave, she was, poor old thing.'

'Well, she is getting on a bit,' says the vicar, pouring himself and then his wife a glass of cider. 'Perhaps she just didn't see you.'

'Oh, there's more to it than that,' she sighs. 'If you ask me, she's missing her daughter. What *was* Pauline thinking? I always thought she was so *brave*. And suicide is such a cowardly act. It's hard to believe she did it. Leaving her ancient mother to manage by herself.'

'You're being very harsh. Pauline must have had her reasons. Didn't her note say something about "being a burden"? And she and Muriel were rather cooped up together. What with having no husband and no children, sometimes I used to wonder whether Pauline was a bit short of friends,' he pontificates between mouthfuls, 'and loneliness can certainly affect a person's judgement.'

'Well it's Muriel who's all on her own now,' says Deirdre, lining up another fishbone on the side of her plate. 'I'll pop over later this week, just to see how she's coping.'

'Excellent thought. I'm sure she'll appreciate your visit.'

Rather than walk through the front of the baker's shop, Vernon Greenleaf slips round the back alley and climbs the metal fire escape to reach the first-floor bedsit. This may be a less salubrious entry route, but it is more discreet. He prefers to reveal the location of his billet on a strictly need-to-know basis. So far, that adds up to just himself and his landlady. And she thinks he's Professor Regis Gearheart, a crime writer doing undercover research for his next novel. 'All terribly hush-hush.'

As soon as he's inside, he fishes a used teacup out of the sink, gives it a cursory rinse under the cold tap, and pours himself a large Scotch. He takes a swig, tops up the cup and then flops down on his unmade bed. He lights a Woodbine. As he slowly exhales, he watches the curl of blue smoke wrap itself around the cobwebs dangling from the ceiling above. He lets out a little chuckle.

All in all, he's chuffed with his morning's work. He didn't expect to win over Muriel Dollimore – 'target MD' – so quickly. Given how frosty she was when she first opened the door, for a few minutes it looked as if he was going to have to make more than one house call before he got his invite to tea. But, there it was. She turned out to be a relatively easy nut to crack. Like his dad always used to say, 'Appeal to their vanity, that's how to do it. You mark my words, Son, doesn't matter how decrepit they look on the outside, on the inside they all think they're Ginger fucking Rogers.' Of course, what he saw on the ID card was a gift. Once he knew she'd been on stage, well, that was his ticket to the front row.

Vernon reflects on his newest soon-to-be conquest. Although MD is unusual in that he got a whiff of background info on her before his masterful lost-and-found scene with the pick-pocketed purse, in other respects she's pretty standard fare: a single woman, in this case doddery and old, with no obvious family or friends, who goes about her daily business with clockwork regularity; someone who is probably quite lonely, and hopefully quite rich. He's glad he chose her and not one of the other characters he's had in his sights of late. The fat blonde lady with her fluffy dog? Too risky. Looks like she's hooked up with a bloke, albeit some miserable-looking narcoleptic who never shifts from his chair. And the grieving mother of that dead teenager who was in all the papers? Too heartbroken to be worth a try. He suspects that particular poor, sad cow has sunk beyond even *his* extraordinary powers of persuasion. No, he's done the right thing, going for MD.

Now that they've met, he must home in – engineer ways to spend time with Muriel while taking care to make it look like it's her idea rather than his. He'll use each meeting to work on her, paying her compliments, offering to run errands. Occasionally he'll decline her invitations. Play a little hard to get. Softly, softly will he approach, until he's gained her full confidence. Then, when she's grown to trust him like her own son... *bam*! In for the kill. Not literally, of course. By 'kill', he means the big heist; milking her for the 'big one', whatever that may be. Sometimes it's jewellery, sometimes cash, occasionally a neat bit of cheque fraud. He sighs in anticipation. But he can't afford to be too pushy. Depending on the target, Vernon knows it can take weeks rather than days to melt down a person's guard. He also knows that the best way to achieve a swift finale is to have a good script and stick to it.

He drains his teacup and stubs out his fag end in the whisky dregs. As always, he'll follow his father's advice.

'Mark my words, Son, the best script is the one life dealt you. Stick to the truth whenever you can. That way you come across as credible. Then they'll believe you when you really have to lie.'

Good old Dad.

*

Over the next few days, Muriel Dollimore gets ready for her visitor. First things first, she sets about tidying her house. A task she finds irksome, but a necessary evil to make it presentable for such a charming new acquaintance. She limits her efforts to the only room he'll need to see, the front parlour. When she surveys the mess, she's relieved that Mr Greenleaf didn't accept her spur-of-the moment invite. Gritting her teeth, Muriel makes a start, but quickly discovers that the bending and stretching required to pick up and put away the wreckage she's generated since Pauline died is beyond her. After a little thought, a solution comes to her. She retrieves a collection of silken shawls from a trunk of *Dolores*'s stage costumes and simply drapes these over the worst of the clutter. As a finishing touch, she stacks a pile of photograph albums on the coffee table, ready for his perusal. Next, she rummages through her wardrobe, taking care to select the most glamorous outfit she can find. She plumps for a floor-length evening gown in emerald green velvet. The zip has burst, and the hem's a bit unravelled, but Mr Greenleaf is surely far too much of a gentleman to notice such things. She spends the rest of her time in the kitchen, baking macaroons and anything else she can think of to tempt his palate.

Vernon's preparations are of a less frenetic nature. He lies low. For his scheme to play out smoothly, it's vitally important he isn't spotted by the target between times. But he knows exactly how to keep out of her way. Since he's been shadowing MD, he's got her daily routine off pat:

1. *Up and about by 9 o'clock*
2. *Spends morning at home, hunkered down in front of TV*
3. *Midday: retires to kitchen at back of house*
4. *3 o'clock (give or take), emerges into outside world: sets off to the corner shop. Uses walking sticks. Usual purchases = cat food and Carnation milk*
5. *On return: more TV*

Additional notes (important):
1. *Choir practice once a week (Thurs evening): St Francis's*
2. *Every other Mon (late morning), goes to high street shops (NB = far limit of MD's stamping ground)*
3. *Visitors to the house v. rare (although NB vicar's wife is one to watch): callers generally sent packing*

Vernon passes his daylight hours in the bedsit. Smoking. Listening to the radio. Once the high street shops close for the night, he strolls out for a pie and a pint, confident MD has safely locked herself inside Number 17.

The venerable oak grandfather clock in the vicarage hallway creaks and groans, like an old man clearing his throat, before it chimes the quarter-hour. On Saturday afternoon, at two forty-seven, Deirdre O'Reilly sets off on her latest charitable mission. She has the sun on her face, a fair wind in her hair – and the cloak of matronly righteousness she puts on whenever she leaves the house is, as ever, a perfect fit.

She's halfway along Atbara Avenue when she becomes aware of someone, a man, walking close behind her. As she passes through the gate of Number 17, she's surprised when his footsteps follow hers… up Muriel Dollimore's short garden path. She turns, expecting to see one of her neighbours coming to call, and finds herself face to face with a complete stranger: a middle-aged man wearing a navy reefer jacket, a Liberty-print cravat and a disconcertingly broad smile.

'Good afternoon,' he says, doffing his fedora. 'The esteemed *Mrs* Reverend O'Reilly, if I'm not mistaken?'

'Why yes,' breathes Deirdre, flushing awkwardly. 'I'm very sorry, but I'm not sure I recall having met bef—'

'Oh, we've bumped into each other several times of late, madam,' he interrupts cheerfully, 'here and thereabouts. Vernon Greenleaf is the name.'

'How do you do, Mr Greenleaf,' says Deirdre, accepting his

handshake. She casts a keen eye over his face. 'You do seem familiar. Are you a churchgoer?'

'Not in this neck of the woods. I attend St Mary Abbots. In Kensington.'

'Then you must be acquainted with its vicar, Gideon Blythe? His wife Virginia and I were at midwifery school together.'

'Can't say we've been formally introduced.'

'Goodness,' laughs Deirdre, a trifle uncomfortably. 'Why wait for a formal introduction? Gideon is the last person to stand on ceremony.'

She waits for the man to speak again or offer some explanation as to his presence, but to her disappointment he remains silent, smiling away to himself, apparently appraising the small, untidy front garden. She grapples with a powerful urge to ask him what brings him to visit Mrs Dollimore, but she can't think of a way of framing such a question without appearing nosy. Perhaps all will become clear once they summon the old woman herself?

'Well, Mr Greenleaf,' she says, gesturing towards the front door, 'shall I knock first, or shall you?'

'Ladies first.'

Deirdre acts accordingly and steps back, making ready to wait before knocking a second time, as she usually does. She's shocked when almost at once the door flies open to reveal the mistress of the house, bedecked in an ill-fitting evening gown, complete with fox-fur stole and tiara.

If looks could kill, then the look on Muriel Dollimore's face would have felled Deirdre O'Reilly where she stood. Deirdre realises she's called at a bad time. 'I'm very sorry for rolling up unannounced, Muriel. I just got it into my head to pop over and say "hello", and perhaps trouble you for a chat, to see if you need any little jobs doing. But I see you're already expecting company.'

The old woman mutters something she doesn't quite catch.

'Please don't apologise, Muriel. The fault is entirely mine. I'll come back another time, when you're not otherwise occupied.'

The old woman mutters something else. Looking past Deirdre, she waves at the man, beckoning him to enter. As he strides across the sill of Number 17, once again he doffs his hat. 'A delight to see you again, Mrs O'Reilly. Good day.'

Before Deirdre has a chance to reply, Vernon Greenleaf closes the door as brusquely as Muriel Dollimore opened it, leaving her standing alone and bewildered on the doorstep.

Vernon Greenleaf is used to squalid living, but he's taken aback by the degree of grime in MD's house. The hall floor feels tacky underfoot, and there are piles of unread newspapers and unopened letters – or bank statements? Those could be useful – stacked up inside the front door. The house also smells bad. A rank, rotting-vegetable stench of blocked drains, mixed with the cloying scent of MD's perfume, almost makes him gag. This is all very gratifying. Very gratifying indeed. It confirms, without him having to ask, that she doesn't have any inconvenient charwoman or the like, checking up on things. And he loves a naturally chaotic target. The greater the muddle she's created for herself, the less likely she is to miss things should they suddenly disappear.

'Mrs Dollimore, I congratulate you on your lovely home.'

'Why thank you, Mr Greenleaf,' she simpers. 'Do come through to my front room. I think you'll like it even better in there.'

And, Vernon concedes to himself, the woman is not wrong. No sooner has he entered the parlour than he's confronted by a tableau of wanton pandemonium. Every surface is covered in dust. The carpet is all but buried beneath countless bits of paper, apparently cut from magazines. Two vases (mid-nineteenth-century, French, if he's not mistaken, nice examples), cringing ruefully on either side of the filthy fireplace, are filled with fusty arrangements of artificial flowers. The walls are decorated with photographic portraits. All are of the same woman (a younger incarnation of the target?), but each is in its own, ornately burnished frame. A handsome mantel clock (English, circa 1800, eight-day bell strike, mahogany case with curl veneers), stands neglected and unwound, its hands fixed at five forty-three. When his eyes land upon a yellowing collection of exquisitely carved chessmen (antique, ivory, Japanese) nestling in a mucky lead crystal fruit bowl, it's all Vernon can do to stop himself from rubbing his hands together in avaricious glee.

'Now, what can I get you?' asks MD, interrupting his train of thought.

'Oh, I'm sure whatever you're offering, madam, will be more than acceptable to me,' he replies, adjusting his cravat.

'Macaroons!' she exclaims triumphantly, bidding him to sit down and get 'comfy' while she goes to fetch the tea things.

He settles himself as best he can into an armchair, which is so *un*comfortable he suspects that underneath its silken throw must lurk a forgotten bag of knitting. As he awaits her return, he peels a sticky clipping – a recipe for plum duff dating back to 1954 – off the sole of his shoe. When he sees it's from *Good Housekeeping*, he suppresses a wry smile at the irony.

Vernon spends the rest of the afternoon at Number 17, enduring MD's scrapbooks from her days as *Dolores* ('Why, you've scarcely aged at all'), eating macaroons ('Delicious. Have you never thought of baking competitively?') and listening to her conceited anecdotes of life as a rising star ('I am in *awe*'). All the while, he makes sure to give the impression he's totally relaxed passing a couple of leisurely hours in her company. In reality, however, he's on tenterhooks, scrutinising everything she says and does: her tone of voice, her body language, the expression in her boggy old eyes. These are the meters of his progress. He flatters her whenever he can but is careful not to overdo it. He reads her reaction to each compliment he pays her. If he senses he's said too much, he pulls back a smidge. If she laps it up, he dribbles on another thin layer of niceties, until she's thoroughly basted.

'You take such an interest in the stage, young man,' MD says, eventually. 'It's lovely to talk to someone who properly appreciates it.'

'I have a confession,' says Vernon conspiratorially, leaning towards his target as if about to share an intimate secret. 'As it happens, acting is in my blood.'

'Aaaah,' sighs MD knowingly. 'I suspected as much.'

'Did you indeed?' laughs Vernon. 'What a very perceptive person you are! I can see there's no pulling the wool over your eyes. You see, my old dad was no stranger to the limelight in his younger days… may I possibly have a third macaroon?'

'Of course. Be my guest.'

Dismissing visions of the doubtlessly revolting state of MD's cooking facilities, he takes a large bite from yet another cake. He chews slowly, as if relishing every crumb.

'Do go on with your story about your father, Mr Greenleaf.'

'If it won't bore you.'

'Not at all.'

'Well, Dad was never *on* stage, mind you, but he's been very much behind it. Watching from the wings, scouting for talent.' Vernon sighs, warming to his subject. He allows his eyes to shift from the target, distracted by his own reminiscences. 'That's how he made his living at one time. He'd find stars in the rough, polish them up and help them on their way up the ladder. And when they found fame and fortune, well, a little of their shine would rub off in his direction. He's retired now, of course, but he's as sharp as he ever was. "Mark my words, Son," Dad says, "I can still recognise a diamond in a bucketful of baubles". Do you know, Mrs Dollimore,' he continues, brushing flakes of desiccated coconut from his moustache, 'I'd like to think I've inherited his eye for old-fashioned quality.' He hazards a wink at her.

To Vernon's disquiet, the gesture falls flat. He becomes aware that, while he was talking, the mood in the room has changed. MD is looking at him strangely. She's not frowning, exactly, but she's not smiling either. He shifts in his seat. Has he inadvertently revealed too much about himself and given the game away? He doesn't think so. Up until now he's told the truth… more or less… like Dad taught him. Apart from a couple of minor details, he's stuck to the script life dealt him.

'Dear lady, I see I've tired you out. Do forgive me. I shall take my leave.'

'No, don't go!'

Vernon is relieved that he doesn't seem to have fallen out of favour, but his instincts tell him to back off for today. 'I insist. I have been thinking only of myself and taken far too much of your time.'

'When will you be back? I have so many more pictures.'

'You've already been too kind.'

'What about next Saturday?'

'Next Saturday is out of the question. I'll be in Rome. Or is it Munich? I shall have to check my diary.'

'The following week, then? I'll make more macaroons.'

Decisively, he rises to his feet. 'Saturday after next it shall be!' He wags his finger teasingly. 'Once again I fear I am to fall victim to your delicious baking. However, perhaps I could telephone you to confirm what time?'

'Why yes, my number is nine, nine, two, three…'

Vernon fumbles in his pockets for a Biro but comes up empty-handed. 'May I trouble you for the wherewithal to jot this down?'

'Yes. Of course.' She nods towards a bureau. 'Help yourself from the top drawer.'

He does as he's bidden.

'Ready?'

'Yes thanks.'

'It's nine, nine, two, three, six, double-O.'

As MD sees him out, once again she appears distracted. He takes her hand and kisses it. 'It pains me to tear myself away.'

He's almost reached the gate when she calls after him. 'Where did you come by the name "Greenleaf"?'

The shock of this question, so direct and close to the mark, almost strikes him dumb. Now is the time to start lying. 'Why, it's my father's name, of course.'

As the old lady closes the front door behind him, he hears her mutter a few words that he doesn't quite catch.

The vicarage door slams shut with such force that Desmond O'Reilly's pipes rattle in their rack. The weight and speed of his wife's footsteps as they approach the sitting room confirm she's returned from her ministering in less than top form.

'Deirdre,' he hails her as she enters the room, 'how was your visit to Number Seventeen?'

'It wasn't!' she snaps, throwing herself into an armchair. 'I was surplus to requirements.'

Desmond puts down *The Innovative Churchman*, removes his glasses and gives her his full attention. 'How do you mean?'

'She had another visitor, so I was summarily dismissed.'

'By Muriel Dollimore? Surely not?'

'Of course not by *her*,' snorts Deirdre. 'Muriel was very apologetic about not being able to ask me in. But her visitor! Well there was definitely something off about him.'

'Why?' He straightens up, indignation rising in his chest. 'What did he say to you?'

'Nothing,' says Deirdre crossly. 'He was *horribly* polite.'

'What an ordeal for you,' he teases.

'Actually, I'd say he was polite *and* dismissive, all at the same time.'

'Who was this master of incongruity?'

'That's just it. I've not the faintest idea. Some spivvy man who rolled up on Muriel's doorstep, who said he knows me, but I'm as sure as I can be that I don't know *him*. And he'd clearly no idea who Ginny Blythe is.'

Desmond's even more confused. 'What has your old bridesmaid got to do with this?'

'Oh,' sighs Deirdre, her temper settling, 'nothing much. He

said he goes to St Mary's church. But the thing that struck me as *most* odd,' she adds thoughtfully, 'was how his feet didn't match his body.'

'Now you've really lost me,' he laughs.

'He looked respectable enough, I suppose. But the way he had on a smart jacket yet such tatty shoes – it just made me uneasy. My father always told me that a gentleman dresses from the ground up. If you have on good footwear, well polished, it speaks volumes about who you are as a person.'

'Really?' says Desmond, eyeing his own threadbare felt slippers. 'I thought "manners maketh man".'

'Well, they do help. But they're not the whole performance. And I'll tell you another thing, now I think of it: I recognised his cravat. It was just like the one Trixabella Cartwright gave you for Christmas.'

'A smashing cravat it is too.'

'Well I never liked it. That's why I gave it to the charity shop. And now this man is wearing it, or one remarkably like it, when he comes calling on Muriel.'

'Did he give any indication of how he knows her?'

'Not so much as a hint. But it was clear from everything he *didn't* say that he wanted Muriel all to himself.'

'So, you've been made to feel the gooseberry,' the vicar says kindly. 'What of it? If Mrs Dollimore has a wider circle of friends than we imagined, then I for one am grateful. Let's hope she won't seem so lonely.'

'Yes,' says Deirdre, uncertainly. 'Let's hope. Do you forgive me for donating your cravat?'

As soon as her visitor has gone, Muriel Dollimore retires to her bedroom. She opens her bedside cabinet and retrieves the well-thumbed copy of *Madame Bovary* hidden away at the back. With an unsteady hand, she carefully slides out a faded photograph from underneath its dust cover. It's of a short, stout man with slicked-down shiny black hair. Dressed in a tight tuxedo, he has a fat cigar clenched between his teeth and a glass of champagne in his hand. Muriel spends several minutes looking at the image, gently retracing its familiar features with her fingertip, before turning it over to read the precious few words scribbled on the other side. *'Dolores, my little lark, from your VG.'*

'Vinny Grünblatt,' she moans. 'Or is it "Greenleaf" these days?'

Vernon takes a convoluted route back to the bedsit, making sure to give the vicarage a very wide berth. He waits until he's safely inside, door shut, curtains closed, before shaking out his shirt sleeve. He holds MD's fountain pen up to the light, inspecting it carefully for clues to its value. He had thought it might be made of abalone shell, but he now sees its just cheap plastic, and no way is the nib gold. No matter. To have hooked such small fry is totally fine at this early stage in the game. 'Mark my words, Son. It's always best to start slow.' Dad taught him to begin by taking small items of little worth, for example a fountain pen, maybe the odd cigarette holder. 'Test trinkets', just to see whether the target even notices they're gone.

If MD does catch him out, then it's no big deal. He simply hands the thing back, laughing off his light-fingeredness as an innocent mistake. 'Silly me! I have a pen much like this one, only platinum, on my desk at home'; or '*Ha ha*. Must be force of habit made me pocket that cigarette case. I'm strictly a cigar man these days.'

If she doesn't spot the theft – and they usually don't – then he knows it's safe to up the stakes. Next time an opportunity presents itself, he can go for a larger item of higher value.

He smiles to himself, rolling the second-rate pen over and over in his palm. Snaffling this was as simple as taking candy from a baby. And now he knows she keeps jewellery in the bureau. A decent amount of it to boot. So far, the plan is working perfectly.

*

Vernon waits until Monday morning before telephoning MD. Naturally he offers his most fulsome apologies.

'My dear Mrs Dollimore. My housekeeper was just taking my jacket to the dry cleaner's when she came upon a pen, the one you so very kindly loaned me the other day... I must have slipped it into my pocket... so absent-minded... Heaven knows what you must think of me... Although we aren't scheduled to meet again for a little while, I wondered if I might perhaps make an impromptu call, before my business trip... just to return it to you?... I may? That's wonderful! Too kind. Then I shall see you directly, Mrs Dollimore... Very well, I shall see you directly, *Muriel*.'

When Deirdre O'Reilly next calls at Number 17 to ferry Muriel Dollimore to choir practice, she manages to talk her way inside the house.

'Thank you, thank you, thank you, Muriel. I'll make my own way to the kitchen,' she blusters, as she sweeps past. 'I must just help myself to a drink of water before we jump in the car. It feels as if an annoying fly has caught in my throat.'

This is the first time Deirdre has made it beyond the hallway since Pauline died, and she's shocked at what she sees. And smells. Her gaze flies around the room, ricocheting off towers of dirty pots and pans, piles of unwashed laundry, plates of half-eaten food. She whistles under her breath. It's as if a doodlebug's scored a direct hit.

Deirdre expected things to be bad, but not *this* bad. She may not be any Mrs Beeton herself, but the vicarage kitchen has never been in such a state. This brave old lady, too proud to ask for help, is clearly all but overwhelmed. Deirdre thinks about getting a drink, as she said she would, but a cursory inspection of the filthy sink and draining board makes her change her mind. Remembering all Muriel's baked contributions to church cake-stalls, she shudders. It's nothing short of a miracle that no one's died after eating them.

Realising this is a situation that requires a full-on practical response, and not a matter she can tackle now, she returns to Mrs Dollimore's side.

'Now, where did you put your sticks?' she asks breezily, resolved not to let any pity show in her voice.

'Behind the door.'

'And are you going to wear your lovely hat?'

'Not today.'

'Let me get you into your coat then.'

'I can manage perfectly well by myself,' says Mrs Dollimore, muttering something else that Deirdre doesn't quite catch.

'We'll have to see about that,' Deirdre mutters back.

Over the following couple of weeks, Vernon procures an enamel matchbox cover, then moves swiftly on to an Italian glass paperweight, two diamante bracelets, some earrings (real rubies, nine carat), and a mink stole – MD showing not a flicker of a sign she's noticed a single one of these thefts. Ironically, however, the best item he squirrels back to the bedsit is one the target hands over personally.

'Please, Mr Greenleaf, I'm asking you to choose.'

'But these are your special treasures.'

'Nonsense. I would like you to have a picture of me to keep as your own. Take whichever you like from those you see on the parlour wall.'

'Well the choice is obvious,' he says, lifting down the portrait with the weightiest, fanciest, solidest-silver frame. 'I pick this one, as it shows *Dolores* at her very best.'

It's been clear to Vernon since he first took MD on that she's a queer old bird. Nothing he can't handle but certainly one of the more eccentric targets he's dealt with. She's always dolling herself up to the nines, like some gross, over-painted marionette, stumbling about in the mess of memories that litter her stinking house. And she only has two topics of conversation, one being her bygone days in the limelight, the other, weirdly, being his own father. Her appetite for stories about 'Mr Greenleaf Senior' seems insatiable:

'Where was he working between the wars?'

'Does he ever talk about Brighton?'

'How did he meet your mother?'

'Is she dead yet?'

'And how is *his* health these days?'

Although Vernon is unsure why she's fixated on a man she's never met, he's glad to go along with her questions. In fact, it's an idiosyncrasy he plays on. She's so transported by tales of Dad's exploits, they are a useful way of distracting her from the drip-drip-drip withdrawal of her worldly goods. If that's what she wants to talk about, it's fine by him. Besides, as it happens, his dad did work as a talent scout, around the period MD was working on stage – although they were never in the same resorts at the same time, as far as he can tell. And this makes it easy for him to stick to his true-life script. More or less. He occasionally tweaks a few little details here and there, to keep her sweet.

One day, when MD produces a photograph of some short, puffed-up squire in an ill-fitting suit, and comments on his 'extraordinary charisma', Vernon chips in that 'the resemblance to my old dad is uncanny' – an ad lib he's pleased with, given how much it seems to strike a chord with his target.

On a Monday morning, while the rest of the inhabitants of Atbara Avenue stick staunchly to their plans for the day ahead, Muriel Dollimore takes an uncharacteristic detour. She sets off from Number 17 at her usual time, in her usual ill-tempered state, but instead of heading for the high street for her usual loathed grocery shop, she enters Atbara Park. Errands can be put off for another day. She needs time and space to think, and the funny smell inside her house seems to cloud her brain. In search of a quiet spot away from the merry mums and litter-pickers and generally annoying neighbours, she trundles herself quite far into the gardens. This extended walk does nothing to improve her mood. Finally coming upon a vacant bench overlooking the duck pond, she plonks herself down to collect her thoughts.

Ever since the flashy stranger turned up at her door, her head has been in a spin. 'Greenleaf,' she mumbles crossly, using the end of her stick to shoo off a hungry pigeon.

It was hearing his name that lit the touchpaper. At first it seemed no more than a quirky coincidence. A pot-shot from the past that happened to dislodge a few memories. But then came his casual revelation about the theatre being 'in his blood'. As soon as he'd said it, notions long submerged in the deepest mulches of her mind began to shift. And now, when she considers what she's managed to glean about the circumstances of his upbringing: the towns, the venues, the dates… well, *everything* points to one remarkable conclusion. Vernon Greenleaf is Vincent Grünblatt's son! If she'd needed any further confirmation, Vernon's reaction to that photograph was as good as proof.

'My old dad. I'll give him "my old dad"!'

Muriel scans her surroundings irritably, taking in the cheerful rows of bedding plants, the glossy rhododendrons and the sprays of yellow forsythia swaying in the breeze. 'Greenleaf,' she mumbles again. If Vernon Greenleaf is indeed Vinny's boy, why is he using an alias? And such an obvious one at that? There's an infinite number of pseudonyms he could have assumed that wouldn't have aroused her attention. Really! She reckons she could have done better herself, even just plucking a name from thin air. Yet he's plumped for a simple translation from German to English. She finds this confusing.

At last, after sucking her way through three ounces of Pontefract cakes, she comes up with a credible explanation. No doubt it was Vincent himself, rather than Vernon, who made the switch. And he probably did it years ago. What with the wars and everything, distancing one's identity from the Krauts was a very understandable thing to do. She smiles a private, inky-black smile. Of course, there were other people from whom Vinny wished to dissociate. Herself included.

Hand in hand, a pair of young lovers approaches Muriel's bench. They nod dreamily as they go by. Her smile collapses. *'It'll never last.'*

She closes her eyes, letting her mind fly back through the decades until she is, once again, sitting in the stuffy waiting room at Brighton station. Her figure was slim; her skin flawless; her outfit mercilessly tight. No man who passed could resist an appreciative look her way. Normally, the sensation of being centre stage would have amused her, but on that day half a century ago, she was indifferent. Any second, the person she'd got dressed for would be with her, and the rest of her life could begin. She snapped open her powder compact, checking her makeup in the little round mirror. She felt inside her pretty beaded clutch bag, checking her train ticket safe within its folds: Brighton to London, Second Class, one way. 'This time next week, I wonder where I'll be? Crooning the blues at Romano's, or singing at the Savoy?' Suddenly she felt sick. It must have been the wait, the anticipation of what was to come, that unsettled her stomach. Or perhaps something else.

As the next train for Victoria pulled in, the waiting room quickly emptied. She picked up her case and followed the pack into the relative fresh air of the platform. She watched one set of passengers spill out, then another set climb aboard. One by one the carriage doors slammed shut. The guard blew his whistle, waved his green flag, and the train jerked off. Without her.

She looked around, trying to spot her man amongst the thinning crowd, but she never saw him coming. He must have sneaked up on her for, all at once, she was grabbed from behind. 'Gotcha, little lark!' he cried, sweeping her off her feet, swinging her round and round. 'Did you miss me?'

'Oh, Vincent, you're late! That was our train.'

'No worries, sweetheart,' he laughed, lowering her back to the ground. 'We'll catch the next one. Are you all right, girl? You look a bit pale.'

'I think I need to sit down,' she gasped, her heart beating wildly. 'You've got my head spinning.'

He took her elbow and steered her back to the waiting room. They had the place to themselves. He helped her into a seat, sat down beside her and lit a cigar. The smoke made her guts lurch, but she didn't care. Vincent was here to take her to London, just like he'd promised. The rest would be history.

'Are you sure you're all right?' he asked, for the first time looking properly into her face. 'You can't be keeping secrets from old Vinny.'

She hadn't planned to say anything. Not yet. 'Well, I *have* got a surprise for you,' she whispered teasingly, stroking his lapel. 'But it's for later.'

'When's "later"?' he grinned, suggestively. 'It's bad manners to keep a chap hanging.'

'When we get to London,' she smiled. 'You'll just have to be patient.'

'Go on. Just a hint,' he breathed, reaching for her breast.

'Don't be naughty,' she giggled, pushing his hand away. 'If you behave, I might give you a clue when we're on the train.'

'Don't be such a spoilsport, Miss Muriel Edwards. Tell me now, while we're alone.'

'Do you promise to be good?'

'Try me!'

She leaned in and rested her head against his chest. It felt warm and comforting. She inhaled deeply, taking in the scent of his cologne. It smelled expensive and foreign; it smelled like success. He rested an arm about her shoulders and kissed her on the top of her head. And so, in that moment, perched on the very cusp of the adventure she'd dreamed of for so long, she decided to tell him everything. In a few breathless sentences, she told him about the songs she'd been working on and the costumes she had planned to dazzle her new West End fans. She told him how she loved him and adored him, and how she'd always be his lark. She told him about the baby, about how their wedding would have to be soon… it wouldn't be long until she started to show… how he wasn't to worry, as she'd never sung better. 'With you at my side, I can do anything.'

Before she'd even finished her speech, she knew her dream had died. He said nothing, but she sensed his body stiffen. He withdrew his arm.

'What's the matter, Vinny? I know it's not exactly how you planned things, but isn't it good news? You'll be a daddy. I can still be a star.'

'A star? You?' He sounded incredulous. 'Doing what, exactly?'

'Singing. Naturally,' she replied evenly, struggling to remain calm.

Vincent Grünblatt stood up sharply and took a step back. 'Listen, lady,' he said dismissively, slowly looking her up and down, 'it's time for you to get wise. Hell will freeze over before that voice of yours will ever keep you in satin and furs. What you *have* got is a body that men will pay to see. But that, it seems, is about to change. If you think punters will part with hard-earned cash to watch some pregnant, atonal fleshpot waddle about the place, you've got another think coming. They can get that for free from their wives.' He tossed his half-smoked cigar to the floor, grinding it to bits with the toe of his shiny wingtip brogue. 'When's it due?'

'In six months, I think. Or a bit sooner. Vinny—'

'How do I know it's mine?' His voice was stone cold.

'Of course it's yours. Who else's?'

'One of those johnnies who hang around your dressing room,' he spat. 'You've eaten enough of their chocolates and drunk enough of their champagne. I suggest you go and ask one of *them* to buy *Dolores* her dresses, because I'll tell you here and now, I am no one's "Daddy".'

With those words, he tightened his tie, turned on his heels and left.

'*The spineless bastard!*' spits Muriel, opening her eyes. She salvages a grubby handkerchief from the end of her sleeve and scrapes away a tear. She can't remember her walk back to her digs from the station, or how she unpacked her things, but she can remember the day, two weeks later, when she accepted Ernest Dollimore's proposal. It was the saddest day of her life.

She pulls herself up as straight as her curved old spine will allow and summons her thoughts back to the present. She wonders what forces of fate led Vincent's son, of all people on the planet, to recover her purse. Pure happenstance? On balance, she believes that must be so. She can think of no other explanation. She also wonders whether Vernon knows *Dolores* and his father were once 'acquainted'? On balance, she's sure not. Whatever brought him into her life, though, it's provided her with an opportunity she never thought she'd get. A shot at revenge.

Muriel considers how much time she's contrived to spend with Vernon, just so she can milk him about the current whereabouts of Vincent Grünblatt. She's endured a dozen long afternoons, showing him countless pictures of *Dolores*, stuffing him full of her baking and regaling him with animated tales of her life lived under the gaze of admiring fans. All the while, she's given the impression she's totally engrossed in her own recollections, passing a faraway couple of hours in his *delightful* company. In reality, however, she's been on her mettle, analysing everything he says and does: the nervous way he fiddles with his cufflinks, how his smile slips slightly when he thinks she's not looking, the expression in his wily grey eyes as he tries to get the measure of her. He's a chip off the slippery old block, and no mistake. Although she's worked hard at playing the addled old lady, she's been careful not to overdo it. She's read his reaction to each 'eentsy little question' she's asked. Whenever she senses she's gone too far, she's pulled back a touch. But when she's successfully beguiled him with her befuddled curiosity, she's followed up with a raft of further enquiries, all in the name of maudlin nostalgia for the golden olden days.

Muriel admits she's found this fact-gathering exercise tedious. Having to turn a blind eye to Vernon's stealing is especially irksome. The man pockets any little knick-knack that isn't nailed down. And her earrings, too. A gift to *Dolores* from an infatuated young viscount, no less. She sighs. Nevertheless, she judges it's been worth the aggravation. So far, she's learned the following:

It can't have been long after he abandoned her that Vinny married one of his so-called 'discoveries': a singer by the stage name of Adeline. '*Never heard of her.*' She gave birth to baby Vernon while they were on the road. The little family travelled a lot, following Vernon's 'dear old dad' as he, in turn, pursued other acts to add to his stable. Adeline carried on performing for a bit, until she ran off with a sailor. Oh *so* sad. Over the passing years, man and son muddled along, being strong for one another. Raised without a mother, Vernon grew up fast, becoming a master of thinking on his feet. It's not exactly clear to Muriel how he's made his money. Fraud? Gambling? No doubt theft has played a part. But he's done well for himself. Very well. He's now in the gratifying position of being able to support his old dad financially. 'It warms my heart to do right by him, madam, after all the gifts he's given me.'

Muriel lets out a long, satisfied sigh. The bottom line of this touching tale is that Vincent Grünblatt is alive, happy and living in Kensington.

But these are all things she can fix.

Next time Deirdre O'Reilly calls at Number 17, she's armed with scouring powder, rubber gloves and a no-isn't-an-option approach. She can tell from the brusque way she's received that the sweet old lady is clearly embarrassed.

'Muriel, believe me, it will be my pleasure to attack that kitchen of yours. After all the baking you've done for the Church over the years, I feel the whole community owes you a thorough spring clean.'

Mrs Dollimore glares at her fiercely, muttering under her breath.

'I know you're used to muddling through,' continues Deirdre, marching without further ado towards the offending room. 'It's just that kind of gumption that won us the war. But each and every one of us needs a helping hand sometimes.'

The old lady follows, still muttering furiously.

Deirdre is quick to dismiss her thanks. 'That's very gracious of you, Muriel. However, I *insist*. And when I'm all done I shall rustle up a pot of tea for us both. Won't that be nice?'

Mrs Dollimore turns away, no doubt to hide her shame, and shuffles off.

'Quite right. You put your feet up while I get stuck in.'

As soon as Muriel has left the room, Deirdre dons her apron and sets to. The drain pong has got even worse since her previous visit, so the first thing she heads for is the sink. She looks in the cubbyhole underneath and is pleased to find an impressive stock of cleaning products. Now she comes to think of it, she recalls that practically her last conversation with pitiful Pauline was at the ironmonger's. Her basket was laden with every kind of concoction, and here they all were, still brand new by the look of them. Deirdre opens a tin of Drano and gives it a sniff. The astringent smell bites sharply at the back of her throat. Good stuff, but not half so good as caustic soda. One bottle and tin at a time, she goes through the cupboard, looking for the brown paper packet she now remembers giving Pauline. But it's not there. She must have used it. Deirdre's gratified that her little gift was appreciated, all those months ago.

'Oh well,' she sighs, pouring the contents of the tin into the festering plughole. 'Drano it must be!' The pipes make a satisfying series of gulps before swiftly gobbling down the whole lot.

She can't do anything about washing up until she's given the Drano some time to work its magic, so Deirdre confers her exertions elsewhere. The rubbish bin is given short shrift, as are the milk bottles lined up on the sunny windowsill, each containing its own culture of rancid, greening curds. She collects up those dishcloths she deems salvageable and puts them on to boil in a soup of soap flakes. Over the next hours, every cupboard is systematically cleared, wiped down and its contents rearranged. Deirdre is sure Muriel will appreciate the new way things have been organised. The floor is scrubbed, the blackened oven scoured and the reeking fridge thoroughly disinfected.

Eventually Deirdre grinds to an exhausted halt. Flopping down on a chair, she mops her sweaty brow with the hem of her apron and leans back to admire her work. She's happy with what she sees. In fact, it looks like an entirely different room. She looks at her watch. She still has time to confront one last thing before she sees to the dishes. Muriel's pantry. She pulls herself to her feet and tugs open its door. It's crammed from floor to ceiling with every kind of tin, packet and box. It has a nasty, fusty odour. Not as bad as the drains, but bad enough. Damn! Just when she thought the end was in sight, she's uncovered this whole bucket of worms.

She briefly considers putting it off until another day, but guesses that Mrs Dollimore is almost certainly too self-respecting to let her come and clean again. And leaving the pantry undone is out of the question. Some of the food smells so off, it could be downright dangerous. Deirdre would never forgive herself if the old lady were to be poisoned because of her. She realises it's now or never. Girding her loins, she empties each shelf, checking what's still safe to eat and what is not. To her dismay, apart from the canned goods, she ends up having to chuck almost everything. She's relieved when, at the very back of the top shelf, she finds an old metal caddy filled with granulated sugar. At least Muriel can keep that.

Deirdre finds a nice clean sugar bowl, loads it brimful, and puts it in pride of place in the middle of the kitchen table.

Muriel goes to a great deal of trouble with her next batch of baking. She imagines she's on the telly, on *The Galloping Guzzler*. Its host, Julian LeCheval, is delighted to see her. Naturally.

'Great to have you back, *Dolores*.'

'My pleasure, as always, Julian.'

'And what are you going to make for us today?'

'Macaroons. My special recipe.'

'That sounds just grand. Why don't you talk us through it? I'm sure our viewers would appreciate a couple of tips.'

'All right, Julian. Let's start by firing up my cooker.'

After some foraging, Muriel manages to find a box of Swan Vestas in her cutlery drawer. There used to be a whole tin of them on the windowsill but, to her irritation, that seems to have gone. She's not sure whether damnable Deirdre moved it, or if Greenleaf-the-thief has swiped it. Whatever. It's of no real consequence now.

She strikes a match, leans into the oven and sets a light to the gas. With a *phut phut phut*, a row of little blue flames dances into life. 'So, Julian, while we wait for that to heat up to Regulo Mark Three, I shall line a couple of baking trays with greaseproof paper.'

It takes Muriel five minutes to locate the trays, which have been transferred from their shelf in the larder to the bottom drawer of the dresser. *Blast it.* She gives up on her search for the non-stick paper. 'The viewers will find that rubbing their trays with fat will work just as well.'

Not wishing to waste more time looking for the pudding basin she normally uses for mixing, she empties out the contents of a plastic fruit bowl. At least the wooden spoons are where she left them.

'Okay. Here we have a whole pound of shredded coconut,' says Muriel, smiling into the lens of an illusory television camera. 'I bought this at my local corner shop, but you can probably get it cheaper on the high street. To this, I'm going to add a small tin of condensed milk, and a few drops of vanilla extract.' She puts all these ingredients into the bowl and begins to stir.

'People watching at home may be wondering why you're using condensed milk, *Dolores*.'

'It's for extra sweetness, Julian. You *can* use regular Tate and

Lyle,' she continues, pointing to the freshly filled sugar bowl in the middle of the kitchen table, 'but I find milk makes a moister macaroon.'

'Yum!'

Once again Muriel improvises, separating three egg whites into a casserole dish. 'You'll see I'm beating these until they're really, really stiff. My preference is to whisk by hand, but of course a blender would be quicker. Don't forget to pop in a pinch of salt… just a pinch, mind – too heavy-handed, and the flavour will be ruined. I know some cooks might include corn starch, vinegar, or even cream of tartar, but I like to keep to my own tried and tested recipe.'

'May I have a little taste?'

'Yes, Julian. In fact, it's a good idea to do that sooner rather than later.'

'Dee-lish-us!'

'And now, it's time for my special ingredient.'

'I thought that was the condensed milk, *Dolores*?'

'Oh no, it's much more special than that,' chuckles Muriel. She shuffles off to the parlour, ferrets through her handbag, then returns with three full pots of sleeping pills. 'Ideally, I'd crush these with my pestle and mortar,' she tuts as she tips them into the mixture, 'but I'm not sure where it is at the moment. Never mind. I'll just give it another really good stir.'

Once satisfied the tablets are sufficiently mingled in with the other constituents, 'and remembering to make sure my macaroons are evenly sized, and evenly spaced,' Muriel carefully scoops fist-sized balls of her concoction onto the waiting, well-greased trays. 'I'm going to bake these beauties for about half an hour, until their tops are gorgeously golden, and their bottoms are barely brown. Then I'll finish each one off with a lovely, sticky glacé cherry. *Et voilà!*'

'Irresistible, *Dolores*.'

'That's what I'm hoping, Julian.'

*

As always, Vernon Greenleaf is punctual. As always, Muriel is ready for him.

'Dear lady,' he puffs, settling himself into what has become his customary armchair, 'I can't tell you how pleased I am to see you today. Business has been very trying of late. Your company will be a welcome diversion.'

'May I offer you tea?' she asks brightly, with pot (good quality, silver-plated, Mappin & Webb) poised and ready to pour.

'I'd love one,' he replies, surprised to note a striking absence of anything to eat. 'White, no sugar, as usual.'

'I do apologise. Just this once it'll have to be black. The vicar's wife used the last of the milk.'

'Pops round much, does she?' He makes his enquiry sound casual, but underneath he's disconcerted by the news of an impromptu guest checking up on MD.

'Not really. Just one of her flying visits. And what about *your* social life, Mr Greenleaf?' she asks sweetly, handing him his drink in a remarkably clean china cup. Have you seen much of your old dad recently?'

'Just the other day, as it happens. He's exceptionally pukka… asked me to pass on his most particular regards to you.'

'Did he now?' Her voice wavers. 'I wasn't sure he knew about these little rendezvous.'

Vernon notices her colour rise slightly and he's gratified. 'Oh, yes indeed, madam. He gets quite misty-eyed when I tell him about our conversations. Takes him right back to his theatrical days. "Mark my words, Son," he says, "those were the best times of my life." And I say to him—'

'When are you next seeing him?' The old lady cuts him off midstream.

'I don't know.' She's caught him off guard. 'I mean to say, "soon", of course.'

'Oh good,' she says, retrieving a square biscuit tin from underneath a cushion and passing it to him. 'I wouldn't want these to get stale.'

As he takes the tin from her, he finds it's unexpectedly heavy. 'What's this?' he asks, giving it a shake.

'A little gift from me to your father. Take it, please, and be sure to pass on *my* most particular regards to *him*.' She's smiling, but the trace of ice in her voice leaves Vernon cold. 'But it's only for him, mind. So, just this once, don't go helping yourself!'

Unsure whether or not her last remark is a joke, or a worryingly deliberate gibe, he lets out a nervous laugh. 'I assure you I—'

'Have I made myself clear, young man?' she snaps, interrupting him for the second time.

'Perfectly, madam.' He's shocked by the strength of her insistence.

'Oh, thank you, Mr Greenleaf,' she breathes, as if a weight has been lifted from her. 'You've made an old lady very happy.' To his relief, she's once again smiling amiably, and all tension in the room has evaporated as quickly as it arrived. Like a passing thundercloud. Vernon wonders if this target is more senile than he first realised.

Still grinning away, she leans over and gives his hand a gentle pat. 'Now, how about we look at some more photographs of *Dolores*?'

'I thought you'd never ask!'

It's almost midnight. A crescent moon bestows its shimmery light on the houses of Atbara Avenue. Their silver-kissed façades, with shuttered windows for eyes and locked doors for mouths, are shut up in dumb repose. Tortoiseshell pussycats dressed in collars and bells slink in and out of the shadows, searching for rats, while faithful dogs twitch and snore in their kennels. A blackbird perches on top of a street lamp. Several hours must pass until dawn, but his little barrel chest is too full to contain itself. He sings out his heartfelt chorus to the pavements and the dustbins and the empty milk bottles that grace the well-scrubbed front steps – just as if an audience of angels was in his thrall.

Try as she might, Mrs Dollimore can't get off to sleep. She attributes her restlessness to too much excitement in one day. A wry thought enters her head. Perhaps she should have hung on to a couple of those pills? Muttering crossly, she pulls on her dressing gown and totters downstairs to make herself a hot drink.

She flicks on the kitchen light, opens the pantry door and scans her all but bare shelves. '*Shit and buggery!*' There's no cocoa powder. Not because Deirdre O'Reilly threw it away, or because anyone stole it. Remembering her aborted shopping trip, Muriel realises that she has finally run out. With mounting annoyance, she sets about making herself tea instead.

As she waits for the kettle to boil, she wonders how Vernon's old dad received his gift. As she tips the steaming water onto the tea leaves, she wonders if Vincent Grünblatt tucked in straight away, or whether he saved her tender offerings as a treat for later. While the pot brews, she wonders if he's dead yet, or whether he's still slipping into a coma. At this last thought, her mood lifts. Given there's no milk, she decides to indulge herself and have some sugar for a change. She sits down at the kitchen table and scoops one, two... '*oh, go on then...*' five spoonfuls into her coronation mug before pouring on the hot tea.

Stirring it slowly, waiting for the sugar to dissolve, she sings. '*Meet me tonight in dreamland, Under the silv'ry moon. Meet me tonight in dreamland, Where love's sweet roses bloom.*'

Suddenly, Muriel Dollimore falls silent. That was Vinny's favourite tune. They'd dance to it. He'd take her in his arms, waltz her around and around, murmuring how he loved her, how he'd make all her '*dreams come true*'. For a fleeting moment her eyes mist over... but then she shrugs her shoulders and raises the mug to her lips.

At the very same second that MD takes a long, deep gulp of her comfortingly sweetened cuppa, Vernon Greenleaf prises open the biscuit tin and sees exactly what he expected to see: a batch of perfect cakes nestling within their glistening, coconutty juices.

So I'm supposed to hand these over to my old dad, am I? Smiling to himself, he pictures 'Mr Greenleaf Senior', real name Ewan 'Big Mac' McDonald. A tall, red-haired Scotsman, who was the physical antithesis of the oily man in the old woman's faded photograph. Vernon may have been truthful to the target in so far as Big Mac did have a West End career; Big Mac even dabbled in 'talent-spotting'. But that was just one, short-lived chapter in a richly varied life. The times he spent as an antique dealer, then as a used-car salesman and then as a guest of her Majesty the Queen? Well, they were surely of no interest to her? As always, Vernon had followed his father's advice.

'Mark my words, Son, help them believe what they want to believe. That way, everyone's happy.'

He inspects the macaroons. There's no chance of his dad getting his teeth into them any time soon, given he's been six feet under for the best part of eight years. He contemplates binning them but thinks better of it. He's very hungry. Funds have run low, so he's skimped on buying food rather than other, liquid, essentials. He pours a large Scotch. With his drink in one hand and the tin in the other, he sits down on his dishevelled pull-out bed.

He gives the contents of the tin a tentative sniff before cautiously helping himself. Leaning back into his grubby pillow he bites into a sweet, sticky macaroon. It's delicious. He takes another and, as he does so, he notices something – a piece of card, hiding at the bottom of the tin. It has the letters 'VG' on the front. Who on earth is VG? Surely not Vernon Greenleaf? Didn't the old woman make it very clear he wasn't to open the tin, let alone eat what he found inside it? He turns the card over and reads the handwritten message on the other side: *'FOR VINNY. THESE WERE OUR DAUGHTER'S FAVOURITE. ENJOY. YOUR LITTLE LARK. XOX'*

Vinny? Vinny who? None the wiser, Vernon takes a generous swig of whisky and guzzles a third macaroon. He replays MD's barbed comment from earlier that day, the one about 'helping himself'. Chances are, the daft old bat meant nothing by it. But then again, perhaps she's cottoning on? On balance, it's time to move on. A wave of tiredness rolls over him. He closes his weary eyes and allows his thoughts to roam. 'This time tomorrow, I wonder where I'll be…'

As Deirdre O'Reilly stands on the doorstep of Number 17, waiting for Mrs Dollimore to answer her second knock, she feels strangely nervous. She's wondering whether she should be risking this fresh attempt to tackle Muriel's parlour, but she remains steadfast. In Churchill's words, she mustn't take no for an answer. After all, she's sought spiritual guidance from her husband and, more importantly, the sisterhood of the Women's Institute. Consensus was, it would be unchristian to leave their beloved neighbour to fester in her own mess, whatever her aged sensibilities about accepting help.

With a tenacity that defines both prime ministers and vicars' wives, Deirdre raps several more times. Still no response. Her sense of unease grows. It isn't the first time she's found herself, early one morning, banging this very knocker, striving to get the attention of a lonely woman who never comes. She tries the handle and, with a sickening sense of déjà vu, finds the door unlocked. Sheepishly, she pushes it open.

'Muriel!' she calls out. 'It's only me. Is everything all right?' She hears no coherent reply. Just a hoarse whisper coming from the direction of the kitchen, rasping something she doesn't quite catch.

It turns out that one swallow of Tetley tea, sweetened with five spoonfuls of caustic soda, isn't enough to kill a person. Perhaps if the old lady had drunk the whole mug. But she didn't. However, it *is* enough to permanently damage one's throat, especially the vocal cords. Such a tragic fate for a singer. Of course, three special-recipe macaroons are enough to bump off a horse, especially if the horse washes them down with a cheap malt.

Over the following days, while the poor, *poor*, mute Mrs Dollimore languishes in the vicarage, being selflessly nursed by Deirdre O'Reilly – 'Don't even try to thank me, Muriel' – the bloated remains of Vernon Greenleaf lie undiscovered in the bedsit on the high street. Only when the stain on the baker's shop ceiling becomes noticeable does the landlady venture upstairs. She's been simply dying to ask the professor how his crime novel is progressing, and now she has the perfect excuse to tap on his door…

Acknowledgements

As the saying goes, it takes a village to raise a child, and a tribe of very, very, very understanding family and friends to prop up an author during the delivery of their first manuscript. Boy, am I glad I joined the York Novelists group! Conceiving the idea for *A Curtain Twitcher's Book of Murder* was a solo effort. Growing it into anything more has required the tolerance of thick-skinned peers prepared to listen and comment while I freely shared the pains of my labour. To be able to create alongside such talented fellow writers provided me with everything I needed to really get started and, more importantly, keep going. It's been a privilege. To members past and present, I send power to your pens.

Thank you, Helen Corner-Bryant, for looking at my initial draft and seeing in it everything I hoped readers would see. That recognition meant a great deal then, as does your continued encouragement now. I am hugely indebted to you for this, and for introducing me to my agent, Eugenie Furniss.

Thank you, Eugenie, for being quite simply, brilliant. You have taught me many things, probably without even knowing it. Having you in my corner gave me strength through some tough writing times, and it's down to your faith and perseverance that the residents of Atbara Avenue have, at last, come to life within the covers of this book. We're all extremely grateful.

Thank you to Carolyn Mays, my wonderful publisher, for choosing to work with me and for sharing your wealth of experience. I'm humbled by the amazing support that you and all at Bedford Square Publishers have shown me. I do know I'm lucky.

Thank you to my husband and my children, who cheer me on through everything. The loves of my life. Without you, Steve, I'd be far less than half of whatever it is that I am.

April, I miss you.

Finally, thank you Heather Wright, a loyal and wise critic to whom I owe so much.

**Did you read *A Curtain Twitcher's Book of Murder*
for your book club?
Some of these questions might spark discussion
or give you different ideas to talk about.**

1. How does the period the book is set in (1969) contribute to what happens in the novel? Could the same events take place in a similar suburban setting in the present day?
2. In today's society, could a nosy vicar's wife hold the same irreproachable position that Deirdre O'Reilly does? How would the parish react to her if she behaved in the way Deirdre does?
3. Who is telling the story of the inhabitants of Atbara Avenue? Do you think of the narrator as a character living on the street?
4. Are any of the characters likeable? Does it affect your enjoyment of the novel if they are not?
5. There are some dark and serious topics addressed in *A Curtain Twitcher's Book of Murder*. How does the tone in which they are addressed affect the way you think about them? Does it make them more or less shocking?
6. There are unexpected things going on in each of the houses on Atbara Avenue which we see into. What point is the author trying to make about what happens behind closed doors?
7. On Atbara Avenue people commit murder but escape justice because their crimes, veiled by a thick fog of social propriety, go unseen. Perpetrators continue to mix with their neighbours as if nothing happened. Does this occur in real life? How many times, do you think, has your path crossed with that of a killer without you even knowing it?
8. Some reviewers have called this a cosy crime novel; others have said it's not a novel at all but a collection of short stories. Is it cosy? Is it a novel?
9. What do you think happens to the characters after the novel ends?
10. If you had to pick one Atbara Avenue resident to meet for a cup of tea, who would that be? Why would you choose this person? What would you like to ask them?

Bedford Square Publishers is an independent publisher of fiction and non-fiction, founded in 2022 in the historic streets of Bedford Square London and the sea mist shrouded green of Bedford Square Brighton.

Our goal is to discover irresistible stories and voices that illuminate our world.

We are passionate about connecting our authors to readers across the globe and our independence allows us to do this in original and nimble ways.

The team at Bedford Square Publishers has years of experience and we aim to use that knowledge and creative insight, alongside evolving technology, to reach the right readers for our books. From the ones who read a lot, to the ones who don't consider themselves readers, we aim to find those who will love our books and talk about them as much as we do.

We are hunting for vital new voices from all backgrounds – with books that take the reader to new places and transform perceptions of the world we live in.

Follow us on social media for the latest Bedford Square Publishers news.

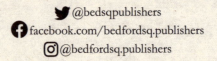

bedfordsquarepublishers.co.uk